Praise for JULIA STUART and

The Pigeon Pie Mystery

"A delicate yet kooky romp."
—Oprah.com, "Book of the Week"

"Stuart's gift is that for all that her setups are ingenious, she never loses sight of the humanity of her characters."
—*The Denver Post*

"Quirky characters, a feisty protagonist, a clever mystery and the requisite historical tidbits combine for an amusing read."
—*Kirkus Reviews*

"[Stuart has] a deft and charming style."
—*The Washington Post*

"Fans of Stuart's novel *The Tower, the Zoo, and the Tortoise* will find the same wit on display."
—*Publishers Weekly*

"Stuart combines vivid historical detail, layers of intrigue, and plenty of humor in this intelligent mystery that will appeal to Agatha Christie fans as well as those who enjoy G. M. Malliet and C. S. Challinor."
—*Booklist*

JULIA STUART

The Pigeon Pie Mystery

Julia Stuart is an award-winning journalist and the author of two previous novels, *The Tower, the Zoo, and the Tortoise* and *The Matchmaker of Périgord*. She lives in London.

www.juliastuart.com

The Pigeon Pie Mystery

A NOVEL

*

JULIA STUART

*

ANCHOR BOOKS
A Division of Random House, Inc.
New York

For my mother, with love

FIRST ANCHOR BOOKS EDITION, MAY 2013

Copyright © 2012 by Julia Stuart Limited

All rights reserved. Published in the United States by Anchor Books,
a division of Random House, Inc., New York. Originally published in
hardcover in the United States by Doubleday, a division of
Random House, Inc., New York, in 2012.

Anchor Books and colophon are registered trademarks of Random House, Inc.

The Library of Congress has cataloged the Doubleday edition as follows:
Stuart, Julia.
The pigeon pie mystery / Julia Stuart.—1st ed.
p. cm.
I. Title.
PR6119.T826P54 2012
823'.92—dc23
2012009998

Anchor ISBN: 978-0-307-94769-7

Map illustration by Laura Hartman Maestro

www.anchorbooks.com

Printed in the United States of America
10   9   8   7   6   5   4   3   2   1

We look at other nations and we pity them because
They're not a little patch on dear old England.
Their trades, their arts, their everything are full of faults
    and flaws,
So different to clever Model England.

—"MODEL ENGLAND," HARRY DACRE AND EDGAR WARD, 1892

Contents

*

Cast of Characters

*

H.H. the Maharaja of Prindur: former ruler of the Indian state of Prindur, with a weakness for shirt-sleeve pudding

H.H. Princess Alexandrina: his daughter, nicknamed Mink, and the best woman shot in England

Pooki: the Princess's large-footed Indian maid and defender against moths

Dr. Henderson: amorous general practitioner and bicycling enthusiast

The Honourable Dowager Lady Montfort Bebb: once held hostage in Afghanistan, and a horror at playing the pianoforte

The Lady Beatrice Fisher: devotee of exuberant millinery and doves, whose apartments are haunted by Jane Seymour

The Countess of Bessington: parsimonious widow in perpetual mourning, with an addiction to ferns

Major-General George Bagshot: former military man with a roving eye, and a Tudor expert who is writing his fourth history of Hampton Court Palace

Mrs. Bagshot: his wife and patron of a school for the blind who takes cures in Egypt

Cornelius B. Pilgrim: the Bagshots' American houseguest, with a woeful grasp of English etiquette

William Sheepshanks: Keeper of the Maze and victim of the success of *Three Men in a Boat,* a novel by Jerome K. Jerome with a scene in the palace's leafy labyrinth

Thomas Trout: Keeper of the Great Vine, who strives to protect his mighty charge from being felled by rats

Mrs. Boots: bronchial palace housekeeper and Keeper of the Chapel Royal

Mrs. Nettleship: Dr. Henderson's incompetent housekeeper, who's even worse at matchmaking

Alice Cockle: the Bagshots' former parlour maid, since demoted to a maid-of-all-work for the Countess

Inspector Guppy: police inspector with an inglorious past

Silas Sparrowgrass: homeopath from East Molesey, and Dr. Henderson's archrival

Charles Twelvetrees: solicitor and coroner for West Middlesex, who's had a gutful of the mysteriously dead

Pike and Gibbs: the butcher's and grocer's delivery boys

The Lord Chamberlain: the Earl of Kellerton, responsible for the allocation of apartments at Hampton Court Palace, and a laudanum addict

The Reverend Benjamin Grayling: palace chaplain, with an appreciation for the communion wine, who's at war with the organist

Mr. Blood: the myopic undertaker who carries a measuring rule tucked under his arm

The watercress seller: hawks outside the palace gate and sleeps in a coffin

Mr. Wildgoose: Dr. Henderson's tailor and taxidermy fancier

The organ grinder: street musician paid by the public to keep quiet

Wilfred Noseworthy: palace turncock and hauler of the push, a sedan chair mounted on wheels used by the palace ladies

Alfred Bucket: bicycling instructor and fancy riding opponent

Horace Pollywog: one-legged dancing master, who trod on a sea hedgehog

Barnabas Popejoy: a butterman of over-generous girth known for his bad jokes

The drunk woman who sells pig's trotters outside the King's Arms

Albert: the Maharaja's monkey, who suits red velvet trousers

Victoria: a hedgehog named after the British sovereign, with a penchant for beetles and Madeira wine

Lord Sluggard: the palace mouser, who wouldn't recognise a rat if he saw one

Gertrude: Silas Sparrowgrass's adored rabbit and reluctant prop for his magic tricks

Trixie: Thomas Trout's leech and formidable weather forecaster

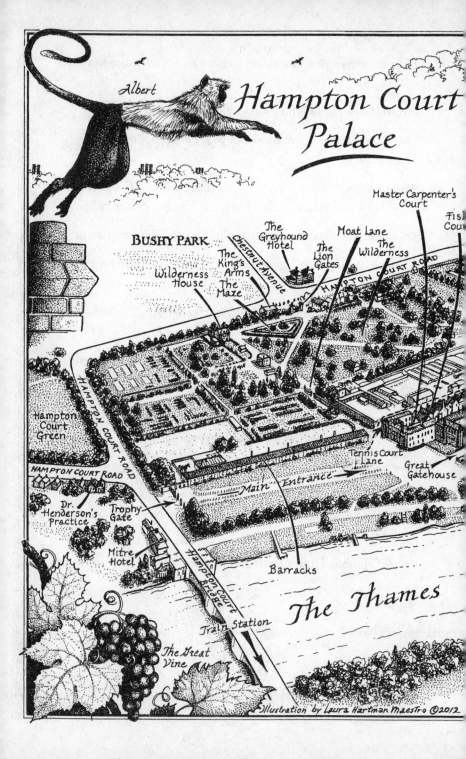

Albert

Hampton Court Palace

BUSHY PARK

Master Carpenter's Court

The Greyhound Hotel

Moat Lane
The Wilderness

Fish Cour

Chestnut Avenue

The King's Arms
The Maze

The Lion Gates

Wilderness House

HAMPTON COURT ROAD

HAMPTON COURT ROAD

Hampton Court Green

HAMPTON COURT ROAD

Tennis Court Lane

Great Gatehouse

Main Entrance

Dr. Henderson's Practice

Trophy Gate

Mitre Hotel

HAMPTON COURT BRIDGE

Barracks

The Thames

Train Station

The Great Vine

Illustration by Laura Hartman Maestro ©2012

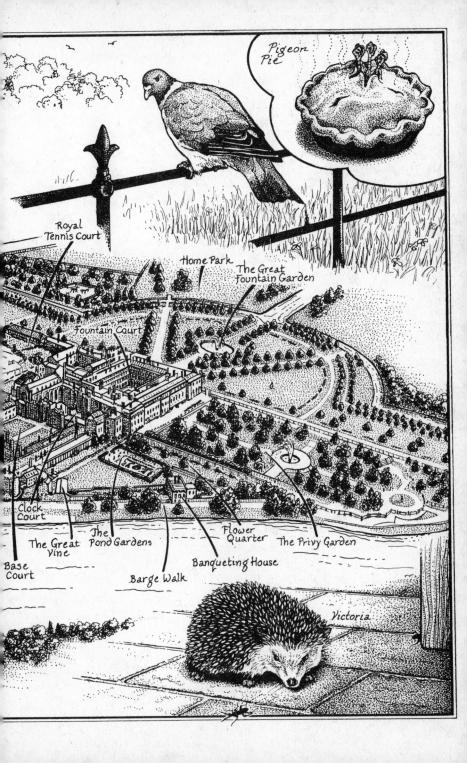

Pigeon Pie

Royal Tennis Court

Home Park

The Great Fountain Garden

Fountain Court

Clock Court

The Great Vine

The Pond Gardens

Flower Quarter

The Privy Garden

Base Court

Banqueting House

Barge Walk

Victoria

The Pigeon Pie Mystery

CHAPTER I

An Elephant, a Funeral, and
More Bad News

MONDAY, MARCH 22, 1897

S the hail bounced on the carriage roof, Mink suddenly
wondered whether she ought to buy mourning knickers.
She thought of asking her maid, who had wept for the
dead Maharaja almost as much as she had. But the sight of Pooki's
stockingless feet emerging from the bottom of her sari changed
her mind. She turned back to the window to distract herself from
the loathsome task ahead of her. Wiping away the condensation,
she watched the shoppers on Regent Street, the gritty downpour
toppling the ostrich feathers on their elegant hats.

The horses began to slow and came to a halt outside Jay's,
the mourning emporium. The Princess had walked past it during countless shopping trips, but never once imagined needing
to go in. As she waited for the carriage door to open, she fiddled
with the buttons on her gloves, avoiding the window display. But
George, the second footman, whose woeful height and lamentable
calves would normally have excluded him from such a position,
took so long she wondered whether he had forgotten her. Finally
the door opened. Lifting up her skirts, she climbed out, determined not to be sold a pair of mutes, for the funeral attendants

hired by the bereaved for their doleful expressions had a reputation for unabashed drunkenness.

A doorbell never tinkled so mournfully as the one at Jay's. A lump was sure to form in even a hangman's throat at the sound of its pitiful wail. The Princess and the maid stood silently in the entrance, shrouded in black drapery, a vase of white lilies engulfing them in the politest scent of death. As they waited to be served, a huddle of pale-faced female assistants dressed in the hue of sorrow stared at them. Those at the back stood on their toes and gazed with envy at Mink, whose arresting looks were the result of an Indian father and an English mother. Her long dark hair was pinned and padded to form a high cushion round her head, and her straw hat was trimmed with daffodils and chiffon, which, they noticed, perfectly matched her green cape jacket. Those at the front stared at her emerald earrings, some of the few family jewels the British hadn't stolen. Added to the colourful spectacle was an older, dark-skinned Indian lady's-maid in native dress, a black plait hanging down her back. She was so skinny she seemed to have been eroded by years of persistent wind.

The hush was broken by a sniff, and the Princess handed Pooki a silk handkerchief, which she took with grateful, bony fingers. Suddenly, as if descended from the overcrowded heavens above, a man appeared. Dressed in the dullest of black, for only tears were allowed to shine at Jay's, he appeared to be executing the humblest of bows. But too long passed before he straightened himself up, and it was soon apparent that he was in a permanent state of humility. His cinnamon hair, the only hint of gaiety in the establishment, was respectfully sleeked to his head. He looked up at his customer from his near folded stance with the pitiful eyes of a drover's dog.

"Ratakins is the name, ma'am," he said, clutching his limp hands in front of him. "How may I be of assistance?"

The Princess looked at him uneasily, and replied that she needed some mourning wear as soon as possible.

"First of all, ma'am," he said, "may I offer you the deepest of sympathies? Some of the lesser mourning establishments may tell you of their regrets, but I assure you that here at Jay's condolences are at their most profound. If I may enquire, at what hour did our loved-one depart?"

The Princess thought back to the previous day, when the butler broke the news. "Some time yesterday afternoon," she replied, her stomach like lead.

Mr. Ratakins scrabbled for his watch chain, and, with a flutter of bloodless fingers, stopped the time accordingly. Slowly he raised his red-rimmed eyes to her once more.

"A tragedy," he said.

The assistants continued to stare.

As silently as he'd arrived, Mr. Ratakins headed down a mahogany-panelled corridor, which the Princess took as an indication to follow. Passing through a doorway, he took up his position behind a counter. A one-eyed ginger cat lay on top of it, a stray the shopkeeper fed out of solidarity for its colour. He swiftly removed it and asked: "If I may enquire, which of our loved-ones has left us?"

Mink swallowed. "My father."

"A tragedy," he repeated, his eyes downcast.

The Princess sat down on the chair next to the counter, clutching her green handbag. "I'm not sure how long the period of mourning is for a parent these days," she said. "None of the women's magazines seem to be in agreement."

"For a parent, we at Jay's recommend a year, six months in crape, three in black, and three in half-mourning." He continued with the speed of a mantra: "For grandparents it's six months, two in silk with moderate crape, two in black without crape, and two in half-mourning. For brothers and sisters it's also six months, but we advise three in crape, two in black and one in half-mourning. For an uncle or an aunt, two months, no crape, black to be worn the whole time. For a great-uncle or aunt it's six weeks, three in black and three in half-mourning. For a first cousin it's four weeks. Black. Three weeks for a second cousin, if you liked 'em."

"I see," replied the Princess, blinking.

"Heliotrope and other mauves are, of course, still very favourable colours for half-mourning, and grey has never gone out of fashion. It is, after all, a most fetching colour for the bereaved. Complements the pallor."

"Tell me," said Mink. "Is a widow still expected to wear mourning for two and a half years, while all a widower does is put on an armband for three months, and remarries whenever he pleases?"

"Something like that, ma'am."

Mr. Ratakins then rubbed his fingers until they shone. There were skirts and mantles in the latest fashions ready for immediate wear, he said, and bodices made to measure in a few hours. He hauled down a roll of black cloth from behind him, and pulled out the end for inspection.

"This is what I'd recommend for you, ma'am. Bombazine. And we use Courtauld's Crape. It will withstand any amount of rain," he said. He glanced at Pooki and lowered his voice. "Bombazet is best for the servants. It's inferior and therefore cheaper. I wouldn't want to waste your money."

With none of the usual pleasure she derived from sitting at a shop counter, Mink chose from the selection of shoes, gloves, mantles, bonnets, toques, hairpins, fans, aigrettes, boas, parasols, bags, purses, mittens, umbrellas, and antimacassars—all the colour of crows.

A young female assistant, her hair scraped back into an unyielding bun, took the place of Mr. Ratakins in order to broach the delicate matter of underwear. Instantly she recognised the Princess from the newspapers, which for years had been captivated by the oriental glamour of the young woman born and raised in England. The female columnists extolled her outfits, quoted her calls for suffrage, and longed for an invitation to her all-women shooting parties, when the laughter startled the grouse more than the beaters.

Opening several drawers, the dry-mouthed assistant draped on the counter a selection of white chemises, drawers, and underpetticoats, all trimmed with black ribbon.

"They're from Paris, Your Highness," she said, glancing at the Princess's earrings.

Mink looked at them. "I'm not of the opinion that everything from Paris is automatically desirable," she replied. "And anyway, no one will know what I've got on underneath."

"You will, Your Highness," said the girl, fingering the lingerie with bitten nails.

"So will I, Your Highness," piped up Pooki from the sofa behind her.

The Princess let out a short, sharp sigh that sent the cat fleeing from underneath her chair, and quickly made her selection.

Mr. Ratakins returned, spread his pale hands on the counter, and leant forward. "And the funeral itself, ma'am," he said, his eyes gleaming. "Jay's can take care of that. We have the best mutes in the whole of London, if you don't mind my boasting. They won't say a word. We keep them down in the basement. There's not much to talk about down there. Except for the spiders."

The Princess shook her head. "My father arranged his funeral years ago, and I'm told he left very precise instructions," she stated. "I can assure you, the last thing he'd want is mutes."

"How will people know that a death has occurred, ma'am, without the presence of mutes at the front door?"

"I'm sure half of London is already well aware of my father's death, gossip being what it is."

The shopkeeper's slender fingers silently traced the counter. "They're coming back into fashion, ma'am," he said from underneath his lashes.

"I dare say."

He looked up. "Ours will squeeze out a tear for an extra twopence."

"They won't be necessary, thank you."

"What about a penny tin of black paint for the horses that pull the hearse?" he asked, producing one from underneath the counter with the flourish of a conjurer. "They come up lovely, ma'am."

"No, thank you."

The tin disappeared.

"May I recommend some black ostrich feathers for their heads?" he asked, slowly pulling one through his fingers. "All the way from Egypt."

"No one has plumed hearses these days expect for costermongers and chimney sweeps."

The shopkeeper foraged under his counter, then stood up triumphant. "We do an unparalleled line in false horses' tails," he announced, holding one up in the air and giving it a hopeful shake.

"Mr. Ratakins!"

The man's eyes fell to the floor, and he lost several inches in height. Suddenly he looked up. "There's one thing I almost forgot, ma'am. A young lady such as yourself, thoughts naturally turn to marriage. We have the daintiest of wedding dresses in bridal black, should the happy occasion fall sometime soon. It's a most fetching shade, ma'am. Just the right tint of hope and despair."

The Princess suddenly thought of the ivory wedding gown with orange blossom at the neck and waist that she had already chosen. She had seen it in a magazine and hidden the picture in her stocking drawer, ready for her dressmaker, should the proposal finally come. But there had been no word from Mark Cavendish since news spread of the scandalous way in which her father had died.

The silence continued as the Princess stared at the floor.

"Her Highness would like to leave now," said Pooki, standing up from the sofa, clutching the cat.

"Well, that seems to be everything," muttered Mr. Ratakins, his eyes flicking from the servant to her mistress as he realised that he was in the presence of royalty. "Your Highness, if I may inform you for next time, we do make personal visits at no extra cost. On receipt of a telegram one of our lady fitters will be with you in no time at all."

Mink's thoughts turned to her mother, who had died of childbed fever just days after giving birth to the sister she'd begged her for, who had also failed to survive. She then imagined her father cold and alone, lying on his back in a mortuary.

"There won't be another time, Mr. Ratakins," she replied, her voice uneven. "All my relatives are dead."

*

A STICKY DRIZZLE WAS FALLING by the time the carriage crunched up the driveway of the vast villa in Holland Park. Its lavish oriental interiors and magnificent grounds had been regularly featured in society magazines. Since the Maharaja's death, however, any hint of gaiety had been snuffed out. The blinds on the windows were drawn, the pots of cheerful daffodils removed from the steps and attached to the door, sheltered by a grand portico, was a wreath, its crape ribbons hanging limply in the damp. Clutching one of her new black-edged handkerchiefs, Mink ran up the steps to the front door. Standing on either side were two white-haired men in top hats, black sashes tied across their matching overcoats, who smelt fiercely of drink.

"Who are you?" Mink asked one of them. The man continued to stare ahead of him in silence. "And you?" she said, turning to the other one. He too refused to speak. "What are you both doing at my front door?" she demanded crossly. The pair remained as quiet as graves, their gazes fixed on the trees in the distance. Suddenly, one of them twitched and rattled, and from out of an eye sailed a solitary tear.

As the Princess stood in the hall furiously unbuttoning her gloves, Bantam, the butler, approached. "The mutes arrived while you were out, ma'am," he explained. "They haven't said a word. We've done our best, believe me. One of the gardeners tried to tempt them with a German sausage, but there was absolute silence. I got in touch with the undertakers, and they agreed that mutes aren't normally required until the day of the funeral. Unfortunately they said it was impossible to call them off. The Maharaja was very specific in his instructions. He stipulated a matching pair, apparently, though I notice only one of them has a beard."

"They already smell of drink, Bantam."

"Indeed, ma'am. They must have come straight from a previous engagement. May I suggest that we tell the mourners not to give them any more, despite the inclement weather?"

"Please see to it." There was a pause. "And my father?" she added.

"They've just brought his body back following the inquest, ma'am. I took the liberty of putting him in the drawing room."

"And the servants. How are they?" she asked.

"Still rather shaken, ma'am. Mrs. Wilson made so many mistakes making breakfast I had to give her the morning off. There should have been potted char. I do apologise."

"Give them all the time they need," Mink replied, looking away for a moment. "And Mr. Cavendish?" she asked, turning back.

Bantam hesitated. "Not a word, ma'am," he said.

The Princess climbed the stairs, feeling a blade turn inside her with every step.

*

SEVERAL HOURS LATER, POOKI KNOCKED on the Princess's bedroom door. "The bodice has just arrived from Jay's, ma'am," she said upon entering. Mink stood in front of the mirror and silently took off her earrings, which would be replaced by those of unpolished jet. As she was helped into the gruesome clothes, she had the impression of being slowly choked by tar. When the maid left, she took a book out of her chest of drawers, and read the inscription written by the man she had imagined would admire her eyes forever.

The Princess and Mr. Cavendish had met one afternoon when their carriages collided in Hyde Park. Mink, who thought the accident to be entirely his fault, proceeded to inform him of the fact. It was when he admitted that women were better drivers than men, who had a tendency to show off, that she noticed the shape of his thighs. When she recounted the incident to her father, he instantly recognised a flame of desire in his daughter's indignation. Up until then, she had rejected all manner of handsome temptations he had invited to the house on the pretext of playing cards. He investigated the background of the erratic driver, and was pleased to find it entirely suitable. Keen to stoke the fire underneath her, he asked him to his forthcoming Highland shooting party, and ordered a new kilt for the occasion.

The first the Princess knew of the invitation was her father's announcement that he had just sent a carriage to pick up Mr. Cavendish from the station. Protesting, she ran upstairs to change, but after several minutes in front of the mirror, she changed back again, much to Pooki's frustration. Unable to speak to the unexpected guest, she contrived not to sit next to him in the drawing room after dinner while her father agreed to the numerous requests to sing. The best woman shot in the country, she refused the following day to hide her talent with a gun to save the man's blushes. By the end of the afternoon she had filled the carts with enough grouse to scandalise vegetarians for miles, and poachers retreated to their armchairs in despair. It was only when Mr. Cavendish was leaving that she finally felt able to talk to him. She stood at the landing window watching the retreating carriage, chastising herself for having so rudely ignored him.

It was her father who lured him to their home in Holland Park with an invitation to see his animals. Inspired by the Tower of London's historic menagerie, the Maharaja had acquired them in the belief that every monarch should own a collection of exotic beasts. But his neighbours weren't the only ones unsettled by the noisy invasion. The still-room maid shook at the sight of the kangaroo that hopped with its baby in its front pocket. The coachman, a tear in his eye, tried to scrub the zebra clean in the belief that it was a white pony that gypsies had painted with black stripes. And the scullery maid fainted when a pair of porcupines walked into the kitchen and raised their deadly defences.

Unaware of her father's scheming, Mink went out into the garden to see the flamingos. Deep pink when they first arrived due to their diet of shrimp, they had now started to glimmer as a result of a weakness for the Maharaja's goldfish. But instead of the long-legged birds, the Princess found Mr. Cavendish, who had not the slightest appetite for the contents of the ornamental pond. Next to him stood her father, who was trying to shake off an orphaned bear cub convinced that the Indian was its mother. The Maharaja insisted that Mink join them on his tour of the grounds, and she followed at a distance, her stomach tight. When she entered the grotto, she found Mr. Cavendish turning in circles, looking for her father, who had disappeared with the mastery of a magician. The couple stood in silence, surrounded by the gloom, and it wasn't until they were joined by the bear cub hunting for its moustached mother that they started to talk.

Mark Cavendish was a regular addition to the luncheon table after that. His hat and exquisite cane became such a fixture in the hall that the servants stirred themselves into a frenzy over an imminent wedding, seeing white satin in every look the couple exchanged. The Maharaja was unable to control himself, and took to reading out loud the florid descriptions of society nuptials in the newspaper. Mink remained silent, the waiting made worse by the expectation that filled the house to its well-swept corners. But since the news of the Maharaja's death, none of them had seen the ivory-handled cane again.

*

THE PRINCESS CLOSED THE BOOK, returned it to the drawer, and braced herself for the task ahead of her. She descended the marble stairs, each bearing the Maharaja's initials in a florid script, the crape on her skirt trembling with every step. The servants had already gone down for tea, and she found herself alone. As she reached for the drawing room door handle, she suddenly remembered the last time she saw her mother. She had just turned six and burst into her bedroom just as the doctor was raising the sheet over her exhausted face.

Stepping inside, Mink instantly felt like an intruder. Swaths of black velvet hung over the colourful Indian silk wall hangings, the French mirror above the fireplace, and the portraits of her ancestors with furious moustaches. The furniture had been pushed back against the walls, and in the middle stood a trestle bearing a short, open oak coffin, as deep as its occupant was stout.

Slowly she approached, fearing what she would see. The Maharaja's moustache had been expertly waxed, his hair parted on the correct side, and the toes of his red slippers pointed to the heavens in two perfect curls. A man who had spent most of his life in a frock coat or Norfolk jacket, he was now dressed in his father's gold robes and pantaloons. Tucked into the unyielding waistband was an ornamental dagger, and several strings of pearls reached his navel. Her hand trembled as she straightened them. Bending towards him, she kissed his forehead, her tears slipping down his waxy cheek, and she wondered how he could have left her.

The Maharaja's final expression of utter contentment had rarely been seen in recent years, except in the company of his daughter. The rage he felt for the Government, and his frustration with the Queen for not having returned his jewels, had grown steadily towards the end of his life as he sat brooding in his study over what had once been his.

When, all those years ago, British troops came at night to seize the state of Prindur, he had been too young to feel the intensity of what later smouldered like a branding iron inside him. His mother, then regent on account of his youth, was shot in the chest during the battle, though for years rumours persisted that she had escaped to the mountains with a sack of foreigners' heads.

The first he knew of defeat was the sight of the awestruck soldiers in the palace treasury, their filthy fingers on the family's jewels, taken by the invaders as financial compensation for having to defeat his army. Prindur and its lucrative mines annexed to British India, the deposed Maharaja was exiled to England. The Queen, seduced by the teenager's charm that was later to be his downfall, painted his portrait, and welcomed him to Windsor Castle and Osborne House on the Isle of Wight. He was invited to the best balls, where he danced with considerable talent with the prettiest guests. Young ladies would crowd round the piano to hear him sing after dinner, such a pure and melancholy sound that even the moon wept. Invitations to his shooting parties were displayed on the most elegant mantelpieces in London, and such was his skill with a gun that even the horses stared at the wagons piled high with the still-warm corpses of so much game.

The Maharaja called his daughter Alexandrina after the sovereign who had propelled him to the top of society, taking the Queen's first name, which she never used. When the Princess began to walk, and would be found asleep amongst her mother's furs, he nicknamed her Mink. After the deaths of his wife and second child, from which he never truly recovered, he made frequent visits to the nursery. Sitting his daughter dressed in black on his knee, he distracted her from her grief with tales of palace life and her grandmother's celebrated talent for hunting tigers. He soon taught her how to play chess and handle a gun, and hired the best fencing instructor he could find. Years later, he sobbed with regret when she left for Girton College, so far away in Cambridge, and he sobbed with pride at her achievements.

*

THREE DAYS LATER, THE NIGHT before the funeral, Bantam came into the servants' hall when the under staff had finished their supper. Standing at the head of the table, the butler warned that he would not tolerate any negligence during the Maharaja's final hours in their care. The funeral procession would travel from the house to Waterloo Station, he explained, where the mourners would take a train to the cemetery for a private burial. With a glance at Mrs. Wilson, he added that anyone who fell short of his expectations would not receive their beer money that week. The perk, long abandoned by most employers, had been maintained by the Maharaja, who enjoyed indulging his servants almost as much as himself.

No one slept that night for fear of the train being missed. Even the canary in its cage draped with black velvet failed to put its head under its wing. Mink was still far from her dreams when Pooki came in with a tea-tray covered with a serviette, bearing a cup of tea, a small milk jug, a sugar basin, and thin slices of bread and butter. The Princess lifted her head to get a better look at her. Having succumbed to Western attire for the occasion, she was wearing servant's mourning, a simple black dress with a crape collar and cuffs. Her hair, with its occasional flicker of silver, was coiled into a plump bun.

"How does the corset feel?" asked the Princess.

"Like I am being tortured, ma'am," she replied. "I have made some mourning trousers for Albert," she added, referring to the Maharaja's tiny monkey.

"He's been hiding in my father's study ever since he passed away," said Mink, sitting up.

"That is where I found him, ma'am," said the servant, putting the tray on the Princess's lap.

Mink looked down. "There's something sticking out of your boot."

"It is a bay leaf, ma'am. I put it there to ward off lightning. It is very inauspicious during a funeral. My grandmother was buried during a storm and her soul has never rested. She comes to see me at least once a week, all the way from India. I thought I was rid of her when she died. While I loved the Maharaja more than I can say, I do not want to see him ever again."

Mink sipped her tea, hoping that the worst of it was over. "All those people who came to the house to pay their respects . . . I can't say all of them were respectful of my father when he was alive."

"Some just came out of curiosity after what was in the papers following the inquest, ma'am," said the maid, attending to the fire. "Everyone was talking about it, and people are very nosey."

"Thank God I didn't go."

Pooki had just laid out her mistress's clothes when the peculiar noise sounded. They both assumed that it was Mrs. Wilson blowing her perpetually blocked nose. The servant, who suffered from an allergy to flour, had spent the last few days baking widow's tears for the mourners, whose appetites for the small pastries dusted with icing sugar matched their inquisitiveness. Mink heard the noise again when she sat down for breakfast, unsettled by her father's empty seat. "That sound is coming from a nose even longer than Mrs. Wilson's," she said, standing up. Abandoning her kidneys, she followed it to the hall and looked out of the window. Standing in the driveway was the undertaker. But instead of four horses, the open-mouthed Princess saw shackled to the hearse a caparisoned Indian elephant, plumes of black ostrich feathers mounted on its head.

The servants spent the next forty-seven minutes flicking their eyes to the clocks as they performed their duties, waiting for the bearers to arrive. Despite the undertaker's insistence that they were on their way, the Princess stood smoking at the morning room window with its view of the drive. Eventually they turned up, blaming a broken wheel for the delay. But the men turned out to be apprentices, which was entirely the fault of the deceased, who had stipulated an age limit for reasons of aesthetics. As slight as clerks, they found themselves unable to shoulder the devastating consequences of the Maharaja's weakness for venison pie and shirt-sleeve pudding. During the struggle, two of their top hats were knocked to the ground, and a muddied gardener was called from his carpet bedding to assist. The coffin pitched and rolled as if on a high sea as it eventually found its way into the hearse. The mourners watched from their carriages, hands over their mouths, pretending not to look.

The procession moved out of the drive, headed by the undertaker dressed in a black overcoat, the crape weepers on his top hat fluttering in the breeze. Next came the mutes, finally extracted from their resolute position under the portico. They were now sunk in a depression as black as their coats, brought on by the drink some of the mourners had slipped them out of mischief behind the butler's back. As they walked, what had started off as the odd fraudulent tear during their time at the front door progressed into a shoulder-shaking flood, which no turncock could halt. They were followed by three feathermen, holding four-foot confections of black ostrich feathers above their heads, who struggled to see where they were going. The elephant-drawn hearse followed, flanked by the exhausted bearers longing for their lunch, muttering that such a beast was the only thing strong enough for the job.

Mink sat alone in the family carriage, bitterly regretting her father's showmanship, which would inevitably get into the papers. A number of the vehicles that followed were empty, a common practice indulged by those unable to attend. But the Princess suspected that some of her father's friends who had enjoyed his legendary indulgences were trying to avoid the taint of scandal. She glanced round, trying to see whether Mark Cavendish was in the cortège. Still uncertain, she stared ahead, and prayed that the lumbering procession would pick up speed so they wouldn't miss the train.

But no one had foreseen the curiosity of the elephant. The bearers found themselves frequently goosed by an inquisitive trunk, which slowed the journey while decency was restored. The children en route sacrificed their penny buns to the colossal animal with wrinkly knees, its sudden halt causing the exasperated drivers behind to yank on their reins to avoid a shunt.

Finally they arrived at Waterloo, rattling over the cobbles of the private terminus of the Necropolis Railway. Its very name unsettled the souls of the living, for its principal passengers never returned from the journey to Brookwood Cemetery. The mourners eased themselves out of their carriages, the men fiddling with their black crape sashes across their left shoulders, an accessory stipulated in the Maharaja's instructions that had subsequently gone out of funeral fashion. By now the Princess had begun to feel sick, as there were only two minutes before the train was due to depart. A whistle sounded, and for a moment she imagined the humiliation of having to return home with the coffin. A quietly furious station-master appeared at her side, his outrage completed by the elephant droppings in his courtyard. He marched them up a spotless stone staircase, flanked with palms, to one of the first-class waiting rooms opposite the platform. While the rest of the party remained standing, the mutes collapsed onto the seats and started to snore. Meanwhile, the coffin was heaved into a once steam-powered lift, which had been broken by the unrelenting weight of aristocratic indulgence. It was now hand-operated by Snub the turner, who set to work and offered up a prayer for a cure for corpulence.

Upstairs the train itched to leave its buffers, impatient smoke billowing down its green flanks. With its first-, second-, and third-class carriages, it looked like any other except for the hearse vans at the rear, one of the doors still open. The mourners for the other funerals were already on board, and a number stuck their heads out the windows, demanding to know the reason for the delay. But Snub was still labouring with his handle, invoking the help of gods in whom he didn't even believe. Passengers in the third-class carriage, realising that the delay was due to the Maharaja's contingent, gave up heckling the station-master, and shouted to them to get a move on. Heads turned away, pretending not to hear, which only increased their fury, and insults started to fly. A carriage door was flung open, and two mourners ran out, only to be herded into a waiting room by the terrified staff.

The foreign deities must have been listening, for the long-awaited coffin suddenly appeared like a divine apparition. The staff winced as they lifted it onto their shoulders and carried it to the hearse van. Eventually the boxed Maharaja slid onto the shelf bearing his name, and his friends, acquaintances, and daughter rushed to their allotted compartment.

As the train pulled out, they sat in silence, looking at their funeral gloves. The vicar, who had baptised the deceased all those years ago, tried to strike up conversation, resorting to the national obsession: "Isn't it a lovely day?" But the only sound came from the slumped mutes muttering in their dreams. Ignoring Mark Cavendish's empty seat, Mink rested her forehead against the window, and watched as men pulled off their caps on seeing the train, and crossed themselves in dread.

Forty long minutes later, they arrived at the cemetery built to alleviate London's overcrowded graveyards. Said to be the largest and most beautiful in England, its five hundred acres of Surrey woodland and expanses of heather and rhododendrons sent the living into raptures. Much was made of the separate burial grounds for certain members of society, including bakers, actors, and Swedes. The train stopped at North Station, where the mourners attending funerals in the Nonconformist and Roman Catholic grounds got out, and, with a backwards glance at the offending party, trooped into private waiting rooms. The train continued to the South Station in the Anglican ground, past sumptuous statuary that would make even an atheist sigh. Once the passengers had left the train, two gravediggers carried the collapsed mutes to a shed and shut the door. United by silence, the Maharaja's party stood in a waiting room, where two women who hadn't been invited joined them. The Princess glanced at their careful ringlets, wondering how they knew her father. She realised their provenance when an official came to escort the party to the chapel. For they blushed at the sign on the door that forbade vagrants, beggars, itinerant musicians, and females of doubtful persuasion to enter.

After the service, the mourners followed the bier down a path, the weak sun failing to warm them. But instead of the freshly dug grave Mink was expecting, she found herself in front of a Portland stone mausoleum resembling the palace of Prindur. They stepped inside, their feet uncomfortably loud on the cold marble floor. The Princess shivered in the frigid air, and watched with dread as the coffin was lowered into a brick hole in the ground that would shortly be sealed. Unable to leave him, she hung back when the mourners left for some cold beef in the refreshment room. As she gazed at the wreaths, her eye was drawn to one of neat white roses, which the Maharaja had feared would never come. Kneeling down, she looked at the black-edged card with a crowned royal cipher on which was written "In Sorrowing Memory." It was signed "Victoria RI."

*

A VISITOR WAS WAITING FOR the Princess when she finally returned home, having slept through most of the journey. He sat eating the last of the widow's tears in the drawing room, where the furniture had been pushed back into position and the windows opened to clear the air. She had never liked seeing Bartholomew Grimes at the house, as the lawyer's visits always left her father in a rage. As she sat down opposite him, she soon realised that his over-consumption of mourning cakes was a result of nerves rather than appetite. It took a while for him to get to the point, momentarily alighting on topics Mink knew had no relation to his visit, including the crisis in Crete and the proposed electric railway running from Kensington to Charing Cross.

Finally he brushed off a non-existent piece of fluff from his trousers, and said that for years her father had refused to listen to his advice, and that it was only out of concern for the family that he had kept returning to the house to give it. He then explained that the Maharaja had routinely spent more than the annual stipend the British Government had paid him since he signed the treaty following the annexation of Prindur. As a result of the Maharaja's frequent appeals, the Government had given him a loan against the house to help repay his debts incurred at the gambling tables. The lawyer held up a sheaf of bills. "As well as at the draper's, the gunsmith's, the wine merchant's, the carriage builder's, the furrier's, the hatter's, the bootmaker's, the goldsmith's, the exotic animal dealer's, and . . ." He squinted to read the piece of paper in front of him. "The corset maker's." The borrowing against the house was on condition that it would be sold on the Maharaja's death, he added, at which point, according to the treaty, the Government pension would also come to an end.

"I trust he never told you?" the lawyer asked, gripping the edge of the papers. The silence confirmed his suspicion.

Eventually the man with crumbs in his whiskers picked up his hat and cane, and left without another word. The Princess continued staring at the floor, seeing the remains of her life finally collapse, having completely forgotten to ring the bell for the visitor to be shown out.

CHAPTER II

Albert Is Sold to a Travelling Zoo

MONDAY, MARCH 7, 1898

T was almost a year later when the letter arrived. For several days it remained ignored, tossed by Mink onto a pile of increasingly exasperated correspondence from the Government demanding that the house be sold. At first the Princess answered their entreaties with a veiled reference to difficult circumstances, and a polite request to stay a little longer. But as no solution presented itself, and the demands continued to arrive, the perfect penmanship on the black-edged replies began to wane. "My father would not have been able to build up such debts in England," she wrote, her nib scratching furiously across the page, "had this country not slain his mother, stolen his land, and exiled him."

By then many of the rooms had been shut up to save having to heat and clean them. Sheets hung over their furniture like frozen ghosts, curtains were tied in hessian sacking, and pictures were covered with brown paper. Despite Mink's habit of wanton spending, a vice inherited from her father, she finally decided that his menagerie had to go. The owner of a travelling zoo came to buy it, and gradually the servants were dismissed. At first a gardener

was given a month's wages, followed by two of the grooms, causing panic amongst the remaining staff, who were already far too
numerous. They started to scrutinise each other, searching out the
dead wood in order to reassure themselves that they wouldn't be
next. The silver had never shone so brightly, bells were answered
within an instant, and the topiary was trimmed to an inch of its
life. Mrs. Wilson resorted to quack remedies to rid herself of her
allergy. George, the second footman, whom the other servants
suspected had been hired on account of the Maharaja's affection
for his mother, invested in padded silk stockings in the hope of
bringing some allure to his disgraceful calves. But eventually even
those two had to go, and tears of regret were shed once more for
the dead Maharaja.

Only Pooki, the longest-serving servant, remained, having
carried out her duties completely oblivious to the jostling of the
other staff desperate to keep their positions. Demoting herself to
a maid-of-all-work, or a slavey, as some called them, she took to
her new role with quiet determination rather than skill. The Princess never once mentioned the dust that hadn't been reached, the
fires that were left to die, and her cooking that was something to
endure rather than extol.

It was while the maid was trimming the lamp wicks that she
noticed the writing on the envelope that came that morning was
different from those which had been arriving for almost a year.
Wearing servant's half-mourning, a black dress with white trimmings, she placed it on the silver salver and offered it again to
Mink, who was reading an old issue of the *Strand Magazine* in the
drawing room, a rug over her knees and her feet in a muff. She
automatically opened it, distracted by the antics of Albert, whom
she couldn't bring herself to sell. Dressed like his mistress in a sor-
rowful shade of grey, he had found his late master's favourite pipe,
and was sitting between the photograph frames on the mantelpiece, inspecting it. The Princess glanced at the letter.

Madam,

With my humble duty, I am directed to inform you that The Queen should like to offer you a grace-and-favour residence at Hampton Court Palace in recognition of her regard for His Highness your late father.

The six-bedroom house is within the palace grounds and has its own garden. The warrant would serve for your lifetime and could be drawn up in due course.

I look forward to your response, at your earliest convenience, which I shall convey to The Queen.

I have the honour to remain, Madam, Your Highness's obedient servant,

Kellerton

"It's from the Lord Chamberlain," said the Princess, her eyes wide as she looked at the letterhead. "The Queen is offering me a grace-and-favour home at Hampton Court Palace."

Pooki frowned.

"From what I remember, it's full of widows whose husbands served with distinction in military or imperial service, and who have fallen on hard times. God knows what they'll be like, but it means I can finally sell the house and get the Government off my back!" continued Mink, beaming.

The servant turned round, picked up the bellows, and squeezed them at the fire. "We cannot live in that palace, ma'am. There are far too many ghosts," she said curtly. "You will have to think of something else."

"But grace-and-favour residents don't pay rent," said Mink, staring at her incredulously.

The maid continued to pump until the embers flushed scarlet. "That is one of the most haunted places in England, ma'am," she said, her back still turned. "Even the dustman knows that."

"But there's a huge waiting list," Mink protested, holding the letter out towards her. "I'm very lucky to have been offered it. It's a six-bedroom house with a garden, for goodness' sake. Most of the other residents live in apartments."

The maid put down the bellows with a loud clatter, and picked up the salver. "Even so, ma'am. It is not for us," she said, marching out with the short steps of a servant, her jaw set.

While the Princess had every intention of accepting the offer, she wasn't going anywhere without Pooki. She glanced at her throughout the day as she performed her duties, but there was no sign of capitulation. "That woman's as stubborn as a dachshund," she thought to herself, as the maid strode past her carrying a coal bucket, refusing to meet her eye. The following morning, after helping herself to breakfast from the sideboard, Mink returned to her seat and peered at the black-and-yellow mixture. "I asked for an omelette," she said, as Pooki came in with a basket of warm rolls. "Is this a new recipe?"

"It is an omelette, ma'am," came the reply. "They are very difficult to make."

The Princess raised her eyebrows. "Are they? Blondin the acrobat managed to make one on a cooking stove while balancing on a tightrope stretched across the Niagara River. Isn't he one of your heroes?"

"Yes, ma'am, but he was French. Everyone knows that the French are born with special cooking powers because their mothers eat snails."

Mink prodded it doubtfully with her fork. "You shouldn't have to be doing the cooking, anyway. Maybe if we sold the house and moved to Hampton Court Palace I might be able to find some money for a cook."

Pooki frowned and headed for the door. "Domestic servants do not like to work in that place, ma'am. It is haunted. I told you that yesterday," she said over her shoulder.

"But there are no such things as ghosts," Mink protested.

The maid turned, her hands on her hips. "Ma'am, my grand-mother visits me more often now than when she was alive. She is the reason why my hair is turning grey. I do not want the spirit of Catherine Howard at the bottom of my bed as well. Some of us have to get up early in the morning," she added, pulling the door loudly behind her.

Later that afternoon, when Mink returned from her walk in Kensington Gardens, she glanced at the servant as she opened the front door and saw that her jaw was still set. Deciding that the only way forward was a bribe, she sat in the drawing room with the newspaper, waiting for Pooki to come in with her sewing. The servant had long abandoned the lady's-maid's sitting room on account of the Princess's terrible loneliness. It wasn't long before Pooki took the seat opposite her, bent her head in silence, and started to mend the seam of a blouse. Five minutes passed and there was none of her usual chatter that made Mink wonder how anyone could have so much to say, let alone a servant, who was only supposed to speak when necessary. Ten minutes later, and not a single tradesman's joke had come from her lips. Mink glanced at her, then cried from behind her newspaper: "Look what they've got on at the Royal Aquarium—performing dogs!"

The needle suddenly stopped and the maid slowly raised her dark eyes.

"I wonder what they get up to," enthused the Princess from behind her paper. "Maybe it's one of those charming dog orches-tras where they all play a musical instrument. Who could resist a fox terrier playing the drums?"

The servant remained transfixed.

"I don't believe it!" gasped the Princess. "It says here that Pro-fessor Finney is performing his great dive from the roof in flames. I hope he doesn't burn to death. And if he survives that, there's always the risk he'll drown."

Pooki dropped her needle, her eyes wide.

The Princess drew the newspaper even closer. "Goodness me.

They've even got Countess X in a den of lions. Imagine if you were sitting in the audience and they bit off her head . . ."

"We must go tomorrow, ma'am, and sit at the front!" Pooki suddenly burst out.

Mink folded up the paper, and pulled the rug up higher over her knees. "I'm afraid there'll be no little treats for us," she said with a sigh. "I'm trying to cut back on any unnecessary expenditure. If we stay here any longer I'm going to have to attend to the gardens, though I don't know what with. If I sold the house, then at least I'd be able to repay the Government their loan. But where would we go then? At this rate I'm not even going to be able to afford to buy you gingerbread."

The maid picked up her needle and bent her head. It wasn't until the following morning that she finally changed her mind. "Maybe they have got rid of the ghosts at that palace, ma'am," she said, doing up Mink's dress. "There are machines for everything these days."

As soon as the reply was posted to the Lord Chamberlain, the house and some of the furniture was put up for sale, along with the carriages, and the oil paintings in the Maharaja's study of women who must have been chilly while they posed. But some simply came to peer at the sumptuous Indian interiors they had coveted in the society magazines, and the bedroom of the man who had died in such unusual circumstances. The owner of the travelling zoo, whose beard was no match for that of his pygmy goat, returned for Albert. However, Pooki left the man standing on the steps and shut the door, refusing the Princess's instruction to fetch the monkey's tiny suitcase.

"Ma'am, you cannot sell Albert," she protested, standing in the hall with her hands on her hips. "The Maharaja had him brought over from India especially. He fell overboard after a mango and even the captain prayed that he would live when they fished him out, he loved him so much."

But the Princess was adamant. She had had several letters on the matter from Mrs. Boots, the palace housekeeper, who also acted as the Lord Chamberlain's representative. "I don't want him to go either, but she was quite insistent. No pets are allowed, apart from lap dogs."

"But ma'am. How will that man with the mangy beard know when it is time for Albert to come out of mourning and put on his red velvet trousers?" she asked, pointing to the door.

"I suggest you tell him, though I'm sure the issue of clothing will be of no interest," said Mink, walking off to the library to avoid seeing Albert go.

FRIDAY, MARCH 18, 1898

When the day of the move arrived, a telegram was dispatched to Mrs. Boots informing her of the time their train was due to arrive at Hampton Court. It followed copious correspondence from the woman, much of which disclosed the torment of her bronchitis, as well as the insistence that they arrive on a Friday, when the palace was closed for cleaning. But when the four-wheeler arrived to take them to Waterloo, Mink invented so many things that still needed to be done that the driver fell asleep and the horse discovered an appetite for the tulips. When no more excuses could be found, the Princess finally tied the ribbons of her grey bonnet and walked down the front steps for the last time. As the carriage slowly headed down the drive, she looked back at the only home she had ever known, blinking away the tears that rose, lost in the bewildering no-man's-land between her past and her future.

The driver of the ponderous growler dropped them at the entrance to the station, choked by a scrum of hansom cabs, carriages, omnibuses, vans, and carts collecting or disgorging passengers. A porter loaded their luggage onto a barrow, and they followed him inside. Newspaper boys yelled the day's news over the thunder of the trains, shoeblacks cast admonishing looks at passengers' boots, and pickpockets slunk past, preying on the confusion. The Princess sought out the bookstall while Pooki, tightly clutching her mistress's jewel case, went to buy the tickets.

"But they're third-class," said Mink, when the maid returned with them.

"Two first-class tickets would cost four shillings, ma'am. Those people who came to the house did not pay what we asked for the furniture, and some just wanted things for free. Ladies also travel in third class on trains. It said so in one of your newspapers."

Mink instantly recognised an attempt to control her extravagances. "It's all very well travelling in third class as long as people know you can afford to travel in first," she replied.

"But ma'am. You were one of the first ladies to travel on the top of an omnibus."

"Yes, but that was for an entirely different reason. Men had had the best view for far too long."

When the dispute was finally settled, and new tickets purchased, the only thing left of their train was a cheerful plume of smoke. The pair stared incredulously at the empty track, then turned and retreated to the waiting room. Easing past the portmanteaux, carpetbags, and parcels, they sat down next to the Bibles chained to the wall lest someone broke the Eighth Commandment. While the passengers and a dog glanced at the curious couple, the mistress and the maid kept their eyes on the ground, silently blaming the other for bronchial Mrs. Boots waiting in vain for them outside the palace. Never once did either suggest a pot of tea in the refreshment room. And when they had waited, they waited some more, for it was an unshakeable truth that no train took longer to arrive than when its predecessor had been missed.

Finally they pulled out of the station, the porter gazing at the generous tip the Princess had pressed into his hand with relief. As the train crossed over the viaduct, she looked down at the London streets and tried to imagine living so far away from the centre of the universe that was Piccadilly. It wasn't long before the Princess, unsure of her future, thought again of the life she had hoped to share with Mark Cavendish, who had offered his love so generously, then snatched it back again with the greed of a miser. Reaching for the novel she had just bought, she opened it to distract herself: she had already wasted too much regret on that man as it was.

Pooki, her face seeming even thinner in her black bonnet, finally broke the silence as they passed through fields in the early thrust of spring. "At least you will be living in a palace, as you should be, ma'am," she said.

The Princess smiled unconvincingly, and then lowered her head back to her book.

The light was starting to fade by the time the train reached its final destination forty-five minutes later. A porter carried their luggage to the fly, a one-horse covered carriage whose sullen driver was wearing a filthy blanket over his knees against the damp. As they headed over the bridge towards the palace, which was already in view, two small boys ran after them, caps in their hands, hoping to earn a penny carrying the bags inside. Wondering why she had never been, Mink gazed at the monument that had been seducing visitors for centuries with its iconic chimney pots, stately cloisters, and romantic courtyards. Once a royal residence, at the front stood a majestic redbrick sixteenth-century Tudor building constructed for Cardinal Wolsey and Henry VIII, and extending from the back was a contrasting late-seventeenth-century elegant Baroque addition commissioned by William III and Mary II. Its gardens, enjoyed by countless sovereigns, were some of the most loved in England.

Despite the brevity of the journey, and the lameness of the horse, when the driver pulled up at Trophy Gate, the main entrance to the palace, he had the temerity to attempt to overcharge them. When Mink threatened to report the forsaken beast to the nearest constable, the man realised what he was up against and reduced his price. He then sloped off to the Mitre Hotel over the road, where he bought a pint of stout and eyed the only women who ever returned his glances.

More prostitutes stood at Trophy Gate, their cheeks rouged and plump curls cascading down their backs, lured by the cavalry-men barracked in the palace's driveway. The Princess glanced at the women uneasily, remembering the pair with the careful ring-lets at her father's funeral. She then spotted a plum pudding of a woman, her shawl drawn up over her bonneted head, and her arms folded across her formidable chest. From the cough that emerged from the bundle, she guessed that it was Mrs. Boots. After intro-ducing herself, she apologised for being late. "You wouldn't believe the effects on the lungs of having to stand outside waiting for people who have missed their train, Your Highness," came the immediate reply. The housekeeper then peered up at the smutty sky. "There's nothing worse than a north-east wind for someone with my condition. It's been howling round me ever since I came outside, which was so long ago it's a wonder Mr. Boots isn't a widower." She fell silent as a young gentleman with dark curls and a black frock coat strode out of the gates. His topper bulged, the telltale sign of a general practitioner who still preferred to carry his short wooden stethoscope in his hat rather than use a bag. A faint yet persistent creak came from his boots as he passed. Reaching the other side of the road, he tipped the crippled crossing sweeper, and, as he headed home, glanced back towards the Princess with eyes that quickened the pulse of a number of his patients.

"Not that Dr. Henderson there has cured me," Mrs. Boots continued, as Mink followed her gaze. "If you ever see him on his bicycle I'd give him a wide berth if I were you. He's one of them scorchers. Got fined for speeding in Bushy Park the other week. And if you decide to have him for your doctor, don't tell him you drink tea. He's an opponent. Says it creates all manner of mischief in the body. Still, he's better than Dr. Barnstable, the last village doctor. Ever so nervy. Trembling hands. He should have prescribed himself one of his useless tonics. Ended up dead as a duck in the Thames just over there by the bridge. One of the watermen found him. It was a right palaver getting him out of the water. His pockets were full of stones. Not that I'm a gossip-monger. Is that all you've got? I expect the furniture's following. I'll take you the long way so you can get your bearings. We'll have to do the tour of the palace tomorrow, given your extremely late arrival. Mr. Boots will be wanting his kippers."

With the speed of a startled pheasant, the housekeeper suddenly took off towards the palace. The Princess and the maid rushed after her, followed by Pike and Gibbs, the butcher's and grocer's delivery boys, weighed down by the luggage.

"Excuse those ladies," Mrs. Boots called over her shoulder. "The gate was put up to stop them coming in, but they still manage to get past the sentry. You would have thought the smell of that thing would put them off." She nodded to a pile of manure from the stables. "Aggravates my chest, I tell you. The residents don't stop complaining about it. Don't blame them, neither, it being a royal palace and all. What we need is the Queen to pay a visit. Then they'd soon clear it."

As they continued up the drive, Mink peered at the Tudor Great Gatehouse ahead of them, but there was no trace of the charm she had seen in countless pictures. The creeping darkness had snuffed out the dusky salmon hue of the bricks, and the crenulations stood brutally against the sky streaked with night. Wondering how it would ever feel like home, she glanced to her left and saw a long, low line of barracks, where several soldiers stood watching her from the doorways, the smoke of their cigarettes twisting up into the damp air. She looked to her right and spotted beyond the railings the silent Thames, its banks now empty of postcard hawkers, umbrella merchants, and peddlers of spurious guides who lay in wait for the excursionists arriving by river.

The palace had been attracting tourists since the reign of Queen Elizabeth, a tip to the Palace Keeper almost always ensuring a guided tour as long as the court was not present or about to arrive. Order was imposed in the eighteenth century with the standard charge of a shilling, and the housekeeper herded visitors around armed with a long stick to point to the paintings and tapestries. But the numbers were nothing compared to the assault on the monument after Queen Victoria announced in 1838 her decision to open the State Apartments and gardens free to visitors. Hordes converged with unfettered glee on the landmark, with its collection of paintings and sumptuous gardens. And still the masses charged, more than two hundred thousand a year, stuffed into railway carriages, omnibuses, char-à-bancs, carriages, dog carts, brakes, vans, costermongers' barrows, steamers, electric launches, sailing boats, and canoes.

As they approached the gatehouse, the housekeeper pointed out the recently restored mullioned windows, which had replaced the sashes installed by the Georgians. "They never did have any taste," she muttered, wrinkling up her nose. Passing through, they came out onto Base Court, a vast empty square overlooked by countless windows where members and guests of the court were once lodged in luxury, their numerous fireplaces the reason for the palace's plethora of chimneys. Shafts of light suddenly appeared as its current residents parted their curtains an inch, drawn by the sound of the women's feet.

Suddenly Mrs. Boots came to a halt and turned sharply to the Princess. "You haven't got any pets, have you?" she asked.

Mink detected a faint odour of smoked eel. "You were very explicit on that point, Mrs. Boots," she said.

"It pleases me very much to hear that, let me tell you," she replied, continuing her moorland scuttle. "There are some residents who completely ignore what I tell them and think they're too grand to follow rules. After years of protests and a petition from the residents the Lord Chamberlain finally agreed to allow lap dogs. You'd be surprised how many of those ladies pretend a Labrador can sit on their arthritic knees. Lady Montfort Bebb took it upon herself to buy a red setter. There were six months of arguments, and the Lord Chamberlain gave in and said she could keep it until it died, after which she would have to get something smaller. She's already replaced it once, and claims that dog is the original. Thinks I was born yesterday. Then there's Lady Beatrice and her wretched doves. Filthy creatures. How they came to be symbols of peace I'll never know. They make General Bagshot positively murderous. Says his windows are all covered in muck. Can't bear her as a result. Nor she him. Not that I'm one for gossip. Four of her birds are missing, presumed dead, so that's a start. Hopefully the cats, which shouldn't be here neither, will get the rest."

Through Clock Court they hurried, without even a pause to admire the famous Astronomical Clock made for Henry VIII, which could tell the time of high water at London Bridge, amongst other marvels. "That's one of the most exceptional timepieces in the country," the housekeeper said, as Mink turned round to look at it. "It stopped as it struck four on March 2, 1619, the moment Queen Anne of Denmark died at the palace. And it's done so every time a long-term resident has expired within the palace precincts. Something in my bones tells me it's about to stop again, but Mr. Boots insists it's the beginning of gout."

Mrs. Boots kept up her pace, believing nothing should come between a husband and his kippers. There were currently forty-six grace-and-favour warrant holders, she called over her shoulder, some of whom had relatives living with them. They were lodged, along with their servants, in apartments scattered throughout the palace, as well as in several houses in the grounds. There were also more than twenty tenanted staff and their families living there, including masons, carpenters, a lamplighter, and a turncock.

The tradition of accommodation being granted by the grace

and favour of the sovereign started in the 1740s, she explained. A select group of courtiers, some of them relatively poor, were given permission to live at the palace in the summer by George II, whose court stopped using it in 1737. George III had no interest in living in the monument either, buying Buckingham House and making Windsor Castle his principal retreat outside London. The palace, apart from the State Apartments, was gradually divided into apartments, and their allocation began formally in 1767 and was organised under official warrants six years later.

At first the residents were fashionable people with good connections, she continued. The wealthy didn't hesitate trying to get their hands on the rent-free apartments. "Dr. Johnson, who wrote that dictionary, was turned down because the waiting list was full. Good job too if you ask me. Why everyone troops to see his boring old chair at the Old Cheshire Cheese chop-house is beyond me." Some of the residents' behaviour left a lot to be desired. Alterations were made to ancient structures without so much as a by-your-leave, apartments were swapped, and some had the cheek to let them to complete strangers. For the last fifty years or so, the residents had almost all been widows or dependents of distinguished military or diplomatic figures whose finances were less than desirable. "Not that they're any better behaved, believe you me."

Suddenly from out of a passageway appeared an old sedan chair mounted on wheels and drawn by a bow-legged liveried chairman, his powdered wig askew. "That's the push," muttered Mrs. Boots, nodding to the contraption. The man pulling it was Wilfred Noseworthy, the resident turncock, who was responsible for turning the water on from the mains, she explained. "He hauls the ladies to their evening engagements for a fee, and charges an extra sixpence if he has to go outside the palace gates in recompense for being seen looking so ridiculous."

As the vehicle passed, the Princess noticed someone peering at her through the window, and she stared back with equal curiosity. Suddenly there was a tapping sound, and Wilfred Noseworthy came to an undignified halt. The window lowered, and the occupant, a woman in her mid-thirties, with a pale, heart-shaped face, her dark hair neatly pinned up, leant out.

"Forgive me for introducing myself, Princess. I'm Mrs. Bagshot," she said in a voice so soft Mink had to step forward to hear her. "It's terribly bad manners, I know, but I'm leaving for Egypt on Sunday morning, and I just wanted to say that I knew your father."

The Princess remained silent, bracing herself for another unsavoury revelation.

"I met him on several occasions and was always very impressed by the charity work he undertook for his fellow Indians," Mrs. Bagshot continued. "Unfortunately that aspect of him has been quite overlooked."

"That's very kind of you, Mrs. Bagshot," said Mink. "I hope you enjoy your time in Egypt. Will you be staying at Shepheard's Hotel? I could sit on their terrace all day watching the passing dragomans, hawkers of sham antiques, and donkey-boys who name their beasts after English celebrities."

Mrs. Bagshot shook her head. "I won't be in Cairo. I'm going to Hélouan-Les-Bains for a little tonic. The sulphur water is as strong as that of Harrogate and contains almost three times as many salts as the waters in Bath. And the tennis never gets rained off."

"Perhaps we could play when you return," Mink suggested.

"I should be delighted. You must join the palace's Lawn Tennis and Croquet Club. I'm the Secretary. I shall return in a month and we'll arrange a game of doubles. If you should require anything in the meantime, please ask one of my servants." She then knocked on the roof. As the chairman resumed his ungainly trot, Mrs. Bagshot turned back and raised her voice. "I hope you've learnt to live with your loss. It's really all we can do."

Passing the resident gas lamplighter, a hare poached from Bushy Park in his pocket, they entered Fountain Court. The square garden was surrounded by a cloistered walkway with numerous doors, each bearing a brass nameplate and a bell. Hanging in the gloomy stairwells were baskets used by residents on the upper floors to winch up their provisions. "Glad I don't live here. The noise from that fountain would send my waterworks funny," muttered Mrs. Boots, their footsteps echoing on the cold flagstones. "And there's nothing Dr. Henderson likes better than peering at the contents of a chamber pot. Me, I'd rather he didn't take quite an interest. It's no wonder some round here call him the Piss Doctor."

Mink glanced at the darkened corners. "Have you ever seen a ghost?" she asked brightly.

The housekeeper stopped again, leant towards the Princess, and lowered her voice. "I've seen none myself, but they're here all right. The residents don't like talking about the spirits, as they make it difficult to keep servants. Eight have just walked out and two more are threatening to go after seeing two new ghosts that spooked them rotten. Horrible moaning. I'd ask you not to talk too liberally about them spectral sightings, if you don't mind. The Society for Psychical Research keeps asking if it can carry out an investigation. They're gentlemen all right, but I wouldn't want them roaming around the palace at night with all that science in their heads."

She suddenly bolted, and the Princess and the maid ran to catch her up again, the two delivery boys lagging behind with their load. "I've worked here for over thirty years, and while I hadn't seen a ghost, I've seen pretty much everything else," she called over her shoulder. "And if I haven't seen it, then my mother certainly did, having been a maid at the palace all her life. You'd be amazed by what the residents try and get away with, and it's me who has to sort it out." By now Mrs. Boots's cage was well and truly rattled, and out flew her grievances like escaping birds. The most tiresome aspect of her duties was her additional role as Keeper of the

Chapel Royal, she moaned. "The ladies are very particular about where they sit, which causes no end of rows. But I won't be having any problems with you. You'll be one of those . . ." She stopped, her eyes flicking briefly to Pooki for inspiration. "What do you call them?" she asked.

"I'm a Christian, Mrs. Boots," Mink replied. "I shall certainly be attending divine service on Sunday, as will my maid."

Nothing of the housekeeper's previous speed matched the sprint that followed, and they came out onto the East Front, where the enormous yews first planted by William and Mary loomed up in the darkness. Turning left along the outside of the palace, the woman scurried past the royal tennis court, the Princess catching the odd phrase, including "dust the Royal Pew," "the residents will be the death of me," "Dr. Henderson," and "piss pot again."

Eventually they reached the Wilderness, an overgrown shrubbery with large elms and criss-crossing pathways. "Keep up so I don't lose you," warned the housekeeper as she entered. "It's dark in here, but I know my way." Mink and Pooki quickened their step, the servant clutching the back of her mistress's skirt as they crept through. Eventually they reached the other side and the housekeeper stopped at a door in a wall that led to a private back garden.

The Princess and the maid peered through the darkness at the large, flat-fronted house looming beyond it. Built around 1700, it offered not an ounce of cheer. The housekeeper followed their gaze. "This is Wilderness House. Yours on account of Mrs. Campbell having just died. Don't ask me about the circumstances. Turns me queer. I haven't eaten brussels sprouts since. Usually there's squabbling amongst the residents when one of them dies. If the deceased's apartments are better than theirs, they fire off letters to the Lord Chamberlain asking to swap long before the body's cold. But Mrs. Campbell has been in the ground for almost three weeks and not a whisper."

She patted herself as she searched for the keys. "This is the back way in. The front door is on Hampton Court Road, but we can't get to it from the palace, as all the gates are locked by now, given your late arrival." She continued clutching at her pockets. "There's no gas. A couple of years ago the residents petitioned for it, but it was thought too dangerous, what with the fires we've had. And electricity is too costly. There's no good complaining. When Michael Faraday lived in a grace-and-favour house overlooking Hampton Court Green, a few doors up from Dr. Henderson's practice, he didn't have any electricity either, despite his discoveries in the field. And don't bother looking for the bathroom. There isn't one. Mrs. Campbell wouldn't pay for one to be installed. She'll have to lug the water up," she said, nodding to Pooki, who immediately frowned. "Hard to believe that Henry VIII had hot and cold running water when he lived here."

"Perhaps Mrs. Campbell didn't have the means," suggested Mink.

"Didn't have the means, or didn't want to spend the money?" the housekeeper asked. "The biggest misconception about this place is that the residents are destitute, despite William IV having called it the quality poorhouse." Residents needed a certain amount of money to afford to live at the palace, she continued. Not only were they obliged to cover the maintenance of their homes and any alterations, but they had to pay for heating, lighting, insurance, as well as an extra supply of water at a constant high pressure in case of another fire. "Some of the ladies end up having to give up their apartments, as they can't afford to live here anymore," she added.

The Princess fell silent.

"You look a little surprised, Your Highness. All the payments and obligations are set out in the warrant that was sent to you."

Mink hesitated. "I'm a little behind in my letter-opening, Mrs. Boots. I did, however, receive your note about all pets being prohibited apart from lap dogs, so we're fine on that score."

"Glad to hear it. If it were me, I'd ban the lap dogs too. It's enough having to put up with that pile of manure at Trophy Gate, without having to dodge all the deposits they leave around the place."

Pooki pointed to the high hedging that ran alongside the house. "What is that?" she asked, speaking for the first time.

"It's the maze," Mrs. Boots replied, handing Mink the keys. "The keeper's just been given an official warning. Someone was stuck in there for two days last week. Apparently he was still walking in circles when they finally escorted him out."

CHAPTER III

The Ominous Arrival of the Undertaker

SATURDAY, MARCH 19, 1898

OLLOWING a night of intoxicating dreams, Dr. Henderson looked at his unruly curls in the mirror and decided that it was finally time to master the plastered look, all the rage in New York. Bending over the china washbowl, he slowly poured a jug of water over his head, the coldness banishing the stubborn remains of slumber. After rubbing his hair with a towel, he carefully parted and combed it, and, with a quick glance at the diagrams in his gentleman's magazine, swathed his head with linen bands. He fetched his cleaned boots from outside the door, carefully closed it again, and pressed inside them two pieces of India rubber he had cut into a pair of soles. Hitching his white nightshirt up to his knees, he then proceeded to tread around the room, listening for the indignity of creaks.

The general practitioner was so consumed by his impolite footwear that he failed to hear the uneven gait of his housekeeper coming down the landing. Mrs. Nettleship was dressed in the black uniform of mourning, despite the years that had passed since her husband sunk silently to the bottom of the North Sea. Her rust-coloured hair, as coarse as a horse brush, stuck out from underneath her white widow's cap. With hands as large and red as a butcher's, she opened the door with unrestrained determination, forgetting, as usual, to knock. She stood staring, her mouth open, as she took in the doctor's wet curls taped to his head, his nightwear drawn up to his knees, and his bare legs sticking out of his boots. Once she had recovered her senses, she quickly pulled the door shut, having instantly recognised a gentleman maddened by love.

But there was no escaping the woman. "Dr. 'enderson," she called, her lips against the crack. "There's people what's waiting houtside the front door. I told them you don't start until nine hon a Saturday, and that no doctor can cure without heggs hin 'is stomach. But they say they'll catch their deaths in the rain. Tom Saddleback says 'e doesn't want to be seen by hanyone, neither. Says 'is nose his pointing the wrong way. North-heast hinstead hof south-west, happarently."

The doctor parted the curtains and looked down to see the palace gardener holding his nose, and suspected he had been brawling in the King's Arms again with one of the monument's warders. "Show them in, Mrs. Nettleship, I'll be right down," he called. "I would be grateful if you would get out the nose machine. It's the small wooden clamp that you mistook for part of my bicycle last week. It should be in the bottom drawer of my desk, though I think I spotted it in the dining room where the cigar cutter should be. And my eggs, Mrs. Nettleship. Please remember that I prefer them scrambled. With cream."

He started hunting for a clean collar, which could have been anywhere, given her penchant for secreting his possessions in arbitrary places. Seldom a week went by without the doctor fantasising about replacing Mrs. Nettleship. But he could never go through with it, as the widow, who insisted on being called his housekeeper despite being a maid-of-all-work, had five children to feed. And then there was the odd occasion when she managed to find the correct ingredients for a ginger cake, and all resentment would vanish as the smell of it baking drifted under the door of the waiting room and sharpened even the dullest of appetites.

Mrs. Nettleship had come with the practice overlooking Hampton Court Green, a handsome house next to the former home of Sir Christopher Wren, the architect commissioned by William and Mary to rebuild their main apartments in the palace. Dr. Henderson had bought it the previous year with no knowledge of its perilous financial state, as by then its owner had thrown himself into the Thames, weighted down like a sack of unwanted kittens. With its close proximity to the palace and its well-connected residents, he had assumed the business would be sufficiently profitable. Aware that an overworked doctor could reach his grave sooner than his coughing patients, at first he insisted on keeping to the hours stipulated on the brass plaque he mounted outside the front door, with the exception of emergencies. But it soon became apparent that he needed all the business he could get. For the grace-and-favour residents treated his bills with the same indifference as those from their milliners. Not only did they assume they could put his services on account, but they refused to attend the practice, unwilling to share a waiting room bench with the unfragrant poor or the ill-bred soldiers. Some of his afternoons were therefore spent on home consultations that not only incurred an extra fee but involved patients who were more difficult to treat, as the higher classes were prone to exaggerate their symptoms. However, the aristocrats, who could afford to pay, wouldn't, and the poor, who wanted to pay, couldn't. And he found himself at night trying to balance the books, the gas turned pitifully low to save some pennies, with only his jar of leeches for company.

He ate his savoury omelette in silence, fearing that any mention of the wrong breakfast would elicit a comment from Mrs. Nettleship about his aborted new hairdo. Once settled behind his desk in his consulting room, he called for the first patient.

After Tom Saddleback left with his nose clamped as straight as a weather vane, a short, young woman with the telltale pallor of a maid took his place. Her eyes travelled over the microscope, the urinary cabinet, and the gynaecological couch kept discreetly in the corner.

"You've got rid of them stuffed birds," she said, looking at the walls.

"They belonged to the previous doctor," Dr. Henderson replied. "I take it you were one of Dr. Barnstable's patients."

"I was for a while, then . . ."

There was silence.

"Then?"

"If you don't mind, sir, I don't care to talk about it," she replied, tucking away a blond strand that had escaped from her bun.

The doctor picked up his pen. "What's the name?" he asked.

"Alice Cockle."

"How old are you, may I ask?"

"Nineteen, sir."

"And you work at the palace, I presume?"

"I'm a maid-of-all-work for Lady Bessington," she replied. "You'd have thought a countess would be able to afford a household of servants. Not her."

"I hope she doesn't overwork you," said the doctor, who had assumed the teenager too well spoken for a maid-of-all-work.

The maid shook her head. "Oh, no, sir, she treats me fair, not like some people down there . . ."

After pressing her further about her symptoms, he called Mrs. Nettleship to prepare her for examination. It didn't take him long to find the cause of her troubles, and she returned to the seat opposite him, her coat drawn back over her grey morning dress.

"Alice," he said gently. "The reason you're vomiting so much is because you're in the family way. And quite far gone."

No amount of soothing could console the teenager that she wouldn't necessarily lose her position. The doctor showed her into the drawing room, where she sat drying her cheeks on his white silk handkerchief as he returned to his patients. When, eventually, she was sufficiently composed to return to work, she made her own way out. Wondering who the father was, the doctor watched her from his window as she headed back to the palace. He then thought once more of the woman he had seen at Trophy Gate the previous evening, the blueness of her eyes contrasting with the rich mellow hue of her skin, and instinctively he smoothed down his curls.

*

MINK WAS STILL DEEP IN her dreams when she first heard the shout. She had gone to bed late the previous night, having had to wait up for the two furniture vans to arrive, as their drivers had got lost. After they had spent considerable time circling Richmond, helped in no part by two schoolboys who wilfully gave them the wrong directions on each revolution, they happened to find themselves on Hampton Court Road through no genius of their own. A further two hours were lost when they asked their whereabouts from the drunk woman selling pig's trotters outside the King's Arms. Despite its location next to the Lion Gates, the main northern entrance to the palace, the woman insisted that they were still miles from their destination. Into the pub they went to escape their frustration, paying her twopence to guard their loads. Eventually, on hearing of their dilemma, a footman sitting at the bar said that if it was Wilderness House they were after they should look out the back window, as it was on the other side of the wall. By the time they arrived, night had long descended and they were forced to work by candlelight, as many of the lamps had broken en route. Such had been their thirst that the dining room sideboard was taken up to one of the bedrooms, the davenport was carried down to the kitchen, and the Maharaja's ceremonial sword was left propped up in the scullery.

When the second shout came, Mink sat up, her long dark plait hanging down the back of her nightdress. Uncertain of where she was, she looked around in alarm. Recognising her surroundings, she lay back down, but immediately heard the voice again. "To the left!" it cried. "That's the *right*, sir. I said to the left. That's it. Follow it down. No, you've gone the wrong way. Turn round. You're still facing the same way. Follow that dog, sir, he's got the measure of it."

She climbed out of bed, walked over to the window, and peered out between the curtains. There, sitting on a chair on a platform, was a man in a navy uniform issuing directions to an increasingly baffled visitor deep within the maze.

"The dog, I said," yelled the keeper. "Don't follow that lady. She's been in there for almost an hour. In fact, ma'am, would you care to follow the dog as well? Not that one. He's as lost as his master. The white one with the boot in his mouth. No, there's no need to hand it in, thank you, sir. It belongs to someone who attempted to tunnel out through the hedging. He won't be needing it, as he's still in custody."

At that moment Pooki came in, carrying a tray bearing the Princess's morning tea and thin slices of bread and butter. "There is someone shouting outside, ma'am," she said. "I was worried he would wake you with all that noise he is making. No one should have that much to say."

Mink tapped on the pane. "It's that man sitting on the chair over there," she replied. "I presume he's the Keeper of the Maze."

The maid put down the tray and joined her at the window. "Why is he shouting at them?" she asked.

"Because they're lost."

Pooki pressed her nose against the cold pane. "Why did they go in there in the first place? It does not lead anywhere and you cannot see over the tops of the hedges."

Mink continued to peer. "To see whether they could find their way out, I presume."

The maid frowned. "But ma'am, why would you pay a penny to enter something just to find out whether you can get out again? And when you can't find your way out, that man in the chair with the long whiskers shouts at you. It strikes me as exceedingly ridiculous."

The Princess stood on her toes to get a better view of the dog. "I wouldn't mind giving it a go. It looks like fun."

Pooki turned to her, hands on her hips. "Where is the fun in getting lost, ma'am? Those people do not look like they are having fun. They are all clustered in that dead end arguing with each other and fighting over the map. I was lost many times in the East End, which is much more difficult to get out of than that thing, and I would not have paid a penny for it. Some people have more money than brains." She walked over to the fire and knelt down to attend to it. "But not you, ma'am," she added. "You have lots of brains but no money."

*

ONCE MINK WAS DRESSED, THE two women set about exploring their new home. Before being turned into a grace-and-favour residence in 1881, Wilderness House had been the official lodgings of palace gardeners, at one time the celebrated Lancelot "Capability" Brown, who complained of the offensive kitchen, and the rooms being small and uncomfortable. If it had appeared mournful in flickering candle flame, daylight did little to improve it. It had been newly painted, but the fresher colours did nothing to disguise its defeated soul. As Mink and Pooki wandered from room to room their excitement soon faded into gloom. Black beetles circled the kitchen floor like ice skaters. The smell of damp was unavoidable, and they soon stopped opening the cupboards, lest it plunge them further into despair. While the maid had risen at six to light the fires, the meagre flames in the tiny grates did little to combat the wind that rattled through the gaps in the sash windows. The ornate carved furniture, much of it from India, looked out of place in the unfamiliar surroundings, and for the first time Mink questioned her father's taste. After their inspection, they sat in silence at the bottom of the staircase, staring ahead of them, the Princess clutching the warrant, which she had finally opened.

"It says that I have to occupy the house for at least six months of the year, or it'll be considered vacant and given to someone else," said the Princess.

"That will not be a problem, ma'am, because you have nowhere else to go."

"Even those tiny clerks' houses have bathrooms these days," muttered the Princess.

Pooki turned to her mistress. "I spoke to the butterman this morning. Apparently Mrs. Campbell did not put her fingers into her purse to maintain this house. I do not know why they thought it would be suitable for the daughter of the Maharaja of Prindur. Moths are very happy in the damp, and I have anxious forebodings about your furs. But do not worry, ma'am, no moth will get the better of me. After breakfast I shall wrap up your furs in linen washed in lye and put them in a drawer with pieces of bog myrtle. Then I will put saucers of quicklime in the cupboards to dry them out. And once we have hung your butterfly collection in the drawing room it will cover those marks on the wall."

As the Princess stared at the chipped hall tiles she remembered the time, many years ago, when her father put a mutton bone under an oak tree to lure down a Purple Emperor. She then thought of the watercolours she had done for him of the jewel-coloured creatures they had caught together, which she found tied with a ribbon in his desk drawer when he died.

"I wonder how Albert is getting on," said the Princess flatly. "He'd soon cheer the place up."

Pooki remained silent.

Suddenly Mink stood up. "I'm going to hang the family portraits," she announced. "We'll both feel much better surrounded by those moustaches." She headed down to the kitchen in the hope of finding some nails, Pooki calling after her that such a task was not suitable for a princess.

*

LATER THAT MORNING, WHEN POOKI answered the front door, she found Mrs. Boots on the step wearing a tight-fitting bonnet that squashed her beetroot cheeks. Before they had exchanged a word, the housekeeper barrelled her way inside, hoisted her skirts, and started up the stairs, elbows pointed. "Just having a quick check," she explained over her shoulder. "You wouldn't believe some of the pets residents try and smuggle in with them."

Pooki stood with her hand on the banister, her mouth open. "But ma'am!" she cried, suddenly running after her. "Her Highness is in the drawing room. You are going the wrong way."

"I won't be long!" called the short, round form. "I can detect the presence of a cat or a dog at a hundred paces."

Leaping up the stairs two at a time, the maid overtook the labouring housekeeper and stood at the top, her fists by her side. "Ma'am!" she ordered. "You must go down!"

But Mrs. Boots swerved and darted into a bedroom with the speed of a ferret. Crouching down, she looked underneath the washstand as Pooki stood helpless in the doorway. She then shuffled to the bed on her knees and lowered her head to the floor. "Birds are easy to find, as they make a noise," she said, straightening up. "The other week I heard my name being called, followed by such a wicked insult I couldn't eat for three days. Stopped me dead in my tracks in the middle of Clock Court, it did. I went to find the culprit, expecting one of the delivery boys, but it turned out to be an African grey parrot in Lady Beatrice's apartments. Needless to say, I escorted that bird off the premises. With any luck it's already been stuffed."

The housekeeper hauled herself to her feet, sailed out, and immediately barged into the next room. "Something tells me that we're not alone," she muttered to herself, hunting behind the curtains.

"Ma'am!" Pooki protested from the doorway. "This is Her Highness's bedroom. You should not be in here!"

But Mrs. Boots sniffed the air, then flung open the wardrobe. "It's got to be here somewhere."

The servant approached her and stood with her hands on her hips. "Ma'am!" she shouted. "You are on a wild goose chase!"

Mrs. Boots turned and looked the maid up and down. "I wouldn't put a flock of geese past any of them," she said, then sank down onto all fours and peered underneath the chaise longue.

Shooting past the maid, she headed out the door and scuttled down the landing towards the attic staircase. "I'm getting warmer," she announced, her cheeks scarlet. But there was no beating the speed of Pooki, who overtook her and stood at the bottom of the steps, her scrawny arms outstretched. "Ma'am, I may be thin, but I am stronger than I look. And you have not seen the size of my feet," she declared.

The housekeeper looked down and raised her eyebrows as she saw what she was up against. Reluctantly she made her way down-stairs, and once she had inspected the rest of the house, finally entered the drawing room. Pooki followed, and stood in the door-way, her bun dishevelled. "Mrs. Boots, ma'am," she announced, brushing a strand of hair from her eyes.

It wasn't until she had hunted amongst the palms, under the grand piano, and behind the oriental screen that the housekeeper noticed the Princess standing next to a ladder watching her. After a double take at the family portraits, she asked whether there were any pets on the premises.

"No, Mrs. Boots," Mink replied curtly. "I've already told you."

The housekeeper folded her arms across her chest. "You'd be

surprised what some residents tell me," she replied. "Lies, most of the time." She then announced that she was unable to give the Princess a tour of the palace "on account of my bronchitis that's taken a turn for the worst." If the Princess were agreeable, she continued, General Bagshot, a resident and Tudor expert who was writing his fourth history of the palace, would escort her. "You'll be better off with him anyway," she admitted. "I get my Georges muddled. Four shows a distinct lack of imagination, if you ask me. They should have called the last one Archibald and have done with it."

*

DRESSED IN HELIOTROPE, WITH A matching toque and pearl earrings, Mink headed out to meet the General at the King's Staircase. As she passed the royal tennis court, built in the reign of Charles I, she was stopped by a milliner's assistant carrying numerous boxes, who asked her the way to Lady Montfort Bebb's apartments. Apologising that she didn't know, the Princess continued and turned in to Fountain Court. As she raised her eyes to the windows, she noticed a number of pale faces at the curtains, which quickly disappeared.

Eventually she arrived in Clock Court, a large empty court-yard flanked on one side by the tall windows and gilded weather vanes of Henry VIII's Great Hall. Following a group of excursionists through a doorway, she found herself at the foot of the celebrated staircase that led to William III's State Apartments. Visitors stood gazing up in awe at the triumphant King and banquet of gods painted on the walls and ceiling by Antonio Verrio. Standing amongst them was Mrs. Boots, who had the perpetual air of someone who was late for her steamer. As soon as she saw Mink, she made much of looking at her pocket watch. Next to her was General Bagshot, a thin, large-nosed gentleman with flamboyant side-whiskers the colour of ash. The buttons of his dark blue morning coat were engraved with his initials, and a heavy gold watch chain with numerous charms hung from his floral-patterned waistcoat. Born at the palace, he had been christened in a bowl on top of a table in the Chapel Royal when it still lacked a font. For a reason the Princess was soon to understand, she took an instant dislike to him.

Once the housekeeper had introduced them, Mink apologised for being late. "There seems to be an awful lot of people here," she said, as the excursionists pushed past them.

"Sundays are the worst," muttered Mrs. Boots. "You're not still thinking of coming tomorrow, are you?" The assurance of the Princess's presence at divine service provoked from the house-keeper a sudden bout of coughing. Her mouth muffled by a blue handkerchief, she explained that she was still waiting for a reply from the Lord Chamberlain as to whether foreign royalty was permitted to use the Royal Pew. If she didn't hear back from him before the service, she continued, she would be obliged to sit with the congregation. "In which case you'll have to take your chance with the seating like everyone else. The ladies insist the soldiers have an odour of the stables about them, and sit as far away from them as possible." Suddenly the housekeeper looked through the doors to the sky. Mumbling that a north-easterly wind was blow-ing, she made her excuses, and then took off through the crowds.

The General's eyes slipped up and down Mink. As he leant towards her, she noticed flakes of dandruff caught in his sprouting eyebrows. "You're a pretty little thing, aren't you? Mrs. Boots quite undersold you. I read so much about your father in the papers last year, though I know next to nothing about you. We must get to know one another," he said, his breath rancid from pipe tobacco and port.

"That's the last thing I want," thought the Princess, as her stomach curdled. She was just about to reply when General Bag-shot turned away and stared through the doorway. She followed his gaze and saw two urchins standing under the colonnade built by Sir Christopher Wren as a stately approach to the magnificent staircase. Bootless and irrefutably mud-streaked, each was holding an enormous basket of whelks. Pushing past the pleasure-seekers towards them, General Bagshot demanded to know what they were doing. "This isn't Billingsgate Market," he roared. "How the devil did you get past the sentry?"

The boys put down their baskets, dragged their caps off their unwashed heads, and clutched them to their chests. They had a delivery for Lady Montfort Bebb, they explained, but had been unable to find her apartments. He gave them directions, then returned to the Princess.

"Quite what Lady Montfort Bebb wants with so many whelks is beyond me," he said. "Have you met her yet? My wife and I have the great misfortune of living next to her. She's learning to play the pianoforte and slowly murders the same tune every day. A deaf elephant wearing mittens would sound more melodious. She was taken prisoner during the First Afghan War, but unfortunately was released. My guess is that she started practising her scales and her captors threw open the door and insisted that she leave."

Passing his cane to a pair of warders behind a desk, who were also collecting bags, parcels, and umbrellas lest they damaged the paintings, he started up the stairs. "The palace was originally founded by Cardinal Wolsey in 1515, who subsequently handed it over to Henry VIII," he announced at such a volume several excursionists turned their heads. "The King enlarged it, passing much of his time here with his six wives."

The Princess followed him. "All of Henry's additions, except the Great Hall and one or two other rooms, were demolished by William III, so I believe," she said, remembering the palace history she had read before arriving.

The General looked momentarily taken aback. "Quite so, quite so," he replied. "In the seventeenth century William and Mary commissioned . . ."

"Sir Christopher Wren," interrupted Mink.

". . . to build the existing State Apartments, copying the splendour of . . ."

"Versailles," she added. "Shall we continue, General? We seem to be holding people up."

They entered the King's Guard Chamber, where William III's gunsmith had mounted almost three thousand pieces of arms and armour on the walls. After looking at Canaletto's Colosseum at Rome, and the life-size portrait of Queen Elizabeth's porter who stood over eight feet tall, they moved on to the King's Presence Chamber. Mink gazed at Sir Godfrey Kneller's portraits of Queen Mary's court, known as the Hampton Court Beauties. General Bagshot stood next to her, his hand momentarily brushing hers. "There's something irresistible about them, don't you find?" he remarked.

"Indeed," Mink replied, stepping away as she felt his hot breath on her neck. "Though they lack the considerable charm of your wife, General Bagshot. I met her when I arrived at the palace on Friday."

"She's off to Hélouan-Les-Bains tomorrow morning. Apparently they've got about a dozen thermal springs. Do you know Egypt?"

"I've been a number of times," she said. "I climbed to the summit of the Great Pyramid a couple of years ago. Two locals pulled me up by the arms, while another attempted to bring up the rear while clamouring for baksheesh. I beat him off with my parasol."

They continued, engulfed by visitors, stopping to admire William III's Great Bedchamber with its sumptuous Verrio ceiling and delicate carvings by Grinling Gibbons. When the General pointed out that the bed looked remarkably comfortable, Mink moved swiftly onto the next room. Eventually they came to the Communication Gallery, where hordes stood admiring the Triumphs of Caesar, nine vast canvases stretching down the length of the room, and the most important paintings in the palace.

General Bagshot stood so close to Mink she could detect his presence simply from the smell. "They were painted by . . ." he began.

"Andrea Mantegna," she interrupted, taking a step away from him.

He advanced again towards her. "Quite so. For . . ."

"Gianfrancesco Gonzaga, the Marquis of Mantua," she added, her voice trailing off as she noticed a huddle of chimney-sweeps, their pitifully red eyes fixed on the paintings. Each had a brush over his shoulder, its filthy bristles perilously close to the pictures.

"Good God!" the General cried. "Just a minute."

As he ordered them out, sending two excursionists tumbling to the floor in the commotion, Mink took the opportunity to slip away. Grateful that he hadn't asked a single thing about her, for she had not the slightest desire to form an acquaintance, she entered the restored Wolsey's Closet, which had once been part of some grace-and-favour apartments and used as a butler's pantry. After staring in amazement at the painted scenes from the Passion of Our Lord, and the magnificent Tudor ceiling, she was just about to head down the Queen's Staircase when General Bagshot caught up with her.

"How the warders never spotted those sweeps is beyond me," he fumed, mopping his forehead with a handkerchief. "I've never met such a disreputable bunch of uniformed men in all my life. Apparently the sweeps were also looking for Lady Montfort Bebb's apartments. What on earth would she want eight for? Really, that woman is as mad as a hatter, and mine has just been carted off to the asylum."

As they started down the stairs, he asked whether she had ever seen a ghost.

"I don't believe in them," the Princess replied dismissively.

"I'm sure you'll change your mind once you've been here long enough," he said, stepping back as a group of cockneys herded past them. He pointed to a door on the right. "Behind that is the Haunted Gallery. Catherine Howard ran along it after escaping from her chamber hoping to persuade Henry VIII to call off her execution, but his guards seized her. She's now said to haunt it." He lowered his voice. "It's closed to the public, but perhaps one evening when my wife is away I could get the key and we could go just the two of us and see whether she appears," he added, rubbing a cold, thin finger against the back of her hand on the banister.

Immediately she pulled it away. "That would be delightful," she replied curtly. "I will be sure to bring Mrs. Boots with me. She's never seen a ghost."

Looking horrified, he continued down the stairs. As they passed along a passageway at the bottom, he pointed to some oak steps. "They lead to the Silver Stick Gallery, which is said to be haunted by Jane Seymour, who died at the palace after giving birth," he said. "Lady Beatrice lives there. Everyone says the ghost has driven her potty. She wore mourning for years, then suddenly took to wearing so many startling colours she looked like a toucan in a zoological garden. You'll spot her soon enough. Now, I must show you Henry VIII's Great Hall, where *Macbeth* was first performed. It will give me the chance to wake up the warders, who, instead of preventing the visitors from damaging the tapestries, will no doubt be sleeping off the effects of their evening in the Cardinal Wolsey public house."

As they headed towards it, a tall woman with high cheekbones dressed in mourning came towards them, her blue eyes standing out against the endless black. Her bonnet tied firmly underneath her chin, she nodded at the General, who raised his hat. As she walked quickly past she glanced with unfettered curiosity at the Princess.

"That was Lady Bessington," he said, lowering his voice. "Have you met her yet? She's obsessed with ferns, and her late husband, the fourteenth Earl of Bessington, who was the last in the title.

We swapped apartments with her and found she'd made the place into a shrine to him. Their initials are entwined in the marble floor in the hall, and the study walls have been painted with the names of all the battles he had fought in. Unfortunately my wife still hasn't got round to getting it all ripped out. A lady that good-looking should have remarried."

The Princess turned and watched the Countess disappear. "I thought it was against the rules to exchange apartments," she said.

"It is," he admitted. "But the Lord Chamberlain eventually agreed. There are only so many letters the poor man can answer, and my wife is a very determined woman. Lady Bessington was always complaining about the cost of heating her rooms, and we were in some poky Tudor apartments in Fish Court with no view to speak of. Everyone else is furious, of course, because we now overlook the river. Still, we do have to endure Lady Montfort Bebb's wretched attempts at mastering the pianoforte. The visitors tramping through the State Apartments below us is nothing compared to that torture. Believe me."

Suddenly a strangled tune sounded above the cheerful din of the tourists. The Princess and the General turned to see the organ grinder who was normally pitched outside Trophy Gate, much to the misery of the sentries who had to endure the same pitiful song played at a staggering variety of wrong tempos. Wearing a billycock hat with a broken brim, he slowly cranked his instrument of torment with a peaceful smile, the frayed ends of his coat sleeves reaching past his knuckles. General Bagshot strode over and demanded to know what he was doing. He had been hired to play outside the window of Lady Montfort Bebb, he explained, still turning, but had decided to give a brief recital on the way in the hope of earning a few extra pennies from the crowds.

Returning to the Princess, the General said he needed to go and see what on earth his neighbour was up to. He then leant towards her. "Do think about our little rendezvous in the Haunted

Gallery. Just the two of us," he added, his eyes lingering on her chest. Before she had the chance to reply he suddenly turned and stared at a bespectacled man in a black frock coat and top hat walking briskly past, a collapsible rule tucked neatly underneath his arm.

"That's Mr. Blood, the undertaker," he gasped. "Who the hell has he come for?"

CHAPTER IV

The Ruinous Consequences of
Shirt-sleeve Pudding

SUNDAY, MARCH 20, 1898

BOTH carrying umbrellas, Mink and Pooki headed out early to divine service, the rain driving up the earthy odours of the gardens. It wasn't Mrs. Boots's warning of having to sit next to one of the malodorous soldiers that hurried the Princess's step. Neither was it the opportunity to thank the Lord for her numerous blessings, for, as things stood, they weren't immediately obvious. What drove her from her sheets at such an unchristian hour was unfettered curiosity over the sudden appearance of Mr. Blood.

A dignified scrum was already standing outside the Chapel Royal as they approached, the hems of their skirts wet from the downpour. Many were dressed in perpetual mourning, while others stood hitching their fur tippets up around their ears as defence against the drafts gusting down the Tudor cloisters. In the middle stood Mrs. Boots, with the exasperated air of a woman who had not only missed her steamer but just discovered that the next one wasn't due for another week. Suddenly the chapel doors opened, and the ladies surged forwards with the determination of dowagers at a draper's sale. The housekeeper remained where she was, her eyes closed as she waited for the storm to pass.

The Princess approached. "I was wondering, Mrs. Boots, whether the Astronomical Clock has stopped?" she asked with a smile.

"Not yet it hasn't," she said. "It will do, though. I'm certain of it. There's gout, and then there's a hunch. I'm not the sort to confuse the two."

"You strike me as a woman with the most dependable predictions, Mrs. Boots. I only ask because the undertaker was at the palace yesterday."

The housekeeper shook her head. "Disgraceful business," she muttered. "I can't bring myself to talk about it."

"Come, come Mrs. Boots."

"Rest assured, all the residents are still very much alive. Though between you and me there are some I wouldn't miss." The arrival of Mr. Blood, as well as all the other tradespeople, was a practical joke, she continued. "Who was behind it, I'm not certain. But my first guess would be the General, given his dislike for Lady Montfort Bebb. Not that I'm one for gossip. I leave that for the residents."

The housekeeper then headed into the chapel. In a whisper more penetrating than her speaking voice she leant towards the Princess and said: "The chaplain is in one of his states, if you get my drift, and has just had another row with the organist. I always lock the communion wine in a cupboard and give the key to the verger before a celebration. But the chaplain must have gone through his pockets."

Lifting her skirts, she led the way up the wooden stairs to the Royal Pew, explaining that the Lord Chamberlain had given her permission to use it. "He said I shouldn't have needed to ask, but how was I to know that foreign royalty counted? I've just had to dust it. It's gone straight to my chest."

Mrs. Boots then scurried away, and the Princess sat down in the private gallery, gazing at the chapel's flamboyant ceiling made for Henry VIII and restored to a brilliant blue. But after a while, she could bear the loneliness no longer and crept back down, her footsteps turning a number of heads.

Sitting at the back next to Pooki, she noticed that all the ladies had pressed themselves into the right-hand side of the chapel, a number of brightly coloured hats standing out in the black mire. Several glanced over their shoulders as the whisper passed along the pews that the Maharaja's daughter was behind them. Slowly the seats in the middle began to fill with gentlemen holding their top hats and officers barracked at the palace. Amongst them she spotted Dr. Henderson, and she peered at the back of his head, trying to work out what he had done to his hair, hanging in strangled curls. Suddenly he looked round and for a moment they held each other's startled gaze. She looked away, but minutes later her eyes drifted back to his neck.

As the soldiers and palace staff took the remaining places, a woman in a large straw hat bearing a pair of stuffed humming-birds entered the chapel out of breath. She hesitated, surveying the seats already occupied by the ladies, who looked at her with an air of victory. Slowly she sat down on the end of a pew next to a man in a cheap ready-made suit whose hands had never known a manicure.

Taking their cue from the hymn number on the board, the congregation turned to "O Gladsome Light" in their books. But when Amos Shoesmith, the organist, struck up, there was not the slightest hint of any light, gladsome or otherwise, coming from his temperance fingers. Uncowed, the Reverend Benjamin Grayling launched into the song at a volume that could part not only the Red Sea but the Dead, the Black, and the Baltic. Meanwhile, the invisible Amos Shoesmith continued thundering out "My Hope Is in the Everlasting" with the impudence of the devil, while the terrified blower, the small boy charged with pumping the organ's bellows with a handle, prayed for deliverance. The congregation wavered, unsure of whom to follow. The choir was equally confused, and for a while the Reverend Grayling sang alone, as if hailing a distant ship through Newfoundland fog. Suddenly allegiances were formed. A number of the grace-and-favour residents and officers joined in with the chaplain in solidarity with his superior rank. However, the choir, made up of boys from the village, followed the organist, who was one of their own. They were swiftly joined by the palace staff and the soldiers of questionable odour, who naturally sided with the commoner. Others hedged their bets, snapping open their mouths like emus to deliver a random note.

But the demolition of the hymn was not the only event that the congregation gleefully recounted upon their exit. For when they all sat down, a young lady remained unequivocally on her feet. She stood for several seconds, swayed left, then right, and finally collapsed with a pitiful sigh onto the black-and-white marble tiles. Dr. Henderson immediately rose to his feet, went to her side, and gently lifted her in his arms. He swiftly carried her out, her eyes miraculously settling on him the instant they were alone.

*

AS POOKI WASHED SOME OF her mistress's lace at the kitchen sink, shaking her feet to rid them of scuttling beetles, the back doorbell rang. Standing on the step holding a plate covered with a white linen napkin was a short maid with delicate features, her blond hair tied back into a bun. She introduced herself as Alice Cockle, the maid-of-all-work for Lady Bessington. "I saw you at divine service and made this for you," said the teenager. "It's a tipsy cake. Her Ladyship's favourite. I used more sherry wine than usual. I thought you might need it living in this place, what with the noise from the maze and the damp. Mrs. Campbell's maid never got used to it."

Grateful for a friendly face, for none of the other palace servants had spoken to her, Pooki let her into the kitchen. Offering her a seat at the table, she set about making some tea.

"You do not seem like a maid-of-all-work," said Pooki, getting out her mistress's best china. "They have a disregard for the letter H, and indulge in vulgar street chaff. Pretty ones like you usually rise to at least a parlour maid."

"You don't seem like a maid-of-all-work either," replied Alice, looking her up and down. "But everyone says you're the Princess's only servant."

Sitting down opposite her, Pooki cut two large slices of cake and handed one to Alice on a plate.

"I used to be Her Highness's lady's-maid," she said, raising her chin.

Alice stared at her incredulously. "You went from being a lady's-maid to a slavey? What on earth did you do? Pawn the family plate?"

Pooki frowned at the suggestion. "Her Highness's circumstances changed and she had to let go of the servants," she said. "I was the only one she kept."

"Blimey, you were lucky. Why do you think she kept you?"

Pooki looked at the ceiling as she considered the question. "Not only am I very obedient, but I am a fearless defender of Her Highness's wardrobe against moths," she said, her eyes closed with satisfaction.

Alice nodded towards the range. "And now you have to do all the cooking and cleaning for less wages . . ."

"It is an honour to serve Her Highness," replied Pooki, sitting up straight. "Her father was the Maharaja of Prindur. When my mother found out who I was working for she cried for three days with pride."

Alice raised an eyebrow. "It's a wonder she didn't cry for three days with shame, considering what happened."

Pooki's jaw set. "I do not gossip about His Highness," she said, pouring them some tea.

"Even so, it can't have been easy for you, suddenly finding

yourself scrubbing the floors," she said. "Why didn't you just get a new position?"

Pooki raised her chin. "My place is with Her Highness. Her sorrows are my sorrows, and her joys are my joys."

Alice stared at her. "You're one of those servants, are you? There aren't many of you left. Her Ladyship is kind, but I wouldn't go that far." She folded her arms and sat back. "I'd love to be a lady's-maid. Think of all those beautiful leftover dresses you get. You'd have to choose your mistress carefully, though. Some don't give their old dresses to their lady's-maid, as they don't like seeing them in clothes they've recently worn."

Pooki dropped some sugar into her tea. "Her Highness gives me hers, but I do not wear them. I look exceedingly ridiculous in them. They are very fancy, and I have big feet. I sell them and send the money to my mother."

Picking up her cake with her fingers, Alice said, "Sometimes I think I should go and work in the colonies."

"Do not fall into the fatal habit of thinking that if you were somewhere different life would be so much better. There are moths everywhere," said Pooki, her mouth full.

"All masters and mistresses aren't the same," Alice pointed out. "Someone will tell you sooner or later, but I used to be the Bagshots' parlour maid. Four years ago the General accused me of stealing. Unfortunately Mrs. Bagshot was ill at the time and didn't stand up for me. She was the best mistress I'd ever had, and had hinted that I would become her next lady's-maid. But he dismissed me without any notice and didn't give me a character either. That's why I ended up working as a trotter for Her Lady-ship. I'm grateful she took me on, no one else would, but she pays me the wages of a German maid. Nasty piece of work, the General is. Don't go anywhere near him."

Pooki poured her some more tea. "So you have gone from being a parlour maid to a maid-of-all-work? That is almost as bad as me."

Alice crossed her arms. "I have to drink in the King's Arms with the under servants, not that many of them talk to me. It's a right dump. I should be in the Mitre with the butlers and housekeepers."

Pooki sat back, holding her cup and saucer. "We are both doing work that is unfit for our station. But we should be grateful that we have a position and that we can help others. In the meantime we should finish this cake before Her Highness sees it. It will prevent her from becoming stout. A good maid should always put her mistress before herself."

Alice took another mouthful and then looked at the floor. "What are you going to do about all those beetles?" she asked. "They make my skin crawl."

Pooki sipped her tea. "I have a plan, and it is one of my better ones."

*

LATER THAT AFTERNOON, MINK STOOD peering up at the bookshelves in the library, searching for her etiquette manuals. While she was naturally well versed in the protocol of calling, the afternoon ritual of social visits, a new set of rules came into play now that she had moved. She took down several volumes and brought them to her father's desk, where she leafed through the commandments. According to one text, when a stranger arrived in a neighbourhood it was the duty of the older inhabitants to leave their cards. If they were desirable acquaintances it was usual for the visit to be returned personally, or by leaving a card, within a week. In large towns, it was common to wait until more was known about the stranger, it said.

However, another guide stated that the opposite was the case in the countryside, and that the newcomer should make the first move. Mink had no idea whether the Middlesex palace abided by town or country rules. The dilemma was further compounded by the fact that as a princess, albeit a foreign one, she outranked them all. But given her treatment by some of her friends and acquaintances in London, she wasn't sure how she would be received. Most of them had stopped calling the moment the scandal appeared in the papers. While fresher gossip had long since replaced the sordid tale, her re-entry into society had been thwarted by the fact that nothing turned upper-class stomachs more than the whiff of financial embarrassment.

She opened another manual but took in none of the words as she remembered the terrible moment, almost a year ago, when her world changed forever. She had just finished writing her letters, and was looking for signs of spring in the garden, when Bantam approached with such a look of concern she assumed that something was missing from the plate chest. With a glance towards the gardener, he asked whether he might speak to her alone. He then steered her towards the bench that circled the apple tree, and made sure that she was sitting before he broke the news: the Maharaja was dead.

But the butler, who prided himself on being able to conceal the slightest emotion, honed from years of eavesdropping at dinner, found himself weeping so profusely that he was unable to continue. Mink offered him her handkerchief and waited, adrift in her imagination until he stopped. Apologising profusely, he led her across the lawn and into the drawing room, his red nose the only visible dent to his dignity. He fetched Mrs. Greensleeves, the housekeeper, who stood in front of the Princess with her hands clasped, searching for the appropriate words. But there was no disguising what had happened: the Maharaja had died in an East End opium den, she explained. Underneath him, in an equal state of undress, was the girl who came in the mornings to clean the boots and the knives.

It wasn't so much the seedy location that set tongues wagging, though it added a certain spice. Rather it was the lowly position of the girl, who spoke far too coarsely to ever get a live-in position, to say nothing of her colourful testimony at the inquest. The hearing attracted so many spectators that a fistfight broke out over accusations of queue jumping. When the doctor who carried out the post-mortem examination revealed that the Indian's death had not been caused by drugs, as many had presumed, but by a massive heart attack brought on by exertion, the coroner immediately called Maud Posset to the stand. Pushing his spectacles up his florid nose, he peered at the servant and enquired how she happened to find herself underneath a dead maharaja.

Wearing her sister's Sunday bonnet, and with an accent that could curdle milk, the teenager explained that Mrs. Greensleeves had employed her on a temporary basis, as the third footman had suddenly taken ill. One morning she was walking down the drive when she encountered the Maharaja looking for one of his porcupines that had escaped. She listened to its description and joined him in the search, curious to see such a beast. It wasn't long before she announced that she had found it, and crawled into a bush. But the Maharaja informed her that the creature she was pointing to was a hedgehog, and removed a leaf from her hair. He suggested that they try the hothouse, where they found the escapee, its snout down a gardener's boot, drawn by its salty sweat. He then offered to show her his pineapples, a result of the head gardener's mania for forcing. They wandered around, gazing at the fruit she had never tasted, his thinning coiffure sleeked with miracle hair tonic, and her dull brown curls clumsily pinned. Eventually the heat and the sweet aroma made her feel giddy, and he found her a bench and patted her hand. Before long, he was patting elsewhere, and declared her ripe enough to pick. Mesmerised by the man who smelt of frankincense, she felt his manicured fingers travel up her stocking and under her drawers, seeking the softness of her thigh. Her cheeks inflamed by the tenderness of his touch, she turned her lips to his, and all decorum was lost. The porcupine raised its quills in fright at the Maharaja's gasp of ecstasy, and three overripe pineapples fell to the ground with his final exalted thrust.

Every subsequent morning, once she had cleaned the boots and the knives, Maud Posset slipped into the hothouse to meet her master. She left with so much bruised fruit that Mrs. Wilson started complaining that there was not enough for the table. Suspecting a thief, the head gardener announced he was going to make regular patrols of his crops. The Maharaja caught the girl on the way to meet him and asked her to wait instead at the end of the road that evening. They travelled by hansom to Limehouse, in the East End, where shops with Chinese names sold ginger resembling swollen hands, and bottles of medicine made of animals that customers had never seen. Eventually it stopped outside an opium den, where washing hung between the upstairs windows like filthy bunting. Passing the counter, with its brass scales and selection of tobacco, they headed for the back parlour, screened off with a stained blanket. The reclining regulars didn't stir at the entrance of the portly Indian in the Savile Row suit, and the teenager whose third-hand bodice failed to reach the top of her skirt. Gradually a Chinaman looked over while stirring a stew in a saucepan used to cook opium. The Maharaja pressed some coins into his tarnished hand, and the couple climbed the stairs to the upper floor, where they made their love nest in a room empty apart from a chest belonging to a sailor who had never returned. The Maharaja spread on the floor the piece of silk he found inside, and placed on the windowsill the shells the missing man had collected for his wife. The pair took their pleasure to the boisterous sound of the docks, the scent of the drug curling up through the floorboards. As weeks turned to months, they eventually expressed their love in words, and both surprised themselves by meaning them. It was then that the Maharaja apologised for the grubby surroundings and offered to take Maud Posset to a hotel. But the girl refused, preferring the room with its graffiti written in languages she didn't understand, longing for sweethearts on far-away shores.

When the coroner asked her about the day in question, the teenager explained that the Maharaja was halfway through his usual exertions, when he came to an abrupt halt and collapsed on top of her. She prodded him in the buttocks, but he failed to respond, and when she attempted to move she realised she was pinned to the floor. The wails of a hungry baby next door drowned out her pleas for help, and it wasn't until her knuckles were raw from knocking on the floorboards that help eventually arrived. When the Chinaman finally rolled off the Maharaja, there were no more tears left in her to cry.

"What were you thinking while you were trapped underneath him for all that time?" asked the coroner, his curiosity having got the better of him.

The jury leant forward, and a member of the public produced an ear trumpet so as not to miss a word from the girl in the mis-matched boots.

"That 'e shouldn't 'ave heaten so much shirt-sleeve pudding," she replied.

The coroner did his utmost to stem the howls of laughter that followed, but he was forced to announce an adjournment while order was restored. Once the gentlemen of the jury returned from their deliberations, the foreman cleared his throat and returned a verdict of natural causes. But that was by no means the end of it. The George pub next to the opium den renamed itself The Boots & the Knives; dealers in exotic animals had to draw up a waiting list, as there was a sudden run on porcupines; and the Savoy's pastry chef created a pineapple meringue pie called Fat Maharaja. But more damaging of all was the tale's inevitable eruption into the music halls, where songs were performed in perfect renditions of the offending accent. The most popular were hummed on the top of omnibuses, along picture galleries, and eventually in the queues at the Bank of England. And, a year later, the chorus could still be heard from revellers swaying out of pubs at closing time:

The Maharaja loved ladies and pies
But his appetite was his own undoing
For he died in mid thrust, and his love he did crush
Because 'e shouldn't 'ave heaten so much shirt-sleeve pudding

*

THE PRINCESS WAS STILL HOLDING the etiquette book when Pooki appeared at the library door looking flustered. "The Countess of Bessington, Lady Beatrice Fisher, and Lady Montfort Bebb are here to see you, ma'am," she said.

Mink stared at her, taken aback. "Have you shown them in?" she asked.

"Yes, ma'am. They must like the portraits of the ancestors very much, because they keep staring at them."

The Princess wondered whether she had time to change, but dismissed the idea, as there was nothing more irritating than having to wait while the lady of the house fussed over her dress. Entering the drawing room, she found the three visitors sitting next to one another on the sofa by the fireplace, gazing around at their surroundings. Immediately they rose to their feet.

Standing in the middle with the help of a cane was Lady Montfort Bebb, her smoke-grey hair and loose skin under her powdered chin betraying her almost eighty years. There was an unmistakable air of defiance about her that had kept her from her grave. Her jacket sleeves were puffed at the shoulder and tightly fitting, as fashion dictated, and her matching hat had the restrained air of a dependable milliner. The lowest in social ranking of the three visitors, she introduced herself in a voice more indomitable than a schoolmistress's, before turning to the others.

"Princess, may I introduce the Countess of Bessington," she

said, indicating the woman in mourning half her age. Mink immediately recognised her from the tour of the palace with General Bagshot. The Countess, who outranked the two other visitors, raised her blue eyes and smiled, its warmth momentarily lifting the pallor of her skin drained of life by the black trappings of loss. Framing the inside of her bonnet were dark curls marbled with premature grey.

"And Lady Beatrice Fisher," Lady Montfort Bebb added. Mink remembered her as the woman wearing the hummingbird hat who arrived late for divine service. It had been replaced by one of equal size bearing several butterflies. Three years short of her sixtieth birthday, across her nose was a shower of freckles that no patent remedy had come close to shifting in decades. Lady Beatrice smiled, her fingers fussing with her golden blond false fringe that failed to match the rest of her hair, dyed an unfortunate shade of mustard.

As Mink took her father's armchair opposite, the women settled back down on the settee like a flock of birds. Resting a hand on the quartz knob of her cane, Lady Montfort Bebb said that she hoped the Princess didn't think their visit improper, but they had been somewhat confused over the regulations of calling, given the circumstances. "One would assume that we should call on you, being as though you're a newcomer to the palace. However, as a princess, it is, of course, for you to call on whomever you deem fit."

Lady Beatrice leant forward, her eyes wide. "But we weren't sure whether that was correct, as none of us was certain which of the foreign titles conferred precedence in England. So we wrote to the Lord Chamberlain, and asked his opinion."

"And he said that in the majority of cases, when the foreign rank is assured, courtesy dictates that it be taken into account," explained the Countess, holding her black-gloved hands in her lap. "But he went on to add that the etiquette of calling was as labyrinthine as the palace maze, and he wouldn't attempt to understand it. As it was a habit most indulged by ladies, he suggested that we sort it out amongst ourselves. After considerable discussion we were still unsure, so decided to come anyway," she added with a triumphant smile.

The Princess watched as Lady Montfort Bebb raised her lorgnettes to a pile of books on the side table. "I see you admire Mr. Dickens," she noted, her nostrils flared.

Lady Beatrice leant forward again and lowered her voice. "None of we residents read Mr. Dickens."

"You don't?" asked Mink, taken aback.

The three visitors shook their heads.

"Not after what he wrote about us," explained the Countess, holding a hand to her throat.

"And what was that?" asked Mink.

"He called us gypsies!" hurled Lady Montfort Bebb, her chin wobbling.

"And suggested that we were all waiting for a better offer," continued the Countess, blinking with indignation.

"In *Little Dorrit*," explained Lady Beatrice, her eyes wide. "We much prefer Mr. Wells and his *War of the Worlds*. When the Martians come to Surrey they wreck Woking Station, and burn Richmond town, but leave Hampton Court completely untouched, as any right-thinking monsters would."

The other two looked at her uneasily.

Lady Montfort Bebb then surveyed the room, noting the French mirror over the fireplace, which was taller than it was wide, as taste dictated, and the Indian clock on the mantel, covered with a glass jar to protect it from soot. "I must say, you've made it perfectly charming. What a pity Wilderness House used to be inhabited by gardeners. I'm not sure that Mrs. Campbell ever lived it down."

The Countess and Lady Beatrice shook their heads.

"Mrs. Boots mentioned that poor Mrs. Campbell had some kind of accident," said Mink.

The women glanced at one another. It was such an unfortunate business, they explained. She was standing on the top of an omnibus when the driver suddenly moved on, and she tumbled over the back rail.

"But that wasn't the end of it. She was then struck by a costermonger's barrow," said Lady Montfort Bebb, closing her eyes. "If that wasn't bad enough, it was piled high with brussels sprouts."

"At least the costermonger was a former solicitor," said the Countess. "Albeit one who had been struck off the rolls."

Lady Beatrice gazed into the distance. "If one were to be run over, one would hope it would be by a carriage and four, with a nice pair of tall footmen with elegant calves," she said with a wistful smile.

The other two visitors glared at her.

Despite the circumstances, said Lady Montfort Bebb, turning back to Mink, Mrs. Campbell's funeral in the Chapel Royal had been very well attended. "It's hard to believe that the Authorised Version of the Bible was conceived at Hampton Court Palace, given the unholy behaviour in the chapel this morning," she added. But the feud between the chaplain and the organist was not the only impropriety, she told the Princess. The seating used to be strictly by rank and precedence, and supervised by the housekeeper, but there were so many arguments about who was superior to whom that the Lord Chamberlain decided to make it a free-for-all. Unless one arrived early, there was no guarantee of avoiding sitting next to the palace's foreman bricklayer. She turned to Lady Beatrice. "You ended up next to the vine keeper again this morning. You must get there at least forty minutes before it starts. Bring your embroidery or a novel. *War and Peace* springs to mind, given this morning's events."

Lady Beatrice smoothed down her dress. "My cook failed to

wake me in time. She overslept," she muttered. "I still haven't been able to find a replacement for my parlour maid. Why she would take fright over two new ghosts is beyond me. She was quite used to Jane Seymour."

"Well, don't get another Parisian," suggested Lady Montfort Bebb. "They're always flighty. Try a Swiss maid next time. They're much more dependable and don't suffer from grand ideas. As for your cook, if she continues to oversleep, you must get her the bed I remember seeing at the Great Exhibition that was especially designed for servants. It had a clockwork device which, at the appointed hour, withdrew a support from the foot of the bed and threw the occupant onto the floor."

Lady Beatrice fiddled with her fringe. "I could use one for my daughter," she replied. "I can't prise her from her sheets. I've no idea what's wrong with her, but fortunately each time she faints in the chapel Dr. Henderson always comes to the rescue. It's high time she were married, but it isn't easy finding a husband these days, with so many men having emigrated to Australia, South Africa, India, and Canada. Of course, the situation isn't helped by American women elbowing their way into London society, some pretending to be millionairesses, and walking off with the best catches. And it's not just we English who have to suffer them. They have already married half the nobility in Europe. Princess di San Faustino, Princess Colonna, and Countess von Waldersee, a grocer's daughter no less, are all Americans."

Lady Montfort Bebb closed her eyes. "Thank God the Prince of Wales is already taken," she said with a shudder.

Lady Beatrice turned to her, still burning with indignation. "Remember when we were at Euston Station last year and all those American women arrived for the Diamond Jubilee over-loaded with trunks and hatboxes? They were wearing diamonds in the morning!"

"Don't," begged Lady Montfort Bebb, lifting a hand to the

side of her head. "Just the memory of the noise they were making makes my ears ring."

"There's a lot to be said for Americans," Mink interrupted. "Their literary men aren't actively hostile to their female rivals, sons and daughters usually inherit equally, women have full suffrage in four States, and many of them are ahead of us in their professions. Only this morning I read about an American mother and her three daughters, all of whom are lawyers."

"That'll be their English heritage," said Lady Montfort Bebb.

The Countess leant forward with a smile. "Ladies!" she said. "I've just heard the news from my maid this morning. We have an American in our midst!"

Lady Beatrice reeled back, a hand on her chest. "It's not a lady, is it?" she asked.

"I do hope so," said Mink. "American hostesses are the best entertainers. I knew one who went as far as having the correct tropical birds specially stuffed to order for her ballroom, which resembled an outdoor bower."

"Not only is he a gentleman, but he's a bachelor," the Countess replied, pausing for dramatic effect. "He's the Bagshots' house-guest. Apparently he calls trousers 'pants,' overshoes 'gums,' and domestic servants 'girls.' The maids are quite taken by him."

Lady Montfort Bebb looked at her open-mouthed. "Pants?" she repeated, aghast. "How extraordinary! Has anyone corrected him? I shouldn't leave it to the General. He has no idea how to behave. He invited me to dinner when he first moved into the apartments next to mine, and I regret to say that I accepted. He stood in front of the drawing room fire during the whole time we were waiting to go into dinner. Even a dustman knows that a gentleman should never hog the fire. I'm convinced he was responsible for the stream of hawkers and peddlers who plagued me all day yesterday. The undertaker insisted on measuring me up! He wouldn't believe my footman that I was still very much alive, and thought something fishy was going on. He was about to call the constable, so I was obliged to show myself at the door. I've never been so humiliated. I had to ask my maid to telegraph for some real turtle soup to help me recover. The grocer had quite run out."

The Countess tucked the hair back underneath her bonnet. "Do you think he will bring the American to the Easter picnic?" she asked. "He would have to contribute something, of course. What is it they eat?"

"They're always chewing tobacco," said Lady Beatrice brightly.

The two other visitors shot her a look.

"I very much hope the General brings him. It is our duty to put that man's English straight before he returns to the colonies," said Lady Montfort Bebb. She turned to the Princess and invited her to join them, explaining that the grace-and-favour residents held a picnic every year just before Easter to avoid the hordes that descended on the palace. "We're having it a little early this year, as I still live in hope of an invitation to spend Easter elsewhere. Life would be so much more pleasant if the costermongers kept to Hampstead Heath on a bank holiday. I still remember the riot that broke out when five hundred of them from Peckham brawled outside the Cardinal Wolsey public house before moving on to the Mitre. They had to call in the Hussars to help the police. As if their whistling wasn't offensive enough."

The Countess turned to her. "That was twenty years ago," she pointed out.

"A costermonger is always a costermonger. Some traits cannot be bred out," replied Lady Montfort Bebb, gripping the knob of her cane with both hands. She glanced out of the window. "I do hope the weather doesn't let us down, otherwise we shall have to decamp to the Oak Room. We had a lovely day last year, with only one disaster, as I recall. Someone forgot the gong."

Lady Beatrice fiddled with a ringlet. "I was distracted by my butler carrying the blancmange," she said, with a nervous titter. "He's a little gouty."

Lady Montfort Bebb surveyed her for a moment with a look of disapproval, then explained to Mink that it was a subscription picnic so as to bring a little order to the proceedings, otherwise they would end up with five sets of knives, no plates, too many rolls, and no butter to speak of.

"In fact there is never any butter to speak of," she added, looking at the Countess, whose eyes slowly travelled to the other side of the room. "Each year one of the residents, who shall remain nameless, always offers to bring some. However, it never materialises on account of her habit of not settling her bills with the butterman."

Lady Beatrice leant forward. "One would think the lady destitute, given that she asked her maid-of-all-work to carry home all the food that was left over."

"But it's absolutely not the case," said Lady Montfort Bebb, still staring at the Countess, who was examining the toes of her shoes. "She just won't open her purse. And I'll make no mention about the amount she drank. That's another matter entirely," she added, her nostrils flaring. "Now," she said, her voice softening as she turned to the Princess. "Is there anything you would like to bring?"

Mink hesitated, looking at each of the visitors as she wondered what on earth Pooki would be able to make.

"What about some pigeon pies?" suggested the Countess with a smile. "They're always so delicious at a picnic, and I'm aware that you only have a maid-of-all-work, as I do. I'm sure she will manage them perfectly well. There are so many things one has to avoid without a real cook. I've had to forget that soufflés even exist. Still, at least my cooking brandy is safe."

"God sends the meat, and the Devil sends the cook," said Lady Montfort Bebb, pursing her lips.

Lady Beatrice leant towards the Princess, the butterflies on her hat quivering on their wires with the sudden movement. "If you ever need any extra help, I know an excellent girl who'll come in the mornings to clean the boots and the knives," she said brightly. Almost immediately she covered her mouth with both hands. Mink looked down at the carpet as her cheeks flared, while the other two visitors suddenly took an interest in the ceiling. Eventually the brittle silence was broken by the sound of a banjo coming from outside.

CHAPTER V

An Unfortunate Incident with
the Blancmange

MONDAY, MARCH 21, 1898

GNORING the furtive glances of the soldiers parading outside the barracks, Mink strode swiftly down the palace driveway, the memory of the missed train quickening her step. One pace behind her was Pooki, in silent disapproval of the shopping expedition to the West End. As they approached Trophy Gate, they were spotted by the organ grinder, who grabbed his crank, despite having been moved on twice by the police that morning. The closer the Princess came, the faster the man turned, until the last of the birds fled screeching from the trees. Mink swiftly passed a penny to Pooki, who dropped it into his chipped cup, putting an end to the torment. She ran to catch up with her mistress, unaware of the gaze of the watercress seller, a tiny green bouquet clutched to his heart.

Not a word was exchanged as the pair crossed over the bridge. While Pooki kept her eyes on the ground, the Princess watched the cats' meat seller coming towards them, pulling his barrow piled with horseflesh on sticks, followed by a procession of strays. Once at the station, they sat at some distance from each other on the wooden bench in the empty waiting room, the meagre fire losing against the March drafts.

"We could go for luncheon at the Tea and Tiffin Bungalow. It's just opened in New Bond Street," suggested Mink, hoping a curry might bring her round.

Pooki stared at the ground in silence.

The Princess looked at the top of her bonnet, then tried again: "I wonder whether the owner of the travelling zoo will remember to dress Albert in his red velvet trousers."

Still the maid didn't lift her head. Suddenly Mink's irritation flared.

"I don't know why you expect me to wear my old dresses. It's your duty to see to it that I appear to my best advantage," she protested, plunging back into the heart of the discord. It had started over breakfast that morning, the anniversary of her father's death, when, in order to distract herself from the relentless waves of pain, the Princess announced that her year of mourning was up and she had nothing to wear.

Pooki looked at her and frowned. "It is also my duty to make sure that you do not end up in the workhouse, ma'am," she said. "You have not even worn some of them because you had to go into mourning."

The Princess stared back incredulously. "You don't seriously expect me to walk around with last year's sleeves the size of mutton legs, do you? And anyway, blouses aren't that costly this season," she said, adding that sleeves only needed two yards of material per pair, as opposed to eight.

"I will alter the old ones for you, ma'am," the maid insisted, her voice raised. "I am next to useless with a saucepan, but I am very good with a needle, as a lady's-maid should be. Another letter came from the undertaker's this morning. I recognised the writing. Those people need to be paid. The elephant was very costly, and you will not even open their letters. Then there is the mausoleum to pay for. I have anxious forebodings."

Mink glanced away. "Everyone will get their money in due

course, somehow or other," she said dismissively. "As for my old dresses, the colours are no longer fashionable. You can sell them. And anyway, we need to get something for you too, unless you'd rather go back to wearing your saris. But you said you didn't want to, as the other servants stare at you enough as it is."

Pooki crossed her arms and contemplated the ground again. As the silence continued, the Princess wondered what it would be like to have a maid who didn't argue with her. "At least being early we'll have command of one of the carriage windows," she said, opening her newspaper. "There's nothing more annoying than a man insisting on having it open."

When Mink eventually looked up, she realised that the train had already pulled in. Its sound had been muffled by the brutal noise of the sleeping maid, who had drifted off as the Princess read, having woken just after dawn, worrying about her mistress's finances. Holding on to their hats, they ran for the platform where the guard stood, his whistle in his mouth. Hauling open the door of the nearest first-class carriage, they climbed in and sank down onto opposite seats, unable to believe they had almost missed another train.

As it started to pull away, Mink noticed that they were not alone. Sitting on the other side of the compartment reading a magazine was Dr. Henderson. She glanced at him, but he caught her eye and she immediately studied the view out her window. After a while, she looked again, but their gaze met and both immediately turned away. Suddenly Dr. Henderson stood up, unhooked the leather strap holding up the window next to him, and lowered it several notches. Feeling an undignified gust of country air, Mink got to her feet, strode across the carriage, and hooked it closed.

She had just turned the page of her newspaper when she heard the window being opened again. Immediately she stood up, smoothed down her skirt, and retraced her steps. After shutting it with more purpose than before, she stalked back to her seat. But as she turned back to the view, she heard the unmistakable wallop of it falling all the way down. She sat in silent fury, unwilling to give the doctor the satisfaction of closing it again, and wondered why men were always so intent on making everyone else freeze.

Mink wasn't sure whether it was sitting in such a penetrating draft that did it, or her close proximity to Dr. Henderson. Either way, when the cab dropped them at Marshall & Snelgrove in Oxford Street, she headed straight to the fur section. Taking a seat in front of the counter, she asked the assistant to show her a sealskin jacket. After trying it on, she decided she had to have it, despite the fact that spring had already arrived. She then informed the assistant that she needed to go to the drapery next, and a shopwalker was called to escort her. And so she kept going until she had visited silks, trimmings, outfitting, ribbons, parasols, fancy jewellery, ball dresses, embroideries, and lace.

It was while she was inspecting the ready-made blouses that Mr. Cheeseman, the manager, appeared, his dyed hair immaculately parted. Wearing a morning suit that perfectly fitted his new sleek figure, only the damp handkerchief in his pocket was testimony to his wife having finally left him that morning. He cleared his throat, still thick from weeping, and with the perfect hint of a bow said, "Forgive me for mentioning it, Your Highness, but there seems to be a small problem with your account."

Mink sat up in her chair at the counter. "And what small problem might that be?" she asked.

"The settling of it, Your Highness."

"It'll be settled within twelve months, as it always is, Mr. Cheeseman," she replied dismissively.

The manager held his hands together behind his back and raised his chin. "I'm not referring to today's purchases, though, of course, given their number, I'm duty-bound to take them into consideration. I'm referring to those already on your account, Your Highness. The bill hasn't been settled for well over a year."

Mink frowned. "But my father would have settled it."

There was a pause. "I regret to say that the Maharaja failed to do so. A number of letters have been sent."

The Princess blinked as she tried to take it in. "There must be some mistake."

"Unfortunately not," said the manager, shaking his head.

Mink stood up and faced him, an eyebrow raised. "I very much hope, Mr. Cheeseman, that you will take into consideration my family's unfailing loyalty over the years, and rest assured that the bill will be paid. Otherwise I shall have to consider taking my custom elsewhere. What would my new neighbours at Hampton Court Palace say if I told them I'd switched drapers over the small matter of paying a bill? Why, they may very well wish to accompany me and tell all their friends in the West End. I hear the tearoom in Swan & Edgar is charming."

The manager looked at her aghast, gripping his hands together in front of him. "There's no need for that, Your Highness, no need for that at all. I have no doubt that the matter will be sorted out in a jiffy. Is there anything else you require while you're here? I trust that you've been shown our dainty Japanese parasols. They always look so charming on the river," he said, picking one up and opening it with a flourish. "May I assure you that the tearoom at the establishment you mentioned is no longer what it used to be." He paused, lowered his eyes, and muttered, "I have it on good authority that the rat-catcher was called there last Thursday."

Mink and Pooki left the store as swiftly as they had entered. As the Princess hailed a cab, she glanced at the maid and immediately asked the driver to take them to the Tea and Tiffin Bungalow. She sat during the journey with her eyes closed, wishing that she could go to the Klondike like everyone else and search for gold. The maid, in silence next to her, kept her head turned towards the window, her jaw set. Madame Pheroze Langrana, the owner, greeted them at the restaurant door, still glowing from the article in *The Times* that mentioned the nobility and Member of Parliament who had attended her inaugural luncheon. Not only was she of good stock, the paper had reported, but she came from the most enterprising, and the most devoted to the British Crown, of all the races in India.

After being shown to the best table, Mink surveyed the menu, wondering whether Pooki would unpurse her lips sufficiently to eat. But she needn't have worried. When the curries arrived, the servant's remarkable appetite, which she blamed for the size of her feet, was still very much in evidence. Never once did she falter, despite the number of unsolicited dishes that kept arriving at the table, many of which hadn't been served in England before. It wasn't until the maid finally put down her cutlery that she spoke.

"We are very lucky that we live in the times that we do, ma'am," she said, looking her mistress in the eye for the first time since leaving Oxford Street.

"We certainly are," the Princess said with a smile, assuming the maid had finally come round. "You can eat everything in London these days."

"Thirty years ago you would be headed for the debtors' prison in that sealskin jacket of yours," Pooki continued, wiping the corner of her mouth with her napkin.

*

FOLLOWING A MEETING WITH HIS fellow medical men about the tyranny of homeopaths, Dr. Henderson arrived at Waterloo and headed straight for the train. Ignoring the shoeblack and his admonishing stare at his boots, he walked down the platform hoping that he wouldn't bump into the Princess. What had started out as an innocent desire for some fresh air had finished with his breaking the window strap. He had spent the journey chilled to the bone, mortified by what he had done, and fearing for the health of both her and her maid. Peering into the carriages, he selected one that was empty, sat down in the far corner, and unfolded his newspaper. He glanced at each passenger as they came in, and was relieved when the porter slammed the door and the whistle finally blew. Suddenly the door opened again, and in leapt the homeopath from East Molesey, wearing a top hat with an over-worked brim. Silas Sparrowgrass was instantly recognisable not only by his lack of height but by his Newgate fringe, a style of beard named after the notorious prison, as it followed the chin line of the hangman's rope. Sitting down opposite the doctor, he fixed him with his squint and hailed him as if he were a colleague. He then proceeded to perform a magic trick with a sixpence that even-tually found its way inside an orange, much to the amusement of the other passengers. Dr. Henderson raised his paper, wondering how anyone could believe the theory that like cured like, or that infinitesimal doses could have any effect on a body ravaged with disease. And yet there were plenty who did, and he had lost count-less patients to the charlatan, who not only charged less than him but had not the slightest interest in the contents of their piss pots.

He arrived home, further riled by the homeopath having handed out his cards to the passengers on arrival at Hampton Court Station, and immediately noticed a delicate aroma of orange and spice. Looking into the waiting room, he saw the remains of several slices of bachelor's cake, and immediately asked his house-keeper into the consulting room.

"Mrs. Nettleship," he began. "I believe I have mentioned this several times before, but I fear I must repeat myself. You must refrain from feeding the patients. A number of them are already far too stout as it is. The butterman got stuck in his parlour win-dow last week when he lost his key and attempted to climb in. They had to tie a rope to his ankles and use a corn chandler's mare to pull him out. The grocer's donkey wasn't up to it."

The housekeeper scratched at her rust hair. "I couldn't 'elp myself, doctor. They looked so 'ungry sitting there waiting for you

to come back. I put in hextra raisins, I was so pleased I'd found
'em. Care for a slice?"

Dr. Henderson took off his hat and coat, and took his place
behind the desk. "What I would like, Mrs. Nettleship, is for you
not to feed them. They are not animals in a zoological garden,
though judging from some of their behaviour it may seem so. And
while we're on the subject of baking, you seem to have been making nothing but bachelor's cakes for the last month. Is there something you wish to tell me?"

The housekeeper clutched her butcher's hands in front of her.
"A nice young man like you rattling haround in a big 'ouse like
this. It breaks me 'eart to see you hall halone."

"I'm very much aware of the fact that I'm unmarried. I wish I
weren't, if truth be told, but that's my concern."

Mrs. Nettleship approached. "Is there hanything I can 'elp you
with? The name of a new barber, per'aps?"

The doctor instinctively raised a hand to his hair, swallowed
his indignation, and asked for the first patient. In hobbled a man
in a navy uniform with tarnished silver buttons, clutching a cap.
Sprouting from his cheeks, discoloured by years of rain, was a pair
of Piccadilly weepers. Caught in the unfashionably long side-
whiskers was a constellation of cake crumbs. The man introduced
himself as William Sheepshanks, the Keeper of the Maze, and
explained that he needed a doctor's certificate confirming that he
was unfit for work.

"There's something awful wrong with my legs, doctor," he said
sitting down. "Makes it hard for me to climb up onto my platform.
Some people can't find their way out of the maze unless I'm up
there giving them directions."

The doctor picked up his pen and noted down his name. "You
must otherwise be in rude health, Mr. Sheepshanks. I don't believe
we've met before."

The keeper clutched his cap. "That's because I usually go to
the homeopath from East Molesey," he admitted.

The doctor put down his pen and sat back. "And why, if you don't mind my asking, would you put your health in that man's hands?"

There was a pause. "Because his medicine doesn't taste like sewer men's boots."

"His potions taste of nothing, Mr. Sheepshanks, because there is virtually nothing in them. Now, let's have a look at you."

The patient took off his boots and holey stockings, rolled up his trouser legs, and clambered onto the examining table.

"Do you enjoy your job?" the doctor asked, walking round the desk. "There can't be many maze keepers in the country. I expect you're the only one."

William Sheepshanks lay back and turned his head to the doctor. "Sometimes I sit there wondering what would happen if I just walked away and left them all in there. I've been out in all weathers for sixteen years, and struck by lightning more times than I care to remember. Last time all my hair fell out. It grew back curly."

The doctor peered at the ulcers on his legs. "When did these first appear?" he asked.

The keeper looked at the ceiling. "You'd be surprised how many people don't know their left from their right."

After feeling the man's pulse, Dr. Henderson took out his depressor and examined his tongue.

"The women are quite happy to ask for help if they need it," continued William Sheepshanks, as soon as the instrument was out of his mouth. "It's the men who are the troublemakers."

"How's your appetite?" asked the doctor.

The keeper continued to stare at the ceiling. "They go in there determined to conquer it. Usually it's when they're with a lady."

"Do you sleep well, Mr. Sheepshanks?" the general practitioner asked a little louder.

The patient scratched at his whiskers. "Some of them get into a rage. I see the ladies tugging at their sleeves, suggesting that they ask me for directions. They'd rather cut their own arms off."

Wondering whether the man was deaf in one ear, the doctor walked round to the other side of the examining table. "How would you describe the state of your bowels?" he asked.

"I give them directions anyway," continued the keeper. "There's only so long you can watch a man struggle. But when you tell them to go right, some of them turn left on purpose, as they don't like to be told."

Dr. Henderson leant over him, trying to get his attention. "Do you take much exercise, Mr. Sheepshanks?" he asked, his voice raised.

"Then I go in after them, as they've got to be out before it closes. That makes them incandescent."

The doctor stood for a moment, looking at him. "Are you fond of walking? In meadows, perhaps?" he asked.

William Sheepshanks suddenly turned to the doctor. "I love a meadow, me. Could walk through them all day. Everything's starting to come up at this time of year. Solitude. That's what I like. Not a soul in sight . . . Did you ever read Jerome K. Jerome's *Three Men in a Boat*?"

"I did indeed," the doctor replied, smiling. "I particularly liked the part when Harris gets stuck in the palace maze."

"So did everyone else, and they haven't stopped coming since," replied the keeper through gritted teeth. "That book will be the death of me."

Dr. Henderson strode back to his desk. "Not yet it won't, Mr. Sheepshanks," he said dismissively. "But you might very well find yourself in a much more perilous state if you continue rubbing buttercup juice on your legs, like every other malingerer I know. I'll make no mention of this to the palace. For while you may dislike your position, I imagine you wish to keep it."

The keeper slowly sat up and looked at the general practitioner, the droop of his Piccadilly weepers adding to his air of defeat. "No chance of a certificate, then, doctor?" he asked.

"None," Dr. Henderson replied from behind his desk, his head bent as he wrote in his ledger.

William Sheepshanks attempted a smile. "Not even if I let you into the maze free of charge? You could get yourself a nice bun with that penny saved. Everyone likes a nice bun." The keeper closed his eyes and clasped his hands together. "Imagine the currants, doctor!"

"Absolutely not," Dr. Henderson snapped, writing out a prescription. "This will help clear up the ulcers. I suggest you go and contemplate how fortunate you are to have a position, and one that doesn't involve dealing with time-wasters."

The keeper pulled on his stockings and boots with a sigh, and slowly rolled down his trouser legs. He took the prescription without a word, deposited some coins on the desk, and shuffled to the door. The general practitioner softened as he watched him. "Please try to avoid sitting in the rain, Mr. Sheepshanks," he urged. "And if you speak nicely to Mrs. Nettleship on your way out, she may well darn your stockings. She can't resist the challenge of a hole."

TUESDAY, MARCH 29, 1898

On the day of the picnic, Pooki carefully rubbed her hands with parsley to rid them of the reek of onions, then slipped out the back door. Hoping that the Princess hadn't spotted her, she fled up Moat Lane smelling of violets, still tying the ribbons of her bonnet. When she returned, she crept back into the kitchen and immediately set about reviving her mistress's new hat, trimmed in fashionable turquoise, which Mink had decided to wear that afternoon. It was already suffering from the damp, and she held it next to the range for a few minutes, then dipped a blunt knife into hot water and carefully recurled the feathers. Satisfied with the results, she then put a bone on to boil in order to make some hair pomade.

She was adding oil and citronella to the beaten marrow when

the Princess came down to inspect the pigeon pies, carrying a newspaper. Mink stopped in her tracks, noticing something strange on the floor. Unable to believe what she was seeing, she took a step closer. As she stared, wondering how on earth a hedgehog had got into the kitchen, Pooki stood in front of it, but not even her enormous feet could hide its prickles.

"One of the gardeners found her for me yesterday, ma'am," Pooki hastily explained. "She has come to eat the beetles. I have named her Victoria."

The Princess continued to gaze at the creature, her hands on her hips. "I don't know why you've called her after Mrs. Fagin. That woman still hasn't returned the family jewels."

"Ma'am, you must not let anyone hear you calling the Queen 'Mrs. Fagin,'" said Pooki, wagging her finger. "She gave you a home. There were more than a hundred people on the waiting list."

The Princess surveyed the floor. "Can't you just put down some arsenic or something?" she asked.

"No, ma'am," the maid said, shaking her head. "It is too dangerous. The Maharaja always thought that the British Government was going to poison him, and it was never allowed in the house."

"Well, let's hope Victoria's appetite is as big as yours. And don't let Mrs. Boots see her. That woman's convinced I've smuggled in a pet as it is."

The maid's eyes fell to the floor. "Why would that be, ma'am?" she asked, slowly looking up.

"Goodness knows," the Princess replied. She then handed her the newspaper, and tapped at an advertisement for a fancy dress ball at the Greyhound Hotel, next to the entrance to Bushy Park. "I've decided to go," she said. "I haven't been to one for ages."

Pooki read it and beamed. "That is an exceedingly good idea, ma'am. You might find a husband."

Mink frowned. "I don't want a husband."

"You wanted to marry Mr. Cavendish, ma'am," the maid reminded her. "Everyone needs love. Even Victoria the hedgehog."

"Well, my views have changed," Mink replied curtly, sitting down at the table. "Wives just end up being female valets." She nodded at the paper. "I'm going to go as Boadicea."

Pooki shook her head. "You cannot go as Boadicea, ma'am. Gentlemen do not like such ladies. They are too ferocious for them. You should go as Cinderella."

Mink stared at her. "I'm not going as Cinderella!" she exclaimed.

"You are twenty-seven and still not married, ma'am. You will have to go as Sleeping Beauty or you will die a spinster."

The Princess frowned. "I'm not going as Sleeping Beauty either," she declared. "And I don't need a husband."

Pooki crossed her arms. "Then you shall be Snow White."

The Princess stood up. "I'd rather go as one of the Seven Dwarves. Now, let's see those pigeon pies."

The maid froze. "Ma'am, you do not need to see those pigeon pies."

"I just want to check them before we go to the picnic," said the Princess, looking towards the larder.

Pooki put her hands on her hips. "There is no need, ma'am, as I have already said. You would be better off deciding which earrings to wear."

"I've already decided," Mink replied, studying the maid. "So what's wrong with the pigeon pies, Pooki?"

The maid closed her eyes. "Nothing, ma'am," she said, shaking her head. "They are very, very beautiful." Suddenly she opened them again and looked straight at her mistress. "And even if they happened to be as ugly as Mrs. Boots, there would be nothing you could do about it, as we have to leave in less than an hour and I still need to help you dress and do your hair."

Mink moved towards the larder, but the servant stood in her

way. The Princess darted to the right, but the maid blocked her. She then dodged left, but Pooki was too fast.

"I'm not interested in seeing them anyway," said Mink sulkily, heading slowly for the stairs. Suddenly she turned, and hared round the kitchen table, the duped maid sprinting after her. The Princess reached the larder first, then stood in contemplation, her head to one side in line with the pitch of the pastry, which undulated like the swell of the sea.

Pooki had made them the previous day from a recipe given to her by Alice Cockle, who dropped in with a bag of flour in case she ran out. Pike, the butcher's boy, then arrived at the back door with the delivery of birds, which she lined up in a row on the kitchen table, their clutched pink feet pointing heavenwards. After plucking and singeing them, she relieved them of their pitifully small guts, cut off their wings, necks, and feet, and trussed them up for stewing. Arranging the giblets and a slice of beef in the bottom of each pie dish, she then added the pigeons, stock, ketchup, a glass of port, and, to all except one, boiled eggs. Covering them with a pastry lid, she crimped the edging and placed in the middle a rose made of butter and flour into which she stuck pigeon legs, their feet sticking up into the air.

It took a while for Mink to be able to speak. "Why does only one of them have three legs?" she asked.

The servant peered over her shoulder. "That one is for the General, ma'am," she said. "His butler asked me to make one without eggs, as his master does not eat them, and suggested inserting fewer legs to identify it, as they do every year apparently."

The Princess continued looking at it. "I can't stand the man. He appears to forget he's married." She glanced around the larder. "We seem to have an awful lot of watercress."

The maid froze. Slowly she turned her dark eyes to her mistress and swallowed. "It is in season, ma'am," she replied evenly, then walked swiftly out.

*

WITH HER HAIR SWEPT UP into a well-padded chignon to give her extra height, Mink left Wilderness House wearing a turquoise and seal-brown jacket with a high collar, her matching skirt hugging her hips and flaring from the knee as fashion dictated. Pooki followed in a new black merino maid's dress, with a white apron, cap, collar, and cuffs. They walked in silence, the Princess already regretting having agreed to go on account of the unfortunate-looking contents of the maid's basket. Nor did she know whether anyone would talk to her, apart from the three ladies who had invited her, as none of the other grace-and-favour residents had tried to make her acquaintance.

Eventually they found the Pond Gardens, laid out by William and Mary into small enclosures surrounded by tall hedges to protect the exotics when moved out of the conservatories. Mink immediately spotted the party in a section that remained as a private refuge for the residents. Some stood in clusters, others were propped up in bath chairs, and a number sat on rugs on the lawn. Neatly arranged on a row of trestle tables draped with white linen were silver platters and dishes bearing joints of lamb and beef, veal patties, rabbit pies, lobsters, apple trifles, casseroles of prunes, and Swiss puddings. At one end stood a silver tea urn, and at the other bottles of sherry, claret, beer, lemonade, and soda water. A row of expressionless butlers stood behind with their white-gloved hands at their sides, all of whom had just placed a bet on which resident would disgrace themselves the most.

The Princess approached, wondering whether the three ladies who called on her had arrived. As she stood looking around, she noticed numerous eyes upon her and heads coming together to exchange whispers. She was just contemplating whether to leave when Lady Montfort Bebb caught her eye and gestured to the garden chair next to her and the Countess.

"Do take a seat, Princess," she said, smiling, as Mink approached. "It's always preferable to be off the ground. You get a much better view of the proceedings. We wouldn't want to miss anything exciting. The chaplain and the organist came to blows last year." She then looked the Countess up and down. "Though some behaviour is best forgotten."

The Countess fiddled with the ribbons tying her widow's bonnet. "It would be forgotten were it not for certain people endlessly bringing it up," she said curtly. "The reason I fell from my chair was because the sherry was adulterated. Goodness knows what the merchant added to it. I couldn't get out of bed the whole of the next day."

Lady Montfort Bebb pursed her lips. "May I suggest that you avoid the sherry altogether this year?" she said. "We struggled getting you to your feet, you were so convulsed with laughter. No one else was amused, I can tell you, apart from the butler who witnessed your collapse and found the spectacle so hilarious he fell backwards into a flowerbed. The poor man broke his leg." She looked away, then snapped: "It wouldn't have mattered, except that he was *my* butler."

"I've no intention of going anywhere near the sherry," the Countess replied primly, her black-gloved hands clasped in her lap. She raised herself up from her chair and looked towards the trestle tables. "I shall try the claret."

Feeling the urge for some as well, Mink excused herself and returned with three glasses. She sat down next to the Countess and offered her one.

"Don't encourage her," muttered Lady Montfort Bebb, reaching out an age-dappled hand for a glass, which she promptly drained. "I don't know why I arrange this every year. Something always happens to make me regret it. But I live in hope that one year we will be one happy family and let bygones be bygones."

The Princess glanced towards the path, then lowered her voice.

"I do hope we won't have to spend the afternoon with the General. I find him intolerable."

Lady Montfort Bebb patted her arm. "Don't worry, my dear. Thankfully he finds me intolerable, so we will be spared his presence," she replied. "I'm not at all surprised that you've taken against him so quickly. He has no manners to speak of. He gets into his carriage before his wife, and continues to smoke in the street when he passes a lady. How he can object to my music is beyond comprehension. It never bothered you when you were living next to me, did it?" she asked, turning to the Countess.

There was a significant pause. "Not in the least," she replied, glancing at the floor.

"Goodness knows what Mrs. Bagshot sees in him," Mink continued. "I bumped into her before she left for Egypt. I rather took to her."

"Mrs. Bagshot is adorable," agreed the Countess. "But her husband is another matter entirely. I heard he once slapped a kitchen maid for rejecting his advances. And he was extremely rude about my interior decoration when he and Mrs. Bagshot moved into my old apartments overlooking the Thames."

"So he does have some taste after all," muttered Lady Montfort Bebb, peering through her lorgnettes at the crowd. "I wonder where Lady Beatrice has got to. We're still missing the blancmange. Oh, look, there's Dr. Henderson. Why I should eat luncheon in the company of the man who treats my chilblains is beyond me, but Lady Beatrice insisted that I ask him. It seems her daughter is quite taken with him. Oh, dear, he's coming our way." She turned to Mink. "Let me know if you have no wish to be introduced, and I'll pretend I haven't seen him."

"On the contrary," she replied. "That man needs instruction on the etiquette of train travel."

Once Lady Montfort Bebb had acknowledged him with a nod, the general practitioner approached and raised his hat, revealing his tousled curls. She turned to Mink. "Allow me to present Dr. Henderson. Princess Alexandrina, Dr. Henderson."

Mink looked at him from her seat. "It seems you have a mania for fresh air, Dr. Henderson," she remarked tartly.

"Ventilated air, such as that in a railway carriage provided by an open window, is much better for the health than that which has already been expired by others, Princess," he replied.

She raised her chin. "And what of chills, doctor? Surely one could catch one's death being subjected to a fully open window during a train journey in the month of March?"

Dr. Henderson glanced away, then met her blue gaze. "Strong emotions lead people to act in ways that they often later regret. One can only hope that a victim of such behaviour would find it within herself to forgive such foolishness."

The Princess was about to reply when Lady Montfort Bebb stood up. "Finally!" she exclaimed. Mink turned and saw Lady Beatrice approaching with her daughter, a plain-looking girl much more timorously attired, whose gaze scattered over the guests until it settled on Dr. Henderson. Behind them walked a sweating butler carrying a large pink blancmange on a silver platter as if it were a bomb. Suddenly he appeared to falter, his view of the ground obscured by his tremulous load. All might have been well, had it not been for his woeful over-correction. It was never clear what hit the ground first, but one thing was certain: the servant and the dessert were entirely enmeshed by the time they both landed. Without a backwards glance, Lady Beatrice and her daughter increased their pace and sat down.

"It appears that your butler's gout isn't cured after all," remarked Lady Montfort Bebb.

Mink raised an eyebrow and looked at Dr. Henderson. "He must be your patient, doctor," she said.

"It gets better and better," said the Countess, dabbing away a tear of mirth with a black-bordered handkerchief. "Here's the General, with whom I can only assume is his American guest."

"What on earth has that foreigner got on?" asked Lady Mont-fort Bebb, examining him through her lorgnettes.

Mink sat up and peered. "It appears to be some sort of monkey-fur coat."

The General approached, wearing a bowler hat, a fashionably quiet grey lounge suit, and an unconventional fancy waistcoat arranged with a double row of buttons. He scanned the women, his eyes stopping on Mink. With him was a broad man in a chimney-pot hat and a luxuriant pelt down to his knees. His dark hair was expertly plastered to his head, and over his wide smile perched the politest of moustaches.

"These seats are already taken, General," declared Lady Mont-fort Bebb, gesturing to the empty places beside them.

"By whom, I wonder?" he asked, smiling. "A couple of whelk sellers, or maybe some sweeps? Or the organ grinder? No? Then it must be Mr. Blood! Pity he didn't take you away while he was round on Saturday. Not to worry. It's only a matter of time before he'll be back, with any luck."

Lady Montfort Bebb looked away, nostrils flared, gripping her cane in fury. The General started the introductions, and she reluc-tantly turned back at the sound of her name to find Cornelius B. Pilgrim holding out his hand. She looked at it as if she had caught the tail wind of an elderly cheese. "In England, Mr. Pilgrim, a well-mannered man never puts out his hand in greeting until a lady extends hers," she said pointedly. "Such behaviour is based on the assumption that the lady is the social superior."

The American laughed, slapped her on the back, and took a seat. She sat in stunned silence, looking ahead of her.

"Mr. Pilgrim is a friend of the family and a palaeontologist. He's staying with me for a few weeks while he visits our muse-ums," said General Bagshot, sitting down next to Mink, who immediately froze.

Lady Beatrice leant forward, the pink ostrich feathers on her hat quivering. "You must go and see the life-size dinosaur replicas at the Crystal Palace, Mr. Pilgrim," she suggested. "They were the first in the world, like most things in Britain. I understand the plans for those in Central Park were scrapped."

Cornelius B. Pilgrim thanked her for the recommendation and said he had just been to see them. "I do love English trains. You get much less covered in soot over here," he said.

Mink edged away from the General, who had opened his legs to such an extent that his knee was touching the edge of her skirt. "It's all to do with the coal we use, Mr. Pilgrim," she pointed out. She looked at Dr. Henderson. "Though, of course, it also depends on how far open the window is. Some people insist on having it all the way down, much to the great annoyance of the other passengers."

The doctor's eyes fell to the floor.

"No one ever agrees how much fresh air to let into a train carriage," said Lady Montfort Bebb. "The consumptives are the worst. Do you have any other plans, apart from visiting our muse-ums and manhandling the populace, Mr. Pilgrim? I should avoid the National Gallery when it's raining. The working classes tend to shelter there when it's wet."

"I was thinking of going to see some of the Dickens land-marks," he replied, lounging back in his chair. "Apparently you can still see the steps in *Oliver Twist* on the Surrey side of London Bridge."

Lady Beatrice adjusted her golden-blond fringe. "Much of the rest, I shouldn't wonder, has been trampled to death by foreign tourists. Furnival's Inn, where he began to write *The Pickwick Papers,* was torn down several months ago. At least that's one less mecca for the Yankee hordes."

Cornelius B. Pilgrim scratched his cheek. "I must confess I haven't read it. I'm about to start *Little Dorrit.*"

There was silence as the women exchanged disapproving glances.

Mink turned to him. "I hope you'll feel at home during your stay, Mr. Pilgrim. Jacksons of Piccadilly sells American groceries."

"Should anyone want such things . . ." said Lady Montfort Bebb, looking doubtful.

Suddenly Mink felt an arm on the back of her chair, and the General turned towards her and lowered his voice. "I called yesterday, but your maid said you weren't at home. You weren't hiding from me, were you?" he asked, his eyes skimming her chest.

Her stomach turned as she inhaled the fetid stench of pipe tobacco and port. "Hiding from you, General?" she asked, sitting forward. "To be perfectly frank, I haven't given you a second thought. I was attending a meeting of the National Union of Women's Suffrage Societies."

"Were you, indeed?" he said, looking her up and down. "Woman suffrage is condemned by the Bible."

Mink smiled politely. "I wasn't aware that you had read it, General."

"What on earth does *he* want?" cried Lady Montfort Bebb, staring at Gibbs, the grocer's boy, running towards them, clutching his cap.

Panting, he approached Dr. Henderson. "Mother says to tell you that the baby's on its way," he said. Mink watched the doctor leave, turning away when he glanced back.

"What a pity Dr. Henderson's gone," said Lady Beatrice, looking at her daughter, who was talking to another group of residents. "How she'll find a husband I'll never know." She leant towards the Countess and lowered her voice. "I'm still looking for one for you, of course."

"But I don't wish to remarry," the Countess hissed, glancing around to see if anyone heard. "I've told you countless times. You're a widow yourself, and know perfectly well that it's most agreeable not to have a husband. There's no one spilling tobacco over the carpet, leaving collars in every corner of the bedroom, or forgetting to put their boots out to be cleaned. Why do you insist on trying to push me back up the aisle?"

Lady Beatrice leant towards her. "I'm considerably older than you, not that one could tell with all that grey hair you refuse to dye, and have my daughter for company. You are all alone in those freezing apartments in Fish Court with only your ferns for company. One can only get away with such eccentricity at an advanced age." She then glanced around, opened her handbag, and tilted it towards the Countess. "I have something for you," she whispered. "We ladies have to make the most of ourselves. You're fortunate in that you're a natural beauty, but even nature needs a helping hand."

The Countess peered into the bag with a frown. "It looks like some sort of taxidermy," she muttered.

Lady Beatrice put her hand inside and thrust the contents into the Countess's lap. "It's a false fringe," she hissed. "Put it into your bag. There's no need to pay me back, not that you would. Just keep me abreast of all the gentlemen suitors."

The Countess immediately covered it with her hands. As soon as Lady Beatrice turned away, she dropped it on the floor with the tips of her fingers and went to fetch some more claret. Wanting to escape General Bagshot, Mink joined her. But when she returned, there was no other seat available, and she reluctantly sunk back down next to him.

"I was wondering whether you had reconsidered my offer," he murmured, leaning so close to her she could feel his blood-shot nose against her hair. "I've always found that you natives have such appetites for pleasure. Your father certainly did, as everyone knows. I'm hoping you're just like him."

Suddenly Mink stood up, the contents of her glass spilling onto the General's crotch. He let out a wail, staring in disbelief at the deep red stain on his trousers. The Princess gasped, holding her hands to her cheeks. "Forgive me, General," she begged. "I'm such an oaf."

A butler ran over with a napkin, and General Bagshot snatched it out of his hands and started dabbing at himself while those around them stared. "They're ruined," he seethed, and glared at the Princess. Mink sat down, apologising loudly. She then leant towards him and purred into his ear: "You're absolutely right, General. I am just like my father. I've an excellent aim."

The Countess, who had watched the General's soaking with delight, looked over towards the trestle tables and said loudly: "I wonder whether it's time for luncheon. So much amusement has given me an appetite."

"What a good idea," said Lady Montfort Bebb. "Did you bring the butter this year? Though I don't know why I bother to ask."

The Countess flicked an imaginary speck off her skirt. "Apparently there's a problem with my account," she said, breezily.

Lady Beatrice turned to her. "You should marry the butterman," she said, looking her up and down. "Then we'd all be spared the humiliation of dry bread rolls."

Lady Montfort Bebb headed towards the tables and returned several minutes later, frowning. "No one seems to know where the gong is," she said. She looked at Lady Beatrice. "I can only assume that for the second year running it has been left behind."

Lady Beatrice put a hand over her mouth. "I've had so much on my mind," she said, tittering nervously. "You've no idea the anxiety my cook causes me. She deserted me last week just before a dinner party, claiming she had to see her mother on her deathbed. That woman has been dying for eight years."

As they were eating, the General shouted over to Pooki, demanding to be brought another slice of pigeon pie. As she served him, he turned to her and asked, "So what's the gossip amongst the servants?"

"I do not know, General," she replied, not looking him in the eye.

He frowned. "Come, come. There must be some tittle-tattle with which you can enliven the picnic," he said.

"I do not know of any, General," she replied, shaking her head. "I have already told you."

He surveyed her. "You do disappoint me," he said. "I've always found Indian servants delighted to pass on the slightest hint of a scandal. And what they don't know they make up."

Pooki's jaw set. "There is one thing I heard from one of the delivery boys," she said after a pause.

"Oh, good," said General Bagshot, smiling. "Let's hear it."

The maid looked at him and raised her voice. "He said that you killed some of Lady Beatrice's doves and sold them to the butcher as pigeons."

Lady Beatrice dropped her fork, while Mink stared at Pooki, open-mouthed.

The Countess eventually broke the silence. "Has anyone read the new edition of *The Fern World* by Francis George Heath?" she enquired, looking around. "I do recommend it."

Suddenly the General roared with laughter. Turning back to Pooki, he said, "You'd better bring me another slice, as I might be eating a nice plump dove. I've always wondered what they taste like." He looked over at Lady Beatrice, who immediately got to her feet and walked away. Mink turned to Cornelius B. Pilgrim and asked the first thing that came into her head: "Do American women really wear their diamonds in the morning?"

Not long after Pooki had returned with General Bagshot's third slice, he put his hand against his stomach and declared he was feeling off colour.

Ignoring him, the Countess asked, "Is anyone going to the fancy dress ball at the Greyhound Hotel this year? They always put on such a good spread."

"So it would seem," said Lady Montfort Bebb. "I can't recall a year when you weren't the last person to leave the supper room."

"An English fancy dress ball?" asked Cornelius B. Pilgrim. "What fun! Sure, I'll go."

Lady Montfort Bebb smiled at him and cocked her head. "We'll see about that, Mr. Pilgrim. I'm in charge of selling the tickets in order to keep out the riff-raff."

When General Bagshot complained again that he was feeling unwell, Mink declared, "Isn't it funny how one always fancies some blancmange when there isn't any."

Several minutes later he wrapped his arms around his abdomen and leant forwards with a loud moan.

"Oh, look, there's a kitty cat," said Cornelius B. Pilgrim with a smile, looking at the plump black-and-white creature on top of the garden wall. "How cute."

Lady Montfort Bebb raised her lorgnettes. "That's Lord Sluggard, the palace mouser."

"It looks like he's caught something for once," said the Countess, leaning forward. "I can't quite make out whether it's a rat or a mouse."

The General emitted a much louder groan and doubled over. Everyone sat up in their seats to peer at the animal.

"It's neither," declared Mink. "That's a false fringe."

At that moment came a hideous retching sound, and the ladies quickly withdrew their feet as General Bagshot vomited on the grass. Just as Cornelius B. Pilgrim passed him his handkerchief, the man vomited again, causing the rest of the party to disperse. The American then took his arm and led him back to the palace, watched by the residents and servants, their eyes flicking between the vomit on his boots and his stained trousers. It was considerably later, when one of the butlers was drinking his winnings in the Mitre, that the Astronomical Clock stopped.

CHAPTER VI

A Body in the Palace

WEDNESDAY, MARCH 30, 1898

 HE residents first suspected that someone had died when the myopic undertaker strode through Base Court the next morning, his measuring rule tucked under his arm. The sound of Mr. Blood's determined heels enticed them to their windows, and, glancing down, they found their curiosity rewarded beyond their imagination.

"The undertaker's just arrived! Any idea who's died?" a lady's-maid asked a butler, having been sent next door for information. "My mistress is praying it's not Lady Grenville, as she promised to take her to luncheon at the Savoy."

"Mr. Blood's here. Who's snuffed it?" demanded a housemaid on another doorstep. "Her Ladyship is hoping he's come for Mrs. Applegate, as her apartments overlook the Thames."

A footman leant out of a window. "Apparently Mrs. Boots was diced up at the stroke of midnight and the murderer tried to get rid of her body down the drains," he called to the housekeeper below, who ran back home with the intelligence.

The news of the undertaker's arrival reached Clock Court before he did, and Lady Beatrice's cook burst into the breakfast room with the revelation. The aristocrat looked up from her kippers and dismissed the notion of murder. "It'll be the American. He'll have gone outside to chew some tobacco, fallen into the Thames, and been dragged under by the weight of his monkey-fur coat."

By the time the bier left the palace, numerous letters had been despatched to the Lord Chamberlain asking for the apartments of the deceased, identified as eleven different people. But eventually the truth reached them all: the body in the coffin was that of General Bagshot. The residents retreated from their windows, nursing their disappointment that his home with its spectacular view of the river wouldn't be available on account of his irrefutably alive spouse. If that wasn't deflating enough, his death certificate had stated the relatively pedestrian affliction of English cholera.

The brutal news of her husband's demise was relayed to Mrs. Bagshot in the staccato language of a telegram. Replying that she would return from Egypt as soon as possible, she gave her permission for the funeral to go ahead in two days' time, given the length of her journey, stipulating that it be held in the Chapel Royal, where her husband had worshipped. Out of regard for the widow, the Countess arranged for a different organist to play. Such was the mourners' relief that the hymns matched the music, they forgave the Reverend Grayling for twice referring to the deceased as General Bagpipes during the service. The wind was up when the party reached Hampton Cemetery, and by the time the oak coffin was lowered into the ground only Lady Montfort Bebb had muttered how fitting it was that the deceased was being buried on All Fools' Day. Even Lady Beatrice looked moved, a moment of sentimentality she later dismissed. "It's so much easier to forgive someone once they're dead."

MONDAY, APRIL 4, 1898

Three days after the burial, an anonymous letter arrived on the desk of Charles Twelvetrees, the West Middlesex coroner. A solicitor looking forward to grazing in the pasture of retirement, he glanced at it with disinterest, and continued reading the advertisements in the newspaper for Easter excursions. He then looked at his watch in the hope that it was time to visit the pie shop, and tapped it with disappointment on seeing that there was still an hour to go before lunchtime. Casting his eyes around his office in search of a distraction, he seized the letter, suddenly gripped by the fantasy that it might be from an old flame. But as he read it, he ran an anxious hand through the tufts of white hair that rose from his head like plumes of billowing smoke, and immediately got to his feet.

The two gravediggers complained bitterly when they eventually left the King's Arms and trudged to the cemetery to dig up the General. Labouring in the light of a solitary lantern, their whiskers damp with gin, they swore they recognised each spadeful of soil they tossed to one side with increasing irritation. "I think it's time for a rest," one of them soon declared, and they promptly sat down. Legs dangling inside the grave, they lit their pipes and leant back against the mound of fresh earth. As the puffs rose up into the evening sky, they exchanged tales of bodies they had buried and dug up again, and the perilous state of the coffins. It was when they got onto the subject of their even more rotten love lives that the older one slid the gin bottle out of his pocket. "I once told a woman I was a clerk, but she found me out. I offered to help her with the gardening but got carried away and dug a six-foot grave," he said, taking a swig. He then offered the bottle to his friend, recognising a man not yet resolved to the fact that a gravedigger had more chance of capturing the heart of one of his corpses than a woman's. But with the alcohol came enlightenment, and the younger man started to sob. "I told my ex-fiancée that I was a gardener. But someone ratted me out, and she called off the wedding. She said she'd assumed the smell was my cheese sandwiches rather than the dead."

In an effort to cheer him, his comrade got to his feet and sang a comic song, performing a jig in the soil. But it only increased the other's sense of desperation, and he sat down again. Fearing stoutness was to blame for his lack of finesse as a dancer, he placed both hands on his stomach. "Do I look like I've eaten too much shirtsleeve pudding?" he asked. The other roared so much he almost fell in, and the pair sang their way through every music-hall song they knew until the cats had fled, and the moon refused to come out from behind its cloud.

The horrible sound attracted the attention of the local constable, who naturally assumed someone was being strangled. After a thorough search, he announced that he would take the matter no further on the condition that they didn't attempt another note. "Not even a whistle." Eventually the much more reassuring sound of metal on wood could be heard, and they hauled the coffin up to the surface. The light from the lantern caught the brass nameplate, and the horrible truth that they had got the wrong grave settled on them in silence. Each blaming the other, they lowered the coffin back down and filled in the hole with language fit for a slaughterhouse. Holding the lantern in front of them, they clambered over the headstones in search of General Bagshot's grave until they found it, more than an hour later, in exactly the same place they had left it.

News reached the palace that the General was coming up again long before he had reached the surface. One of the gravediggers told Wilfred Noseworthy on leaving the pub as an excuse for not getting in a round. But the weight of the revelation was too much for the turncock to bear, and he fled at once to Ye Olde Cardinal Wolsey public house and dining rooms on the Green. "They're digging up the General!" he cried to the Superintendent of Hampton Court Pleasure Gardens. The Superintendent then rushed to the Mitre, the bastion of the upper servants. "They're going to perform a post-mortem examination on the General!" he gasped to a housekeeper. The housekeeper then ran home, hoisting her skirts so as not to lose speed. "The General was murdered after all!" she exclaimed to her mistress. The revelation then twice lapped the palace, and the residents who had felt cheated at the pronouncement of death from English cholera returned reinvigorated to their watching posts by the windows.

The first Dr. Henderson knew of the General's second coming was when the coroner requested that he perform the post-mortem examination. Initially Dr. Frogmore, a general practitioner from Thames Ditton, had been asked, as he was the last medical man to attend to General Bagshot on the night he died. But he claimed he was suffering from ague. The truth, however, was that he belonged to a little-known subset of general practitioners who had a dread of autopsies. He justified his aversion by telling himself that he had chosen to become a doctor to cure the living, not to dabble his fingers in the viscera of the mysteriously dead. Dr. Henderson, however, was not in the least afraid of entrails, and, grateful for the fee, bicycled to Hampton Wick Mortuary, where he waited for hours until the gravediggers finally delivered the soil-strewn coffin. When he finished, he was in such a state of shock at what he had found that he returned home on foot, having completely forgotten he had come on his machine.

As word got out that the coroner was going to hold the inquest in the Mitre, having been lured by its famous Thames eels, the residents immediately released a flock of outraged letters to the Lord Chamberlain, pointing out that its bar was frequented by domestic servants. But there was nothing that could be done, given the charred circumstances. The offices of Hampton Wick Urban District Council, which were normally used, were still smouldering after the Keeper of Bushy Park set them alight in retribution for a councillor having bedded his wife.

*

WEDNESDAY, APRIL 6, 1898

More than an hour before the inquest was due to start, a herd of residents waited in the Mitre's lounge, chattering with the animation of wedding guests. They had rushed over from the monument, some without breakfast, hoping to secure a public seat at the hearing. The Countess and Lady Beatrice sat on one side with the other grace-and-favour ladies. On the other stood the palace staff who had either secured a day off or contrived an illness in order to be there, including William Sheepshanks and Thomas Trout. The coroner's officer, a short Scotsman with tangerine hair and a mismatching moustache, stood scowling in front of the door to the bar, refusing admittance. When the time came, he unlocked the oak-panelled dining room, which had been requisitioned for the proceedings, and stood back as a stampede of widows, elbows drawn, rushed in like indignant geese. They draped themselves over the chairs, saving those next to them for their friends. The officer, who had had little sleep on account of his wife, who flipped like a seal in her sleep, immediately ejected those who had parked themselves in the seats reserved for the jury and witnesses. He then steamed over to the dowager duchess settled in the coroner's chair, jerked his thumb, and hissed: "Hop it."

The ladies who had managed to bag one of the places for the public passed along humbugs and polished their opera glasses. Such was their elation, they managed to overlook the fact that some of the palace staff were seated amongst them, and restrained from tutting when they unfurled their napkins and started nibbling German sausages.

Suddenly the door opened, and they nudged their neighbours with the excited anticipation of a music-hall audience. In filed the witnesses as hushed as a congregation, led by Lady Montfort Bebb in sapphire blue leaning on her cane, followed by Cornelius B. Pilgrim in his monkey-fur coat, a copy of the *Anglo-American Times* tucked under his arm. Next came Mink in the new shade of blue-mauve that had been all over the fashion columns, with bunches of violets on her white toque. Walking closely behind her was Pooki, her face dwarfed by an unflattering black bonnet. Amongst the last in was Silas Sparrowgrass, who sat down and offered up a short prayer, keeping his good eye open. He started plucking at his Newgate fringe as soon as the local constable entered with a tall man with a grey waterfall moustache, who immediately took a notebook and pencil from the pocket of his raglan overcoat and surveyed the room. The homeopath's agitation soon afflicted the other witnesses. Nails were bitten, mouths dried, and nervous melodies tapped on the floor.

In trooped the all-male jurors, ushered to their seats by the officer, clutching a pile of court documents. He was just about to confiscate a hip flask from one of them when Charles Twelvetrees appeared, his reading spectacles on his forehead and his hair drifting up from his scalp like mist.

"Gentlemen, the coroner!" the officer barked. The room rose to its feet as the solicitor entered with the weariness of a man who had spent much of his life pondering the circumstances of the inexplicably dead. With a loud sigh, he sat down at a raised table in the middle of the room, and immediately gazed out of the window, wondering what to have for lunch.

As everyone sank back down again, the officer marched to a spot in front of the jury and bellowed in an impenetrable accent: "Oyez, oyez, you good men of this district summoned to appear here this day to inquire for our Sovereign Lady the Queen when, how, and by what means Major-General George Bagshot came to his death, answer to your names as you shall be called, every man at the first call, upon the pain and peril that shall fall thereon."

The jurors frowned back at him as they tried to work out what on earth the Scot had said, and several members of the public tittered. The laughter snapped the coroner out of his gastronomic reverie, and he glared at them. Instantly they fell silent. Dragging his spectacles down to his nose, Charles Twelvetrees then glanced at the list in front of him, and called out the name of the first juror. There was no reply. The coroner peered over his glasses at the jury.

"Barnabas Popejoy!" he barked again.

Wearing a red neck scarf, the butterman, his cheeks as florid as a farmer's, stood up from the two seats he was occupying. "Yes, sir?"

"Why didn't you answer the first time?" Charles Twelvetrees demanded.

The juror swallowed. "I didn't know I was meant to, sir," he replied meekly.

"Were you not listening, man?" asked the already exasperated coroner. "My officer just informed the jurors to reply on the first call."

Barnabas Popejoy glanced at the officer with a frown. "Did he?"

The coroner scowled. "I hope you're not pretending to be deaf in order to get out of jury duty, Mr. Popejoy. It's the oldest trick in the book. I've lost count of the number of ear trumpets that have been carried into my courtroom. Now, sit down at once." Narrowing his eyes, he pointed to the rest of the jurors. "I expect to hear the rest of you loud and clear."

The coroner worked his way through his list, each juror crying a definitive "yes" as his name was called. Once they were sworn in, he laced his short fingers in front of him and rested them on the table. "Now," he said. "The body. I'm very much hoping it's on the premises, as I requested. Otherwise we're going to have to troop all the way over to Hampton Wick Mortuary, which I'm rather loath to do. According to my barometer, we're due for rain."

The officer stepped forward. "I'm afraid it's in the deceased's apartments at the palace, sir," he said.

"What on earth is it doing there?" demanded Charles Twelve-trees, who, after several years of working with the man, no longer found his speech a mystery.

The officer swiftly blamed the Mitre's manager. "Apparently he stood in front of the door when the mortuary assistants tried to carry in the coffin last night, claiming a dead body would harm the reputation of his Thames eels. The assistants didn't want to lug it all the way back to Hampton Wick, so left it in the deceased's apartments. I have it on good authority that the manager bribed them to take it away. They're not usually that obliging, believe me."

"Bribed?" queried the coroner with a scowl. "What with? Beer?"

"Eels, sir."

Charles Twelvetrees raised his eyebrows, pressing a finger against his lips as he thought. "Are they as good as everyone says?" he asked.

"I've never tried them, sir."

The coroner addressed the room. "Has anyone tried the Mitre's eels?"

Lady Beatrice, dressed in yellow with a profusion of daffodils on her hat, immediately stood up. "Oh, yes!" she replied with a smile. "I often come with Lady Bessington when my cook is absent, and we have eels every time. They're not at all costly, which is just as well, as I always end up paying." As she sank back down everyone looked at the Countess sitting next to her, who immediately stared at her shoes.

The coroner tapped his pen on the table. "Either way, I shall be having words with the manager when we've finished." He looked down at his papers. "Now, where were we?"

"The body, sir," said the officer.

"The body, the body, the body," the coroner repeated, trying to remember. "Oh, yes! Let's get the viewing over with, shall we?

At least we haven't got far to go. I'm wearing a new pair of boots, and they nip."

Dr. Henderson stood up and asked whether it was really necessary to see the body. "It doesn't make for pleasant viewing," he pointed out.

"Of course it is!" Charles Twelvetrees exclaimed. "It's not an inquest unless the body has been seen."

"But the lid has been screwed back down."

The coroner looked at him for a moment. "Then it will have to be unscrewed, Dr. Henderson. For all we know, you've got your mother-in-law in there." He paused before adding: "Though I seem to recall you still haven't found yourself a wife. You had better come with us."

The jurors filed out after the coroner without the faintest knowledge of where they were headed, having failed to comprehend the officer's reply when asked the location of the deceased. Silently they made their way across the road to the palace, wondering what was going on. As they passed the fruit seller in Fountain Court, the butterman suddenly felt the urge for some crumble and bought some rhubarb. The procession turned up one of the staircases and climbed to the top floor, where the coroner rang the Bagshots' bell. While they waited for it to be answered, the jurors stared down at their boots in the sudden realisation that they would shortly be inspecting General Bagshot's naked body wrenched from its grave.

The butler opened the door and surveyed the crowd in front of him.

"We've come to view the General," the coroner announced, his spectacles back on his forehead.

"Certainly, sir. He's in the dining room. If you'd care to follow me," said the servant, leading the way down the hall. "I had planned for him to be viewed in the kitchen, but the cook wouldn't hear of it. She locked the door and refused to hand over the key, saying it's no place for a dead body unless it's got a tail. We've had what you might call a mutiny on our hands. A number of the under servants have taken refuge in the King's Arms, and none of the upper servants will enter the dining room. It hasn't been dusted, I'm afraid."

One by one the jurors shuffled into the dining room and stood hesitantly next to the door, staring at the coffin on top of a large mahogany table. A smear of soil was still visible on the nameplate. Sitting at the head of the table was a constable reading the *Surrey Comet*.

"I say, what a marvellous view of the river," enthused Charles Twelvetrees with a smile, striding towards the window. "I wouldn't mind living here myself. Is the palace really haunted?"

"Yes, sir," replied the butler. "I saw one of the latest apparitions myself. Dreadful moaning."

"Any idea who it was?"

"None, sir."

The constable, who had missed his breakfast, suddenly coughed. "The coffin's on the table, sir," he said.

Charles Twelvetrees span round. "Well, let's get it open, man," he snapped. "We can't stand around here all day admiring the view."

"The lid appears to be screwed down, sir," the policeman replied.

The coroner turned to the group of gentlemen, who still hadn't advanced further than the door. "Dr. Henderson, would you kindly do the honours? People will be wondering where we've got to."

The general practitioner approached and traced his fingers lightly on the table. "I don't seem to have a screwdriver on me," he muttered.

The coroner looked at him for several seconds and then addressed the jurors. "Does anyone happen to have a screwdriver on them?"

Pockets were patted, and there was a collective shaking of heads.

The coroner sighed, then turned to the butler. "We're in need of a screwdriver."

"Screwdrivers aren't my responsibility, sir," he replied, staring into the distance.

"Whose responsibility are they?"

"One of the *under* servants, sir."

"Well, go and get one."

"They're in the King's Arms, sir. As I said, I've got a rebellion on my hands."

"For God's sake, someone go and fetch the undertaker!"

The constable, whose stomach had started to rumble, immediately headed for the door. After contemplating the view, the oil paintings, the green carpet, and the red wallpaper, the jurors pulled out the chairs from the table and sat down. After refusing an offer by Barnabas Popejoy to tell some jokes, they started playing cards with a pack they found on the mantelpiece. Citing a law that didn't exist, the coroner gained entry to the kitchen, and persuaded the cook to make him a cup of tea, which he drank in a chair by the range with his boots off.

Eventually Mr. Blood arrived with the necessary instrument, and stood staring at the jurors playing poker around the coffin, on top of which was a bunch of rhubarb.

"Get on with it, man!" barked the coroner. "Otherwise we'll have an adjournment on our hands, and Easter is nearly upon us."

After battling with his tool, the undertaker removed the lid and propped it up against the wall with hands that had touched more of the dead than the living. The jurors winced and immediately reached into their pockets and covered their noses with their handkerchiefs as they peered at the discoloured General. The constable joined them out of curiosity, and lost his appetite in an instant.

*

HUNCHED AGAINST THE RAIN THAT had been predicted by the coroner's barometer, the party headed back to the Mitre. By then, the Countess and Lady Beatrice were sitting in the bar, having informed the officer they were feeling faint and were in need of some fresh air. As soon as they spotted the jury through the window, they knocked back their third sherry and rushed to the dining room, where they reclaimed their seats, landing on them with less poise than before. The witnesses, who hadn't moved, immediately abandoned their contemplation of the ceiling and inspected the jurors as they filed back in looking considerably more sombre than when they had left. After tugging off his boots, the coroner called Dr. Henderson to the stand. The officer approached him and barked: "The evidence which you shall give to this inquest on behalf of our Sovereign Lady the Queen touching the death of Major-General George Bagshot shall be the truth, the whole truth, and nothing but the truth. So help you God."

Assuming the man was administering the oath, the doctor kissed the Bible and gave a brief medical preamble. Finally he got to the point: "I found small traces of arsenic in all of the deceased's organs."

The gossip-mongers suddenly stopped sucking their humbugs.

"Was it sufficient to be fatal?" the coroner enquired. As the pressmen prayed that it was, the residents leant forward, holding an anxious hand up to their throats.

The doctor paused. "It was, sir."

A collective gasp sounded as neighbours were clutched with dread. They stared open-mouthed at the general practitioner for several seconds, after which the room erupted with the clamour of Billingsgate Market.

"All right, all right, all right. That's quite enough," snapped Charles Twelvetrees, raising his voice. He glared round the room, then addressed the jury. "In my experience, out of a hundred cases of arsenic poisoning, around forty-six will be suicidal, thirty-seven homicidal, eight accidental, and the remaining nine are anybody's guess. Let's hope you can determine which it was," he added doubtfully. Turning back to Dr. Henderson, he said that he had come across several cases where poisoners had tried to cover up their crimes by claiming that arsenic had been present in the soil surrounding the coffin, and had been conveyed into the body by water. "Was the body at all wet when you examined it?" he asked.

"No," the doctor replied, shaking his head. "Neither was the inside of the coffin."

The coroner dismissed him, then called Dr. Frogmore. While the general practitioner from Thames Ditton had been in particularly robust health when asked to perform the post-mortem examination, there was no trace of it now. Wiping his bald head with his handkerchief, he waddled over to the stand, his considerable girth no recommendation for the Banting method of weight loss he endorsed. After the officer administered the oath, the doctor merely brushed his lips on the Bible, such was his hurry to press upon the hearing that the symptoms of arsenic poisoning and English cholera were extremely similar.

"When the deceased returned from the picnic he initially asked to see his homeopath, which, of course, did him no good whatsoever," said Dr. Frogmore, his voice as high as an altar boy's. "When his symptoms persisted, his American houseguest naturally insisted that he see a general practitioner. Dr. Henderson was otherwise engaged with a patient, so he sent a carriage for me. By the time I arrived the General had been seized with vomiting and diarrhoea for some time. I was informed that he had just consumed a large amount of a particularly ugly pigeon pie at a picnic. I diagnosed English cholera, which is an acute gastro-enteritis that often appears to be caused by unsuitable ingesta, such as sausages, meat pies, shell-fish, or food in a state of decomposition.

The symptoms are severe vomiting and diarrhoea. Any doctor would have made exactly the same diagnosis," he added hastily.

Charles Twelvetrees peered at him, lacing his fingers. "And how did you treat the deceased?" he asked.

The doctor wiped his head. "I was horrified to learn that the homeopath, a Mr. Sparrowgrass, had asked that he be brought a cup of beef tea. It was utterly, utterly the wrong thing to do. A preliminary purge is out of the question in such instances, and hot drinks excite the actions of the bowels. I gave him arrowroot in plain water with a teaspoon of brandy to cement them. The next step would have been a tincture of opium with ether. But by then it was too late," he added.

After an over-long description of the deceased's tormented bowels, the coroner finally dismissed him. But Dr. Frogmore wouldn't leave. With a glance at the pressmen with their ruinous pencils, he raised his voice and said, "I'm by no means the first doctor to have been caught out by the similarities of arsenic poisoning and English cholera."

"Thank you, Dr. Frogmore," said the coroner.

But still the doctor remained, staring helplessly at the reporters.

"Back to your seat or I'll ask my officer to remove you," Charles Twelvetrees snapped, and called Silas Sparrowgrass.

The homeopath from East Molesey scuttled to the stand wearing a long black overcoat with a short cape that had once belonged to a Burlington Arcade beadle. As he stood, his squint spiralling round the room, the jurors peered at him, trying to work out which way he was looking. The oath administered, he bent his head and kissed the Bible. Just as the officer was about to take the book away, he kissed it again, producing a loud smacking sound, and he continued pressing his lips back and forth against the cover until the coroner looked up to see what was the delay.

"Mr. Sparrowgrass!" he barked. "You're in a court of law, not behind a privy with a landlord's daughter."

Slowly the witness raised his head and wiped his lips on the back of his sleeve.

"Now," said the coroner. "I understand you were the first person the deceased asked for when he took ill." He then looked towards the jury and added, "Just to help you along, a truly suicidal man would never call for medical intervention."

The jurors nodded in appreciation.

Silas Sparrowgrass coughed loudly and waited until he had the room's attention. "That poor sweet man. Dead!" he whimpered. After asking if he could take a moment, he wiped the corner of his good eye, then continued. "I was indeed the first person the deceased asked for. After Dr. Barnstable died last year, only I have treated him. You would have thought the General would have chosen Dr. Henderson over there as his medical man, being as though he lives so close to the palace and has all those fancy letters after his name. But he wouldn't hear of it."

Everyone turned to look at Dr. Henderson, who frowned.

"And why was that, do you think?" the coroner enquired.

The homeopath caressed the remains of his Newgate fringe. "People say Dr. Henderson's medicine smells like gravedigger's breath and you'd be paying twice the amount for the pleasure of it. Look at all those patients he's got. If he could cure them, they wouldn't keep coming back. I never see the majority of mine again."

The general practitioner crossed his arms and scowled.

"Quite so, Mr. Sparrowgrass." Charles Twelvetrees nodded. "No doctor has ever got to the bottom of my piles. No pun intended. And how did *you* attend to the deceased?"

The homeopath tugged down his checked waistcoat. "The General informed me he had eaten a large amount of pigeon pie. Should vomiting arise from over-repletion, or from indigestible food, the best course of action is a hot drink or tickling the throat with a feather until the offending material is expelled," he added.

Charles Twelvetrees tapped his pen. "And did you tickle the General?"

"I did, sir."

The coroner made a note. "Continue."

"As for the diarrhoea, evacuations following over-indulgence at the table should not be interfered with. In the event that atmospheric influences were also at play, I gave him some white bryony, for Silas Sparrowgrass is a man of infinite subtlety. It would have worked, too, if he hadn't died so quickly. I then advised him that people liable to diarrhoea should always wear flannel abdominal-belts, and offered to perform a little trick to raise his spirits. But he was too busy vomiting."

The coroner raised his eyebrows. "A little trick?" he repeated.

"Yes, sir. Everyone loves a bit of magic."

The coroner leant forward with a smile. "You perform magic tricks, Mr. Sparrowgrass? How splendid! Let's see one," he said, slapping his hand on the table.

A murmur of excitement ran round the room. The homeopath immediately called for a hat, and a member of the jury swiftly reached under his chair and passed him one. Opening his arms, Silas Sparrowgrass declared: "And next, ladies and gentlemen, I shall require five florins."

There was a flurry of activity as the coroner, the jurors, the witnesses, and the public reached for their pockets and bags. Silas Sparrowgrass held up his hands. "Do not trouble yourselves, ladies and gentlemen," he begged. "I sense there is so much money in this room I shall help myself." He then strode over to Lady Beatrice and picked up her foot. "Why, there's a florin underneath this lady's shoe," he announced. She tittered behind her hand as he dropped a coin into the hat. "And there's one in these Piccadilly weepers," he announced, reaching into the whiskers of William Sheepshanks, sat behind her, and dropping a coin into his topper. The Keeper of the Maze gave an embarrassed smile.

Approaching the Countess, the homeopath cried, "Look, there's one in this bonnet!" He stretched out his hand and threw another coin in his hat as the aristocrat beamed and felt for more. The homeopath then ran across the room, watched by his entranced audience, and produced a florin from the butterman's ear. He then approached Charles Twelvetrees, plucked one out of thin air in front of him, and dropped both florins into his hat, cocking his ear as they landed. Raising his hat above his head for all to see, he overturned it onto a pile of court documents on the table, and out rolled five florins.

The room erupted into applause. "Excellent!" declared Charles Twelvetrees, beaming. "Perhaps we should have one more? It is raining, after all."

There were loud calls in agreement.

Silas Sparrowgrass pulled down his waistcoat. "For my next trick, ladies and gentlemen, I shall require a watch," he announced. His squint spiralled around the room as he added, "It only works with a gold one."

"Use mine! Use mine!" begged Charles Twelvetrees, fiddling with his chain and handing it to him.

The homeopath then drew back his sleeves, plucked a red handkerchief from his top pocket, and fluttered it in front of his audience. He placed it over the watch and gave both objects to the mesmerised coroner. Grasping a corner of the handkerchief, Silas Sparrowgrass then held it in the air, turning round so that all could see. The bewildered coroner stared at his empty hands, then clapped wildly. "Thank you, Mr. Sparrowgrass, most entertaining," he said, beaming. "I suppose you'd better take a seat."

The homeopath pocketed his florins, executed a deep bow, then turned his good eye towards the public. "You can find Silas Sparrowgrass, a man of infinite subtlety, at number five Vine Road, no appointment necessary. Magic tricks extra."

The coroner repeated the address in case anyone missed it, then looked down at his list and called Dora Cummings, the Bagshots' parlour maid. The teenager, wearing her uniform and her dark hair drawn back into a bun, was still pale, having vomited twice that morning on account of her nerves. Her hands clenched into fists by her sides, she told the court in a Cornish accent that the poisoning could not have been accidental, as the deceased never allowed arsenic in the house. Nor could it have been in anything served at breakfast, she stated, as both General Bagshot and his houseguest had eaten and drunk the same things. "The American has tea like everyone else. He says English coffee tastes like liquorice and has a purple tint to it."

Everyone frowned at the foreigner following the affront to the nation's coffee.

"Did they drink from the same pot?" enquired Charles Twelvetrees.

She nodded vigorously. "Yes, sir, and he's still alive," she added, pointing to the American.

The coroner narrowed his eyes as he studied the man in question. "Let's see for ourselves. Cornelius B. Pilgrim, please take the stand."

As soon as the American was sworn in, Barnabas Popejoy put up his hand and said he had a question.

"Already?" asked the coroner. "The man hasn't given his evidence yet. Well, let's hear it."

The butterman got to his feet, clutching his rhubarb. "What does the witness's middle initial stand for?" he asked. The resulting laughter was such that Charles Twelvetrees had to wait to be heard. Convulsed men clutched their stomachs, while heaving women reached for their handkerchiefs, their cheeks wet with merriment.

"Ladies and gentlemen," he bellowed. "Please show the witness some courtesy. He is a guest in our country. While the American habit of flaunting the middle initial may very well be a cause of mirth in England, I will not tolerate such behaviour in my court-room. Please accept my apologies, Mr. Pilgrim."

"Sure, no problem," the witness replied, smoothing down his moustache.

The coroner then gazed into the distance, and not a single question emerged from his lips. "Dash it all," he said eventually. "Mr. Pilgrim, would you please inform the court of your middle name so we can all stop wondering what it is and move on?"

The room held its breath, and those on the back rows stood up to witness the disclosure.

"Benjamin," came the reply.

"Cornelius Benjamin Pilgrim," said the coroner, trying it on his tongue. "Most agreeable." He then leant forward with a frown and laced his fingers. "Now, what have you got to say for yourself?"

The witness cleared his throat. "I've known the deceased a number of years, and he invited me to stay as his houseguest," he said, his voice raised. "We went to the residents' picnic together and shared a couple of bottles of beer. Around half an hour after eating several slices of a pigeon pie that had been made especially for him, he started to vomit."

The coroner interrupted and asked Dr. Henderson whether the timing of the deceased's vomiting was in keeping with the pie having been poisoned.

The doctor stood up. "It was, sir," he replied, and sat down again.

Mink glanced at Pooki, who suddenly looked at her hands.

"Mr. Pilgrim, are you quite sure that the only food consumed by the deceased, and by the deceased alone, was the bespoke pigeon pie?" the coroner asked.

"Yes, sir. He told the servants not to let anyone have any of it."

"And you had no ill effects from the beer you shared?"

He shook his head. "None, sir."

"Very well. Continue, if you will."

"I took the General home, and when his symptoms didn't improve following the visit from the homeopath I went to ask his neighbour, Lady Angela, if she knew of a doctor." He paused, looked around the room, and added: "I think I know who killed the General."

There was stunned silence. Several women covered their mouths with their hands, while others exchanged looks with their friends.

Charles Twelvetrees stared at him over his glasses. "I beg your pardon."

The American looked round the room again and raised his voice. "I think I know who did it."

"No, no, you said something before that."

"I asked Lady Angela to suggest the name of a doctor."

Charles Twelvetrees scowled. "You asked whom?" he demanded.

"Lady Angela," Cornelius B. Pilgrim repeated, nodding to her.

The coroner paused. "Do you happen to mean Lady Montfort Bebb?" he asked incredulously.

"Sure do."

The coroner leant forward. "The woman to whom you refer is the widow of a baronet, Mr. Pilgrim, and should therefore be addressed as Lady Montfort Bebb," he snapped. "If she were the daughter of an earl, marquess, or duke, then you would be correct in addressing her as Lady Angela. But as it is, I'm afraid you've committed a vulgar error, which I hope the lady in question will have the fortitude to forgive in this instance. I shall excuse her from giving evidence, as such a breach of etiquette is quite enough to contend with for one day. I would like to instruct the gentlemen of the jury to overlook the foreigner's transgression, and not to view his testimony as in any way unreliable. That will be all, Mr. Pilgrim."

The American raised a hand. "But I know who . . ."

"Thank you, Mr. Pilgrim. Please take your seat."

"But . . ."

The coroner pointed to his chair with a jab of his pen. "It's over *there*, Mr. Pilgrim. We'll hear no more from you."

He looked down at his papers and called Mink to the stand. "Whom I very much suggest that you address as Your Highness in the first instance, and ma'am thereafter," he added, glaring at the American. "Not that we more senior members of English society need to go to such an extreme."

The Princess stood up, having listened with increasing anxiety to the coroner's interest in Pooki's pie. As she crossed the room, several women raised up from their seats in order to see her dress. After being sworn in, she answered the coroner's questions in a clear voice, explaining that she had recently arrived at the palace and had been invited to the picnic by three of the residents. "I was sitting next to the General when he was taken ill," she added.

"And what was your opinion of the deceased, Princess?"

Mink raised her chin. "I thought him an utter boor and was amazed that a man of his standing had got through life with such poor manners," she replied.

Charles Twelvetrees tapped his pencil as a shocked murmur ran through the room. "I see," he said. "And was it your idea to provide the pigeon pies for the picnic?"

The Princess hesitated. "Actually, they were Lady Bessington's suggestion."

All heads turned towards the Countess, her smile at Mink's verdict of the General suddenly vanishing.

"And it was your servant who made them?" continued the coroner.

"It was."

"And where were you when she was preparing them?"

"In London, attending a meeting of the National Union of Women's Suffrage Societies."

"I see." The coroner's eyes suddenly dropped to the floor. "What the hell is that?" he asked. He stood up, padded round to the front of the table in his stocking feet, and stared. "Would the person who has lost a rabbit come and collect it at once?" he cried, his hands on his hips. "It's nibbling my toes!"

Silas Sparrowgrass stood up with an apologetic hunch of his shoulders. Cooing the name Gertrude, he crept with the light-footedness of a burglar towards the white creature twitching her nose. As he approached, she suddenly took off and tore round the dining room, her colossal ears flat against her head. The homeo-path leapt after her, his arms outstretched in vain, until she disap-peared underneath a skirt.

"Mr. Sparrowgrass! I suggest you take possession of your rabbit at once or I shall deliver it in person to the pie shop," shouted the coroner.

The homeopath yelped in horror. Holding his hands together underneath his chin, he turned to Charles Twelvetrees with the most angelic of smiles. "Would it be possible for everyone to stand on their chairs?" he asked, with a flutter of his eyelashes. The coro-ner sighed loudly, then nodded. Complaining bitterly, they got to their feet, and each rested a hand on the back of their seat and hauled themselves up. As the ladies clutched their skirts, Ger-trude, who was under Lady Montfort Bebb's chair, started wash-ing her ears. Suddenly the aristocrat jabbed at the creature with her cane, nostrils flared, and she shot off again round the room. The homeopath made two further revolutions in pursuit, then pounced. By the time he struggled back to his feet, he was holding the creature by her ears. Raising her aloft in victory, he kissed her twice, then plunged her back into his inside pocket, and scuttled to his seat.

Charles Twelvetrees turned to the Princess, then scratched the back of his neck. "I've no idea where we were," he admitted. "You'd better sit down."

It was too much for the Countess, who stood up smelling

fiercely of sherry and shouted to the coroner, "Come on, I want to find out who the murderer was!"

"So do I!" cried Lady Beatrice, standing up beside her.

"And me!" came another voice from the public seats.

"Get on with it!" jeered someone else. "We've been here for ages!"

Charles Twelvetrees stood up, his face crimson with fury. "Members of the public, if you do not keep quiet I shall instruct my officer to remove you from my courtroom. Now, let's hear from the servant who made the pies and get this over with. It's almost lunchtime, for God's sake."

Pooki approached, clutching the sides of her dress, and stood with her eyes on the floor while she confirmed that she was indeed a Christian. After the officer read the oath, she kissed the Bible, then explained that the General's butler had asked her to make a pie without eggs, as his master didn't eat them, and she had inserted only three legs into the pastry in order to distinguish it from the others.

"Did anyone else consume any of this bespoke pie?"

The maid shook her head. "No, sir. In fact, nobody had any of the pigeon pies apart from the General. One of the butlers said it was because they did not look fit to eat," she added with a frown.

"I see. And what was *your* opinion of the deceased?" he asked.

The servant stuck out her chin. "I did not like him, sir. There was a rumour that he had killed Lady Beatrice's doves and sold them to the butcher."

Several ladies gasped and covered their mouths with their hands.

Charles Twelvetrees fixed her with his gaze. "And did your pies contain doves rather than pigeons?" he demanded.

"I am not sure of the difference, sir."

The crowd looked uncertain.

Sucking on his teeth for a moment, the coroner then turned to the witnesses and informed them that he would still regard them as being under oath. "You all saw the legs sticking out of the pies. In your opinion, did they appear to be those of doves or pigeons?" he asked.

One of the butlers stood. "I would say they were pigeons, sir. They were rather on the ugly side. Like the pies."

Pooki scowled.

Dr. Henderson sprang up. "I didn't see the feet for long, but they struck me as most elegant. A charming pink colour."

Holding his coat shut with both hands, Silas Sparrowgrass immediately joined him. "I've never seen a pigeon or a dove with elegant feet. They're all gnarled and sharp-nailed like my mother's."

Cornelius B. Pilgrim started to get up, but Charles Twelvetrees gestured to him to remain where he was. "We'll not hear from you, thank you, Mr. Pilgrim," he barked. "Once was quite sufficient."

The members of the public were unable to resist the debate, and it all came to a head when Lady Beatrice raised her hand and said, "The feet sticking out of the pies looked just like those of the flying squirrels I saw in the Zoological Gardens in Regent's Park last week." Once the laughter eventually subsided, and Charles Twelvetrees could finally be heard, he turned back to Pooki.

"Were you alone in making the pies?"

"Yes, sir," she replied.

"Was there any period when the General's pie was unattended by yourself?"

Pooki glanced at Mink. "Yes, sir. For a while I was up in one of the bedrooms."

"I see," said the coroner, tapping his pen. "And what happened to the General's pie after the picnic?"

"I threw it out as soon as we got back home, sir."

The coroner banged his fist on the table. "Why on earth did you do that?" he demanded. "It could have been analysed!"

The maid blinked. "I did not know that the General had been

poisoned and was going to be dug up again, sir. Usually bodies remain where they are once they have been buried. It is their spirits that get up again."

"But why did you throw the pie out immediately?" the coroner continued to press her. "That's a bit fishy, isn't it?"

There were several nods.

The servant's eyes drifted momentarily to the Princess. "It is inauspicious to eat things with only three legs," she replied.

The Countess roared with laughter and immediately covered her hand with her mouth. But it was one distraction too many for the coroner, who clicked his fingers at his officer, then jabbed his thumb towards her. The officer marched up to the aristocrat, hauled her to her feet, and escorted her out of the hearing, which only increased her mirth as she headed back to the bar. Charles Twelvetrees looked at Pooki, and with no idea where he had got up to, dismissed her. He then surveyed the remaining witnesses. "Have any of you got anything of any relevance to say? I'm very much hoping you don't."

They glanced at their pocket watches and shook their heads.

"Just as well," he muttered. After summing up the case while tugging on his boots, Charles Twelvetrees then headed out, and the officer escorted the jurors to an adjacent room for their deliberations. The coroner had just been served some eels when he was informed that the jury had reached its decision. "Already?" he despaired, and returned to the hearing, his napkin still tied around his neck. The jurors trooped back in again and took their places. The foreman stood up, glancing nervously around the room as all eyes fixed on him. The pressmen's pencils were poised.

He cleared his throat and looked ahead. "The deceased met his death by arsenic poisoning. There is no evidence as to how the poison was obtained," he announced, before sinking back down to his chair. There were loud murmurs of disappointment. Raising his voice above them, the coroner swiftly brought the proceedings to a close, and, after wishing everyone a happy Easter, fled out of the door.

As soon as he had left, the public and the witnesses rounded on the jurors.

"The poison was in the pigeon pie, you ninnies," said one.

"It was the American, you twits," shouted another. "There's something about that coat that's just not right."

Cornelius B. Pilgrim tucked his newspaper under his arm and stalked out.

"No, no, it was Lady Bessington," hurled another. "She asked for the pies in the first place. And she got herself thrown out. She's probably gone to tamper with the evidence."

"I reckon it was Lady Beatrice," declared one. "The General killed her doves. People get very attached to their pets. They love them more than humans."

Lady Beatrice tittered nervously.

"It was definitely Lady Montfort Bebb," came a voice.

"Me?" she asked, spinning round, trying to find her accuser. "What have I done?"

"My money's on the maid with the big feet," cried someone else. "She destroyed the evidence."

The room fell silent and everyone turned to stare at Pooki, who immediately looked at the floor. Mink quickly grabbed her arm and marched her out of the room as all eyes followed them. But none was watching the maid as closely as the stranger with the waterfall moustache leaning against the wall, slowly tapping his notebook with his pencil.

CHAPTER VII

Things Aren't Looking Good for the Maid

THURSDAY, APRIL 7, 1898

INK woke, stirred from her dreams by the interest the coroner had taken in Pooki's pigeon pie. As she lay on her side, she heard footsteps going downstairs. Getting up, she looked at the clock on the mantelpiece and saw that it was only five-thirty, an hour earlier than the maid normally started her duties. Returning to the warmth of her sheets, she wondered whether the servant was also worried. As the Princess thought over the testimonies, the maid opened the curtains, then descended to the kitchen and polished the range while the fire was drawing up. As the kettle boiled, she attacked the boots and knives, then cleaned the grate, fire irons, and fender in the breakfast room. After lighting the fire, she rubbed the furniture, washed the mantelpiece, and scattered damp tea leaves on the carpet to collect the dust before sweeping it.

Mink must have fallen back to sleep, for the next thing she knew Pooki was standing next to her with a tray bearing her morning tea. Sitting up, she realised instantly that all was not well when the maid passed it to her without a single enquiry about her dreams, in which she always saw a prophecy. The state of Pooki's nerves became all too apparent when Mink spotted the ubiquitous garnish while helping herself to breakfast. "It must be a good year for watercress," said the Princess, standing at the sideboard. The maid instantly dropped the milk jug she was carrying, and they both listened to the immaculate silence that follows the shattering of porcelain.

Hoping some fresh air would clear her head of the smutty residue of a poor night's sleep, Mink headed out for a walk in the grounds. As she started to cross the Wilderness, something made her look round, and she saw Pooki coming out the back gate and hurrying down Moat Lane. Wondering where she was going, she continued to the Great Fountain Garden, where packs of school-children were chasing one another round the enormous yews. As she strolled, her eye was caught by the hat of Lady Beatrice, who was sitting with Lady Montfort Bebb on a bench in a sheltered spot against the palace wall known as Purr Corner. The nook was given the name by the Duke of Wellington, whose mother had been a resident, on account of its being a venue for female gossiping. The Princess strode over, anxious to know what people were saying about Pooki.

"Thank goodness women aren't allowed to sit on juries after all," she said, taking a seat next to them. "We've all been spared the sight of the General without his clothes on."

"The most gruesome sight in those apartments wouldn't have been the body, I can assure you," replied Lady Montfort Bebb, her red setter lying at her feet. "It would have been the hideous interior decoration. Mrs. Bagshot never altered a thing after she swapped apartments with Lady Bessington, who is charm itself, but her taste is unfathomable."

A sudden silence descended as the Countess rounded the corner and sat down. "To think that we have a murderer in our midst!" she exclaimed, tucking her grey hair into her black bonnet. "What would the Queen say? It wasn't me, by the way, despite what someone said at the inquest."

"Nor me," replied Lady Montfort Bebb, adjusting her mink tippet. "It'll be a servant, mark my words. They'll be the death of us one way or another. If it's not poison, then it'll be exasperation. I'm not at all convinced that these labour-saving machines are a good thing. One of my maids has just asked for a night off a week and every other Sunday out!" She turned to Mink. "I must say, things don't look very good for yours. Pity, I'd rather taken to her after her performance at the inquest."

"It still hasn't been proven that a murder has actually taken place," said the Princess quickly.

"Well, it didn't appear to be accidental," replied Lady Montfort Bebb. "And the General wasn't exactly one for taking his own life, to the rue of many, I've no doubt."

"Poor Mrs. Bagshot, having a husband and a child in the same cemetery," said Lady Beatrice. She turned to the Princess and explained that several years ago Mrs. Bagshot lost a daughter when she was only a few months old. "Her little heart gave up. I can't tell you how gruesome the funeral was."

"We must give her all the support we can at such a terrible time," said Lady Montfort Bebb. "Let's just hope the police are capable of getting to the bottom of it, though I very much doubt it, given their inability to handle the roughs outside the King's Arms on a Saturday night."

The Countess leant forward. "Apparently there's already a police inspector asking questions in the palace. The butcher's boy spotted him in Tennis Court Lane earlier."

Mink stared at her, immediately worried for Pooki.

Lady Beatrice fiddled with her fringe. "He's probably questioning the American as we speak. You can't trust a man who calls overshoes 'gums.'"

Suddenly there were footsteps, and the women turned to see Dr. Henderson. They nodded to him, and he raised his hat as he passed, his dark curls bobbing.

As soon as he was out of earshot, Mink asked, "What on earth is wrong with that man's hat?"

"It's far too big for him," replied the Countess, still watching him.

"Maybe his head has shrunk," suggested Lady Beatrice. The other women looked at her. Suddenly she frowned and peered into the distance. "Who the devil is that?" she asked. They all turned. Walking towards them was a tall man with a grey waterfall moustache who was wearing an open raglan overcoat, its wide shoulders giving him a slouched look.

"It's that man who was standing next to the constable at the inquest," said Mink. "He seems to be coming over."

"Oh, my, what an unforgivable suit," declared Lady Montfort Bebb. "It's the colour of a costermonger's donkey."

Inspector Guppy stubbed out his cigarette and introduced himself. Glancing at his untrimmed whiskers, his bowler hat with the shiny brim, and his ready-made trousers, the women offered reluctant smiles of acknowledgement. But it was only Mink he wanted to see. Standing up, she bid the others good morning and smoothed down her dress. As she walked with him along the East Front to Wilderness House, she made little effort to engage with his small talk, and by the time they arrived, news that the policeman had come to see the Princess had fluttered all the way to the Tudor section of the palace.

Pooki was hanging out of one of the bedroom windows when she first heard the front doorbell. "You must advance for several paces, sir," she shouted to an excursionist deep within the maze. "Then take the turning on your left or you will never see your wife and children again."

When the bell rang again, she swiftly shut the window and ran downstairs to answer it. She stood staring at the visitor until she remembered herself and stepped back to let them in. Mink led the way to the drawing room, and gestured to the settee by the fireplace. But Inspector Guppy sat down in her father's armchair.

"Would you care for some tea, Inspector, or would you be worried that something had been slipped into it?" asked the Princess with a smile, taking a seat on the settee.

Declining the offer, he placed his hat on the side table.

"I must say, it came as a bit of a surprise that the General died from arsenic poisoning," she said. "What was it that the coroner said? Forty-six per cent of cases of arsenic poisoning tended to be suicides? That's almost half. Perhaps the General took his own life, then. What do you think?" She smiled and added, "You've got so much experience in these matters."

The Inspector remained straight-faced. "I wouldn't want to comment, Princess."

"Do you really think the General was murdered?" she continued nevertheless. "He wasn't the most popular resident, but I can't imagine why anyone would want to kill him. Can you?"

The Inspector lightly traced the edge of his armrest with his fingers. "I can imagine all sorts of things," he said. He looked up at the portraits of her ancestors. "It must be over a year now since the Maharaja died."

"That's correct."

"Terrible business."

"Indeed."

He paused, then asked, "It was the girl who came in the mornings to clean the boots and the knives, wasn't it?"

Mink studied him for a moment. "I suggest you get to the point, Inspector, or I shall have to ask you to leave."

Sitting back, he said that it was her maid he wanted to see. The Princess got up in silence and rang the bell. Pooki appeared within minutes, and stood hesitantly by the door until Mink asked her to come in. She sat so closely to her mistress that their skirts touched.

"How did you come to be in this country?" Inspector Guppy asked the maid, opening his notebook. Clutching her hands in her lap, she explained that she had worked as a nurse, accompanying British mothers and their children back to England, but during one trip found herself alone in London without a passage home.

"So the family abandoned you without paying your return, did they?"

"Yes, sir."

"And why was that?"

The maid swallowed. "I do not know, sir."

"Was the lady displeased with your work?"

"No, sir."

"Did you get too close to another passenger or one of the crew, perhaps?"

"Inspector!" the Princess protested.

Pooki shook her head. "No, sir."

"You must have been upset when you found yourself abandoned."

"I was, sir. I did not know what to do."

"Was that what prompted your dislike for the British? I understand you've worked for an Indian family ever since."

"And where, may I ask, were you born, Inspector?" interrupted Mink.

"Calcutta, as it happens."

"I was born and raised in England," the Princess continued. "Some would say that makes me more English than you are."

The Inspector turned back to Pooki. "And how did you make a living while you were abandoned in London?"

"I was a fur-puller, sir."

"You don't earn much pulling fluff off rabbit skins. Did you try your hand at anything else?"

"No, sir."

"There are much easier ways for your sort to make money . . ."

"Inspector!" snapped Mink. "I will not tolerate your speaking to my maid in this manner."

He looked at the maid. "You said in your testimony that you didn't like the General."

"I only spoke to him once, sir. That was at the picnic."

"As I recall, that was the occasion when you publicly humiliated him by alleging that he had killed Lady Beatrice's doves and sold them to the butcher."

"He asked me whether I knew any gossip. He laughed very much, sir."

He paused. "You don't like the British much, do you?"

The maid nodded. "I do, sir. Her Highness is half English. Before the Maharaja died she always gave me extra beer money."

"So you like a drink?"

"No, sir. I sent the money to my mother in India."

"Were you aware that the General fought in the Indian Mutiny?"

"Yes, sir."

"Who told you?"

"Alice Cockle, Lady Bessington's maid-of-all-work. She has told me lots of things about the residents."

The Inspector studied her for a moment. "How many Indians were killed during the mutiny, do you think?" he asked. "Tens of thousands? Hundreds of thousands?"

"I do not know, sir. It was thirty years ago."

"Do you think the General took part in the slaughter? Did he order convicted rebels to be tied over the mouths of cannons and blown into smithereens, or did he just hang them?"

The maid shook her head. "I do not know anything about that, sir."

"Don't you? Is there any arsenic in this house?"

"There's none, Inspector," Mink interrupted. "Apart from my Dr. MacKenzie's Arsenical Complexion Soap. You see it advertised everywhere."

He looked at her. "I know the one. My wife uses it. I presume you won't mind if my constable and I search the premises?"

"Go right ahead, Inspector," she said. "Oh, and if you find my collection of Sherlock Holmes stories, do let me know. I can't find it anywhere. I'm in the middle of the one with the police inspector who literally hasn't got a clue."

The Inspector walked out to fetch his constable, pulling the door loudly behind him. Mink and Pooki remained where they were, then slowly turned and looked at each other.

*

GRABBING HIS HAT, DR. HENDERSON pressed inside his short wooden stethoscope and rushed out, uttering assurances to his housekeeper that he would be back shortly. "No feeding the patients, Mrs. Nettleship," he warned as he pulled on his coat and shut the door behind him. Trotting next to him was a red-faced maid who had run all the way from the palace to tell him of the emergency that had befallen her mistress, a dowager duchess, whom he had never previously treated. Unsure of what he would encounter, for the servant was largely incoherent, he had with him his pocket case containing a clinical thermometer, a female catheter, a small pair of forceps, a hypodermic syringe, a tongue depressor, lunar caustic, a probe, and a case of needles. In his other pocket, just in case, was a bottle of strychnine to start the aristocrat's heart. Hoping that he wouldn't be too late, he ran down Barge Walk, turning the heads of two punters idling on the Thames.

The doctor and the maid soon reached the riverside entrance of The Banqueting House, built in the palace gardens by William III as an after-dinner retreat, which had since been converted into a grace-and-favour residence. The sweating servant showed Dr. Henderson into the drawing room, where he sat catching his breath, looking at the silk wall hangings the mistress of the house had erected on either side of the fireplace to hide the naked ladies in Verrio's spectacular murals.

The maid soon returned and took him up to the principal bed-room, where the curtains had been drawn against the view of the water. Once his eyes had adjusted to the gloom, he made out the patient sitting up in bed wearing a white nightcap, an untouched bowl of gruel on the floor next to her. Lying in the corner was a spaniel, its head on its paws. Before Dr. Henderson had a chance to order the pet's ejection from the sick room, the Dowager Duchess proceeded to list her symptoms as if running through her order with the fishmonger. When she finished, he performed the five cardinal duties. But after feeling her pulse, examining her tongue, and inquiring about her appetite, sleep, and bowels, he could find neither the cause of her symptoms nor indeed any trace of them. The woman continued elaborating on her misfortunes until he was forced to use his tongue depressor in order to be able to think. He then trod around the room, emitting the faintest of creaks, staring at the floor in the hope that the answer would come to him. It was then that he noticed the dog's discarded bone, its watery eyes, the bulge of its belly, and its tail that refused to wag.

Immediately understanding the real reason why he had been called out, he grabbed his coat with irritation and started putting it on, watched by the open-mouthed aristocrat. He then turned to her and said, "Your Grace, you are in a particularly robust state of health. However, your dog, it seems, is suffering from worms. I suggest that you consult the vet in future, even though his charges are higher than mine and he lives further away. I should like to inform you that my fee for patients with four legs is twice that for those with only two, and requires immediate settlement. I shall wait in the drawing room."

Dr. Henderson strolled back down Barge Walk, warmed by the inner glow of victory. Not only was his fee snug in his waistcoat pocket, but while he had been waiting to be paid he had pulled back one of the wall hangings and peeked at a bare-breasted lady. Just as he felt his dignity had been restored, he sensed again that something was wrong with his hat. He took it off, looked at the label, and immediately saw that it was not his own. Hoping he was

mistaken, he returned it to his head. But there was no doubting
its unsatisfactory fit. He thought back over the numerous home
calls he had made, during which time he had left his topper in the
hall with several others, and wondered which visitor had made
off with his by mistake, or indeed taken it as a better option. As
he passed Trophy Gate, he saw Pike and Gibbs smirking at him,
elbowing each other in the ribs. He then thought of all the other
people who had seen him that day, and to his utter mortification
suddenly realised that he had walked past the Princess while she
was sitting outside.

Once home, he was prevented from reaching his consulting room by Mrs. Nettleship, who was brandishing a devastating smile that revealed a ruinous row of cheese-coloured teeth. A
woman whose brain had been softened by a surfeit of romantic
novels, she was now of the conviction that not only was the doctor
in love with the Countess, but that his affection was requited. She
had reached the woefully misguided conclusion that morning following a visit from Alice Cockle, who came to return the doctor's
monogrammed handkerchief. Not knowing he had lent it to the
servant, the housekeeper assumed he had given it to the girl's mistress as a love token. All reason was lost the moment she brought
it up to her nose and detected a scent.

"Doctor!" she said, blocking his way, a telltale streak of flour
across her nose. "I believe you 'ave some good news to tell me."

"Yes, indeed, Mrs. Nettleship. The Dowager Duchess paid her
fee."

"It's not that I'm meaning. Lady Bessington's maid 'as brought
back your 'andkerchief!" The housekeeper waited for his reaction
with a smile of such satisfaction that for a moment he doubted
her sanity.

"Very good, Mrs. Nettleship," he said, distracted by the number of people in the waiting room. "Now, please send in the first
patient. There's rather a backlog."

But the housekeeper didn't move. "There's a sweet smell to hit," she said, her eyebrows raised.

"To what?"

"The 'andkerchief!"

"Such as it should be, Mrs. Nettleship. That's what laundresses are for."

"It smells of hambrosia," she continued. "I'm certain of hit."

The doctor frowned. "Ambrosia? What does?"

"The 'andkerchief, doctor!"

He looked towards the waiting room. "I'm sure it's all perfectly agreeable. Now, if you don't mind, I must get on."

The housekeeper remained where she was. "It will gladden your 'eart to know that hambrosia means 'love returned' hin the language of flowers. I looked hit hup."

The doctor stared at her for a moment, wondering whether she had gone mad. "Thank you for informing me, Mrs. Nettleship," he said evenly. "I very much encourage your interest in flowers. We all need something other than work to occupy the mind. With no pleasurable diversions it becomes exhausted, and we risk no longer being in charge of our facilities. Now, if you'll excuse me, I really must attend to the patients."

Mrs. Nettleship raised an eyebrow. "There's a lot to be said for marrying a mature widow, doctor," she said, leaning towards him. "They 'ave so much love to give."

The general practitioner gazed at her, his mouth open, finally understanding her strange utterances. Mrs. Nettleship had fallen in love with him and wished to be his wife. "I really must ask you to step aside!" he cried.

She relented and headed for the kitchen, humming to herself loudly. The doctor immediately sought the sanctuary of his consulting room, closing the door firmly behind him. He sat in shock, for there was nothing more perilous than an amorous housekeeper. A knock on the door suddenly stirred him from his doom, and a man introducing himself as Thomas Trout, the Keeper of the Great Vine, walked in, his beard clipped with the care of a privet hedge. The doctor recognised him as the man sitting next to William Sheepshanks at the inquest.

"And what can I do for you?" he asked, glancing at the primrose in the lapel of the man's coarse suit.

Without a word, he pulled off his cap and looked up. The doctor followed his gaze and saw that his head was as naked as a full moon. As he studied the smooth pink expanse, he remembered the article he had recently read stating that a former pupil of Pasteur had put the cause of baldness down to a microbe, which was pointed at both ends. The only thing that could be done to halt its spread, the scientist claimed, was to make a clearing around the infected patch, like pulling down a house to stop the spread of a fire, in the hope that the microbe wouldn't leap over it. But in the case of Thomas Trout, Dr. Henderson could see that there was not even an outdoor privy to demolish.

He tapped his pen on his desk as he thought. "Are you married?" he asked.

The keeper shook his head.

"About to be?"

"No, doctor."

"Any hopes to be?"

"None."

The doctor sat forward and rested his elbows on the desk. "Then I wouldn't be so troubled by your lack of hair, Mr. Trout. Baldness is a common plague. And if you were at all bothered about your appearance as far as ladies are concerned, they are very understanding on that score. It's obnoxious-smelling feet, snoring, and corpulence that trouble them."

"Hair keeps my head warm, doctor."

"I would have thought it quite hot enough in that glasshouse of yours."

"Not in the winter, doctor. I turn the boiler off so the vine goes to sleep and gets some rest."

"I see." The general practitioner reached for his pen and wrote out a prescription for a stimulating scalp lotion made up of two drachms of tincture of cantharides, one ounce of spirit of rosemary, one ounce of acetic acid, and rose water to make eight ounces. "Apply a little at night and in the morning," he advised, handing it to him.

Thomas Trout thanked him, handed him his fee, and headed for the door clutching his cap.

"I hope she appreciates it," the doctor added, without looking up from his ledger. The keeper quickly pulled the handle behind him, his blush rising all the way up to his uninterrupted scalp.

*

ALICE COCKLE, THE LAST PATIENT of the day, sat down on the edge of the chair in front of Dr. Henderson. It was the second time she had come, having found the doctor absent when she returned his handkerchief that morning.

"It's the baby," she said, her blond hair in need of a wash.

"Yes?"

She clutched her shawl around her with fingers that bore traces of blacking. "I was wondering whether there was anything you could do about it?"

The doctor looked at her in silence as he took in what the teenager was asking him. She would lose her position, she continued, and the rest of her family depended on her wages, since her father had died in a railway accident the year before. "Davey's not turned two yet."

"You're considerably far gone, Alice. What about the child's father? Does he know you're in the family way?"

The maid shook her head.

Dr. Henderson looked down at his desk knowing the terrible

risks servants took to rid themselves of unwanted pregnancies, and the threat such efforts posed to their own lives. He thought of the law that forbade him from carrying out her wishes, then glanced up at her pale face, and saw that she was not much older than his sister. He then looked at her hands gripping her shawl so tightly her knuckles were white. Slowly he reached for his pen, wrote out a prescription, and handed it to her. The girl took it, deposited some coins, and was out of the consulting room before he could say there was no charge. He watched the door close, trusting that the girl's Latin, if she had any, would not stretch to translating the words "dandelion tea."

As he tidied his desk, his thoughts found their way back to Mink, who seemed so different from the other women he had met, whose conversation never progressed much beyond their last visit to the zoo. Deciding that it was time to smarten himself up, he quickly rubbed the shoulders of his frock coat with sandpaper to remove the shine from too much wear, grabbed his cane and the stranger's hat, and pulled the front door behind him. As he headed for the West End, his conscience whispered increasingly loud reminders of his straitened finances. By the time he walked to Hampton Court Station he had managed to silence them, for, according to his copy of *The Gentleman's Guide to Politeness and Courtship,* in order to attract the attention of the fairer sex a gentleman should put as much thought into his attire as he did into his choice of club. While enduring the black smoke and stifling gas of the Underground, he admired the elegance of other men's suits. As he approached his old tailor's, comforted by the thought that he wouldn't have to endure the indignity of being measured, he remembered the manual's warning of the dire consequences of a coat fitting too well: the resemblance to a tailor's assistant.

At the sound of the bell Mr. Wildgoose appeared at his highly polished mahogany counter. Mounted on the wall behind him was a glass case containing a plover, one of numerous stuffed birds displayed around the shop. The clean-shaven tailor, whose short legs failed to show off the precision of his cutting, stared at the doctor, his eyes magnified to staggering proportions by the strength of his spectacles. He greeted his customer with a smile intended to hide the full extent of his dismay.

"Given up running with beagles, have we, sir?" he asked, his eyes travelling down to his customer's waistcoat.

Dr. Henderson thought of the miserable sport, indulged by health zealots, which involved sprinting through soggy fields along with a pack of dogs in pursuit of a hare, while the hunt followers simply walked along behind. "Yes, I went off it. How did you know?" he asked.

Mr. Wildgoose tapped the tips of his delicate fingers together. "Just a guess, sir."

Resting a hand on the counter, the doctor explained that he needed a new coat and trousers.

"I can see that, sir. While you've left it a little long since your last visit, if I may say, at least you've come to the right place. So many gentlemen who have failed to make their mark on the world go to one of the more humble establishments in order to save a few pennies. But no man has ever made a name for himself in a coat that wasn't cut within half a mile of Piccadilly."

Fixing his customer in the eye, he then came out from behind the counter, slowly pulling his tape measure from around his neck.

"But you already have my measurements," Dr. Henderson protested, taking a step backwards.

"Just need to make sure, sir," said Mr. Wildgoose, continuing his advance.

"I assure you that I'm exactly the same height I was the last time I came," insisted the doctor, walking round a tailor's dummy.

But there was no escaping the diminutive man, who came round the other way. Suddenly he disappeared, and the general practitioner looked around him in alarm. He glanced down and saw him kneeling at his feet, brandishing his weapon.

"Few men have the moral fortitude to transcend the effect of an ill-cut trouser, sir," warned Mr. Wildgoose, measuring the inside of his leg.

The doctor fixed his eyes on the plover as the tailor did his worst. "I'm after something a little more in keeping with fashion," he said, his voice pitched slightly higher than usual. "Something more . . . alluring. I understand that trousers worn with a frock coat are in good style when cut rather close. I'd like them tapered evenly to the boot and set well over the instep so as to avoid flopping. I can't bear flopping. I quite fancy a dark cashmere cloth with a relief stripe of a lighter shade. It's much more dressy."

"To be too much in fashion is as vulgar as to be too far behind it," replied the tailor, slipping his tape round the doctor's waist. "I would stick with a pure black background and a white stripe with your figure, sir."

The doctor frowned down at him.

"Up by three inches, sir, just as I feared. I spotted it the minute you walked in."

"Three?" the doctor exclaimed. "That's my housekeeper's doing. She will insist on baking cakes."

The tailor tapped his fingers together. "If I may, sir, I would suggest that you resist them at all costs."

"I do bicycle, you know," said the doctor indignantly.

"Perhaps you should pedal a little harder, sir. Avoirdupois is ruinous for a man who has not yet made it to the altar."

The doctor looked at him aghast. "How do you know that I'm still not married?" he asked.

"A tailor can always tell, sir," said Mr. Wildgoose, passing his instrument of torture around the doctor's back.

Dr. Henderson looked into the distance. "Well, maybe an improvement in matters sartorial will help in that regard. They do say the tailor makes the man." He raised his eyebrows. "I've read that the Prince of Wales and the Duke of York both have braid-edge coats. Braiding rather takes my fancy."

Mr. Wildgoose tutted. "That's not for the likes of you, sir. We wouldn't want to draw too much attention, as the correct style in frock coats is rather shapely at the moment." He peered at his measuring tape and announced, "Two inches off the chest. Most apparent to the trained eye."

"*Off* the chest?" the doctor asked, his hands on his hips. "Are you sure?"

The tailor looked back at him with his huge unblinking eyes. "The tape measure never lies, sir. We leave that to the customers. Don't worry, you're in good hands. By the time I've finished, you'll look just like my young assistant over there."

When, eventually, it was over, Dr. Henderson pulled the door swiftly behind him and was just about to cross the road when he suddenly remembered something. As he opened it again, Mr. Wildgoose was running a feather duster over a case above the fireplace bearing a white pheasant. The tailor turned and held him with his enormous pupils.

"Perhaps you've realised that you also need a new waistcoat, sir, since the correct vest these days is double-breasted and buttoned rather high," he said, holding his duster aloft. "But with you, sir, there's a much more pressing concern."

"What?"

"There's only so much strain a buttonhole will take, sir."

The doctor pulled in his stomach. "If you don't mind, I was actually after a recommendation."

"And what might that be, sir?" Mr. Wildgoose asked, tilting his head to one side.

"I need an unimpeachable hat."

The tailor put down his duster, gazed heavenwards, then gave his pronouncement: "Try Lincoln and Bennett of Piccadilly, sir.

I would recommend a straight topper rather than the bell shape, even if it has been popular for the last three years. Even such dressy men about town as the Duke of Newcastle and Lord Francis Hope have stuck with level lines for many years. A chimney-pot hat has a morally superior look about it. It might help you get a wife, sir."

The doctor swiftly closed the door behind him, then immediately poked his head back in. "As a matter of interest, how mad should one's hatter be?"

Tapping the tips of his fingers together, Mr. Wildgoose considered the question. "You would expect some degree of madness, of course, sir. But we advise our customers to stay clear of the certifiable. They have a tendency to overcharge, and many struggle with the brims. Just nicely mad, sir. That's what you want. Just nicely mad."

CHAPTER VIII

The Pleasure and Peril of a New Pair
of Gentleman's Stockings

GOOD FRIDAY, APRIL 8, 1898

O one had waited for Good Friday with more long-ing than the inhabitants of London. They greeted the arrival of the sober Christian festival of fasting and pen-ance warmed not only by a hot cross bun in their stomachs but, for the fortunate, a four-day holiday stretching out in front of them. But that wasn't the only blessing. For the sun, notoriously coy on a bank holiday weekend, threw off its clouds and flagrantly exposed itself. It was only then that they got down on their knees and offered up a gleeful prayer of thanks. Debts were forgotten and husbands forgiven as the working classes armed themselves with sandwiches and beer bottles and herded to stations for cheap excursion tickets. Meanwhile, the rich, stuffed into four-wheelers weighed down by portmanteaux, trunks, fishing rods, and hat-boxes, headed to estates in the country. The city was as silent as a Sunday, and even the muffin man's bell failed to ring.

Only the grace-and-favour residents of Hampton Court Palace cursed when they peered out of their windows and saw the excep-tional weather. Lamenting their failure to have secured themselves an invitation elsewhere, they braced themselves for the start of the Easter stampede, their dread inflamed by announcements in the papers that the *Queen Elizabeth*, the luxurious saloon steamer, would be running trips from London Bridge on both Good Friday and Easter Monday, swelling the armada arriving at their banks.

Children were already blowing penny whistles in the Privy Garden as Mink walked through its normally tranquil alleys formed by overgrown yews. The first of the south gardens created by Henry VIII, it had been opened to the public five years ago, much to the irritation of the residents. The Princess took little notice of the jolly visitors with their over-trimmed hats and thumbs in their waistcoat sleeves, her mind still on Inspector Guppy. She had not heard from the police since they searched the house, and was anxious for the matter to be closed so both she and Pooki could get a decent night's sleep.

Hoping to escape the latest scandal to engulf her, she opened the gate of a small garden next to the river, one of the few private retreats that remained to the residents. But as she walked in, she found that she was not the only one to have sought refuge there. Many of the seats were already taken, and several bath chairs were parked in the sun. She was about to turn back when she heard her name, and turned to see the Countess beckoning her over. As she approached, Lady Beatrice and Lady Montfort Bebb moved aside to make room for her on the bench.

"I see you have come to hide, like the rest of us," said Lady Montfort Bebb. "On Easter Monday we will be completely overrun by 'Arrys and 'Arriets. We're all praying for rain."

"The palace at Kew will be open to the public soon. Hopefully it'll lure away some of the visitors," said Lady Beatrice, holding up a parasol to protect herself from acquiring more freckles. "I think they should reinstate the toll on Hampton Court Bridge. It used to put off so many of the destitute. I shall write to the Lord Chamberlain and suggest it."

The Countess leant forward, placing a hand on her arm. "Point out that it should be free for residents," she insisted. She turned to the Princess and asked her how things had gone with the Inspector.

"Such an odious man," Mink replied. "He smells of cheap tobacco. I had to open all the windows after he left."

"He was rather preoccupied by your maid when he questioned me, I must say," continued the Countess, fiddling with the ribbons tying her black bonnet. "I hope for your sake you don't lose her. We struggle so much retaining domestic servants here, what with the ghosts. Thankfully my maid-of-all-work is made of stronger stuff. She's turned out very well, considering how she came to me."

"Was she from the workhouse?" asked Mink.

The Countess shook her head. "Alice used to be the Bagshots' parlour maid but was dismissed for stealing. I haven't had the slightest trouble with her. I put a sovereign under the carpet when she first arrived and she never took it."

"She'd need it, all right, being as though she's only paid the wages of a German maid," said Lady Montfort Bebb, looking ahead of her, both hands on the top of her cane. She turned back to the ladies. "I'm not sure that one can ever fully trust domestic servants. When I was married I always made a point of choosing plain ones."

Mink sat up. "The point is not whether one can trust one's parlour maid but whether one can trust one's husband or the male houseguests," she pointed out. "I've never met a young girl yet who has found the sight of a gentleman leering at her from his morning bath in the least bit alluring. Yet plenty find themselves hauled in with them."

"Oh! What fun!" exclaimed Lady Beatrice, covering her mouth as she tittered.

All three women looked at her.

A plump elderly woman, clutching a tiny trembling dog on her lap, entered the garden in a bath chair, pushed by a sweating maid. The Countess excused herself and went to talk to her. As soon as she was out of earshot, Lady Montfort Bebb lowered her voice. "I don't wish to suggest that Lady Bessington is mean, but apparently she refuses to pay for her skirts to be lined in silk. Instead she uses glove lining from William Whitely in Westbourne Grove, and has a strip of silk sewn onto the bottom in case it shows." She sat back, eyebrows raised, to let the revelation sink in.

Lady Beatrice glanced at the Countess, then leant forwards. "It's quite understandable," she whispered.

Lady Montfort Bebb looked at her in surprise. "It is?" she asked. "We've never understood her miserly ways before."

"She has her trousseau to save for!" Lady Beatrice hissed. "I just heard this morning."

"Her trousseau?" repeated Mink.

"I have it on the best authority that she has stolen Dr. Henderson's heart!" gushed Lady Beatrice. "His housekeeper is most assured of the fact. She told my cook this morning. He gave Lady Bessington one of his handkerchiefs as a love token, and she sent it back, fragranced. While I'm naturally delighted that she's found love again, I must admit I'm a little hurt she never told us, particularly as I've done my best to find her a suitor and she has rejected them all. I even suggested that charming homeopath from East Molesey after he produced a florin from her bonnet at the inquest, but even he was of no interest, despite the fortunes he finds."

Lady Montfort Bebb gripped the top of her cane. "I suggest you inform your daughter that Dr. Henderson is taken to prevent any further fainting in the Chapel Royal. It's happened so often I could set my watch by it." She glanced at the Countess and lowered her voice. "But Lady Bessington shouldn't be wasting her time on a mere doctor. She needs to find someone of equal standing, or marry up, if possible, to improve her financial position. That being said, I do like a wedding. If nothing else, it's the best way of terminating undesirable acquaintances. I sent out numerous cards without a new address on them notifying people of my marriage. I can't tell you what bliss it was never to hear from them again."

As Mink turned to look at the Countess, trying to imagine her and Dr. Henderson as man and wife, Cornelius B. Pilgrim wandered into the garden with the defeated air of a man in need of sleep. Having gone to bed in the early hours of the morning, he was woken by a hideous scraping sound that left him clutching the top of his bedsheet. As his heart pounded, he looked around him, wondering whether it was the ghost of General Bagshot unsettled by having been hauled out of the ground and diced by an inquisitive doctor. Unable to find his dressing gown due to the uprising amongst the servants, he put on his monkey-fur coat and grabbed his gun. He started to search the apartments, peering round doors for the white traces of a spirit before daring to enter. Eventually he tracked down the sound to a sooty urchin holding a mystifying apparatus that disappeared up the library chimney. Standing in his bare feet, Cornelius B. Pilgrim brandished his weapon and asked the teenager to identify himself and state his purpose. The terrified youngster explained that he was a chimney sweep and had been let in by the butler. Unconvinced, the American scanned the room, then proceeded to ask him what a chimney sweep was. He listened, transfixed by the lad's tale of serpentine flues, smoking chimneys, and the time when children were forced to climb up inside.

The sweep blinked his red eyes as he stood listening in wonder to the American's account of chimneys in his homeland with straight flues that neither smoked nor needed to be brushed to reduce the risk of fire. He immediately went home and told his family, who assumed he was making it up, and enquired what he was wearing. He replied that it was a monkey-fur coat, which the American had given him out of pity for his profession. But the family, who had only ever seen the tiny flea-ridden creatures owned by organ grinders, refused to believe that such a luxuriant monkey existed. Unsettled by the pelt of the mysterious beast, they made him return it, certain it was cursed. Before he left they warned him never to repeat his fanciful tales of straight flues, lest the nation's builders saw their folly and put every sweep out of business.

Cornelius B. Pilgrim stood hesitantly in the garden, a copy of the *Anglo-American Times* tucked underneath his arm, looking wearily at the taken seats.

"Oh, look, it's that American without his coat. I suppose that's one reason to be grateful for such lovely weather," said Lady Montfort Bebb.

"I'm going to call him over," said Mink, sitting up and peering at him. "According to his testimony at the inquest, he knows who the murderer is."

Lady Montfort Bebb looked him up and down uneasily. "If you must. Though goodness knows what he'll call me this time."

Turning his head at the sound of his name, Cornelius B. Pilgrim approached and slowly lowered himself onto the chair next to the Princess. She leant towards him, cocked her head to one side, and said, "How shabbily you were treated at the inquest, Mr. Pilgrim. Fancy your knowing who did it and not being allowed to enlighten us all. Do tell. We're all desperate to know."

Cornelius B. Pilgrim looked down. "Oh, I've no idea."

"Come, come, Mr. Pilgrim," Mink urged, leaning even closer towards him. "Don't disappoint me, I've never met a shy American yet. Fill us in, if you don't mind, otherwise we'll all keep suspecting one another."

The American looked from one lady to another.

"Don't look at me, Mr. Pilgrim. I'm innocent," snapped Lady Montfort Bebb.

"So am I," piped up Lady Beatrice. "At least of this."

But he refused to be drawn. "I really don't know what came over me. I guess I got carried away with the magic tricks. We don't have them at inquests in America," he said. "Everyone else seems to know how the General met his death, though." There were dozens of rumours circulating the public houses, he added, all of which the butler relayed to him in great detail while waiting on him at dinner. As a result, he had chronic dyspepsia. "I'm looking forward to Mrs. Bagshot's return so that I can pass on my condolences and get the hell out of here."

Lady Beatrice held up a hand and closed her eyes. "Do not count your chickens, Mr. Pilgrim," she warned. "The British police are very thorough. You may very well be in custody by then."

Cornelius B. Pilgrim stared at her, a hand on his chest.

"Of course Mr. Pilgrim has nothing to do with it," said Mink, turning her eyes on him again. "Tell me, what of your research? I expect you've been to see the dinosaurs at the Natural History Museum. I haven't been there for months."

"They're wonderful," he replied.

Lady Beatrice leant towards him underneath her parasol. "If you ever go to the British Museum, you may be interested to know that there's an American section. Though I expect you'd prefer the Reading Room. It's always cluttered with Americans hunting through the records in the hope of finding a titled ancestor."

Insisting that he had an appointment, Cornelius B. Pilgrim suddenly stood up, tucked his newspaper back under his arm, and bid them farewell. Mink turned to watch him striding out of the gate, and wondered why her question about the Natural History Museum had made him blush.

*

WHEN THE PRINCESS RETURNED TO Wilderness House, Pooki opened the door with a look that instantly worried her.

"That policeman is here, ma'am," she said. "I told him I did not know when you would be back, but he insisted on waiting."

On entering the drawing room Mink found Inspector Guppy sitting in her father's armchair, flicking through his notebook.

"There you are, Inspector. Did you find my Sherlock Holmes

book?" she asked, sitting down on the sofa opposite him, irritated that he was in her seat.

"I didn't, as it happens, Princess," he said, stroking the armrest with the tips of his fingers as he looked at her.

"Don't worry, I can guess the ending," she said, eyebrows raised. "He solves the crime before the policeman has even worked out who's been killed."

The Inspector gazed at her in silence for a moment. "What I did find, however, was a bonnet box on top of your maid's wardrobe." He nodded towards the door. "I think you'd better ask her in."

"Show me a woman who doesn't have a bonnet box in her bedroom, Inspector, but if you insist," she replied, getting up to ring the bell.

Pooki came in, clutching her hands in front of her, and sat down next to Mink, their dresses touching.

Inspector Guppy turned to the servant. "Do you know anything about a bonnet box on top of your wardrobe?" he asked.

"Yes, sir," she replied, sliding her palms down her apron to dry them.

"Did it contain fly papers?"

The maid nodded.

"Are you aware that fly papers contain arsenic?"

"Yes, sir. And sugar. You soak the papers in water, the flies are attracted to the sugar, and then the poison kills them. It is very clever."

The Inspector made a note and then looked up. "A servant's room is a rather strange place to keep them, don't you think?"

Pooki's gaze fell to the floor.

He continued to press her. "Can you explain why you had fly papers hidden in your room?"

"They can't have been hidden or you wouldn't have found them," Mink interrupted crossly.

"Does it not strike you as odd that your maid should have such items in her room?"

She frowned. "Not at all," she replied. "They were probably something to do with warding off moths. What I do find odd is your making such a fuss over it."

"It's April, ma'am," said Inspector Guppy, with a glance towards the window. "There aren't that many flies around."

"I saw one this morning."

He tapped his notebook with his pencil. "A gentleman dies of arsenic poisoning after eating a pigeon pie made by your maid. I find a large quantity of arsenic in her bedroom, despite your insisting there was none in the house. Added to that is the fact that she clearly has a dislike of the British. There's only one servant she talks to, so I'm told."

"The others don't talk to her," the Princess snapped.

The Inspector looked at Pooki. "And why is that?"

"Most people prefer the glamorous Indians with diamonds," she said meekly. "I am poor and my skin is dark."

"Can you account for having a quantity of fly papers in your room?" he continued.

Her gaze fell to the floor.

"Did you soak any of the ingredients in the General's pigeon pie in a solution obtained from fly papers?"

"No, sir."

"Did you poison the General?"

"No, sir."

"You're quite certain?"

Finally she looked up. "Yes, sir."

The Inspector studied her for a moment in silence. Smoothing down his moustache with his palm, he picked up his hat from the side table and got to his feet. "I see you like Dickens," he said, looking at the pile of books.

The Princess followed his gaze. "His novels, yes, though I'm not quite sure about the man after he put out the word that his wife was suffering from a mental disorder when his marriage failed. Has your wife ever questioned *your* sanity, Inspector?"

"Not to my knowledge," he replied.

Mink raised her eyebrows. "You do surprise me. Not even after that last case of yours when that poor innocent man was hanged? It was all over the papers. Goodness knows the damage it did to your career."

The Inspector tapped his hat against his leg with agitation, then looked at the maid and jerked his head towards the door. She immediately got to her feet and showed him out. Returning to the drawing room, she stood by the grand piano. "I did not poison the General, ma'am," she said quietly.

The Princess looked up from the sofa. "I know," she said. "You would have strangled him."

There was a pause.

"Ma'am?"

"Yes?"

"I have anxious forebodings," she said, clutching the sides of her dress.

Mink got up and lit a cigarette from a tortoiseshell box on the mantelpiece. She walked to the window and stood staring at the view, taking nothing of it in. As she smoked, she thought of the day when Pooki first came to the family twenty-one years ago, after being rescued from an unsavoury death by the Maharaja. Born in Prindur during the rainy season, it was no surprise to the maid's parents when she eventually took to the high seas. Working as a travelling ayah, a nurse who accompanied mothers and their children back to England, she made the return journey thirty-two times. She was so used to the rhythm of the ocean that whenever she reached dry land she instantly felt seasick, unable to tolerate the ground that remained irrefutably motionless below her. On one occasion she was shipwrecked, and found herself floating in

the Indian Ocean inside an empty tea chest. She cried so fero-
ciously she feared the sea would rise, and such was her terror she
had never shed a tear again.

It was from her thirty-third journey that she never returned
home. Having safely escorted her charges back to the motherland
in time for the school term, and nursed their mother, who had
vomited herself dry in her cabin, she turned round in the docks
and found that she had been abandoned. With neither the promised passage back to India nor the means to buy one, she wandered
London's backstreets uncertain of what to do. It wasn't long before
men with gin on their breath whispered suggestions to her from
the shadows. She refused them all, punched one, and was eventually befriended by a woman who took one of her gold bangles
in exchange for a position with a respectable family. But the job
didn't exist, and she resorted to eating the seeds that fell onto the
pavement from the birdcages of the rich.

It was a single act of kindness that saved her. When the park-
keeper found what he initially thought was a bundle of colourful
rags, he carried her into his shed. Once the fire had warmed her,
she was able to hold the cup he offered, and she drank the tea as if
it were her last. He suggested that she take off her bracelets, and,
lacking the strength to refuse, she handed them over with the self-
recrimination of the duped. But he told her to hide them in her
sari, and gave her the whole of his lunch.

She left him when she was able to walk, and took to the streets
again. As night fell, she slipped into a back door to escape from
the cold. When she woke, she found herself next to a pile of dead
rabbits and was offered a job as a fur-puller. She sat on a stool
and copied the family as they pulled the loose down off the skins
to prepare them for lining jackets. Bootless children dared each
other to go in and see the woman with an earring in her nose. The
fluff got up it, and down her throat, but she kept on pulling in
honour of the park-keeper who had saved her. But she was soon

dismissed, as her catastrophic sneezing made the family jump out of their own skins and fear for their hammering hearts.

Eventually she found her way to Soho, where newly arrived Turks, Persians, Russians, and Syrians in native dress carried their luggage to their lodging houses, their eyes raised in disbelief at a sky so stubbornly grey. Passing Cossack horse whisperers, Andalusian dancers, and Dutch diamond-cutters, she peered through the shop windows at frogs' legs sold on long sticks, snails bred in Frenchmen's gardens, and Italian cheeses that smelt of the dead. It was as she was crossing the road that she fainted again. When she opened her eyes, her head on the filthy ground, she saw the thundering hooves of an approaching horse pulling a hansom cab. Unable to move, she waited for death, her last thought for her mother so far away. The next thing she knew she was being pulled to the side of the road by a short, stout Indian in a black suit. The Maharaja carried her back into the bar he had just left, where he wiped the mud and blood from her face. He gave her a glass of brandy, which the absinthe drinkers watched her empty, never having seen a woman so thin. When he discovered she was from the state of Prindur he led her to his carriage and took her to the Old Cheshire Cheese, the steak and chop-house off Fleet Street. He marvelled at her appetite for beefsteak pudding, which matched his own, and showed her the preserved chair of Dr. Johnson, whom he explained was a distinguished lexicographer. Ignoring her blank look, he then offered her the position of nurse to his six-year-old daughter, adding that the woman currently holding the position had handed in her notice, unable to bear the silence of the little girl who hadn't uttered a word since the death of her mother. Pooki simply helped herself to more custard, and when she had finished her marmalade pudding, said, "Your daughter will speak when she has something to say. It is the same for chickens."

It was Pooki who blew a gust of happiness into that house of sorrow. After the first week, having witnessed the lay of the land, she hid the key to the wine cellar. When the butler was summonsed to explain its disappearance, she told the Maharaja that it was she who had taken it, as a father drinking himself to death was no good for a child. When she found him reading his old love letters from his wife, tears smearing the words, she sent him up to the nursery, where he discovered his talent as a storyteller. Sitting Mink on his knee, he described her grandmother riding on top of an elephant while hunting tigers, and the gasp of the birds when they saw her dazzling jewels. Dressed in black, the girl listened in silence, her eyes never leaving him for a second, and each day he returned with another spectacular episode. Several weeks later, at the dining table no longer set for three, Mink spoke, asking the name of the elephant. It was then that the Maharaja realised how much he had rather than how much he had lost, and he abandoned the absinthe drinkers in Soho. Eventually there came a time when neither could remember Pooki being a stranger, and when the Princess grew up, she asked her to be her lady's-maid, and never once did the servant allow her to wear rabbit.

Mink blew a final mouthful of smoke against the windowpane. "Don't worry," she said, without turning. "I'm going to find out who did it."

Pooki remained by the piano, still clutching the sides of her dress. "Will you be able to, ma'am?" she asked, her voice uneven.

"You just watch me," she replied, and went to the study to draw up her list of suspects.

*

DR. HENDERSON WOKE JUST BEFORE lunchtime, happy in the knowledge that he would get through the day without seeing neither a boil nor his housekeeper. The previous night, he had put up a sign on the front door saying that he would attend emergencies only on Good Friday, and had given Mrs. Nettleship the day off, for his sake as much as hers. Not only was he unsettled by the sudden onslaught of her ardour, which had continued with undisguised hints about the merits of mature widows, but he was still furious about the anti-masturbation device. He had left it out to give to one of the soldiers, but when he went to fetch it, it had disappeared. He eventually tracked it down to a kitchen drawer, next to the potato ricer. With no hint of an apology for the protracted search, she took it out and thrust it at him as if it were a lost umbrella.

The woman was clearly suffering from a sudden derangement, he concluded from his bedsheets, for it was the only tool of his profession that she normally refused to touch, claiming such proximity would sully the memory of her husband at the bottom of the North Sea. Turning onto his back, he wondered whether there was any way that he had encouraged her. Suddenly he remembered her coming into his bedroom while he was attempting to master the New York plastered look. Then there was his copy of *The Gentleman's Guide to Politeness and Courtship* next to his bed, which doubtless she had seen and also misconstrued.

Unable to bear the harrowing thought any longer, he threw back his blankets and hunted for his new cycling costume. Lured by an advertisement bearing a gentleman in nifty socks, he had first visited the City branch of Isaac Walton & Co., the high-class tailors and colonial outfitters. But as soon as he walked in, the staff immediately reached for their instruments of humiliation hanging around their necks. "I'm after ready-made," he hastily explained, backing out. "You'll be needing the Newington Causeway branch, then, sir," came the reply, and he closed the door and followed the directions. Such was his delight at not having to be subjected to the terrifying touch of a tailor, he returned home with knickerbockers, a Norfolk jacket, and a waterproof cape. He chose flannel lining, aware that cotton or linen damp from perspiration or rain chilled the bones. Only the previous week he had read of several bad cases of inflammation of the kidneys that had been traced directly to the linen waistband of knickerbockers. But that wasn't the end of it. Before he realised what he was doing, he had also picked out a matching cap, a sweater, a shirt, a belt, a tie, a silk sash, and two pairs of diamond-patterned hose. It wasn't until he was presented with the bill that he was brought back to his senses, and the fantasy of the Princess seeing him charmingly attired while in command of his machine vanished as swiftly as the man at the cash desk took his considerable payment.

Once he was dressed, Dr. Henderson looked at himself in the mirror, trying not to see the extra inches on his waist and those that had vanished from his chest. But the more he ignored them, the more they presented themselves, and he decided to forgo breakfast. All misgivings vanished, however, the moment he put on the finishing touch. For there was nothing more satisfying than a new pair of stockings clinging joyfully to the calf, still too young to have developed the evil habit of sliding down the leg and producing ugly rucks. He rubbed a piece of yellow soap over the joins and edges to prevent them from rubbing, then padded downstairs, admiring his splendidly patterned shins. While making tea, he noticed the freak arrival of the sun, and decided not to delay any further. Slipping a meat biscuit into the pocket of his Norfolk jacket for emergencies, he then peered into his tool bag and checked that it contained an oil can, a wrench, a repair kit, a screwdriver, extra nuts, a piece of copper wire, a pair of bellows, and a yard of string. After removing his nose machine, which had mysteriously found its way inside, he debated whether to bring his cyclist's tea satchel with its kettle that was guaranteed to boil in a gale. Deciding against it, he put on his shoes and headed to his bicycle in the garden shed with the happy anticipation of his last purchase, a Pattisson Hygienic Cycle Saddle. As he prodded it with eager fingers, he hoped that it would live up to the manufacturer's claim and conquer the wheelman's most troubling lament: perineal pressure.

He checked that the saddle was at the correct position, for too long a reach obliged the rider to depend upon momentum to carry him over bad spots, increasing the chance of a tumble. Carrying the bicycle through the house, he climbed on in the front garden and headed up Hampton Court Road. He glanced at the crowd of drinkers outside the King's Arms, where the drunk woman had almost sold out of pig's trotters, and just before the Greyhound Hotel turned left into Bushy Park. He pedalled down the famous avenue of stately horse chestnut trees, which would shortly be in full blossom, attracting hordes of annual admirers alerted by excited reports in the newspapers. Dodging the waggonettes plying their way through the park, he wondered how to adopt measures to bring himself to his fair one's notice, as his courtship manual advised.

Eventually his path was clear and he shot off, the wind whipping the hair protruding from his cap into even tighter curls. He straightened up so as to avoid the unbecoming doubled-up, chest-contracted position assumed by so many, as his bicycling instructor had encouraged him. Alfred Bucket had been recommended by the shop where he had bought his machine. The doctor now realised that he should have taken the disfiguring blue marks on the man's face, caused by falling on cinders, as a warning. As they stood in the shed behind the shop, the doctor's initial query about how to use the brake, which he had read was often employed when descending hills, had been met with a distrustful look. Alfred Bucket then told his pupil with the solemnity of a sage that the most useful lesson in managing a machine was to jump ship the moment you felt it running away with you. "Spread your legs wide apart and throw yourself backwards," counselled the teacher, who then proceeded to demonstrate the emergency rearward dismount.

The next clue as to the fate of Alfred Bucket was the title of his second lesson: the art of falling. "When all hope is lost of a dignified dismount at high speeds, the wheelman should avoid all obstructions," he warned the nervous doctor. "A series of somersaults, while ungentlemanly, will not do as much damage to the ego as coming to a dead stop against a dustcart."

It wasn't until the third lesson that Alfred Bucket finally broached the subject of getting the thing to move. Taking it out of the shed, he pointed at his pupil. "Never underestimate the importance of artistic ankle action," he urged. "Very few bother to master it, resulting in their looking slovenly and not being in control of their mount."

It wasn't until Dr. Henderson took to the roads alone that he discovered that back-pedalling slowed down a bicycle. He soon got the hang of the manoeuvre and returned to the shop to share the revelation with his instructor. But he was too late. For upon approaching the counter, the shopkeeper looked at him mournfully and shook his head. "I'm sorry," he said, his voice unsteady. "Mr. Bucket is dead." He went on to explain that the instructor had lost his life, not in an undignified heap at the bottom of an incline as he had always feared, but stationary at the top of a hill, where he had been mowed down by a runaway tricycle complete with rider.

Having executed numerous high-speed dashes, his saddle positioned a few inches back in the perfect position for scorching, the general practitioner headed for the sedate towpath bordering the Thames. As he pedalled alongside the punts and canoes filled with couples in splendid boating costumes, a steam launch approached, laden with happy excursionists singing to the strains of an accordion. Infected by the gaiety of the river, he decided to practise bicycling with one hand. First he lifted his right, and then his left, but found that it was not the slightest challenge. Next he attempted the no-handed method of wheeling, for it was an undeniable truth that a gentleman who relied on his hands for steering never rode as gracefully as one who steered with the feet alone. He found it so simple, he wondered whether he was suitably proficient to take up bicycle polo.

The deafening answer came minutes later, when he was suffering the consequences of his fateful decision. When he had recovered, and the full horror of what he had done hit him, he put his woeful lack of judgement down to his excitement over his new diamond-patterned stockings. Whatever the reason, as Dr. Henderson made his way down Barge Walk, he suddenly decided to indulge in an offshoot of the sport known as "fancy riding." Alfred Bucket had warned him of such peril in his final lesson, lowering his voice and gripping the doctor's arm to impress upon him the dangers. "The temptation comes to every wheelman, but you must resist it at all costs," he warned, his blue scars even more harrowing in the shed's candlelight. "Such things never end well, even for some of the most celebrated entertainers." But it was useless. As soon as the thought entered the doctor's windswept head, there was no getting rid of the urge to attempt to balance on the handlebars and raise his legs while still moving. It didn't take long for him to fully comprehend the reasoning behind Alfred Bucket's dark warning. For, without even time to throw himself off backwards, Dr. Henderson was in the Thames.

When, eventually, he surfaced, he wiped his eyes of riverwater and saw Mink staring at him from the bank, a hand over her mouth and her walking costume soaked. It was then, as the passengers of the honking steam launch stood up to gawp at the curious obstruction, that he finally mastered the New York plastered look.

Spewing out a mouthful of the Thames, the doctor, weighed down by his new bicycling attire, started inching towards the towpath in a series of movements that only the generous or inebriated would term "breaststroke." Within seconds he suddenly found himself deposited on the bank, battered by waves from the passing steam launch, its mischievous passengers throwing pennies at him as they had done to the mudlarks. Looking up at the Princess, he wondered whether he would appear more ridiculous out of the water than in it. But he had no time to decide, for she bent down and tugged him out. He stood on the bank, his sodden hose around his ankles, while his cap bobbed cheerfully in the wake.

Mink shook her hands to rid them of water, then looked at him, an eyebrow raised. "Good afternoon, Dr. Henderson. I shall excuse you not raising your hat, being as though it's almost reached the other bank."

The doctor wiped his mouth with the back of his sleeve but found it to be equally wet.

"Bicycling is a preoccupation of yours, I understand," she said.

"Exercise is extremely beneficial to the heart," he replied, as he dripped. Lowering his mahogany eyes, he added, "That, and having someone special who it beats for."

The Princess gestured to the towpath. "There are so many attractive ladies out enjoying the weather. You've certainly caught their attention now. How fortunate Lady Bessington wasn't around to witness you capsize."

He frowned, trying to understand what the Countess had to do with it. Before he had time to ask, Mink turned to leave.

"Don't stand around too long in these wet knickerbockers, doctor," she warned, as she headed towards the palace. "You'll catch a fever and I'll have to fetch the homeopath from East Molesey. No doubt he'll have just the cure."

HE invasion on Good Friday was nothing compared to the storming of the palace on Easter Monday. The siege began by those who came by road, having set out early for 'appy 'Ampton to avoid the bank-holiday congestion with a joyful wave to those left behind. They were joined by passengers rammed inside nineteen special trains put on by the London & South Western Railway, the overhead racks piled with picnic baskets, the sandwiches eaten long before they arrived. The numbers soon swelled with those advancing by river. Men in boating costumes and cheerful red stockings, and women wearing muslin skirts carrying Japanese parasols, appeared in a perpetual flotilla of gaily decorated vessels that disgorged passengers onto the banks, and into the reach of the beaming postcard hawkers and peddlers of spurious guides. By mid-morning the landmark was overrun by cheesemongers, pawnbrokers, and asylum keepers, all in a state of glee. More than sixteen thousand excursionists herded through the State Apartments, their infernal tramping causing misery to the residents of nearby apartments. Their despair was matched by that of the umbrella merchants, who sat on the grass with their unfurled wares, looking reproachfully at the capricious sun that continued to blaze.

Determined to clear Pooki's name, Mink sat at her desk and contemplated her list of suspects. Rather regrettably, given her fondness for the women, it included her new friends. Lady Montfort Bebb had never disguised her antipathy of the General, and clearly resented his bile about her piano playing. But was that really a reason to poison him, or was there something more behind it? Then there was Lady Beatrice, whose doves General Bagshot was said to have killed. Had she heard the rumour before the picnic? She had dropped her fork and walked off as soon as it was mentioned. But was that just a ruse to deflect suspicion away from her? Neither had Lady Bessington hidden her dislike of the man, telling her how he had hit one of his servants and been offensive about her interior decoration. Did she have a motive Mink didn't yet know about?

But if any of them were guilty, how on earth did they manage to poison the pigeon pie, which appeared to be what had killed the General? Hadn't Pooki been at home all day? And why on earth did she have fly papers in her bonnet box? She had already asked her twice, and both times she had clammed up, suddenly finding a chore that needed to be done in another room and closing the door firmly behind her. If she didn't know the servant better, even she might think she were guilty. It was time for Pooki to answer some questions.

Mink rang the bell, and the servant swiftly arrived at the study door. Since the Inspector's discovery of the contents of her bonnet box, she had transformed into the perfect maid. There had been no pointed comments about unnecessary expenditure, no encouragement to open the post, and never once did she tell one of the butterman's jokes. Instead, she had gone about her chores in silence, keeping her head bowed while polishing what had already been polished, dusting what had already been dusted, and sweeping what had already been swept. Whenever the Princess asked how she was, she simply replied that she was suffering from a sore throat.

"Would you close the windows for me? The noise from the maze is insufferable," Mink said. Without a word, Pooki walked to the nearest one and reached up.

"You told the coroner that you went up to one of the bedrooms when you were in the middle of making the pies for the picnic," the Princess said, watching her closely. "What were you doing?"

"I noticed that the Keeper of the Maze had fallen silent, and went to see what had happened," said the servant, pulling down the sash. "I was worried that he had fallen off his chair on account of his bad legs. When I got to the bedroom I could not see him, and there were so many people clustered at the dead ends that I took pity on them and gave them directions so they could get out."

"How long were you there for?"

The maid walked to the next window. "Quite a while, ma'am. Some of those people did not know the difference between backwards and forwards."

"Did anyone call at the house?"

Pooki looked at the ceiling as she tried to remember. "As well as the General, Alice dropped off some flour, and Pike brought the birds and beef."

"Pike?"

"The butcher's delivery boy. He helped carry the luggage when we first arrived."

"Oh, yes." The Princess frowned. "Why would Alice bring round some flour? We're not that poor."

"I think she was trying to be friendly, ma'am. Not many of the other servants talk to her, since she was dismissed for stealing."

"Did you use it?"

"No, ma'am. I told her I did not need it."

"But she was hanging around the kitchen with you while you were cooking?"

"Just as I was starting, ma'am."

The Princess wrote down Alice's name. "Did you leave the house at all that day?"

The maid immediately turned and shut the window. "Yes, ma'am. I went for a walk," she said, her back still turned.

Mink studied her, tapping her pen on the desk. "Why did you go for a walk when you were in the middle of cooking?"

There was a pause. "Sometimes a maid needs to clear her head, ma'am," she replied, looking out of the window.

The Princess sat back and folded her arms as she continued to watch her. "It's usual for a servant to ask permission to leave the house."

"You were at the meeting in London, ma'am."

"And when you went for this mysterious walk of yours, did you see anyone around?"

"Yes, ma'am," said Pooki, finally facing her. "The Keeper of the Maze was trimming the top of the hedges, and Lady Montfort Bebb was walking that dog of hers."

Mink wrote down his name. "I presume you locked the back door when you left," she said.

The maid shook her head. "No, ma'am. It is inauspicious to lock the back door when there is a crow in the garden."

"A crow?" Mink repeated.

The servant nodded. "It was a big one, ma'am," she said, her eyes wide.

Mink put a hand on her hip. "So its size makes it even more unlucky, does it?" she asked.

Pooki frowned. "Ma'am, that bird looked at me."

The two women stared at each other in silence.

"I bet it wasn't even a crow," said the Princess, striding towards a window. "Look at that tree over there. See the bird on the branch with the mistletoe on it?"

The servant peered. "Yes, ma'am. It is a crow."

"It's a blackbird."

"It is a crow, ma'am," said Pooki, shaking her head.

"It's a blackbird," Mink exclaimed, exasperated. "Look, that's a crow over there. See? It's much larger. That," she added, tapping on the glass, "is a blackbird."

The maid squinted at both.

Mink turned to her. "The next time you decide to leave the house open to all and sundry I would be grateful if you would first make sure that your ornithology was up to scratch," she said, returning to her desk. "They were pigeons you used, weren't they?"

Pooki nodded, closing her eyes. "Yes, ma'am. I know a pigeon when I see one. They are grey."

"That's one thing at least," said the Princess with a sigh, reaching for her pen.

There was a pause.

"Unless they were doves, ma'am."

*

LATER THAT MORNING MINK STRODE towards Trophy Gate against the tide of excursionists, bracing herself for the mangled melody. But the organ grinder was nowhere to be seen, having been paid by the sentry to stay away for the day because of his urge to throw himself into the Thames. Neither were the ladies plying their musky trade, lying instead on picnic rugs in Bushy Park, the sun reaching into the shadowy depths of their cleavages.

The Princess walked across the bridge, past trippers nibbling bunches of watercress as they watched the antics on the river below. Arriving in East Molesey, she looked for Vine Road in the hope that Silas Sparrowgrass would be able to tell her something of interest that the General had said as he was dying. She eventually found number five, the only terrace house surmounted by a weather-cock. When there was no reply, she pushed open the door with her fingertips. Such was the stench of elderly fish, she was momentarily lost for words, and stood staring at the homeopath. Wearing his beadle's coat, he was absorbed in perfecting a magic trick with a duck that had flown into his garden and refused to keep quiet in the depths of one of his coat pockets. At the sight of the Princess, he hastily set the creature on the floor and flicked rabbit droppings off a chair, which scattered noisily across the floor like beads. He then offered her the seat and peered at her with his good eye.

"Mr. Sparrowgrass," she said, a hand against her cheek. "There's something dreadfully wrong with me, and only a man of your considerable talents can help. I'm not at all convinced of the merits of a certain local general practitioner, mentioning no names." She turned her eyes slowly in the direction of the practice on Hampton Court Green.

The homeopath smiled, revealing a missing front tooth that had been knocked out during his pursuit of Gertrude at the inquest. "Not to worry, Your Highness, you've come to the right place. Silas Sparrowgrass, a man of infinite subtlety, is at your service. What is the nature of your ailment, if I may be so bold?"

Hunting for inspiration, the Princess looked around the room, as cluttered as a pawnbroker's warehouse. A coiled snake lay in a cage on a pile of empty orange boxes, brooms with worn-out bristles stood in a coalscuttle, and a tailless stuffed fox in permanent mid-step balanced on top of a broken mangle. Sitting on the summit of a mound of handkerchiefs, a number of which had been doctored in the pursuit of magic, was Gertrude, her nose furiously twitching. Raising her eyes, the Princess noticed a row of smoked mackerel nailed to the beams by their tails.

"I've lost my sense of smell," she said brightly.

Silas Sparrowgrass frowned and cocked his head to one side.

"I assumed they'd cleared away the pile of manure at Trophy Gate, as I could no longer smell it. But then I saw it, as high and fresh as ever, and realised something must be wrong with me," Mink continued.

The homeopath's squint spiralled round the room. "You can't detect a slight hint of . . . fish, perhaps?"

Mink raised her eyebrows. "Fish, Mr. Sparrowgrass?"

Silas Sparrowgrass stood beside her, his hands clasped together. "The street fishmonger is currently lodging with me, Your Highness, on account of his new wife having just thrown him out. He made the mistake of telling her she would get used to the smell. She says it's got into the walls and beams, and she can't get it out. Apparently her bonnet stank of old turbot when she went to visit her sister and a crowd of cats followed them round the park. She has my sympathies. My sister married a cobbler and can still smell boots in bed at night." He shook his head. "Needless to say, it's a childless marriage."

The homeopath then raised his nose and sniffed twice. "There's a load of herrings in the bath in the kitchen going cheap on account of the colour they're turning. The constable came round this morning, as the neighbours were convinced there was a dead body in here. Are you sure you can't smell anything?"

Mink inhaled deeply. "I would have sworn the flower seller had moved in. I can smell roses," she said.

He stared at her with his good eye. "If I may be so bold to enquire, Your Highness, what did you smell when you were at Trophy Gate?"

The Princess looked over his shoulder, and noticed a tin on an overcrowded shelf. "Butterscotch," she said.

"And what does that smell of?" he asked, pointing to a bucket of pig's swill.

The Princess walked over, bent down, and sniffed. "Coal," she declared, and returned to her seat.

Silas Sparrowgrass caressed his Newgate fringe. "It's not the loss of smell that's afflicting you, Your Highness, but the perversion of it.

"Odoratus perversus, odoratus perversus," he muttered as he

picked up his snake-charmer's basket, bought, complete with contents, in an auction of items left in railway carriages. Placing it on the table, he removed the duck that had settled on top of it.

"What we need is monkshood in a low dilution," he concluded, lifting the lid as the animal walked around the table.

"I must say, Mr. Sparrowgrass, I so much enjoyed your performance at the inquest," said Mink, as he searched through his bottles. "What a man of many talents you are. How unfortunate the General wasn't well enough to enjoy your gift for magic during his final hours. It sounds as though you were very fond of him."

"I couldn't bear the man," he admitted, his head still buried. "He's been my patient for a year, and never once did he want to see Gertrude appear in my top hat. I take that as an insult. Have you ever seen anything more beautiful than her? Once I treated him before luncheon and he said he fancied rabbit stew. I had to lie down for the rest of the afternoon."

"I imagine he talked to you, his entrusted medical man, about his private life," she said.

"Not a sausage," he replied holding a bottle up to his good eye and returning it to the basket again. "I like a little chat with my patients. You never know what you'll discover and be able to pass on to an interested party. But he never said anything to me beyond his symptoms. Still, I'm sorry to see him go. He always paid promptly. You'd be surprised how many carrots that rabbit gets through."

"Come, come, Mr. Sparrowgrass," coaxed the Princess. "He must have divulged something to you, the soul of discretion, when you treated him after the picnic. Did he mention anyone's name, perhaps?"

The rummaging continued. "He didn't say much, on account of his bouts of retching," came the muffled reply. Suddenly the homeopath raised his head from his basket. "Hold on. You're right, Your Highness, he did say something."

"What?" asked the Princess, holding her breath.

"He said how relieved he was not to have called Dr. Henderson," he said, his squint sliding across the room.

*

SHORTLY AFTER LUNCHEON, MINK SAT at her desk, still irritated at having got nowhere with Silas Sparrowgrass. She stared at her list of suspects, which had grown longer now that she knew Pooki had left the back door open when she disappeared for her mysterious walk. Anyone could have opened the door in the garden wall, snuck across the lawn, and into the house. Pooki had seen both Lady Montfort Bebb and the Keeper of the Maze in the vicinity that morning. Was it the keeper? After all, he had been interested enough in the General's death to attend the inquest. As she considered him, she was suddenly struck by the silence in the house. She raised her head and listened. There had been none of the usual sounds of Pooki moving around, nor had she come in with the post. Wondering what she was up to, she went down to the kitchen, but all she found was Victoria stalking a beetle. After searching the house, she climbed the unfamiliar attic stairs to the servants' quarters. Pushing open a door, she found Pooki sitting on the edge of a single iron bed. Underneath was a pile of old newspapers, used as extra blankets. She was holding a photograph of her mother, so worn from sea crossings that the woman's image was scarcely visible. Next to her was an open suitcase containing bundles of letters from India tied with string, a pair of sandals, some books, a crucifix, and the Maharaja's visiting card showing him dressed in his father's gold robes and pantaloons, an ornamental dagger tucked into the waistband. The Princess thought of the last time she had seen him wearing it: lying in his coffin with the waxy pallor of death. She stared at the only person left to her. "You're not leaving, are you?" she asked, horrified.

The servant looked at her, the hollows under her eyes even

more pronounced. "I am getting my things ready for when they take me away, ma'am. Will you send the case to my mother when I am gone? She is not a Christian, but she might be able to sell my crucifix. And while it will be hard to find a woman with feet as large as mine, I would like her to have my sandals nonetheless."

"But nobody's going to take you away," the Princess protested.

"Ma'am," she said quietly. "They are going to hang me."

The Princess swallowed, suddenly realising how much she loved her for all that she was: stubborn, superstitious, and as loyal as a mother.

"They'll have to hang me before they hang you," Mink said, her voice uneven.

They continued to look at each other until Mink dropped her gaze and headed for the door. "Put that suitcase away," she said. "You're not going anywhere. I'll find out who poisoned the General and put a stop to this nonsense."

*

WITH POOKI'S SUITCASE BACK UNDER the bed, the two women headed for Hampton Court Green.

"It is very good of you to offer to take me to the fair, ma'am," the maid said, her mood already lifted. "I know how much you dislike such things."

"I'll grit my teeth, given the circumstances," replied Mink, hoping she would bump into one of her suspects.

It wasn't long before the full gaiety of the Easter carnival hit them. Into the resolutely blue sky rose a colourful helter-skelter, down which shrieking children slid. Women sat side-saddle on a steam-powered merry-go-round, the trimmings on their hats fluttering as the horses dipped and rose, their red nostrils flaring. Above the sound of the blind fiddlers and hurdy-gurdy players came shouts from the showmen, shiny rings on their fingers, luring visitors to the coconut shies, the shooting galleries, and the ghost show, the carved winged demons on its ornate frontage casting sinister shadows.

The Princess and the maid stood watching a group of men in boating costumes throw sticks at the clay pipe of an Aunt Sally, a wooden figure of a woman. Moving on, they came across a sea-on-land roundabout, where ships pitched and dipped as if travelling a wild ocean. Pooki immediately asked whether she could have a ride, and they sat next to each other in a vessel with a white sail. Mink clung on, hoping that no one would see her, while the servant sat with her hands in her lap, remembering her time as an ayah.

They wandered through the crowds, stopping the muffin and crumpet maker so that Pooki could try his fare. As the maid nibbled, she noticed a red-and-white tent and headed towards it. Mink followed, looking round for any of her suspects.

"It is a wild animal show with rare and savage beasts from the most impenetrable jungles and forests of the world!" exclaimed Pooki, reading the sign. "We must see them, ma'am."

They joined the huddle in front of a man in a frayed silk top hat adorned with a string of large, ivory-coloured incisors. With his thumbs in the pockets of his strained green waistcoat, he announced that the last living example of the world's rarest creature, the long-legged golden lyrebird, was in the tent behind him. In a voice more penetrating than an omnibus conductor's, he warned that no loud noises were to be made, lest the notoriously timid bird die of shock, bringing the species to a tragic end. For centuries, the barbs of its feathers had been spun into a gold thread used to embellish the wedding gowns of Arabian princesses. Its voice, which could only be heard in springtime, was said to be the most beautiful sound ever heard by man. As a result, the Ottomans had put them into baskets and carried them into battle, opening the wicker doors the moment they met their enemy. Pacified by the tender rhapsody, they would drop their guard, enabling the Ottomans to wield their devastating swords. The trick was so successful that they ruled for more than six centuries. But such was the breed's delicate constitution, the showman hollered, it had all but died out. Much to his amazement, the only remaining specimen had just that morning laid an egg. Despite its incalculable value to collectors around the world, in honour of the holy festival of Easter, he had decided to give it to a member of the audience.

"Ma'am, I have never seen a long-legged golden lyrebird," said Pooki, turning to her mistress. "We must go inside. And if I am given the egg, I will sell it and settle all the bills. Then they will stop sending you those letters."

"Maybe the reason why you've never seen a long-legged golden lyrebird is because they don't exist," suggested Mink, her eyebrows raised.

"They must do, ma'am, as even the Ottomans knew about them," said Pooki, her eyes wide. "You think ghosts do not exist either, but my grandmother comes often to my room. Even if I have managed to sleep through her visit, I know she has been because the room smells of cardamom in the morning. I was hoping she might not know I had moved to Hampton Court Palace, but she found me."

The Princess sighed.

Pooki stuck out her chin. "We need that bird's egg, ma'am."

With a glance at the man's patched coat, the Princess reluctantly paid him their penny entrance fees, and he pulled the door flap to one side with a flourish. Entering the unsavoury-smelling gloom, they made out several cages stacked round the edge of the tent, and went over to look at the contents. As Pooki peered at the swans and ducks, the Princess muttered: "I bet they got this lot from Leadenhall Market."

The maid sat down in the row of seats closest to the stage, followed by Mink holding a handkerchief to her nose to mask the stench. As they waited, Pooki wondered out loud whether there would be an Indian elephant, as she hadn't seen one since the Maharaja's funeral. Suddenly a spotlight appeared on the faded green velvet curtains, and a familiar-looking man walked onto the stage, wearing an old red hunting jacket. As he delivered his introduction, the Princess tried to remember where she knew him from, catching the odd phrase including "an extremely cunning animal that I personally saved from the cooking pot of a man-eating tribe in Ceylon."

The curtains parted, and the man thrust his arm at the still empty stage. Two porcupines eventually sauntered on, a pair of hands flapping behind them from the wings. After their initial steps, the creatures stopped and looked at the audience. Suddenly there was the sound of a boot banging on the floorboards, and they scuttled to the other side, their quills raised. Next up was a zebra, ridden bareback by a smiling dwarf in a red turban and matching harem trousers. It was followed by a kangaroo, which made only a brief appearance before hopping back the way it came. It wasn't long before the man in the second-hand jacket reappeared and called for silence. In a voice Mink was certain could be heard in Kingston, he announced the entrance of the long-legged golden lyrebird, which could die in an instant of fright. The audience shuffled forward on their seats and craned their heads as he wheeled on a box draped with black velvet, on top of which stood the avian marvel. As they peered at the creature with the large bill, the bird stared back, blinked, then cocked a knee backwards. Instantly the Princess recognised one of her father's flamingos, still shimmering from a diet of goldfish. Suddenly there was the noise of a handle being turned off stage, followed by the strains of a house sparrow, as the miracle's beak remained irrefutably closed. Once the applause had died, the man who had shaved off his mangy beard that was no match for that of his pygmy goat plunged his hand into his pocket. He drew from it a brown chicken egg, admired it in the light like a flawless ruby, and presented it to Pooki with a low bow.

As they stood outside, the stunned maid cradling the prize in both hands, the Princess suddenly spotted the Keeper of the Maze, instantly recognisable by his Piccadilly weepers. Thrusting a penny at Pooki for some gingerbread, she told her to meet her by the skittles, and hurried after William Sheepshanks. If she were going to get to the bottom of the case, she would have to get on everyone's good side, including his. Wondering how to tackle the keeper, she threaded through the crowds, following his bowler hat until she found herself outside the ghost show. With a glance at the panels depicting the terrifying scenes that could be witnessed within, she lifted her skirts and climbed the steps to the pay-box. She found the keeper inside, and sat down at the back behind him as the front benches began to fill. Eventually the organ stopped and the torn curtains opened with a squeak. William Sheepshanks quivered each time the spectre appeared, courtesy of an actor below floor level reflected onto the stage with the help of a light and a sheet of plated glass. He forgot to breathe when the Ghost of Christmas Past stood perilously close to Scrooge, gripped the bench until his knuckles turned white when a wispy King Hamlet beckoned his son to follow him with a long, bony finger, and almost fainted when the spirit of Napoléon I drew his sword and looked in his direction.

When it was over, the audience begged for more, then reluctantly got to its feet. Still trembling, William Sheepshanks was just about to return his hat to his head when Mink introduced herself and asked whether he was the Keeper of the Maze. He flushed, having been caught away from his post on one of the busiest days of the year.

"I thought it was you, Mr. Sheepshanks," she said, with a smile. "I'm so pleased to see that you've taken some time off. You poor man. All I hear all day is you giving those hopeless visitors directions out of the maze. What do these people do? Leave their brains at home before they set off for the palace? Why, some of them don't even know their left from their right!"

He looked at her and blinked. "You're right, Your Highness. They don't," he replied. "I shout left and they turn right, and then they blame me when they're still stuck in there half an hour later and they've missed the last launch to London Bridge."

The Princess shook her head. "Silly oafs! And once you've kindly shown them the way out, do they thank you for it? No!"

William Sheepshanks stared at her. "How did you know, Your Highness?" he asked.

Mink threw up her hands in despair. "I've watched them from my windows, Mr. Sheepshanks."

"Some even try to tunnel their way out!"

"With the state of that hedging?" the Princess asked, eyes wide. "The maze needs replanting, if you ask me. I bet the palace won't pay for it to be done. And there's you having to defend it to all those rude people who say they've got healthier weeds in their gardens and ask to be let in for free. You should take the whole week off, Mr. Sheepshanks, not just the afternoon!"

The keeper put his hat on the bench next to him and explained that he never expected to end up on a chair exposed to the vagaries of the English weather, giving instructions to people who had no sense of direction. He had followed his father into service, starting off as an under-groom to a Field Marshal. He worked his way up, eventually becoming the youngest footman in the palace. When the valet was dismissed after being caught with the butler in the attics, the Field Marshal offered him the position, which entitled him to his master's discarded clothes, a lucrative perquisite. When the old man became ill, shortly after the death of his wife, it was William Sheepshanks who carried him up and down the stairs. When things worsened, he organised the sick room, sleeping in a chair next to his master's bed, and fetching another handkerchief when he coughed up blood. But nothing could save him, and he died clutching the servant's hand. "He'd always been very gener-ous, and left me enough money to open a small shop. I'd even chosen it. But his relatives disputed the will on the grounds of insanity. None of them had visited him for years. He was as sane as you and me."

He wanted nothing to do with the upper classes then, and, without a care for the fall in status, applied for the position of Keeper of the Maze. The palace authorities liked the idea of a valet being in charge, as his predecessor, a gardener, had been over-possessive of the hedging, leading to complaints from visitors about being lectured. Such was his elation when he was given the job, he bought everyone in the King's Arms a drink, including the drunk woman who sold pig's trotters. After so many years spent indoors on his feet, which had given him varicose veins and the hue of the dead, he sighed with contentment as he sat in his chair in the tender spring sun, listening to the melodies of the birds. In the summer he was warmed further by the happiness of the excursionists, and thanked the Lord every night in his prayers. As autumn approached and the evenings darkened, he grew a pair of whiskers to keep out the damp, and marvelled as the leaves turned gold in front of his eyes. And when the first snow fell, he tilted back his head and caught the spiralling flakes on his tongue.

Initially he found his income, made up of the penny entry fees, entirely sufficient. But when his mother became ill, there was not enough to cover the medical costs, and he started to allow people into the maze after hours to earn a little extra. Eventually he was found out, hauled before the Lord Chamberlain, and given a fixed salary. But it failed to match his previous gains, and he was forced to use the homeopath from East Molesey. "Mother died shortly afterwards," he said. "I was on duty at the time. The neighbours came to get me, as she'd stopped crying out with pain."

The Princess offered her condolences. "How were you found out?" she asked, watching him closely.

"One of the residents heard someone laughing in the maze when it should have been closed, and wrote to the Lord Chamberlain. I'd told them to keep it down, but they'd just been to the King's Arms," he replied.

"Fancy writing to the Lord Chamberlain, Mr. Sheepshanks. What a spiteful thing to do," she said. After a pause she asked lightly, "Who was it?"

The keeper looked away. "It's not something I care to talk about," he said.

Suddenly one of the actors entered. "You'll have to pay if you want to see it again," he said. "Unfortunately there won't be any ghosts. The man who plays them has just been brawling with the sherbet seller, who's not as puny as he looks."

As Mink made her way back to Pooki, she wondered whether it was the General who had complained to the Lord Chamberlain. It certainly seemed the sort of thing the dead man would have done. Had the keeper refused to name him, knowing that it would instantly give him a motive? She was still debating how to discover the resident's name when she found Pooki a short distance from the skittles booth, gazing at a sign propped up outside a small, filthy tent.

"Madam Sharkey, the world-famous fortune-teller, has come here all the way from Mesopotamia!" the servant said excitedly. "Mole-reading is her speciality. I would like my mole read, ma'am."

"I bet she's come all the way from Whitechapel," muttered Mink. "And anyway, I can tell you precisely what's going to happen to you. Absolutely nothing."

"You do know quite a few things, ma'am, it is true. But you do not know everything like the world-famous Madam Sharkey."

"She can't be that famous. I've never heard of her. Wouldn't you rather go and see the mermaids?" she asked, looking round at the other tents.

The maid stuck out her chin. "No, ma'am. I have seen mermaids before. They are women with tails instead of legs. I want to see my future."

Drawing back the tent flap with the tips of her fingers, Mink entered, followed closely by Pooki. Sitting behind a table was a heavily lined woman, smoking a clay pipe and wearing an ill-fitting wig. Several glittering chains hung down into her battered cleavage. But the carats were no match for those in her head. For when Madam Sharkey removed her instrument and smiled a bored greeting, she revealed two rows of golden teeth. Pooki sat down next to her mistress, her eyes not leaving the woman's mouth for an instant.

"I knew you'd come," said the fortune-teller, with the mangled vowels of a cockney.

"Your talent is exceptional, Madam Sharkey. We've only just decided ourselves," said the Princess. "I was wondering if you'd be so kind as to tell my maid her fortune."

The woman slowly unfurled her palm, revealing stained nails that curled like cat claws. The Princess dropped into it a piece of silver that immediately vanished.

"So, 'ave you got a mole?" the woman asked, turning to Pooki.

The maid nodded, clutching the egg in her lap.

"Where is it?" she asked.

Pooki didn't reply.

"It ain't time to be modest. Where's your mole?" demanded Madam Sharkey.

"It is on my thigh."

"Lemme see."

Pooki hesitated.

"I needs to see what shape it is," the clairvoyant insisted. "If it's round, you can expect plenty of good fortune. If it's got angles, a mixture of good and bad. And God 'elp you if it's oblong. The deeper the colour, the deeper the good or bad luck will be. Then, of course, there's the question of whether the thing's 'airy or not. A bald mole indicates good 'ealth. If it's got a few long 'airs, it means you can leave service 'cos there's prosperity on the way. And if it's a sprouter, then I'm afraid to say your goose is well and truly cooked."

Slowly Pooki stood up, hitched up her dress and petticoats, and raised her knicker leg. Madam Sharkey shuffled round the table and bent down, both knees cracking.

"Just as I thought," she muttered. "A stubborn character." She peered even closer. "The shape and colour indicate someone who will fall in love, and 'er love will be reciprocated. However, this is a secret love, and there will be all 'ell to pay when it's found out. Now, as for the question of 'airs . . ."

Pooki interrupted her. "I do not want my mole read after all, Madam Sharkey. I, like my mistress, do not believe in such nonsense. I would like my dreams interpreted. That is what I believe in."

Madam Sharkey hauled herself up again, clutching the table. Returning to her chair, she unfurled her hand and looked at the Princess. Mink held her gaze through the tobacco smoke, and slowly dropped another coin.

"So, what do you dream of?" the woman asked, sitting back with her arms crossed over her collapsed bosom.

Pooki thought for a moment. "Last night I dreamt of milk," she said.

"Love affairs," replied Madam Sharkey.

"The night before it was myrtle."

"Declaration of love," she shot back.

"But most often of all I dream of nightingales."

"An 'appy and well-assorted marriage."

Pooki gripped the egg to almost cracking point. "I have just remembered that, like my mistress, I do not believe in the interpretation of dreams. It is just trickery. Tarot cards. That is what I believe in."

The East End prophet looked at Mink, who returned her gaze, tapping a coin slowly on the table before sliding it to her.

Drawing a pack of grubby cards from her pocket, Madam Sharkey shuffled them, muttering what could have been a shopping list. As the woman cut them, she asked Pooki to think of the question she wanted answering. She then spread four cards on the table, and turned one over. All three women looked at the grim reaper.

"I don't think you shuffled the cards correctly, Madam Sharkey. Would you mind doing so again?" asked Mink.

"That's what I calls cheating, but if you insist," the fortune-teller replied, scooping the cards towards her, and shuffling them into the pack. As she cut them, she asked Pooki to think once more of the question, then dealt again.

All three women stared at the same card.

The soothsayer adjusted her wig. "Best of three?" she asked, with scarcely a glimmer of gold.

When the skeleton and scythe appeared for the third time, Madam Sharkey quickly picked up the cards with trembling hands. Reaching into her skirt pocket, she pulled out the coins and handed them back to the Princess with an entreaty never to return.

"What stuff and nonsense," said Mink, once they were outside. "Let's see what else there is. I saw a booth of marvels earlier."

But as they approached, Pooki had no interest in the five-legged pig, the tattooed couple having tea, or the perpetually sobbing man.

"How about a false nose?" asked the Princess, spotting the hawker. "They usually cheer you up. I still remember that All Fools' Day when you woke me up wearing one, and I got you back by asking you to tell the cook I wanted some plaice without spots."

"I do not want a false nose, ma'am," said the servant, her head lowered.

Mink glanced at her. "Why don't you tell me one of the butter-man's jokes?" she suggested, bracing herself for the torment.

The servant shook her head, and they continued wandering round the fair. It was a while before she spoke again.

"They will make a waxwork of me, ma'am, and put it in Madame Tussaud's Chamber of Horrors with all the other murderers."

The Princess glanced at her. "They would never find enough wax for your feet," she joked.

But Pooki didn't smile. "When will you find out who did it, ma'am?" she asked, her head still lowered.

"Soon," replied Mink, looking away to hide her unease.

Pooki turned to her. "How soon is soon, ma'am?"

The Princess didn't reply.

"If it is all right with you, ma'am, I would like to go home now," said the servant.

As they started back towards the palace, passing the sherbet seller and the fire-eater, Pooki peered at a group of men. "There is that doctor who soaked your walking costume, ma'am," she said. "I do not know whether it will ever recover."

Mink looked over and saw Dr. Henderson at the try-your-strength machine. The mistress and the maid stopped to watch as he lifted the mallet and brought it down. The puck limped up without the slightest sound from the bell and fell. He tried again, but it rose even less high than before. The soldiers standing behind him, who had just come out of a drinking booth, started to jeer. Abandoning the hammer, he walked off to the neighbouring stand as the bell finally sounded, courtesy of one of the soldiers. Passing a coin to the showman, he picked up a rifle and aimed it at the display of clay pipes. But after several attempts they remained irrefutably intact.

"Excuse me for a minute while I put that man out of his misery," Mink said to Pooki.

She walked over, took the gun from him, and aimed. Immediately the pipe in the middle of the top row shattered. The moment of silence that followed was soon drowned by rowdy applause and calls for the Princess to have another go. She looked the doctor in the eye, handed him back the weapon, and disappeared into the crowd without a word. He watched her until she was out of sight, and was so lost in his thoughts he failed to hear Silas Sparrowgrass offering him a pair of spectacles for his next attempt.

CHAPTER X

The Impolite Shooting of Lady Montfort Bebb

EWS spread as fast as one of the palace fires that Mrs. Bagshot had returned. After her carriage was spotted drawing up at Trophy Gate, word reached her neighbours at the back of the monument before her and her extensive luggage. Shortly afterwards, one of her maids was seen in the post office sending a telegram to Peter Robinson, Jay's rival in Regent Street. Its black carriage duly arrived, bearing a chalk-faced female assistant sitting amongst a morose swamp of mourning paraphernalia, including ready-made dresses, gloves, mantles, and widow's bonnets.

Glancing at the carriage, Mink climbed into the waiting fly and asked the driver to take her to Dr. Frogmore's practice in Thames Ditton. As she settled back, she wondered again whether General Bagshot had said anything significant to him in his last moments alive. Perhaps he had confided in the doctor, telling him a secret that the medical man hadn't revealed at the inquest with all the reporters there. Almost certainly he would be more reliable than Silas Sparrowgrass, whom, given his mendacity and dislike of the General, she had promptly added to her list of suspects, his only saving grace being his adoration of his rabbit. Glancing back at the mourning carriage, she wondered whether she really would be able to discover who had killed the widow's husband. Her stomach turned as she imagined what might happen if she failed to do so. She then thought of everyone else she had lost: her mother, her day-old sister, her father, and finally Mark Cavendish. As the tide of abandonment threatened to engulf her, she turned to face the front and contemplated the view to distract herself.

She didn't have to wait to see Dr. Frogmore. Since his spectacular misdiagnosis had been reported in the newspapers, not even lowering his fees had enticed all of his patients back. His waiting room was as deserted as his bald head, and he sat with the haunted look of the ruined at his dusty desk, piled with dirty dishes. Wearing her most frivolous hat, and an extra dab of Penhaligon's Hamman Bouquet eau de toilette, Mink lowered herself into the seat opposite him. She reached into her bag and drew out a box of Charbonnel et Walker chocolates, one of three rapid purchases she had made in the West End that morning. Placing it on the desk in front of her, she opened it eagerly, then gazed at the selection, a finger on her chin as she deliberated.

"I think I'll try the Butter Fourré," she declared. "All that butter and chocolate ganache . . ." She popped it in her mouth. "Oh, my," she murmured, her eyes closed. "Such heaven!" The general practitioner swallowed, looking from her to the chocolates.

Suddenly she opened her eyes and trained them on her prey. "Dr. Frogmore," she said, with a smile even sweeter than her lure. "I saw you at the General's inquest and was struck by your integrity. I have no time for quacks or homeopaths, which, in my mind, are one in the same."

The doctor beamed.

"I was wondering whether you possibly have a cure for corpulence?" she asked, her head tilted to one side.

The doctor scratched his stomach, which reached his desk long before the rest of him. "I recommend the Banting System, Princess, which you've no doubt heard of. It prohibits sugar, fat, and starch," he said, in his high-pitched voice. "Don't let the fact that Mr. Banting was an undertaker put you off. He moved in the right circles: he built the Duke of Wellington's coffin. Of course I add a little twist of my own, which my patients find most beneficial. I advocate the drinking of vinegar and thorough mastication," he said, his eyes flicking to the chocolates. "But the patient will have to come to see me in person."

"I am the patient," Mink replied coyly.

The doctor looked her up and down admiringly. "But, Princess, you are not in the least corpulent. Au contraire."

Mink put a hand on the desk and leant forward. "Dr. Frogmore," she said, her eyes wide. "I am on my way to being so, and when I get there I want to be ready. There are certain things in life that one cannot, and should not, resist, and Charbonnel et Walker chocolates are one of them."

She lowered her eyes to the box and pondered. "It will have to be the English Violet Cream," she said, picking it up and pushing it through her rouged lips. She chewed slowly, then murmured, her tongue thick with flowery fondant: "So traditional, yet so exotic."

The doctor dabbed his forehead with his handkerchief.

"For years I've resisted their establishment," the Princess continued. "Then one day I was buying a fan in New Bond Street and went in on a whim." She held up a hand. "Do not venture through their door, doctor, if you wish to keep your comely figure. I have hardly been out of the place since, and my corsets are quite tight. We ladies must keep ourselves trim, trim, trim, unlike you gentlemen, who remain so utterly desirable whatever your size," she added from underneath her lashes.

Dr. Frogmore lowered his numerous chins and smiled as he turned a faint shade of pink. He kept his eyes on her as he slowly opened a drawer, groped inside for a sheet explaining the diet, and passed it to her. "Masticate thoroughly, and don't drink anything during meals so when the food is swallowed it becomes mixed with undiluted gastric secretions," he advised, with a glance at the open box. "And drink lots of vinegar, of course."

The Princess handed him some coins, but he refused them with a waggle of a finger and a flash of his dimples. "There's no fee for you, my Princess."

She quickly folded up the sheet and stuffed it into her bag. "Thank God there's always tomorrow," she declared, and bit tenderly into her next selection. The doctor swallowed at the sound of the breaking chocolate. "The Crown, my favourite!" she oozed, her eyes half closed. "Chocolate, hazelnuts, butter, marzipan, and whisky. What bliss!" She turned her gaze on the doctor, holding the other half aloft. "Did you know that the Prince of Wales met Madame Charbonnel in Paris and was so impressed by her chocolates he encouraged her to come to London to make them here?"

The general practitioner, who was trying to catch a glimpse of the Crown's succulent centre, shook his head. The Princess put it into her mouth and chewed loudly. "I can quite understand why he was so desperate to get that woman over here," she said, licking her fingers. Leaning towards him, she added: "What a pity they don't have a branch in Thames Ditton. You'd have to take the train all the way to Charing Cross, then struggle through the traffic, if suddenly you were gripped by the urge to try one."

She got up to leave, holding the box. The doctor flicked his eyes between the patient and her purchase, unable to decide which departure he regretted most. Suddenly, she sank back down again and leant forward, emitting a waft of Hamman Bouquet. "Speaking of the inquest, doctor, I was rather struck by your insistence that the symptoms of English cholera resemble those of arsenic poisoning. I wondered whether that really was the case. So I went into a bookshop this morning and picked up a copy of *Principles of Forensic Medicine* written by those professors," she said, bringing the book out of her bag. "And here it is on page five hundred and thirty," she continued, flicking through to the passage and reading from it. "It says that the symptoms so closely resemble those of English cholera as to avert suspicion from the minds even of intelligent and well-informed physicians." Mink sat back. "Why, that's you, Dr. Frogmore. Intelligent *and* well informed. What hope was there of your knowing that the General had been poisoned? Absolutely none! And there was everyone at the inquest looking at you as if you had single-handedly sullied the name of the entire medical profession. You are completely vindicated in my mind, doctor, and I shall tell all my friends."

The general practitioner held his head in his hands. "Any doctor would have made the same diagnosis," he despaired. "The General wasn't even grateful for my help. He kept shouting at me, telling me how useless I was. Frankly, I'm glad I'll never have the opportunity to meet him again."

The Princess bit into an English Rose Cream and pointed to the doctor with the remains, flashing its pink centre. "I must say, I never took to him either," she said, finishing the chocolate. Suddenly she held a hand to her cheek. "I wonder what he said when he was dying, Dr. Frogmore!" she exclaimed. Slowly she pushed the box towards him. "People always like to get things off their chest in their final hour. At least they do in all those silly novels I devour."

The doctor watched the box approach. "He didn't talk much, except to insult me," he muttered.

"Did he call out the name of a lover?" she gasped. "Do tell, Dr. Frogmore. You know how we ladies love to fill our heads with romance."

His tongue traced his bottom lip. "It would be a breach of trust if I told you," he insisted.

The box suddenly came to a stop. "Come, come, doctor," she coaxed, tilting her head. "The brute is dead! Perhaps he knew too much and had to be silenced. Did he curse his enemies with his final breath? They seem to do that a lot in books."

Dr. Frogmore swallowed. "He did say one thing," he said, gazing at the chocolates.

She slid them towards him. "Yes?" she asked, eyes wide.

The doctor reached over with his sausage fingers and snatched one. "How bitterly he regretted being under the care of the homeopath from East Molesey."

*

POOKI OPENED THE FRONT DOOR with a frown. "I have seen the new hair comb in your room, ma'am," she said, her voice croaky, stepping back to let in her mistress. "You must have bought it this morning."

"I spotted it in a window in New Bond Street. I couldn't believe how cheap it was," Mink replied, with a dismissive wave of the hand. The maid raised her eyebrows as she closed the door behind her. "I do not think so, ma'am. Nothing is cheap in New Bond Street, as we know from the many times we have been there. It looks like real tortoiseshell."

Mink let out a short, sharp sigh. "I had to buy real tortoiseshell. There was a story in the paper about a lady who was curling her fringe with some tongs and the celluloid comb she was wearing exploded with the heat. You don't want me to die, do you?"

Pooki shook her head. "No, ma'am. I do not. You have to find out who killed the General. How did it go with Dr. Frogmore?"

The Princess walked to the mirror and unpinned her hat. "Fine, thank you," she replied curtly.

"I hope so, ma'am," said the servant, standing next to her and looking at her reflection. "I hope that 'fine' does not mean he did not tell you anything useful, like that homeopath yesterday. Apparently the Inspector is in the palace asking questions. Gibbs, the grocer's boy, told me. He said he was surprised to see me, as he thought I would have been arrested by now."

Wishing she had never told her about her consultation with Silas Sparrowgrass, the Princess thrust her the hat and strode to the study. She sat down and opened her silver cigarette case engraved with a woman riding on top of an elephant hunting tigers, a present from her father. Too agitated to sit, she smoked, looking out of the window, thinking about her three new friends, whom she had invited for tea in the hope that something might slip out. It was Lady Montfort Bebb she particularly wanted to probe. There was something behind that piano playing. Why had a woman of her convictions been so affronted by the General's complaints? She then looked at her watch, stubbed out her cigarette, and rang the bell for Pooki to help her change.

*

"EXCELLENT," CONCLUDED LADY MONTFORT BEBB, returning her cup to its saucer. "So many people serve tea that's far too strong these days. It's quite out of fashion."

"The trick is to ask the servants to bring it up as soon as it's made," Mink replied, sitting opposite her at a small table covered with a white linen cloth in the drawing room.

Lady Beatrice picked up her cup. "Dr. Henderson says that tea wreaks terrible damage on the body," she said, taking a sip. She turned to the Countess, the pale blue ostrich feathers on her hat dancing with the sudden movement. "I expect he's spoken at length about it to you, my dear."

"I've never admitted that I drink it. I'm quite aware of his stance," the Countess replied, biting into a piece of rolled bread and butter.

Lady Beatrice leant towards her. "There should be no secrets between a man and a woman. Neither, I hasten to add, between old friends. What are friends for if you can't share with them the secrets of the heart?"

"Quite so," replied the Countess, easing the bonnet ribbons under her chin to make it more comfortable to eat.

"Speaking of friends," said Lady Montfort Bebb. "I understand Mrs. Bagshot has ordered her mourning cards, so we will no doubt hear from her shortly. It's been such a dreadful business, what with the disinterment. At least her being away meant she missed her husband's second coming."

The Countess helped herself to some seed cake. "I spotted her on the way to the cemetery earlier," she said. "I've never seen such a smartly cut cape. I felt quite shown up. Mourning wear is so in keeping with fashion these days that if it weren't for the crape one wouldn't have the faintest clue that a lady was bereaved. But Mrs. Bagshot has always had such immaculate taste. I didn't have to do a thing to her apartments when we swapped. And, of course, she's done nothing to mine," she added, with a smile.

"Perhaps she hasn't had time," muttered Lady Montfort Bebb.

Lady Beatrice looked at the Countess. "I expect you'll be out of mourning shortly," she said.

The Countess blinked. "I see no need."

"And what, may I ask, does Dr. Henderson say of that?"

"I've not discussed it with him," she replied, frowning. "It's none of his concern."

Mink watched them, her eyes moving from one lady to the other. Clearing her throat, she said, "I understand Inspector Guppy was at the palace earlier. Does anyone know whom he questioned?"

"Well, it wasn't me," said Lady Montfort Bebb, the skin underneath her chin wobbling with indignation. "No one could possibly suspect me of creeping around with a bottle of poison like an aggrieved maid." She looked at Mink. "I'm glad to see that you've still managed to hang on to yours. Everyone is adamant she'll be arrested at any moment. I do wish that grubby little policeman would get on with it and charge someone. The suspense is killing me."

The Princess picked up her cup. "I expect he wants to make

sure he gets it right this time. He made a mistake in his last case and the wrong person was hanged."

"Let's hope she's spared the hangman," said Lady Beatrice, holding her hand up to her neck. "Such an unfortunate way to go."

Pooki, who had just entered with a plate of macaroons, placed them on the table with a trembling hand. The ladies kept their eyes lowered until she had closed the door again.

Lady Beatrice leant forwards and whispered loudly, "I'm convinced it was Mr. Pilgrim. The watchman told my cook that he's always sneaking about the palace at night. They caught him in Base Court last night carrying a ball of string, which I suspect was to garrotte someone. I've already made my findings known to the police."

Lady Montfort Bebb put down her cup, her nostrils flared. "That American tried to shoot me last night!" she said.

All three women turned and stared.

"I'd just got out of the push in Fountain Court and suddenly he appeared from the shadows with a gun," she continued. "His aim was rather woeful, but I hit him with my cane nonetheless. I, too, shall be informing Guppy of his behaviour, though how that policeman can spot a clue and yet remain oblivious to his less-than-immaculate collars is beyond me."

"Why would he point a gun at you?" Mink asked.

"I have no idea. But if there's one thing in life I'm used to, it's being shot at."

The Princess studied her, wondering. "I understand you were held hostage during the First Afghan War," she said. "What an ordeal."

It was so long ago, she replied, glancing out of the window, but the worst memories were just as vivid. "Four and a half thousand British and Indian troops and twelve thousand camp followers massacred. The horror of it . . ."

In 1839 an imperial force of about twenty thousand men invaded

Afghanistan, accompanied by thirty-eight thousand servants and supporters, she explained. Eventually they reached Kabul, and as regiments settled into garrison life, their families were summoned to join them. Lady Montfort Bebb was newly married and had just turned twenty. "Things were made as pleasant as they could be, considering where we were. There was horse racing, cricket, and polo."

Eventually a rebellion against the British broke out and it was decided that the entire garrison in Kabul would leave in return for a promise of safe conduct to Jalalabad, eighty-five miles away. More than a hundred personnel, mainly married officers and their families, were forced to remain behind as hostages, she explained.

In January 1842 four and a half thousand fighting men and twelve thousand civilian men, women, and children started the journey, the snow thick on the ground. Most of the ladies were carried in litters and palanquins at the front, while Lady Montfort Bebb rode with them on horseback. The rear guard was fired upon as soon as it left the cantonments. Sepoys and camp followers were slain, and some dropped out of the column, waiting to be killed or die from the cold. Babies were scattered on the snow, abandoned by their mothers, who lay dying further on. Some of the soldiers and camp followers, with neither fire nor shelter, froze to death that first night. "I'll never forget the cold. Even the cavalry had to be lifted onto their horses, as they could hardly move."

With so many bearers dead, the ladies could no longer be carried, and most sat in panniers slung on camels, some with their children, exposed to the continuing gunshot. "A number were only wearing nightdresses. We started drinking sherry to keep out the cold." The slaughter began when they entered the five-mile-long Khoord Kabul pass. "I was shot in the leg. I was fortunate. About five hundred soldiers and more than two and a half thousand camp followers perished."

Three days after they set out, she continued, the Afghan leader proposed that the ladies and children be made over to his protection, and that the married officers accompanied their wives. "Some of the ladies were nursing babies only a few days old." It was agreed, and the rest continued on towards Jalalabad. But only one man survived the ensuing carnage, arriving alone and exhausted, to the shock of his waiting comrades, who asked where the army was.

The hostages were marched along a road strewn with bodies, some of whom they recognised. "A number were still alive, frostbitten and out of their minds." For nearly three months they were held in five filthy rooms in Budiabad, up to ten in each one. Others slept in sheds and cellars. "We were allowed to take a little exercise, and had a few packs of playing cards. Some made backgammon boards." In April they were moved on and stayed near Kabul in much better conditions. There was even a garden. "But our anxiety never ended." At the end of August they were moved again, this time to Bamian and back to squalor. They were finally rescued in September.

"My husband also survived, but died two years later in battle," she said, her head lowered. "I never married again. The pain of losing him was too great."

There was silence as Lady Montfort Bebb's gaze drifted back to the window. The other women looked at the tablecloth.

All the time that they were held hostage, they never knew whether they were going to be killed from one day to the next, she continued. It was the simple things she missed most, such as playing the piano. She had never been particularly proficient, and vowed to take lessons if she lived. Once released, such was her guilt for having survived, she devoted herself to charity work, which she still carried out. "The day I stop will be the day I die."

It was only recently, on realising that she was towards the end of her life, that she remembered the promise she had made to herself, and she started taking piano lessons. "Each time I play, I play in memory of those sixteen thousand people who were butchered or froze to death, and I hope they would think I had done something worthwhile with my life which fate, for some reason, spared," she said.

*

DR. HENDERSON WAS WASHING HIS thermometer, wondering what to wear to the fancy dress ball, when Mrs. Boots shot in and sat down in the chair in front of his desk.

"I fear there's something awful wrong with me, doctor," she said, her eyes wide.

Once her coughing had subsided, he listened to her lungs. Returning to his seat, he advised immediate bed rest, as well as frequent applications of mustard and linseed poultices to the back and front of the chest. "Each should be left in place for at least half an hour, followed by fresh ones every three or four hours. And take some antimonial wine if you have difficulty bringing up the expectoration, Mrs. Boots," he added, picking up his pen.

The housekeeper looked at him in horror. "I can't be taking to my bed, doctor, I've got too much to do, what with the residents breaking the rules and my having to deal with all their complaints. I've got one lady moaning that her kitchen is across a draughty courtyard and her cook is threatening to leave, and another is convinced that people are bathing naked in the Thames in front of her window."

The doctor started writing out a prescription. "You need a few days' rest, Mrs. Boots."

The housekeeper leant forward. "It's worse than you think, doctor," she insisted.

"How so?" he asked, looking up.

The housekeeper lurched back, gripping her armrests. "I'm seeing things!"

"I'm aware of the recent spate of hauntings at the palace, but such visions are not injurious to the health."

"It's not ghosts I'm seeing."

"What is it?"

The housekeeper blinked. "A monkey."

Dr. Henderson tapped his pen on his desk. "Have you had hallucinations before?" he enquired.

"Several times, doctor," she said, wrapping her shawl more tightly around her. "And it's always the same. A monkey in red velvet trousers sitting on one of the chimney pots."

"While I've advised taking sherry in the past, Mrs. Boots, you must not overdo it. Inebriation is a terrible thing. Too much drink leads to full workhouses, prisons, and asylums, to say nothing of crime, poverty, and mental degeneration. The wholesome benefits of sherry can only be reaped by taking it in moderation, and by making sure you purchase it from a reputable merchant, otherwise there is the risk of adulteration. In retrospect I would suggest that you stay clear of antimonial wine," he said, making out a prescription for camphorated tincture of opium instead. "This is just as effective," he added, handing it to her. "Let's hope that the only monkeys you see in the future are those at the zoo, Mrs. Boots."

Once the housekeeper had left, Dr. Henderson looked up to see the Reverend Grayling in a black suit and white clerical collar entering stiffly. The doctor tried to repress his antipathy of the man. It was bad enough that he refused to heed his warnings about drinking too much, as he was sailing perilously close to gout. But what incensed him more was the clergyman's endorsement of quack remedies, an infuriating habit of ministers of the Church, whom the doctor believed ought to stick to the miracles in the Bible. Much to his irritation, the village chemist had just stuck in his window advertisements of nostrums bearing the chaplain's enthusiastic pronouncements. "No clergyman worthy of his pulpit would be without Dr. Nightingale's Voice Pills," claimed one.

"I truly confess that I am a very great admirer of Mr. Steadfast's Nerve Tonic, which I always take before giving a sermon," stated another. "Gluttony is a sin, and I am trim because of Madame Maigre's Corpulence Pills," pronounced a third.

Holding on to both arms of the chair, the chaplain lowered his considerable girth with a grimace. "It's my knees, doctor," he said, looking at him through tiny spectacles. "I only just made it here."

Asking him to roll up his trouser legs, the general practitioner walked round the desk and gave each knee a gentle squeeze, asking whether it hurt.

"Yes," came the strangled reply.

"Thought it might," said the doctor, returning to his seat, having resisted the urge to give them a second, much harder, pinch. "You have the worst case of housemaid's knee that I've ever come across. Either you're in need of a domestic servant, or you've been overdoing the praying."

The clergyman ran a hand through his neat, grey hair. "I suppose I have been asking for forgiveness a little more than usual."

"Oh, yes?" said the general practitioner, raising an eyebrow. "What exactly have you been up to?"

"Murder," the chaplain replied.

The doctor, well used to being privy to his patients' darkest secrets, kept his composure. "The General's?" he asked.

"No, Mrs. Boots's."

The doctor sat up. "But I've only just seen her."

"Oh, I haven't carried it out," he replied. "I just fantasise about it. The woman doesn't stop meddling. She keeps locking Lord Sluggard out of the chapel. She says his hairs get on the altar cloth."

"Lord Sluggard?" The doctor frowned. "I don't believe I've met him."

"The palace mouser. I've got a terrible problem with rats. And she will insist on locking up the communion wine."

The doctor nodded. "For good reason."

"We all have our vices, doctor, which is just as well, otherwise you and I would be out of a job."

Dr. Henderson explained that treatment involved the application of blister plasters. The irritant they contained would cause the skin to blister, absorption would be induced, and the swelling would disappear. Resting the knees was also vital. "You'll have to pray on your back, I'm afraid," he said, sitting back with his fingers laced. "Just imagine you're one of those tomb effigies in Westminster Abbey."

Once the clergyman had hobbled out, the general practitioner set about preparing himself for his appointment at Wilderness House. After applying pomade to his hair, which instantly sprang back into curls, he put on his new frock coat and looked at himself in the mirror. He turned to one side, and then the other, but there was no escaping the impression of a tailor's assistant suffering the consequences of a surfeit of bachelor's cakes. He then put on his new topper, his heart falling even further as he contemplated the results, and he regretted the unquestionable sanity of his hatter.

Grabbing his pocket instrument case, he peered out of the door, hoping to avoid his housekeeper. Ever since realising that he was the object of Mrs. Nettleship's affections, he had been trying to keep out of her way, fearing he might encourage her. But the more he ignored her, the louder she hummed, until disaster struck and she launched into song without the least regard for anyone's feelings. As the broken notes invaded the waiting room, a cowkeeper went deaf in one ear, an ale taster's blood pressure shot up, and a birdcage-maker declared that life was no longer worth living and left not wanting a cure.

The doctor was just about to close the front door, already congratulating himself on having made a safe getaway, when suddenly it was prevented from moving by a boot.

"You'll be hoff seeing your patients hat the palace, I presume?" said Mrs. Nettleship, her red hair in uproar around her white widow's cap.

"That's right, I'd better not dilly-dally," he replied, taking a step backwards.

Clutching her hands underneath her chin, she asked, "And 'ow his Lady Bessington?"

"Still suffering from acute pteridomania, I'm afraid, but there's nothing much I can do about it."

The housekeeper smiled. "Whatever that condition his, doctor, hit must 'ave been brought hon by love."

"You're quite right, Mrs. Nettleship, pteridomania is all to do with love. Specifically, it's the love of ferns. Fern madness, if you like. She's at an advanced stage, I'm afraid. But as far as obsessions go, it's quite harmless. It gets you out and about in the fresh air in search of specimens, which is good for the constitution," he added, starting down the garden path.

The housekeeper ran to catch up with him. "Love for an holder woman, particularly one what's already lost 'er first 'usband, needs to be 'andled with the most tender hof care. But I fear things haren't progressing, doctor. A widow hin such a position naturally thinks of matrimony."

Dr. Henderson turned to her. "Things are certainly not progressing, Mrs. Nettleship, and it pains me to say this, but they never will. You must understand that."

She clutched his arm. "Maybe there's something I can do to 'elp," she said. "Per'aps I could see hif that new 'atter of yours will give you your money back?"

"There is absolutely nothing you can do," he replied, shaking himself free. "You really must desist. There is nothing between us. Now, if you'll excuse me, I must press on," he added, striding off.

"I won't give hup, doctor," she called after him. "A nice young man like you deserves a widow's hembrace."

*

ONCE THE THREE LADIES HAD left Wilderness House, Mink
went in search of the palace's biggest gossip. She eventually found
Mrs. Boots in the Chapel Royal, polishing the choir stalls. The
organist struck up the moment she called her name, so she tapped
her on the shoulder. The resulting shriek woke Lord Sluggard and
sent him fleeing from the altar in terror, his tail as stiff as a flag
mast.

The housekeeper lowered herself down onto a pew, a hand over
her heart. "Was that a monkey I saw running out, Your Highness?"
she asked.

"No, Mrs. Boots, it was a cat," said Mink, sitting down next to
her. "What a pity it ran out. I do so love animals. If I had my way
I'd have a huge menagerie."

The housekeeper shuddered. "The only animals I like are those
slaughtered and on my plate, preferably with a bit of mustard."

Mink shook her head. "Not me, Mrs. Boots. You should have
seen what I wanted to bring with me to Hampton Court Palace.
Great. Fat. Hissing. Snakes."

The housekeeper turned to her, open-mouthed.

Mink nodded. "Oh, yes. Five of them. Well, I would have
started off with five, but undoubtedly one would have gone missing, and slithered away into someone's bed. Perhaps even yours."

Mrs. Boots slumped back.

"I must confess, I was going to sneak them in, thinking you'd
never notice. But my maid explained that rules were rules, and
there must be a very good reason why pets were forbidden in the
palace. She asked me who I thought I was, thinking that *I* was
above the regulations? Well, she had a point. No one is above the
regulations."

"No one," agreed the stunned housekeeper, looking ahead of
her, still thinking about a reptile in her bed.

"That maid has saved me from myself more times than I care
to remember," Mink continued. "Some mistresses never stop com-

plaining about their domestic servants, but I count my blessings with Pooki. It's most unfair that everyone is pointing a finger at her, just because she's in service. I remember your saying that your mother was a maid at the palace, so you'd know all about the injustice of it all."

Mrs. Boots folded her arms across her billowing bosom. "I feel for that maid of yours, I really do," she said. "Too many servants have taken a fall for the doings of their master or mistress. My mother was once accused of pinching a silk handkerchief when it was her mistress who had dropped it in the carriage. The palace servants are running a sweepstake on who they think did it, and every one of the suspects is a grace-and-favour resident."

The Princess leant towards her. "No one knows the people in this palace better than you, Mrs. Boots, with all the responsibilities you have. Who would you put your money on?"

She thought for a moment. "I'd say any of the grace-and-favour lot was capable of it, apart from Lady Beatrice, despite her harbouring a parrot. That woman has too much taste when it comes to hats to kill anyone. I'm surprised she hasn't been interviewed by that inspector, mind, being as though she bought some arsenic from the chemist not so long ago. His char, a very good friend of mine, looked through his poisons register immediately after the inquest and saw her name on it. Not that I'm a gossip-monger. Now, what was it you wanted?"

*

MINK HADN'T BEEN HOME LONG when Pooki showed the visitor into the drawing room. "Ah, Dr. Henderson, there you are," she said, putting down her notebook and gesturing to the settee opposite her. "Did you come on foot or on that machine of yours?"

"On foot, Princess," he said, his gaze dropping to the floor. "My bicycle needs a little repair work."

"That's a relief. Goodness knows how many walking costumes have been spared." She then beckoned to Pooki, who was still standing hesitantly at the door. "It's my maid who's unwell. She's very hoarse. We've tried Dr. Nightingale's Voice Pills, which the chemist recommended, but they didn't have any effect."

Resisting the urge to comment, he took out his tongue depressor, and asked the servant to open wide. She did as she was told, her eyes seeking the reassurance of her mistress. After peering down her throat, he asked her to speak. The strained reply, enquiring what he wanted her to say, told him all he needed to know.

"I'm afraid you have a rather serious case of clergyman's sore throat," he told her. "It's usually associated with the prolonged use of the voice and straining of the vocal cords. I'm at a loss as to how a domestic servant might develop it."

Pooki looked at Mink, who rolled her eyes and said, "I'm afraid to say she's been shouting out of the window at the excursionists lost in the maze whenever the keeper is absent. Apparently she feels sorry for them."

"I see," said the doctor, glancing at the servant. "I would suggest resting the voice, repeated inhalations of creosote in the vapour of steam, and a tonic for the whole system. If things don't improve, we could consider the application of electricity to the throat. However, the best internal remedy is glycerate of tar combined with . . ." He paused before adding, "Minute doses of arsenic."

All that could be heard was the ticking of the clock on the mantelpiece.

"Well, I think resting the voice sounds a very good idea, and we'll try the inhalations," said the Princess, quickly standing up.

Once Dr. Henderson had written the prescription, Mink approached and thanked him for coming. "I'm most grateful. Do send the bill when it's convenient."

The general practitioner looked out the window, searching for the words. "I must apologise for soaking you on the towpath the other day," he said. "Perhaps you would allow me to make it up to you in some way?"

The Princess held up a hand. "I wouldn't say a word more, doctor. You'd only be wasting your breath, and you might need it if you end up in the Thames again on the way home."

He glanced at the floor with a smile. "You're an excellent shot," he said, looking up. "I don't think that showman of the fair had seen anything like it. Me neither."

"Then it's a good job I wasn't aiming for your heart, Dr. Henderson," she replied.

He glanced at the maid, then lowered his voice. "You've already captured it," he said.

"Then I shall see to it that it's returned immediately," she said, her blue eyes defiant.

He held her gaze. "I won't give up. I believe you're worth fighting for."

She took a step closer to him. "Some battles are lost before they've even begun, doctor. Pooki will show you out."

After closing the front door behind him, the servant searched for her mistress and found her sitting at her desk in the study, staring down at her notebook, her head in her hands.

"Ma'am," she croaked from the doorway. "You will have to start thinking about finding a new maid. Everyone is saying that the police are going to arrest me at any minute. Even the man who came to buy the dripping said he was surprised that I was not in prison."

The Princess didn't move. "I've no need of a new maid. You're not going anywhere."

"Do you know who did it, ma'am?" Pooki persisted, clutching her hands in front of her.

"Give me a chance."

The maid remained where she was. Not having heard the door shut, Mink looked up and asked whether there was anything else.

"Yes, ma'am."

"Well?" she asked, raising her eyebrows.

Pooki took a step forward. "I did not realise that you liked the doctor in that way, ma'am."

"I don't like him," Mink protested. "And what do you mean 'in that way'?"

"I have seen it all before, ma'am. You were also rude to Mr. Cavendish when you were falling in love with him," she added, and swiftly left the room.

CHAPTER XI

Cornelius B. Pilgrim's Secret

 EITHER woman was certain when the letter was slipped under the front door of Wilderness House. Pooki spotted it before breakfast, and brought it on a silver salver to her mistress, who had just sat down at the table. The Princess simply glanced at it, then picked up her knife and fork. After waiting silently at her side, the maid suggested that she open it, as the writing didn't resemble that of her creditors.

"It might be a love letter from that doctor who soaked you, ma'am," she said, her voice still hoarse. "And if it is, you must reply to it, because the policeman is going to take me away and make sure I am hanged. Then you will be all alone and I will weep for you from heaven."

Mink looked again at the envelope. "It's not from Dr. Henderson. His penmanship leaves a lot to be desired if his prescription is anything to go by," she said, cutting off the burnt edge of her cod fishcake.

"Ma'am, if you do not open it, I will. And it is not my place to do so," said the servant.

Muttering that it wasn't too late to ask Dr. Henderson to perform his electricity treatment on her throat after all, Mink put down her cutlery, grabbed the opener, and worked it across the envelope's spine. She held the letter up to read. "Someone wants to meet me this morning at the hotel on Tagg's Island," she said, taken aback.

"Who, ma'am?" asked Pooki, her eyes wide.

"It doesn't say," the Princess replied, getting up to change.

"Ma'am, you cannot meet a stranger on an island," said the maid, following her upstairs. "Everyone gossips in this palace. It is what keeps the old ones alive."

Mink opened her wardrobe and selected a dress. "It might have something to do with the General," she said dismissively.

Pooki frowned. "Ma'am, you cannot risk your reputation for me."

"My reputation is already ruined," she replied, putting on turquoise earrings in keeping with the craze for gems that matched the eyes.

"Then I will come with you, ma'am. The Maharaja would not like you going on your own."

*

AS THE FLY PASSED HAMPTON COURT GREEN, its trampled grass the only reminder of the travelling fair, Mink refused to turn her head when Pooki pointed out the doctor's practice.

"Ma'am, my throat is feeling a lot worse. I think we should go and see the doctor on our way back," suggested the servant.

"That's strange, considering you said earlier it had improved a little. Maybe you should rest your voice, as Dr. Henderson suggested," came the curt reply.

They passed Ye Olde Cardinal Wolsey public house, and stared at the chalet brought from Switzerland to house the guests of a local landowner. The carriage then stopped opposite a small island named after Tom Tagg, who had established a boat-building business there, as well as a hotel that attracted boating people, pleasure seekers, and the more glamourous members of society. Taking the calloused hand of the ferryman, who had been barred from the Wolsey following a number of high-profile capsizes covered by the *Surrey Comet*, the Princess climbed in, followed by Pooki. As he started to heave them across the silent water, Mink looked at the cheerful houseboats moored to the island, still wondering who had sent her the letter, the ostrich feathers on her toque fluttering in the breeze.

In the hotel's lounge, where potted palms stood between clusters of chairs, the Princess chose a seat by the window so that she could see the whole room. After ordering tea for three and some seed cake to keep Pooki quiet, she studied the ladies in spring hats gossiping in thickets. Several glanced at her with the usual mix of curiosity and envy, but each turned back to their conversation. The only person alone was a gentleman sitting in the far corner, his face obscured by *The Times*. He was wearing a modish nut-brown checked Duke of York lounge suit, its jacket expertly cut with square corners. On the table in front of him were the remains of a piece of shortbread. As he turned the page, she saw to her surprise that it was Cornelius B. Pilgrim, whose dress sense had hitherto left a lot to be desired. As she continued to look at him he held her gaze and quickly folded up his newspaper.

"Mr. Pilgrim, won't you take a seat?" she asked, when he approached. She immediately poured him a cup of tea and passed it to him. "You're quite right in that English coffee is perfectly vile."

Once he had sat down, she tilted her head to one side and asked, "Forgive my asking, Mr. Pilgrim, but have you been to Savile Row?"

Cornelius B. Pilgrim beamed and ran a hand down his double-breasted waistcoat that buttoned fashionably high. "I have, actually, Your Highness."

She looked him up and down. "I must say, you look quite the man about town. But we can't give the tailor all the credit. Some gentlemen never achieve a cultivated look no matter how much money they throw at Mayfair. Why, I was only reading the other day that certain Americans have been wearing plum-coloured dress-suits with a lighter shade roll collar again, with the usual lack of success. It's the third time they've attempted it in six years, apparently. You, however, Mr. Pilgrim, do the British tailor proud. Why, you look as though your family would take up several pages of *Burke's Peerage*."

Pooki raised her eyebrows.

His smile broadened. "Nice of you to say so," he replied.

Mink leant towards him and lowered her voice. "You look so elegant, I almost mistook you for the Prince of Wales!"

The maid choked on her seed cake as the American turned pink with pleasure.

"I must say I was rather fond of that fur coat of yours," the Princess continued. "Did you shoot that monkey yourself? There's something about you that suggests you would be a good shot, Mr. Pilgrim. Those broad shoulders of yours, perhaps."

Pooki scowled at her as she wiped her lips.

"Actually I didn't," he said, picking up his cup. "Despite what Lady Montfort Bebb thinks, guns aren't really my thing."

"I never doubted it for a moment. Why would you want Lady Montfort Bebb dead?" She paused before adding: "Or anyone else for that matter?"

Leaning towards her, he explained that he had sent her the note in order to test how serious she was about clearing her maid's name. He had some crucial information, which he didn't want falling into the wrong hands. "That's why I said nothing when you asked me who I thought the culprit was when we were in the garden with the other ladies. One of them might be in on it."

Mink asked why he hadn't gone to the police.

"Having been interviewed by them over the incident with Lady Montfort Bebb, I'm not at all convinced they're up to it."

He then looked behind him to make sure that he wasn't being overheard, and lowered his voice. "It was me who sent the anonymous letter to the coroner suggesting foul play," he admitted. "I didn't name the person who I thought responsible, as I didn't have any proof. Then I got so frustrated at the inquest I decided to tell the coroner there and then, hoping he'd get to the bottom of it. But I didn't get the chance. What I hadn't foreseen, however, was that someone else entirely would become the focus of the investigation." He glanced at Pooki, who raised her chin.

Mink leant towards him. "How clever of you to have discovered who the culprit is, Mr. Pilgrim. None of we English have a clue," she said. "Who is it?"

"Thomas Trout," the American whispered. "The week before the General was poisoned, he came twice to the apartments, which struck me as rather odd, given that he's a gardener. Both times they argued so loudly I could hear them as I walked past the study. I couldn't make out each word, but on the keeper's second visit I heard him saying something about a lady's name being ruined."

"Whose?" asked Pooki.

They both looked at the servant, who immediately lowered her eyes.

"Whose?" Mink repeated.

"That's the problem," he replied. "I have no idea."

The Princess poured them some more tea. "I very much appreciate your telling me, Mr. Pilgrim. You must be a very busy man, what with all the research you're doing. Tell me, what do you think of the brontosaurus at the Natural History Museum?"

"Oh, it's a wonderful specimen."

The Princess looked at him. "That strikes me as rather curious, as there's nothing of the sort there."

The American smoothed down his moustache.

"Why would an eminent palaeontologist not bother going to see the country's leading collection, yet make the effort to go all the way to see the dinosaur statues at the Crystal Palace when everyone now knows they're not all anatomically correct? Even I know that the horn on the iguanodon's nose is its thumb spike." She paused. "Perhaps you don't want to go to the police with your information because you're not who you say you are."

Cornelius B. Pilgrim slid his palms down his trousers.

"Who are you, Mr. Pilgrim?" she demanded.

Slowly he raised his eyes. He was indeed a palaeontologist, he said, or at least he had been. As a teenager he developed a fascination for natural history, and went on to study mineralogy and anatomy. Eventually he became a fossil hunter, and his findings added much to the world's understanding of dinosaurs. He was most well known for his discovery of the kerasaurus, which he donated to London's Natural History Museum.

It was years later that he realised the error that was to haunt him forever. While looking at a photograph he had taken of his prehistoric beast, which he had joyfully assembled, thinking of the wonders it would do for his career, he saw that he had mixed up two of its appendages. He stared aghast at its tail, surmounted by a head, protruding from its shoulders, and its neck extending from its rear end.

"I couldn't believe what I'd done," he said. For five nights he couldn't sleep as he thought of all the people who had viewed it at the museum in South Kensington, and the damage it would do to his reputation if anyone found out. But that wasn't the end of it. When he mustered the courage to look at the photograph again, it was then that he noticed the pinnacle of his folly.

"It suddenly occurred to me that the spiral horns I had attached to its skull were those of a goat which must have died nearby," he said, his voice a whisper.

The realisation that he had mixed up the remains of a primeval monster with those of a nineteenth-century ruminant was too much to bear. Turning his back on palaeontology, he burnt all his academic papers and returned every box of bones and fossils unopened to their curious senders. But soon he was gripped by a more insidious obsession. His mind still disturbed by the realisation of his error, he started dabbling in vegetarianism, seduced by the tantalising petals of an artichoke. Suddenly he renounced brisket and all hope of sanity was lost. It wasn't long before he found himself drawn to the shady underworld of spiritualism. He grew a beard and started to socialise with mediums who smelt of violets, and clairvoyants who, despite their visions of the future, never knew he was coming.

His mother saved him from a life of cabbage and fictitious messages from the dead. Dropping in on an unexpected visit, she took one look at him and marched down to the kitchen. She found the cook on the verge of handing in her notice, claiming it wasn't natural to work in a household that banned eating anything with a tail. The mother immediately sent for the butcher's boy, and never had the kitchen seen such activity, as the cook made up for four barren months armed solely with a vegetable peeler. By the time the dinner gong sounded, the whole household knew what was to come, except for Cornelius B. Pilgrim. When his mother ladled out the Albert soup, made with young fowl, lean ham, oysters, and the hind leg of an ox, he immediately bolted for the dining room door, but found that it was locked from the other side. He looked at his mother through his uncut fringe and understood at once what he was up against. It was the aroma of the dish that broke him. He hung his head and wept for his topsy-turvy kerasaurus and the enthralled public who had queued to see it. He wept for his abandoned career that had so fulfilled him. And he wept for all the sausages he had steadfastly spurned.

Wiping away the tears that had run into his raggedy beard, he picked up his soupspoon and started to eat. It took a week for his senses to be completely restored, and he forswore his monstrous whiskers. Venturing back into his study, the seat of his shame, he decided to put his scientific talents to good use again. He started to investigate the supernatural, revealing the tricks of the country's greatest hoaxers and frauds. It was he who exposed the table-rapper Esmeralda Shufflecock, who for years had been stunning audiences not only with her talent but also her beauty, as most of her contemporaries ran to nineteen stone. One evening, as he watched her sitting at a table transmitting messages from the dead, he strode onto the stage and hauled up her skirts, much to the horror of the crowd. The gentlemen in the audience made much of covering their eyes, and when they peeped through their spread fingers saw to their dismay the knocking instrument irrefutably strapped to her shapely calf.

But Cornelius B. Pilgrim's biggest triumph was revealing the true nature of Esmond Winterbottom, the celebrated prophet of spiritualism. Such were the man's powers, he claimed he could summon the sleeping ghost of Shakespeare. Disguised with a false beard and spectacles, Cornelius B. Pilgrim obtained a seat at one of his séances and waited for the dead bard to appear. The lights were dimmed, and the slumped Mr. Winterbottom wasted no time in falling into a trance. Suddenly the sound of a harpsichord could be heard, though no instrument was present. A prostrate figure of poetic countenance rose from the ground and proceeded to drift out of the open window feet-first. It turned, continued for several yards, then came back in again through the adjacent window. After several revolutions, Cornelius B. Pilgrim rose from his chair, whipped the quill from the spectre's grasp, and proceeded to tickle its seventeenth-century toes. The music was drowned by shrieks of mirth that gave way to uncontrolled hysteria. They were soon followed by a loud thud as the convulsed dramatist fell off his apparatus. The investigator then mounted the tracks, lay down, and proceeded to waft in and out of the windows boots-first while reciting *Hamlet*. Esmond Winterbottom suddenly snapped out of his trance, and fled through the trap door in the floor. The last that was heard of him was that he had renounced America and was living in Peebles, Scotland, dressed in the tartan of a clan that never existed.

Cornelius B. Pilgrim became so well known as a result of his successes that his disguises failed to work, and he was turned away from séances before even reaching the parlour. So he changed tack and set himself up as a ghost hunter, specialising in haunted houses infested by strange knockings, chain-rattling, and impossible footsteps.

He took a sip of tea. "I came to Hampton Court Palace to investigate the new ghost sightings at the request of the General, who wanted to include them in his history of the palace," he admitted. "He told me not to tell anyone the real reason why I was here, as not only would I need permission for an investigation, but I would come up against resistance from the residents who loathed any interest being taken in the spirits, as they made it difficult to retain domestic servants. I had been sitting in the dark in Fountain Court, waiting for an apparition, when I heard a strange sound and drew my gun, which was exactly the moment when Lady Montfort Bebb emerged from the push. I'm not sure who was more terrified, though I certainly came off worst," he added, his fingers reaching for the bump on his head. "I'm surprised she left any of those poor Afghans standing."

Insisting that he had an appointment, he then got up to leave and headed for the door. As Mink watched him, she was struck by the superior cut of his jacket. Why would a man so apparently intent on seeking justice for his dead friend go to the time and trouble of ordering a new suit? If he were simply taking advantage of being near London, home to some of the best tailors in the world, why didn't he just put it in his trunk and wear it when he got home? Wasn't it a little vulgar to be so concerned with his appearance when his host had just died? As the ferryman heaved her back across the Thames, the breeze lifting the ruffles of her dress, the resounding answer came. Somewhere, in all of this, was a woman.

*

RETURNING TO THE PALACE, the Princess ignored the hopeful look of the watercress seller, made her way to Clock Court, and headed up the stairs to the Silver Stick Gallery. A flushed cook with a bloodstained apron and a trail of flour across her forehead eventually opened the door. Glancing at the Princess's turquoise earrings, she informed her that Lady Beatrice was not at home. She would be able to find her in the Flower Quarter, which was part of the Pond Gardens, and for the private use of the residents. "I've got to go, Your Highness," she added. "There's a joint of beef in the kitchen what needs seeing to. The sooner Her Ladyship gets a new parlour maid, the better. I've got more important things to do than answer the front door. And by the way, let me know when they arrest your maid-of-all-work. My niece is looking for a position."

Mink eventually found the walled garden and spotted Lady Beatrice sitting on a bench in the shade, a basket next to her. Her eyes were closed, and she was wearing a large, battered straw hat that had clearly been demoted to gardening-wear. As she looked at her more closely, she noticed she was not enjoying a rest in the spring sunshine as she first thought. She was clutching a pair of secateurs, and there was a tenseness in her jaw line. Was this woman with a fondness for false fringes and exuberant millinery really capable of poisoning the General? she wondered.

Suddenly Lady Beatrice turned to her. "I'm so glad it's you, Princess," she said, a hand against her heart. "When I heard the gate, for a horrible moment I thought it was that police inspector again. I could really do with a brandy, but I suspect my cook has already polished it off."

"She was still coherent a moment ago when I called, though quite what state she'll be in by the time that beef is cooked is anyone's guess," said Mink, sitting down next to her. "What did that awful inspector want?" she asked casually.

Lady Beatrice explained that he had discovered that she had recently bought some arsenic from the chemist's. "Unfortunately, I'd completely forgotten, as I do most things, and it was only when he said that my name was on the poisons register that I remembered. He seemed to find my initial denial very suspicious, and started scribbling in that infernal notebook of his. I explained that I was the daughter of a marquess, and that my late husband had not only been a captain in the Army but Keeper of the Crown Jewels. But apparently none of that matters when it comes to murder," she added indignantly.

In the end she had been compelled to tell the Inspector the truth: she had bought the arsenic because the palace cats were a constant threat to her birds. "But I only got as far as mixing some up with milk. I then thought of all my neighbours whose laps those creatures keep warm in winter, and the companionship they brought them, and I just couldn't do it. I feel very ashamed that I even considered it," she said, lowering her head.

The Princess assured her that she wouldn't tell a soul. "I must apologise for my maid blurting out the rumour that some of your doves had been sold to the butcher. It must have come as a shock," she added, watching her carefully.

Lady Beatrice gripped her secateurs. "I'd already heard it," she replied angrily. "Lady Bessington's maid told my cook. I was furious, as you can imagine, but not altogether surprised. The General had sent numerous letters about my birds to the Lord Chamberlain, who asked Mrs. Boots to see to it that I got rid of them. But I continue to ignore her."

"And so you should," said the Princess, sitting back. "Our pets are very precious to us. I once had a canary. Such a sweet little thing." She paused. "What made you decide to keep doves?"

Lady Beatrice fiddled with a mustard-coloured ringlet. "One of the palace staff gave me a pair," she replied. "Apparently he's a good friend of the birdman. Luckily the pair mated. It's such a fascinating ritual." She then stood up and turned to the Princess. "I suppose I'd better make a start before the next shower brings up yet more weeds. That policeman has quite delayed me, though at least it has kept him away from your maid. Apparently some of the residents have a sweepstake on how long it will be before he arrests her. I told my cook just this morning that she doesn't look the sort. Big feet are no indication of criminality, I told her. It's a funny-shaped head you need to look out for, though Cornelius B. Pilgrim seems to be the exception. Maybe it's different for foreigners."

She picked up her basket. "The funny thing about that whole episode this morning is that when that awful little policeman asked me to show him the bottle of arsenic, I took him to the kitchen and it was no longer there."

*

POOKI OPENED THE GARDEN DOOR and peered out. She hadn't wanted to leave the house, for just as she tied the ribbons on her bonnet the Princess had sneezed three times. She hung back in the hope that she would sneeze again in order to break the bad omen. But eventually Mink could contain her exasperation no longer, and told her that if she really wanted to avoid being carted off in a black maria, she had better leave immediately to see what information she could extract from Alice Cockle. For not only was she the maid's only friend in the palace, she was a considerable gossip.

Seeing that Inspector Guppy wasn't around, Pooki walked quickly down Moat Lane towards the Tudor section of the palace, head bent and hands gripped into anxious fists. She had already come close to death on several occasions during her life. While working as a travelling ayah she had been tossed with such violence during screeching storms she had been convinced she would never see her mother again. Twice she had seen the glint of a knife while walking the perilous East End streets after she had been abandoned, and twice destiny had found her a place to hide. Then there was the time when the Maharaja pulled her out of the path of a hansom cab in Soho as she lay in the filth of the road, unable to move. But nothing filled her with more dread than the thought of being hanged. Her dreams, when she finally fell asleep, were invaded by images of her neck not breaking completely after the trap door opened, and her being caught in a monstrous half-death as her life was slowly dragged from her, her feet hanging limply from the bottom of her dress. As she continued, she imagined her mother being told of her degrading end, heaping shame not only on her family but on that of the Maharaja.

One of the soldiers showed her the way to Fish Court, a tall, narrow, redbrick passageway once used to store raw ingredients for Henry VIII's kitchens. There were telltale signs of occupation. Several window boxes were filled with spring flowers, and the odd curtain moved at the sound of her feet. She found the Countess's apartments by its nameplate, and stood with her hands clutched in front of her as she waited for the door to open. Suddenly she heard footsteps behind her and span round. But it was only Pike, the butcher's boy, on his rounds, holding his basket on his shoulder.

Alice appeared at the door and immediately stepped back to let her in. "We're in luck," she said, as they climbed the stairs. "Her Ladyship is at a British Pteridological Society meeting, which is something to do with ferns. She's crazy about them, and even has them on her tea set." She took her into the drawing room and showed her the numerous specimens perched on plant stands, and pointed out the Wardian case underneath the window, filled with lacy fronds curling up towards the glass.

The servant then led the way up to her room in the attic, where they sat down on her single iron bed, over which hung a portrait of the Virgin Mary. Asking whether Pooki was hungry, she opened a cupboard and drew out a tin of Hovis biscuits. "Apparently they're good for the bones, brain, flesh, and muscles," she said, offering them to her.

"I do not believe advertisements," said Pooki, taking a couple. "Dr. Nightingale's Voice Pills are meant to give you the voice of a clergyman, but I do not even sound like a sexton. If Dr. Henderson's treatment does not work, he will fire me up with electricity. Her Highness says she will be able to light the drawing room with me."

Alice leant back against the wall, her feet dangling over the side of the bed, and straightened out her white apron. "What's she like?" she asked. "One of my cousins once met that girl who came in the mornings to clean the boots and the knives."

Pooki leant back next to her, her feet dwarfing those of the teenager. "She is a very good mistress, but sometimes I have to tell her what to do," she said, with a weary shake of the head.

Alice suddenly turned to her with a frown. "A servant's voice should never be heard by the ladies and gentlemen of the house, except when necessary. And then as little as possible. You should know that," she said.

Pooki raised her chin. "Her Highness is always very grateful for my advice," she said.

Alice looked at her. "You don't talk to her when you're bringing up coals or laying the cloth, do you?"

Pooki nodded, biting into a biscuit. "They are my favourite times, as well as when I am dusting," she said, her mouth full.

The teenager stared ahead of her in amazement. "It's a wonder she doesn't pick up a book every time you come in the room."

"She does, but my mistress can read and listen at the same time," Pooki replied, brushing crumbs from her lips.

"You'd better keep quiet or she'll get rid of you and you'll end up working for a shopkeeper's family," Alice warned with a frown. "That's what happened to a friend of mine. She kept telling her mistress the tradesmen's jokes."

"My mistress does not like the dripping man's jokes, the dustman's jokes, or the rag and bone man's jokes. But she very much likes the butterman's," said Pooki, with a smile of satisfaction. "When I am telling them she raises her newspaper so that I cannot see her laughing. She finds them so funny she begs me not to tell them to her. Often I tell them twice in one morning just to amuse her."

"I'm surprised she doesn't leave the house to get away from you."

"She does," said Pooki, biting into another biscuit. "Sometimes she has to go out into the garden to compose herself."

Alice looked at her dubiously.

"Why is an umbrella like a pancake?" asked Pooki, smirking.

The other maid shrugged.

"Because it is seldom seen after lent!" she said, a hand over her mouth as she snorted.

Alice remained straight-faced.

"Her Highness loves this one: why can a gentleman never possess a short walking stick?" asked the maid, her shoulders already shaking.

"No idea."

"Because it can never be-long to him!" she cried, clutching her stomach.

Alice looked at the ceiling.

"And this one is my favourite: what kind of gaiters should a professor wear?" asked Pooki, her voice rising as she tried to stifle her laughter. But she didn't wait for an answer. "In-vesti-gators!" she screeched, wiping away her tears with both hands.

Alice touched her arm. "Here, you'll never guess what happened this morning," she said, changing the subject.

"What?" asked Pooki, still laughing.

"Dr. Henderson's housekeeper came round with some flowers for Her Ladyship."

Pooki's face fell.

"She said they were from the doctor and made a big point of telling me they were La France roses, which means 'meet me by moonlight' in the language of flowers," Alice continued, her eyes wide. "Her Ladyship didn't know what to do with herself when I gave her the message, and told me to hide them behind the curtains if anyone called. Nice as she is, I'm not sure what he sees in her, her being so much older than him and always complaining she hasn't got two pennies to rub together."

Pooki frowned, the thought of the doctor sending flowers to anyone apart from her mistress immediately sobering her up. As Alice went down to make some tea, she remained on the bed, helping herself to biscuits, each of which she told herself would be her last as she brushed away the crumbs. Remembering what she had come for, she got up and looked under the washstand and bed, feeling uneasy about searching the room of her only friend. She then went through the chest of drawers, moving aside stockings and pieces of underwear. There was nothing there. Suddenly she heard footsteps and sat back on the bed.

As Alice came in with the tea-tray, Pooki got up and opened the cupboard. "I am putting the biscuits away, otherwise I will eat them all and my feet will get bigger," she explained. There was something inside that stopped her. Reaching in, she drew out a bottle of arsenic. Instantly Alice's cheeks flushed. "I was just about to get rid of that," she said, setting down the tray with unsteady hands.

Sitting on the bed, she told how she had been in Lady Beatrice's kitchen borrowing some arrowroot when the bell rang and the cook went upstairs to answer it. Feeling hungry, she looked around for something to eat, and found the bottle of poison. "I put it in my pocket in case the cook got blamed for killing the General. Servants are always being found guilty of things they never did. You like your tea strong, don't you?" she asked, picking up the pot.

Pooki stood up. "I had better get back to Wilderness House. Her Highness will be wondering where I have got to," she said flatly.

After Alice closed the front door behind her, Pooki headed along Fish Court, her heart even heavier than when she had arrived. She glanced back, wondering whether it were possible that the girl had poisoned the General and left her to take the blame. And as she looked up she noticed Alice standing at the drawing room window, watching her.

CHAPTER XII

Pooki's Dying Wish and Trixie Predicts Rain

OLLOWING a night of fitful sleep, Mink watched from her bed as Pooki poured hot water into the bath. The servant seemed even thinner than usual in the grey dress she wore in the mornings to hide the dirt of her heavier work. When she had emptied the final can and retreated downstairs to get on with her other chores, Mink took off her white nightdress and stepped in. Leaning back in the water, she cast her plait over the side, where it hung several inches from the floor. Hoping for some escape, she closed her eyes. But all she could think about was how utterly desolate she would feel without Pooki, and she took not the slightest pleasure from the warmth of the water or the smell of the soap.

It was while the maid was preparing breakfast that the Princess decided to bring up the contents of her bonnet box again, having previously been given a variety of explanations, none of which she found convincing. She came into the kitchen, instantly catching the maid off guard as she battled to make kedgeree. After asking numerous questions about the recipe, which further unsettled her, Mink started pacing up and down perilously close to Victoria, producing nervous glances and warnings to watch her feet. When it seemed that the maid was at the most crucial point in the proceedings, Mink suddenly asked, "So why did you have fly papers in your room?"

Distracted by the boiling eggs, the simmering rice, the poaching haddock, and a hedgehog in jeopardy, Pooki immediately blurted out with the truth. "To make me prettier, ma'am," she replied, without turning round.

"Prettier?" the Princess repeated, incredulous.

"It is a beauty treatment some German maids once told me about," the maid said, lifting the lid of the copper fish kettle and peering inside. "They soak fly papers in elderflower water and put the solution on their faces with handkerchiefs to improve the complexion."

"Have you done it before?" the Princess asked.

Pooki continued to stir the rice. "No, ma'am. This was my first time."

Mink sat down at the kitchen table, relieved at such a reasonable explanation. "So why didn't you tell the Inspector that? It seems perfectly understandable to me."

There was a pause, "Because of you, ma'am," Pooki replied.

"Me?" asked the Princess, staring at her.

"You would have wondered why I wanted to be prettier, ma'am."

After a moment it came to her. "Have you got a follower?" Mink asked, suddenly standing up.

The only sound was the rattling of the eggs. "Mistresses are not the only people who fall in love, ma'am," the servant replied over her shoulder.

The Princess put her hands on her hips, immediately wondering whether he had something to do with the poisoned pie. "Has this friend of yours been in the kitchen?" she asked crossly.

The servant nodded. "I once invited him round to try a pound cake I made because it tasted as it should do and it might have been the first and last time."

Mink paced the room. "You know very well that having a male friend in the house is not permitted. My father never allowed it either. Was his visit before or after you made the pigeon pies?" she asked, her voice raised.

Pooki continued battling at the range. "It was after the inquest, ma'am, so it could not have been him."

The Princess folded her arms and looked at the maid, who still had her back to her. "I suppose this man was the reason for your mystery walk while you were making them. Would you care to tell me who it is?"

Pooki turned round, clutching the wooden spoon. "It is the watercress seller, ma'am," she muttered.

The Princess walked to the window and looked out. "At least that explains why the larder is full of cresses. I suppose I should be thankful you haven't fallen in love with the cats' meat seller, or we would be up to the rafters in horseflesh." She turned back to the maid. "So what is it about this man that you find so endearing?"

Pooki's gaze dropped to the floor. "He has nice eyes, ma'am." She paused before adding: "And he says my feet are just the right size."

The Princess sighed. "And how serious is this love affair?" she demanded.

The servant looked at her. "I am not keeping company with him, ma'am, only walking out," she insisted.

"Well, thank goodness there isn't a marriage on the horizon." The Princess folded her arms. "Is there anything else you'd like to get off your chest while we're at it? We may as well get everything out in the open."

The maid nodded.

"Well?" asked Mink.

"I have burnt the fish, ma'am."

*

THE PRINCESS CLOSED THE GARDEN DOOR behind her and walked swiftly through the Wilderness, ignoring the admiring glances from the gentlemen excursionists. They weren't the only ones who noticed her. Heads turned as she passed Purr Corner, where several residents were gathered, and even the gardeners in the Privy Garden raised their eyes from their beds. As she crossed through the Pond Gardens, she remembered the picnic and wished she had never gone, her stomach turning at the implications for Pooki. Headed towards the Great Vine, she thought again of the arguments Cornelius B. Pilgrim had overheard between the General and the keeper. She had no idea whether they bore any relation to his death, or indeed if they even took place. But it was certainly curious that Mr. Trout had attended the inquest. And, she suspected, he had a rather intriguing secret.

She stopped to read the notice nailed to the door of the Vine House: "The person showing the vine is permitted to take a small fee." Slipping inside, she stood alone behind the barrier, staring up at the celebrated plant. As she glanced around, she noticed the short, stocky legs of Thomas Trout, who was up a ladder, snipping off a tendril from one of the branches clinging to a wooden frame against the roof. He bent down, looked at her, and scratched his neat moustache with the tip of a gloved finger. Immediately she got out her purse. "There's no need, Your Highness. That sign's for the visitors."

As he resumed his work, he apologised for not stopping and explained that the vine was currently growing at almost an inch a day and he had to control it, as it produced more shoots than could fit into the hothouse. Of the Black Hamburg variety, it was planted in the 1760s by Capability Brown to produce grapes for the table of George III, he explained. It had been grown from a cutting of a vine at the Valentines Mansion in Essex, its branches now covering more than two thousand square feet. "Some say it's become so big because the roots have got into the cesspool, and it's been nourished by sewage. But it's nonsense. It's all down to the variety," he said.

Each September he had a mature crop of more than one thousand bunches, which were presented to the Queen, who usually sent a share to hospitals. "The residents are always after them. I have to keep the door locked after hours, or there'll be none left."

Mink looked around her. "What a responsibility you have keeping such an historic plant alive, Mr. Trout," she said. "Why, you've got one of the most important jobs in the palace. I don't know how you do it. It would give me sleepless nights. I do hope you're appreciated."

Thomas Trout suddenly lowered his arms and looked down at her. "They have no idea of the enormity of it, ma'am," he replied. "You wouldn't believe the amount of dust the visitors give off. They should be kept behind a glass panel, but no one listens to me. About ten thousand of them turn up on bank holidays, all pushing and shoving in and out of that door." There were pests to control, which he did by painting the vine in the winter with soft soap impregnated with nicotine. Mildew was another huge problem, which he kept away by spraying the plant with sulphur. Then he had to keep an eye on the temperamental boiler, which supplied hot water to the pipes heating the glasshouse and threatened to blow any minute.

"But do you know what keeps me awake at night?" he asked, coming down his ladder and standing with his hands on his hips. "Rats," he said, without waiting for an answer. "Nothing tempts them faster out of their holes than hunger. If one gets in here after those grapes, it's all over. I've even seen them nibbling the toes of the statues of Mars and Hercules in the Privy Garden, as lead tastes sweet." He then pointed to the corner of the glasshouse. "See the vine's stem? It's thirty-eight inches in circumference.

A rat could get through that before you could say 'the Pied Piper of Hamelin.' And will the palace get the rat-catcher in? No, they won't go to the expense. So what did they give me instead? Lord Sluggard, the laziest mouser I've ever had the misfortune of having to feed. That cat would rather let a rat tie its whiskers than get up and chase it."

Thomas Trout glanced at his pocket watch. "If you'll excuse me, ma'am, I'm going to have to lock up so I can nip home for a quick cup of tea before the palace opens." He looked up at the sky through the leaves. "It's going to rain today, according to my leech barometer, so hopefully that will keep some of them away."

"Leech barometer?" repeated the Princess.

"It was inspired by Dr. Merryweather's tempest prognosticator, which he showed at the Great Exhibition," he explained. Fashioned in the style of an Indian temple, it featured twelve bottles of water, each containing a leech that rang a bell when a tempest was expected. "That man was kind enough to place the bottles in a circle so that the leeches didn't have to endure the anguish of solitary confinement. He advised the Government to establish leech-warning stations around the coast, but unfortunately they ignored him. My version's a lot more humble than Dr. Merryweather's, but it works."

"Oh, Mr. Trout, it does sound fascinating. I should love to see it," enthused Mink. "May I?"

The keeper hesitated. "You'll have to excuse the state of the place. The charwoman didn't come this morning," he said.

"Don't worry about a thing. I'm sure your home is as well cared for as that vine of yours."

The keeper led the way to an adjacent cottage, covered by the Great Wisteria, which eclipsed the vine during its brief annual flowering. "Dreadful business about your maid," said Thomas Trout, unlocking the door. "My money's on one of the residents. Or their houseguest."

"Mr. Pilgrim, you mean?" she asked, watching him carefully as she stepped inside.

He nodded. "I went to see the General a couple of times before he died, as he wanted some information about the vine for the book he was writing," he said, closing the door behind them. "That American was always creeping around the place. There's something not right about him. Maybe it's just the monkey-fur coat."

He took off his cap, revealing the utter ineffectiveness of Dr. Henderson's scalp lotion, and offered Mink a seat in the parlour while he busied himself in the kitchen. As soon as he was gone, she stood up and looked around her at the unlovely furniture and age-dappled mirror. She peered inside a work-basket on the rocking chair but found nothing of interest amongst the needles and threads. Checking that he wasn't coming back, she opened a cupboard next to the chimneybreast and poked through the candles, tobacco, and tiny fold-down ships that hadn't yet made their way into bottles. Quietly closing the doors again, she crept to the other side of the fire and, with a backwards glance, opened the other cupboard. Moving aside a ball of string and an old pair of men's leather gloves, she drew out a book entitled *Full Revelations of a Professional Rat-catcher After Twenty-Five Years' Experience*. She had just turned to the section on drugs and chemicals when she heard a sound. Her heart thudding, she quickly put it back again and closed the door.

The Princess was standing in front of the fire, peering at a solitary black streak in a plain bottle on the mantelpiece, when Thomas Trout came back in with a tea-tray. "Is this your leech barometer, Mr. Trout?" she asked. "It does look intriguing. How does it work?"

"If the leech is coiled up at the bottom, we're due for fine, clear weather," he explained, setting down the tray. "If it's formed a half-moon when out of the water and stuck to the glass, then there's a tempest on its way. If it keeps moving, we can expect thunder and lightning. If it moves slowly, a cold snap is due. And if it bolts, strong winds will blow when it stops."

"What if it has climbed up to the neck of the bottle?" asked Mink, staring at the inhabitant.

"A sure sign of rain."

The Princess returned to her chair. "Who would believe that leeches were such visionaries, Mr. Trout?" she asked. "There was I thinking that their only use was to suck out my blood whenever I had a sprain. What a pity Dr. Merryweather's invention wasn't taken up. I can just see those leech-warning stations dotted along the British coastline. Imagine all the disasters that would have been averted! Some people's talents are never recognised." She paused and tilted her head. "A bit like yours, Mr. Trout."

The keeper blushed.

Mink raised her eyebrows. "Does your leech have a name?"

"She does, actually," he admitted with a shy smile. "Trixie."

Mink clasped her hands together. "How perfectly charming!" she exclaimed. She paused before adding: "Trixie is short for Beatrice, I believe."

The keeper looked at her, his smile vanished. "I named her after the Queen's daughter," he added hastily.

Mink leant forward and smiled reassuringly. "Just as I thought, Mr. Trout. You and I are two of a kind. I have a hedgehog called Victoria, and up until recently a monkey by the name of Albert. Any more pets and we'll have our very own Royal Family!"

As the keeper poured the tea, Mink surveyed the room. "What lovely flowers," she said, looking at the vase on the mantelpiece. "Are you married, or is that the hand of the charwoman I detect? Whoever it is has a lovely eye for flower arranging."

"My wife died nine years ago," he replied, adding that he had five children, two of whom still attended the palace school in Tennis Court Lane.

"Your children must be a great comfort, Mr. Trout. Loneliness is a terrible thing. It can wither the heart. I should know," she said, opening her bag and pulling out a handkerchief. "At one time I thought I was to be married. But I was wrong." She dabbed the corners of her eyes. "There must be lots of widows in the palace hoping to find love again. Do you think I will find my heart's desire, Mr. Trout?" she asked, her eyes wide.

"I'm certain of it, ma'am."

"Are you, Mr. Trout? Are you? I do hope you're right." She put down her cup and wiped her nose. "Sometimes I wonder whether Lady Beatrice is lucky enough to be in love. Do you know her?" she asked, clutching her handkerchief with both hands.

Thomas Trout shifted in his chair. "The palace staff get to know all the residents sooner or later," he muttered.

The Princess sniffed. "Apparently, after years of mourning, she suddenly started wearing all the colours of the rainbow, often at the same time. I don't like to gossip, Mr. Trout, but nothing suggests the presence of a man more to me than a widow who takes a sudden fancy to over-trimmed hats and false fringes. I do so envy her good fortune."

The keeper picked up his cup and saucer and held them in front of his face.

"But what surprises me most about Lady Beatrice is her being consistently late for divine service, when everyone knows you have to get there early to avoid sitting next to someone beneath your station," Mink continued. She leant forwards and whispered conspiratorially. "One might almost believe that she did it on purpose!"

The keeper took a sip of tea and flicked his eyes to the corner of the room.

"I believe she's sat next to you on several occasions."

His gaze travelled to the other corner.

"Mr. Trout!"

He jumped, his blush rising to the top of his bald head.

"Why, it's not you, is it, Mr. Trout?" she gasped. "If so, you're extremely fortunate. Not everyone finds love. To find it twice is a double blessing." She paused before adding: "Should such a love be permitted, of course."

Eventually Thomas Trout found the words. When his wife died he assumed the pain would never leave him, and was resolved to spending the rest of his days alone. Two years ago, he was tending the Great Vine when Lady Beatrice came in one morning before the palace opened, looking for Lord Sluggard, as her cook had opened the range to find a rat asleep on the cinders. At that moment a spattering of rain hit the glass, and Lady Beatrice, who was still wearing mourning, said she would have to stay until it was over, as wet weather was ruinous for crape. The shower quickly turned into a storm. As they watched it through the branches of the Great Vine, she remarked that thunder always reminded her of her late husband, who, despite his braveness on the battlefield, had a secret fear of it. "I told her that my late wife was always frightened that it would curdle the milk." By the time the final flicker slashed through the sky they had both told each other something that they had never admitted to themselves: part of them had also died when they lost their spouses.

Before she left, he asked her whether she liked flowers, adding that there was an old saying that she who planted a garden planted happiness. Two days later he spotted her in the Flower Quarter and fetched her an English spade, explaining they were rightly considered the best in the world. The following week, he warned her against moving a peony, as uprooting one was said to bring ill fortune. As the grapes began to darken, she entered the Vine House and asked how to care for her passionflower. Holding her gaze, he explained that it refused to be fertilised by its own pollen but could be helped along by softly stroking its stigma with the pollen of the same species using a camelhair brush. She then looked at the crop left to hang while the sugar developed, and asked whether she could taste it. He reached up and offered her a grape with his rough gardener's fingers. But instead of taking it, she opened her mouth, and as he passed it between her lips they both realised that what had been dead inside them was now very much alive.

He didn't see her during September's frantic harvest, and was so distracted by her absence he found himself reaching for berries he had already picked. With the passing of autumn, the residents deserted the Flower Quarter, and the weather seemed much colder than usual. Fearing he wouldn't make it through the winter without seeing her, he sought her out as she strolled in the gardens, watching her out of sight, as his lowly position prevented him from approaching her. It was quite by chance that he saw her the following spring in the Great Fountain Garden coming towards him in the Lime Walks, for centuries the favourite haunt of lovers. Surrounded by the lusty scent of the trees, he stood in his grubby work clothes, his beard tangled from a winter of weeping. As rooted as the trees, he was unable to move, fearing that time had chilled her affection. She stopped in front of him, and asked how he was. When the terrible truth came to him, he found himself asking her to marry him. But what surprised him even more than his proposal was her immediate acceptance.

There was never a question that their marriage would be anything other than secret, given their opposing classes. After a long search, they found a country vicar who agreed to marry them, and they travelled in separate coaches so as not to be seen. Lady Beatrice carried a bouquet of Great Wisteria, explaining that it meant "I cling to thee" in the language of flowers, and she would never let him go. And when she returned to the palace, she found his wedding gift waiting for her in the hall: a pair of doves that was never to be parted.

When Thomas Trout finished his tale, they sat in silence for a moment. Mink then put down her cup and said it was time for her to go. As he reached for the front door latch, he turned to her and asked, "You won't tell anyone, will you, ma'am? Some people wouldn't view our happiness as right."

The Princess shook her head. "I wouldn't dream of telling a soul, Mr. Trout. I can quite see the problems it would cause if anyone found out."

*

NOT LONG AFTERWARDS, AS MINK sat at her desk writing up her notes, it suddenly occurred to her that if Lady Beatrice's secret marriage became public, she would have much more to lose than status. Opening a drawer, she fished out her warrant to check that she had remembered the wording correctly. "The apartments shall revert to the Crown on the event of the marriage or re-marriage of the occupier, unless it shall be Her Majesty's pleasure to renew this Warrant," it said.

Wondering whether the two lovebirds were in on it together, she reached over and rang the bell, as she felt the urge for some sherry. But there was no response. She rang again, but still the maid failed to appear at the door. Putting down her pen in irritation, she went to look for her. At first she tried the kitchen, and then worked her way up the house until she eventually reached the attics, noticing a half-eaten penny bun on the stairs. Slowly she pushed open the door to Pooki's room and found her tying her bonnet, her suitcase standing next to her on the floor, along with Albert's. The pile of newspapers under the bed was gone and her bed stripped of its sheets. Glancing around the room, the only trace the Princess saw of the maid ever having been there was a small box on the mantelpiece.

Pooki turned to her. "You do not need to dismiss me, ma'am, for I am going. I should not have had a follower in the house. It is against the rules. I have left you the egg of the long-legged golden lyrebird to thank you and your family for everything you have done for me," she said, pointing to the box. She glanced uneasily at the tiny suitcase and turned to her mistress. "I hope you do not mind, ma'am, but I kept Albert's suitcase."

"But I've no intention of dismissing you," Mink said, aghast. "I suggest you come downstairs and make sure both doors are locked after I leave. I won't be long."

Pooki shook her head. "There is the other matter, ma'am. People are talking about me on the omnibuses. If they are talking about me, they will also be talking about you. The Maharaja would not have rescued me if he knew the shame I would bring on his family. You should not risk your reputation further by trying to help me. Do not tell my mother what became of me, as it would be the death of her. Please send her my suitcase so she has something to remember me by. That is, if she wants to remember me when it is all over," she added as a tear slipped down her cheek.

Unable to bear seeing her so upset, Mink looked at the battered suitcase filled with the pitiful belongings of the servant who had spent more than half her life looking after her. "Unpack your things and we'll say no more about it," she said, her voice uneven.

The maid shook her head, wiping her face with the back of her hand. "You should be spending your time with Dr. Henderson, not trying to save me, ma'am. He is your future. I am not."

The Princess could stand it no longer. "Take off your bonnet, and I'll see you downstairs in a minute," she replied, walking out to put an end to the discussion.

"Ma'am?"

"Yes?" Mink called from outside the door.

There was a pause. "Servants are not meant to love their mistresses, but sometimes they cannot help it," came the tentative voice.

Mink swallowed. "And mistresses aren't meant to love their servants, but sometimes they can't help it either," she replied, and headed quickly down the stairs.

*

A LITTLE LATER THERE WAS a knock on the study door.

"Ma'am?" called Pooki from the doorway, her hand still on the handle.

"Yes?" Mink replied, not looking up from her notebook.

The maid hesitated. "I have a dying wish."

The Princess didn't stir. "I've no idea why that would be. Your death is no more imminent than mine. Did you remember to ask the butcher's boy for some mutton for the mock venison we're having tonight?"

But Pooki wouldn't be derailed. "I would like you to take me to the Royal Aquarium."

Mink span round. "The Royal Aquarium?" she repeated, horrified.

The maid nodded. "That is my dying wish. I cannot die without seeing whether those lions bite off Countess X's head," she said, her chin raised.

"For all we know she's already had it bitten off."

Pooki shook her head. "It would have been in your newspaper, ma'am. I read it every night and it has not been mentioned."

Turning back to her list of suspects, the Princess muttered about possibly going the following week.

"Ma'am, I might not be here next week. I need to go this afternoon."

"This afternoon?" Mink repeated. She paused, then looked out the window. "I really don't think we should go out, Pooki. Look, there's a crow in that tree."

The maid approached the window and peered. "That is not a crow, ma'am," she replied, tapping the pane. "That is a blackbird."

*

AS THEY SAT IN TRAFFIC, Mink gazed up at Big Ben through the greasy window of a hansom cab, unable to believe where she was going. When, in 1875, a music and dancing licence was sought for a grand new aquarium in Westminster, the owners insisted that Londoners needed more than just fish. There would be a summer and winter garden, and the ignorati would not only be entertained but enlightened with a concert hall, a theatre, and a picture gallery. The composer Arthur Sullivan, whose operatic collaborations with W. S. Gilbert would invoke a craze for pirates, was lined up to direct the musical arrangements of the band. A division bell in direct communication with that in the House of Commons was installed in the conviction that the venue would be patronised by both Houses of Parliament. Respectability would be further ensured by not admitting unaccompanied women after dusk.

However, on the day of opening, the tanks in the vast hall with its magnificent glass and iron roof contained neither fish nor water. It wasn't long before the great Mr. Sullivan no longer appeared with his baton, and the public, never keen on self-improvement, remained indifferent. The vision to educate the masses clouded, and an altogether different means of attracting them hove into sight. They duly showed up, this time in an undignified stampede, lured by women shot out of cannons, fasting Italians, alligator charmers, bulls that could climb ladders, and performing fleas. Drunks, pickpockets, and prostitutes also joined in the jamboree, and so much fun could be had that one year the council refused to recommend the renewal of its licence, until it was pointed out that the often fishless aquarium was just as tawdry as everywhere else.

After the Princess reluctantly paid their shilling entrance fees, Pooki turned to her and said, "Ma'am, we must go and see Professor Finney's famous dive immediately, as he only performs it once a day and I cannot miss it." They squeezed past the visitors and women hawking curiosities in matchboxes, and sat as close as they could to the tank of water sunk into the floor. Within minutes the entertainer appeared on a high platform underneath the aquarium's dome, wearing a misshaped suit. After tweaking the ends of his elegant moustache, he climbed into a sack and pulled it up over his head. His vertiginous manager then appeared, called on at the last moment, as the maestro's assistant was prostrate following a misguided attempt to juggle some wine casks. With trembling fingers the substitute tied the sack, struck a match, and held it against his gold mine. He then kicked the professor in the shins and started praying. At the signal, the flaming performer tipped forward and plunged headfirst towards the water, black smoke billowing behind him. Much to the disappointment of the audience, the human inferno was extinguished as soon as he entered the tank. But it wasn't the end of their excitement. For he started to thrash around, attempting to break free from his sack before drowning. Once out of it, he struggled in the water to rid himself of his forsaken suit, ruined by so many incandescent flights ending in cold plunges. Finally he hauled himself out of the tank, his moustache collapsed, smoldering yet triumphant in a jaunty bathing costume. A Russian strongman then climbed up the steps to the platform, tossed the manager over his shoulder, and carried him down, a feat the audience wildly applauded on account of the man's staggering corpulence. It wasn't, however, part of the spectacle. For the manager, whose future earnings rested on the professor's ability to outwit his reef knot, had long since fainted.

Her palms red from clapping, Pooki then insisted on seeing the performing dogs, and took off through the crowd, Mink struggling to keep up. They arrived just as a fire broke out in a small wooden house on the stage. Two collies on their hind legs then fetched the fire escape and placed it against the wall of the blazing building. Ralph, the four-legged fireman, leapt up the ladder, jumped into the flames, seized a doll, and carried it back down the ladder. The hero then promptly rolled over onto his back, paws in the air, seemingly dead. As Pooki clutched the Princess's arm, his canine colleague stalked off on two legs and returned with an ambulance and a policeman with a hairy muzzle. The body was put onto a bier, and Ralph's whiskered widow appeared, dressed in full mourning, and stood inconsolable next to it. The dearly departed was then loaded into the ambulance and wheeled off to the melancholy strains of a funeral dirge.

It was too much for Pooki. As the audience left their seats, she remained where she was, waiting for a happy ending, despite Mink's insistence that the show was over. "I've just seen Ralph cocking his leg against a contortionist," the Princess added. But there was no appeasing the servant, and not even the offer of a piece of gingerbread improved her mood.

"Let's go and watch the Champion Jumper of the World," Mink suggested, changing tack. "Then we can go and see whether Countess X still has her head."

The servant perked up the moment she saw the diminutive Henri Flight dressed in a splendid red leotard and white tights, his hair slicked to improve his trajectory. He sprinted up to a non-chalant grey horse that had seen it all before, took off with both feet, and hurled himself over it, landing politely on the other side. Even the Princess held her breath when he proceeded to negotiate a row of eleven chairs, rising five feet into the air and travelling for fourteen over them. When the applause finally faded, he turned to the audience and asked for a volunteer. Before Mink realised what she was up to, Pooki started for the stage with the fearlessness of a woman whose days were numbered. Taking off her bonnet, she put on the top hat offered by Mr. Flight, who promptly lit the candle protruding from the crown. Not once did she flinch as he jumped over the table behind her, extinguished the flame with a gentle tap of his tiny feet, and landed on the ground in front of her with the grace of a dove.

Two tall assistants then walked on, and the athlete turned to the audience and requested a volunteer to perform the "human obstacle." The crowd went silent, fearful to move, lest they be deemed willing. On her way back to her seat, Pooki suddenly darted to the stage before Mink could grab her. She was promptly hoisted into a horizontal position between the assistants, her feet and head resting on their shoulders. The entertainer charged at them, rose into the air like one of the Maharaja's kangaroos, and sailed over the maid, who didn't so much as blink.

Praising his volunteer's fearlessness as she returned to her place, the almighty jumper then called for half a dozen brave men to take part in the final act: the human wall. Not to be upstaged by a skinny Indian servant, six men with wives in the audience strode onto the stage and lined up one behind the other as instructed. However, an argument soon broke out, as none was willing to stand at the end. "Stay where you are," the Princess ordered the servant, but Pooki shot out of her seat and took the position at the back. As Mr. Flight thundered towards them, the men grabbed one another, shut their eyes, and swore, while the maid gazed in awe as he passed over her head like a shooting star.

When Pooki returned to her seat, the Princess immediately grabbed her arm. "If you want to see Countess X, we'll have to go now, as it's time to leave," she hissed. They found the woman standing inside a caged arena, head intact, wearing a faded ball gown and grubby evening gloves. Encouraged by the rips in the Countess's dress, the maid insisted on sitting in the front row. A door shot open at the back and three bored lions wandered out, dragging their tails. The artiste cracked her whip, and they lumbered up onto their podiums, where they yawned, revealing their devastating teeth. The whip sounded again, and the beasts sat on their haunches, raising their clawless paws as if shooing away butterflies. After another crack, they lowered themselves to the sawdust and started to drag themselves around the ring with the reluctance of children taken to a picture gallery.

As the ponderous procession continued, one of the lions suddenly came to a halt and flicked its ears forward. Swishing its tail, it stared at the spurious aristocrat. The entertainer frantically waved her whip, but the beast let out an almighty roar. Suddenly it sprang into the air with even more ease than the Champion Jumper of the World, and landed in front of the Countess. She staggered back in dread, all too aware of the horror that was to befall her. But it was useless. Before she had time to raise her arms in defence, the king of the jungle had licked her on the nose and settled down for a snooze at her feet.

"Perhaps we should come another time, ma'am," suggested Pooki, standing up without bothering to clap.

"I think once in a lifetime is quite sufficient," the Princess replied curtly, heading for the exit. As they passed a sign for the Living Freaks, who refused to go out in daytime in order to retain their mystique, Mink held onto Pooki's arm. But the servant had not the least interest in entering on account of the three-legged man. "The General's pigeon pie had three legs, and it has caused me a lot of trouble," she said.

They had almost reached the exit when the servant came to a sudden stop. "Ma'am, there is the doctor you like," she said.

The Princess followed her gaze and saw Dr. Henderson talking to a man with a snake draped around his shoulders. "I've no idea what you're talking about. I don't like him at all. And anyway, he's in love with Lady Bessington," she replied, looking quickly away.

Pooki continued to stare at him. "He has seen you, ma'am, and is coming over."

Mink turned her back. "Then let's pretend we haven't seen him."

"It is too late for that, ma'am, because I have given him a wave."

The Princess turned round and acknowledged the hesitating general practitioner with a nod. He smiled as he approached and raised his hat.

"Dr. Henderson, how lovely to see you," Mink said. "I expect you've come to watch the bicyclists performing tricks on their machines."

"I'm actually here on a professional basis, standing in as the on-

duty doctor as a favour for a friend. The sword-swallowers sometimes take things a bit too far."

The Princess held his gaze. "Men do have a tendency to show
off."

The general practitioner glanced at Pooki and took a step
towards the Princess. "I understand you're trying to clear your
maid's name. Please let me know if there's anything I can do."

Mink raised her eyebrows. "Don't worry yourself about that,
doctor, I can manage perfectly well on my own. I've no need of
anyone. Particularly you."

"Everyone needs someone, Princess," he said.

"What rubbish," she snapped.

He paused. "There's no greater poverty than a loveless life," he
said tenderly.

The Princess looked away, then turned back. "How seductive,
Dr. Henderson. I fear you've been spending too much time with
the snake-charmers," she replied tartly, and headed for the exit.

Once they were settled in a hansom, Pooki gazed out the window and said, "You must be very much in love with Dr. Henderson, ma'am. You were even ruder to him than you were the last
time."

Mink looked at her. "You do realise that a servant should never
talk to her mistress unless to deliver a message or ask a necessary
question?" she snapped.

"Ma'am, I am no ordinary maid," she said, turning round. "I
am at death's door, and it is my duty to speak out, because soon I
will be silenced."

"You've always spoken to me like this. And anyway, you're
completely wrong about Dr. Henderson," she replied, looking at
the view.

Pooki shook her head. "I do not think so, ma'am. You are going
to have to risk your heart one day. It is the only way to mend it."

Mink suddenly turned back. "Speaking of love, I still haven't
forgotten that business with you and the watercress seller."

"I do not talk to him anymore, ma'am. I do not want to waste his time, as I am going to the scaffold."

"We'll see about that."

They continued without a word.

"Ma'am?" came a shaky voice after a while. "You will have to hurry up and find out who did it. It said in your newspaper that the Queen has taken an interest in the case, as the General died in her palace. That policeman needs a culprit."

The Princess continued looking out the window. "It's a pity she can't interest herself in returning my family's jewels."

"Ma'am?"

The Princess was lost in her thoughts as the rain started to fall.

"Ma'am?"

Eventually the Princess turned.

"They are going to hang me," said the maid, tears coursing down the hollows of her cheeks.

CHAPTER XIII

The Hazards of a Stuffed Codpiece

FRIDAY, APRIL 15, 1898

R. HENDERSON woke to find Mrs. Nettleship bending over him, her smile revealing a flagrant disregard for dentists. Gripping his sheet, he silently hauled it up to his nose and remained perfectly still.

"Hit's time to get hup, doctor," she said. "You've hoverslept. There's patients what's waiting to see you. Mrs. Bagshot's parlour maid his down there. I hexpect she wants those freckles getting rid hof hon haccount hof that nice-looking 'ouseguest. Silly girl. Hamericans like a lady with a title."

"I'll be right down," said the general practitioner, from behind his sheet. "And Mrs. Nettleship, I must ask that you knock before entering. I have mentioned this on numerous occasions."

"I did, Dr. 'enderson, but you didn't 'ear me. Snoring like a magistrate during a trial, you was. Still, at least you got your beauty sleep hin time for the fancy dress ball. Oo are you going has, may I hask?"

The doctor hesitated. "Romeo," he muttered.

The housekeeper beamed and clasped her butcher's hands together. "Most fitting, doctor, most fitting, hit being a full moon tonight has well! I expect hit's got a codpiece. I've got some hoily rags hif you need hit stuffing. Let me know hif you want some 'elp. I can't tell you what a pleasure hit would be."

Once Mrs. Nettleship had closed the door, Dr. Henderson threw back his bedclothes and started hunting for a clean collar, his ability to second-guess where his housekeeper had put them impeded by his lack of sleep. After returning home from the Royal Aquarium, he had gone straight to bed but was unable to sleep following the Princess's rebuttal. He had only just drifted off when the night bell woke him. Lighting a candle, he pulled on his dressing gown and groped his way downstairs, expecting an anxious father come to tell him of the imminent arrival of a baby. But through the speaking tube came the shrill voice of Mrs. Boots. "I've just seen a monkey in red velvet trousers looking at me through the bedroom window," she shrieked. Fearing that the woman was finally fit for the asylum, the general practitioner quickly unlocked the door and led the way to the consulting room in his bare feet.

After lighting a lamp, he took his place behind the desk and asked her to tell him what she had seen as calmly as she could. Swathed in a shawl, her white shins exposed in the gap between the bottom of her nightdress and the top of her boots, the palace housekeeper clutched the armrests and disgorged her harrowing vision. The words came out in such a deluge that the doctor eventually asked to see her tongue in an attempt to dam them.

Unable to detect the smell of sherry, he suggested that the apparition was simply the product of sleep. "When one is dreaming, Mrs. Boots, each side of the brain acts independently, and as one conflicts with the other the most curious fantasies present themselves. In fact, the dreamer could be said to be in a state of transient insanity. Rest assured that there is absolutely no cause for concern. Dreaming can also often be traced to a physical cause, such as indigestion or constipation." The doctor, his uncombed curls standing on end, then leant forward with a frown. "May I enquire into the state of your bowels?"

The housekeeper folded her arms across her considerable chest. "I'm not telling you such things, doctor! It's enough your being interested in the contents of a lady's piss-pot."

"All I'm suggesting, Mrs. Boots, is that perhaps you have been eating too many sausages," he said, sitting back and fiddling with his pen. "They're extremely indigestible, and many a death has been traced to their consumption. If you must indulge, stick to those you've made yourself. It's the only way of knowing what's in them."

The housekeeper shook her head. "I saw that monkey with my own eyes. Lit up by the moon he was, eating a penny bun."

"Did Mr. Boots see it?"

"He was snoring so loudly I thought the ceiling was going to cave in, hence my being awake at such an ungodly hour."

Watching his patient closely, the doctor asked, "Are you in the habit of drinking tea?" The woman's eyes immediately fled to the corner of the consulting room.

The doctor sat forward with a frown. "I cannot overstate the evil effects of tea-worship. Not only does the tannin ravish the throat and stomach, but it can also induce melancholia and suicidal monomania. According to a recent study, the increase of lunacy amongst the lower classes is considered partly due to the amount of tea they now drink. Their teapots are never off the hob. Where is yours, may I enquire?"

The housekeeper refused to look at him. "On the hob," she muttered.

"I suggest you go home and take it off at once. We'll say no more of it."

*

HAVING FINALLY FOUND A CLEAN COLLAR, Dr. Henderson finished dressing and went straight to his consulting room without any breakfast. He was still wondering how to keep Mrs. Nettle-ship away from his codpiece when the last patient of the morning sat down in front of him. The young soldier flushed violently, his eyes rooted to the floor. Finally he looked up and broached the delicate matter of nocturnal emissions. The doctor cleared his throat. "They're not injurious to the health," he stated. "However, they are believed to be caused by a mental disturbance combined with a derangement of moral faculties and should therefore not be encouraged. The problem can easily be solved by sewing a bobbin onto the back of your nightshirt."

The soldier looked confused. "I don't follow."

"It will prevent you from sleeping on your back," the general practitioner explained.

"I see," said the soldier. "But I haven't got a bobbin. Would that housekeeper of yours give me one?"

The doctor pointed at him with a frown. "Steer clear of that woman, whatever you do," he warned.

Once the soldier had left, Dr. Henderson glanced out the window and saw Silas Sparrowgrass walking past in his beadle's coat, a pair of long white ears protruding from his inside breast pocket. He stared at the homeopath, sensing something different. As he peered, he saw that he was wearing a much smarter topper than usual, which didn't quite fit. Convinced that it was his own, he stood up with such indignation his chair fell over. As he picked it up, Silas Sparrowgrass turned to him and raised his hat with a cheerful smile, a muffled quack emerging from deep within his coat.

The doctor immediately sat down and reached into his drawer for his copy of *Modern Homeopathy, Its Absurdities and Inconsistencies,* and placed it on the desk to face his patients. As he fiddled with his stethoscope, as hunched as a tailor, his thoughts eventually turned to the ball that evening. He wondered again whether the Princess would be there, having pledged his now rusting machine at the pawnbroker's to pay for his costume. Suddenly he regretted not having taken the advice of *The Gentleman's Guide to*

Politeness and Courtship. "It is exceptionally bad manners to go to a ball unless accomplished in the art of dancing," it warned. "Suitors should go to the expense of taking private dancing lessons rather than risk exposing their incompetence to their fair one." Instead, over the last few weeks, he had attended the academy in Kingston, its cheap fees soon explained by the wooden leg of the master. A former sailor with a perpetual sway, Horace Pollywog gave cursory consideration to the correct placement of the feet, made no mention of the necessity of maintaining a dignified carriage, gave scant instruction on the dangers of an unregulated pace, and offered absolutely no warning of the hazards of knocking a lady's knees with one's own. There were times, when the attic was filled with the smell of rum, that he seemed more intent on demonstrating his mastery of the sailor's hornpipe, a solo dance imitating nautical duties such as hauling ropes and climbing rigging. His renditions were so earnest that Dr. Henderson found himself treating the man's solitary bunion with his leeches, having waived his charge out of pity for the man who had lost his other foot after stepping on a sea hedgehog. As the dancing master lay on the worn floorboards with the trouser of his good leg rolled up, he suddenly stopped humming a sea shanty and declared he was about to die. The doctor informed him that he was more likely to die from a sausage than a bunion, but the ex-mariner was insistent: if a man knew the precise moment when a storm was due, despite a cloudless sky, he could foretell something as intimate as his own death. In an effort to reassure him, Dr. Henderson reached for his pulse, but it was so feeble he could barely detect it. The teacher then looked him in the eye and said he had something of utmost gravity to tell him, and the general practitioner braced himself for a harrowing deathbed confession.

Holding up a trembling finger, the instructor warned in a whisper: "Never, ever attempt the Lancers. The average person has not the faintest knowledge of the steps. It's the shortest known route to pandemonium on the dance floor, and it's almost impossible for a woman to forgive a man who has made her look ridiculous." After requesting that he be buried at sea, his hand fell upon his chest and Horace Pollywog had danced his final polka.

*

AFTER INSTRUCTING POOKI TO LOCK herself in the butler's pantry if anyone called, Mink put up her umbrella against the downpour and hurried along Moat Lane to luncheon with the Countess, hoping something would come out of it. As she splashed through the puddles, she cursed herself for still not having discovered the identity of the murderer. Was it Lady Montfort Bebb, who had taken exception to General Bagshot's criticism of her piano playing, which was all to do with her guilt for having survived the First Afghan War? Or was it Lady Beatrice, who had purchased some arsenic before the General's death and whose wedding gift he was supposed to have killed? Not only that, but she would lose her home if her marriage was discovered. What about her husband, Thomas Trout, whom Cornelius B. Pilgrim claimed to have heard arguing with the victim? Did he fear that if she lost her glamourous address she would leave him for someone who could offer her a lifestyle he never could? Did Silas Sparrowgrass, who had treated the General for a year, have a motive she had not yet uncovered? Was there anything in Thomas Trout's suspicions of Cornelius B. Pilgrim, whom she was sure was hiding something else? Then there was William Sheepshanks, who blamed General Bagshot for his mother's death. She had still to find out who had written to the Lord Chamberlain informing him that the keeper was allowing visitors into the maze after hours. And what about the Countess? Why had she never remarried, given the amount of suitors she attracted? Just as Mink was wondering how to catch her alone, she saw Inspector Guppy striding towards her. She watched him approach through the rain, her heart thumping, hoping he wasn't on his way to Wilderness House.

"I hear you've been asking people questions, Princess," the Inspector said over the drumming on their umbrellas.

Mink raised her eyebrows. "It appears the police need all the help they can get."

"It's not a job for a lady," he said. "Their place is in the home." He glanced over her shoulder at Wilderness House. "How's that maid of yours?"

The Princess moved to obstruct his view. "I do hope you get the right person this time, Inspector. Goodness knows the effect another wrongful conviction would have on your career, what with the Queen taking such an interest in the case."

Inspector Guppy glared at her. "Take my advice and leave it to people who know what they're doing," he snapped.

"If only one could, Inspector," she called, continuing on her way. "If only one could."

After turning in to Tennis Court Lane, Mink stood outside the school, looking for the door that led to Fish Court. Hearing her name, she glanced round and saw a tall, pewter-haired gentleman in a frock coat and silk hat running towards her without an umbrella, his shoulders hunched against the rain. On a rare visit to the palace, the Lord Chamberlain had the flushed cheeks and cemented bowels of a man who had resorted to dosing himself with laudanum to cope with the residents determined to get their own way.

Raising his voice above the downpour, he introduced himself. "I understand that an arrest in connection with the General's death is imminent, Princess," he said. "Inspector Guppy is adamant of a conviction, which is just as well, as the Queen is anxious that the matter be brought to a close as soon as possible." Taking a step closer, he peered at her through rain-streaked spectacles, his pupils like pinpricks. "It would be better for you, and for the palace, if you dismissed that maid of yours. There are some scandals from which it is impossible to recover."

Mink sheltered him with her umbrella. "You're absolutely

right, My Lord, I never thought of it like that," she said, a hand against her cheek. "This is Her Majesty's palace, and its reputation has to be upheld. Neither do I wish to be the subject of any more gossip. That woman never was any good in the kitchen anyway." She smiled. "How kind you are to think of me when you've got so much work. Sometimes I wonder whether the grace-and-favour residents have even read their warrants. If I come across anyone renting out their apartments, or leaving them vacant for more than six months, rest assured that I will inform you immediately."

"I'd appreciate that very much. Some think the regulations apply to everyone else except themselves," he said with a frown. "You'd be amazed how many of them insist they've seen the Prince of Wales recently and that he's adamant they need more suitable rooms."

The Princess shook her head, the rain driving against her skirt. "I wouldn't believe them for a second. And it's not just the residents who flaunt the rules. I understand the keeper used to let people into the maze after hours to earn a few extra pennies. Whatever was that man thinking of?"

The Lord Chamberlain gazed for a moment at the downpour. "Mr. Sheepshanks needs to be careful that I don't replace him with a turnstile. It was actually one of the residents who helped put a stop to it. He caught him red-handed."

"Did he?" asked Mink, her eyes wide. "How terribly clever. Who was it?"

"The General."

*

AS MINK HEADED ALONG FISH COURT, she found Lady Montfort Bebb waiting at the Countess's front door under an umbrella, holding her skirts up out of the wet. "I can't imagine Lady Bessington has invited many of us," muttered the elderly aristocrat. "I hope you've already eaten. It's the only way of ensuring one doesn't faint with hunger when one gets up to leave."

Alice showed them into the drawing room, where the Countess was sitting with Lady Beatrice. Mink immediately wondered where Cornelius B. Pilgrim was. Wanting to probe him further, she had suggested he be invited to give Mrs. Bagshot some time to grieve alone. Taking a seat next to a tall fern, she looked at the fashionable William Morris wallpaper depicting a green and gold vine, and then at the wax orange blossom the Countess had worn on her wedding day, preserved underneath a glass bell.

"We're all here, apart from Mr. Pilgrim," announced the hostess, looking at the clock on the mantelpiece next to a bust of her husband.

"Maybe he's been delayed in the West End, trying to find himself a lady with a title," suggested Lady Beatrice, following her gaze.

"Mr. Pilgrim has been in the palace all morning," said Lady Montfort Bebb. "I saw him sketching in the Privy Garden from my window before it started to rain. I do fear for his sense of perspective."

"Is he coming to the ball this evening?" asked the Countess.

"I thought it only proper to sell him a ticket, being as though it's for charity," replied Lady Montfort Bebb. "I'm afraid to say that some of them have gone missing. I hope they don't fall into the wrong hands. There's nothing more injurious to a ball than finding oneself in the presence of one's dustman dressed as a Zulu chief."

"Do you all have your costumes ready?" asked the Countess. She then looked at Lady Montfort Bebb. "I understand the more competitive have been ransacking the pictorial archive at the South Kensington Museum in search of inspiration."

Lady Montfort Bebb glanced at her white widow's cap. "Fortunately for you it's not an expense you have to bear."

When the five minutes' grace allowed for the late arrival of luncheon guests had passed, the Countess stood up and followed her guests down the narrow corridor to the dining room. Shortly after they had taken their seats, Cornelius B. Pilgrim rushed in, the shoulders of his new dark blue frock coat soaked. The women stared at the hat and cane he was clutching, which, according to the holy laws of etiquette, should have been left in the hall upon arrival. He slowly followed their gaze. Instantly realising his mistake, he thrust them at Alice, who was standing next to him, waiting for them to be surrendered.

"While you're in England, Mr. Pilgrim, you might find it more useful to be armed with an umbrella rather than a pistol," remarked Lady Montfort Bebb. "Fortunately for you our hostess hasn't lit the fire, despite the gale howling around my ankles, otherwise you'd positively steam throughout luncheon."

He sat down and joined the other guests in peering with dismay at the dishes on the table. A solid-looking dessert stood in the middle, which the Countess identified as American snow pudding. "I thought it would make Mr. Pilgrim feel at home," she explained triumphantly. "My maid assures me that the lumps in the custard are meant to be there."

Lady Montfort Bebb turned to him. "Well, Mr. Pilgrim? Do put us out of our misery. Should the lumps be there or not?"

He leant forward to have a closer look, then glanced at the Countess. "Absolutely," he replied.

Next to the pudding was a selection of cheeses that wouldn't have tempted a mouse with its ribs showing. It was surrounded by bowls of melancholy salad and plates of cold meat that were clearly the remains of the previous night's dinner.

"I don't think I've ever seen beef so thinly sliced," observed Lady Beatrice. "I could read *The Times* through it."

"If Mr. Pilgrim would care to serve us . . ." suggested Mink, turning to him.

"May I offer you some meat, Countess?" he asked.

She appeared momentarily taken aback. "Thank you," she replied graciously. "A little bit more, perhaps."

"Mr. Pilgrim!" barked Lady Montfort Bebb.

The American froze, then turned to look at his accuser, the slice suspended in mid-air.

"It would not be polite for our hostess to point out such a vulgar error, so I must take it upon myself to inform you that in speech the title of countess is wholly incorrect," she continued. "The only exception is when it needs to be mentioned, such as in a formal introduction. For the benefit of all our sensibilities, I would be most grateful if you would address our hostess as Lady Bessington." She furiously shook out her napkin and placed it on her knee. "One more aberration and my appetite will have completely vanished."

After they were all served, the Princess asked, "How are you finding our restaurants, Mr. Pilgrim? I understand visitors admire and abuse London's cuisine in equal measure."

"I've tried what I believe is termed 'dinners from the joint.' All that meat and potatoes . . . I find it . . . How should I put it? . . . Filling . . . Yes, that's the word. Filling."

"That's more than can be said for some luncheons," muttered Lady Montfort Bebb.

"And how is the research going?" asked the Countess.

He glanced anxiously at Mink.

"It's going splendidly, isn't it, Mr. Pilgrim?" said the Princess. "Tell me, have you been to see a play yet? No visit to London is complete without a trip to the theatre."

"I've been to a couple of matinees," he replied hastily. "But unfortunately I wasn't able to see a thing on account of the enormous hats the ladies in front of me were wearing. In San Francisco there's a by-law prohibiting women from wearing hats or bonnets at public performances."

Lady Beatrice reached for the salt. "I understand that *The Stage* magazine is publishing a list of ladies considerate enough to remove their hats during matinees. Please shoot me, Mr. Pilgrim, if ever my name appears on it."

Lady Montfort Bebb turned to him. "While I understand the police asking you to remain here until their investigation is concluded, I do wonder, Mr. Pilgrim, whether it is in Mrs. Bagshot's best interests that you stay in her apartments with no husband to protect her. I would have informed her of your attempt on my life, but she is not yet receiving callers. Please remember that you are not in Chicago now. This is Her Majesty's palace."

"I wouldn't dream of hurting Mrs. Bagshot," protested the American. "As I've explained to both you and the police, I was not trying to kill you." He then put down his cutlery, and admitted the real purpose of his visit.

There was silence around the table.

"But we don't want our ghosts investigated, Mr. Pilgrim," said Lady Beatrice eventually. "The least said about them the better. I have been without a parlour maid for longer than I care to remember. There are far too few good female servants as it is. Education has ruined them. They stipulate no washing, knife cleaning, or window cleaning in their advertisements for a position and expect to find employment. And even if one does find a maid prepared to work for her wages, it is highly unlikely she will live in the palace. My butler is too gouty to answer the door, and in the absence of a parlour maid my cook is running the ship. We are perilously off course as a result of her affection for brandy. So I for one, Mr. Pilgrim, would be grateful if you would leave our spirit world alone."

Lady Montfort Bebb wiped the corners of her mouth with her napkin. "I do wonder what the Lord Chamberlain will have to say about this. I shall write to him as soon as we have finished luncheon." She surveyed the table. "Which, by the looks of things, won't be much longer."

"But why did you come all this way to investigate our ghosts,

Mr. Pilgrim?" asked the Countess. "Surely we have enough experts of our own."

"The colonies have a tendency for ideas above their station," remarked Lady Montfort Bebb. "Look at the Welsh. They wish to be represented in the Royal Coat of Arms, and have even taken it as far as the House of Commons. They'll want us to visit them next. I'd rather go to Whitechapel in the dead of night."

"As Mr. Pilgrim said, it was the General who asked him to investigate them," said Mink. Turning to him, she asked, "Tell me, how did you two meet?"

The visitor shifted on his seat. "It was through Mrs. Bagshot, actually. We were introduced in America years ago, when she was visiting with her father."

"So you knew Mrs. Bagshot before she was married?" the Princess asked breezily.

His subsequent query about why the English didn't use napkins at breakfast provoked such a debate that only the Princess noticed that he had failed to answer her question.

*

MINK OPENED THE DELIVERY FROM the costumier, which had just arrived at the palace with a batch of others wrapped up in brown paper, and stared at the contents in disbelief. Instead of the Boadicea costume that she had had fitted, inside was a flowing blue silk gown with pointed elbow sleeves, a gold girdle, and a low-cut bodice.

"This isn't mine," she exclaimed, laying it out on her bed. "Who on earth is it meant to be anyway?"

Pooki picked up the pearl-and-velvet headdress. "It is Juliet, ma'am," she replied with delight.

"Juliet?" repeated Mink, aghast. "I can't go as Juliet. You'll have to get in touch with the costumier's immediately and tell them they've made a mistake."

But the maid was having none of it. By the time her correct

costume had been found and dispatched, the ball would be well and truly over. "You will have to wear it, ma'am," said Pooki, starting to undo the back of her dress. "I will make it fit. If you do not discover who the murderer is at the ball, at least you might find yourself a husband."

*

THAT NIGHT, AT AROUND ELEVEN O'CLOCK, a curious procession started to make its way through the palace to the Greyhound Hotel. The drunk woman selling pig's trotters outside the King's Arms was the first to spot Cardinal Wolsey, Henry VIII, and William III coming out of the Lion Gates. She immediately ran to tell the landlord, believing they were ghosts, and such was her shock that she endured a whole week of sobriety. A boisterous crowd immediately gathered, swaying out of the public house to witness the spectacle of costumes, the result of weeks of clandestine endeavours during which servants were sworn to secrecy and false rumours were spun.

Several carriages disgorged their contents, provoking murmurs of disappointment at the predictable Esmeraldas, Carmens, and rouge-et-noirs. But it was when the rest of the palace residents started to arrive that their wait in the damp night air away from their pint pots proved worthwhile. Soon after the kings and cardinal came a Klondike prospector, wearing a sieve fashioned into an elaborate hat from which hung nuggets of gold. He was accompanied by Electricity, wearing a dark blue velvet dress covered in silver lightning flashes, with battery-fuelled lights in her hair. Admiring eyes followed Queen Elizabeth, whose spectacular ruff had taken a team of women six weeks to copy from the Armada Portrait. After a surfeit of peasants from Bulgaria, Moldavia, and Burma came a herd of fish-themed revellers, including a Dutch fishwife, a Newhaven fishwoman, and a pecheuse de Calvados. Amongst them were a number inspired by the view from their window, who came dressed as a drizzle, a shower, and a catastrophic downpour. The women in the crowd stood on their toes when the officers of the 1st Royal Dragoons barracked at the palace arrived in uniforms of the previous century. But it was the lobster, its pink claws lit up by the moon, which produced the loudest cheer, and the drinkers returned to the pub satisfied it couldn't be beaten.

Just as Mink reached the Lion Gates, planning to catch the Countess on her own at some stage in the evening, she heard a commotion behind her. Turning round, she saw Wilfred Nose-worthy hauling the push, swearing like a Billingsgate eel merchant. There was a sudden sound of knocking, and the liveried turncock brought the vehicle to an abrupt halt and approached the window. The occupant, unwilling to pay the additional sixpence to cross the palace boundary, informed him that she wanted to walk. Adjusting his sweaty wig with irritation, he opened the door, and out swept Britannia in a blue-and-white satin gown and gold helmet, clutching a trident and shield. After passing the man a shilling, Lady Montfort Bebb turned to Mink and said, "You've come as Juliet, I see. I would avoid any balconies if I were you, Princess. You might attract the wrong sort."

The two women deposited their shawls in the hotel's cloakroom and, squeezing past one of three Henry VIIIs, headed to the refreshment room. "No doubt we'll find Lady Bessington in here somewhere," said Lady Montfort Bebb, looking around. Sure enough, the Countess was sitting at a table with a glass of claret cup and a large slice of cake. Next to her was Lady Beatrice, who was attracting a number of glances due to her grey tunic fashioned into wings and covered in feathers. Tied round her waist was a red ribbon bearing a letter.

Lady Montfort Bebb studied her. "Given the circumstances of the General's death, I do wonder whether it's in good taste to have come as a carrier pigeon," she remarked.

There was a sudden flutter as Lady Beatrice reached for her

glass of champagne. "I've been collecting feathers for this costume since last year. At least it's topical, which is more than can be said for yours," she said, looking Lady Montfort Bebb up and down. She glanced round at the crowd. "Goodness knows why I brought my daughter, wherever she's got to. Men no longer attend balls as they used to. I suppose if they work all day in the city they can't dance all night, but it doesn't help young ladies with an eye on matrimony. Unless the prettiest girls are around, the men who do come just hang about the refreshment room, and leave immediately after supper. I hope the young widows don't hog the few who bother turning up. Dr. Henderson is here, I see."

The Countess immediately knocked back the rest of her claret cup, and asked the waiter for another. "Let's watch the dancing," she suggested.

As they entered the ballroom, hung with red drapery and Chinese lanterns, Portia and Friar Tuck, closely followed by the Queen of Sheba and Oliver Cromwell, galloped past. As soon as the dance was over, the floor was stormed by a glut of Pierrots and harlequins, the lack of imagination in their choice of costumes made up for by their enthusiasm.

"Dancing isn't what it used to be," muttered Lady Montfort Bebb. "People just seem to charge round the room nowadays."

"Thank goodness they haven't waxed the floor," said Lady Beatrice. "We were all rooted to the spot last year, and our gowns ruined."

As Mink took a seat next to the Countess, she noticed Charles Twelvetrees stride past dressed as Julius Caesar, tufts of white hair billowing up around his laurel wreath. He was scrutinising the dancers for any sign of the telltale beard of Silas Sparrowgrass, who had refused to answer his door each time he called for the return of his gold pocket watch. It wasn't long before Lady Beatrice swirled past, the feathers on her tunic flying, clutching onto Charles I wearing a black satin coat and breeches, cavalier boots,

Vandyke lace collar and cuffs, and a large plumed hat. Clearly not all the tickets had fallen into the right hands after all, Mink noticed. For, as she watched, she realised that under the long curled wig was the irrefutable bald head of Thomas Trout.

A South Sea Islander with a grass skirt and Scottish accent asked her to dance, but she declined, biding her time with the Countess, who made several trips to the refreshment room to replenish her glass. Sitting down next to the Princess even more heavily than before, she unfurled a black fan and fluttered it at her flushed cheeks.

"I always prefer a candle-lit ballroom. Gas is always too hot," she complained.

The Princess, who didn't feel in the least over-heated, suggested that they go outside for some fresh air.

"I couldn't do that!" exclaimed the Countess. "There's a full moon, and I might meet Dr. Henderson. I've been dreading it all day."

"Lady Bessington, as strange as Dr. Henderson is, I very much doubt that he will turn into a werewolf."

Leaning towards Mink, the Countess whispered, "The man sent me some flowers!"

"But wouldn't that please you?" the Princess asked.

The Countess recoiled. "Absolutely not! He's considerably younger than me, and goodness knows who his tailor is. I assure you any feelings he has for me are completely unrequited."

The Princess frowned. "But he gave you a handkerchief and you returned it, fragranced."

"He gave it to my maid when she went to see him for some ailment or another. Hopefully she was after a cure for her rampant appetite. She's eating me out of house and home. I do fear for the tread on my stair carpets. Anyway, I saw her using it and insisted she return it, lest he charge me for it. Any scent was the laundress's doing."

Suddenly the Countess hid behind her fan. "That's him now, and he's come as Romeo!" she whispered. "I have a horrible feeling he's going to ask me to dance. Neither my nerves nor my corns will stand it. You must do something."

Dressed in a green velvet doublet and breeches with white silk hose, the general practitioner stood hesitantly in front of them, trying to muster the courage to ask the Princess to dance. He had long debated his choice of costume, as the chapter on fancy dress balls in *The Gentleman's Guide to Politeness and Courtship* stated that it was imperative to choose a character and style of dress suitable to the wearer's face, figure, and personality. "Without considerable forethought, the chances of looking absolutely ridiculous in an inappropriate guise are extremely high," it warned. There was a long discourse on the recklessness of not being correct in historical detail, particularly when it came to beards. "Do not make the grave error of wearing hair upon the face with a powdered wig," it urged. "You will remain without a wife forever."

To help the hopeless, a handy guide explained the styles of facial hair from the Ancient Britons to the Georgians. It included a long tangent on the Elizabethan period, when it was possible to determine a man's occupation by his beard. Churchmen wore the cathedral beard, soldiers the stiletto, bakers the loaf, and tailors the thimble.

Fearful of falling into the trap of inappropriate whiskers, Dr. Henderson flicked through the suggested list of characters until he chanced upon clean-shaven Romeo. However, the costume came with a dark warning: "Any gentleman who chooses the most famous star-crossed lover in English history should do so at his own risk. Utmost care must be taken over the codpiece. One that is under-stuffed and wont to flap suggests a distinct lack of mettle, whereas one that is over-stuffed is the mark of a braggart." Just as the doctor wavered, he read the next sentence and immediately headed to a West End costumier for an outfit that best evoked the

House of Montague. "When successfully adopted, the guise of Romeo will stir the amorous inclinations of a fair one more than any other. There is no more irresistible sight on the dance floor."

That afternoon he had given Mrs. Nettleship the rest of the day off so as to avoid having to defend himself from her butcher's hands when it was time to get ready. But when he went upstairs to change, he found a pile of oily rags outside his door with a note saying that she had asked a friendly taxidermist to come round, as there was no more expert a profession for stuffing. When the doorbell rang, he opened the bedroom window and looked down to see a short man with spectacles and squirrel-coloured hair carrying a leather bag in his gloved hand. The doctor shouted down that his services were not required, but the man took it badly and said that he understood that a lady was at stake. "Apparently you still haven't found yourself a wife, sir," he called back. Several passers-by stared at the doctor, and an old woman burst into tears. He slammed down the window and sat on the bed, head in his hands, wondering how life had turned out the way it had. He then thought once more of the Princess and told himself to pull himself together. Opening a drawer, he pulled out one of the new diamond-patterned stockings he had been wearing when his foray into fancy riding went so hideously wrong. Since reduced to a fifth of its size by his housekeeper, who boiled it for two days to get rid of the smell of the Thames, he put the finishing touch to his costume.

Standing in front of the Princess, he eventually found his courage. "Would you care to dance?" he asked her, while distracted by the cowering Countess. Assuming he had addressed Lady Bessington, the Princess immediately rose to her feet and offered her hand to save the Countess from having to partner him. Still suffering from a lack of sleep, it was then that all of Dr. Henderson's terrors collided and he was suddenly struck by the irrational fear of his shrunken stocking dropping out. As the couple walked to the dance floor, the revellers started whispering that Romeo had found his Juliet. They whispered even louder after the dancing started, for one false turn could spoil the Lancers, and there, much to their delight, was the ruinous spectacle being played out in front of them. It was never known when Dr. Henderson first went wrong. Some claimed it was as early as his initial attempt to turn round. Others insisted it was a little later, when the couples were changing places. The more mischievous ran with the rumour started by the homeopath from East Molesey that the doctor botched the very first move, which was simply turning to his partner and bowing. Whenever it was, one thing was certain: when it was time for the side couples to divide, and for a lady and gentleman from each to join the top and bottom couples, the general practitioner was nowhere to be found. For by then he had worked his way jauntily down the ballroom in a spectacular misguided bluff, hoping that the gods would deliver him to his rightful position and that nothing would poke its way out of his crotch during the procedure. Instead he found himself in front of Silas Sparrowgrass dressed as an astrologer in a wide-sleeved gown, a pointed cap entwined with a gold snake, and long shoes curling upwards. The befuddled doctor immediately offered him his hands. But the homeopath refused to partner him, and prodded him away with his wizard's wand. It was then that the dance unravelled, and the disorder was such that the conductor, dressed as the Artful Dodger, was compelled to bring a halt to the music that served only to highlight the carnage on the dance floor.

When Mink returned to her seat in silent humiliation, she found the Countess collapsed with mirth. The more she tried to control herself, the worse it got, for each time she recovered her composure the vision of Dr. Henderson's labyrinthine leaping round the ballroom would return, with its numerous false starts, wrong turns, and hopeless dead ends. Sitting up, she wiped her eyes on a black-bordered handkerchief, then hiccoughed loudly, blaming dyspepsia. "Since receiving Dr. Henderson's flowers, I haven't been able to face seeing him for treatment," she explained, fanning herself frantically. "I'll have to get some Fowler's solution, but Lady Montfort Bebb, who's taking it for psoriasis, has misgivings. She's a little worried that all that arsenic is darkening her complexion, and she'll end up looking like an Arab, or that lobster over there. Who *is* that, by the way?" she asked, peering at the crustacean standing near the band.

As the dancers started heading towards the supper room, Mink was suddenly filled with dread that Dr. Henderson would attempt to escort her, having been his last partner. She suggested that they go outside, and the Countess immediately agreed, declaring herself too bilious to eat. As they walked past the open doorway, the hiccoughing aristocrat looked longingly at the tables laden with roasted fowls, oyster patties, savoury jellies, cold salmon, tongue, lobster salad, veal cakes, game pie, boiled turkey, snowy creams, trifles, and jellies. "Such a lot of food. What a pity I can't take any of it home," she muttered.

Sitting on a bench on the terrace, they gazed in silence at the avenue of chestnut trees stretching out in front of them, drenched in moonlight. Mink turned to the Countess and asked how long she had lived at the palace.

"Thirteen years," she replied. "Ever since I lost my husband. Thankfully the Queen offered me some apartments not long afterwards. They had wonderful views of the river. I'm sure all the other residents were hoping I would die at any moment so they could get their hands on it."

"It must have been a wrench to move to Fish Court, given all the memorials to your husband in your old home," said Mink, watching her closely. "You must have been very much in love."

The Countess glanced away. "There are certain advantages to having a smaller place," she said. "It's much less costly to heat, and one needs fewer servants. My ferns are doing a lot better since I moved too. There was one room where they always failed to thrive. It must have been the damp."

"I was in love once," Mink continued, sitting back. "At least I thought I was. Now I'm not so sure. You never thought of remarrying in all that time?"

There was silence. The Countess bowed her head and looked at her empty glass. The dark secret that had been tunnelling inside her for years finally found release, and before she knew it she had unburdened herself. "I'm still married," she admitted, her voice uneven. The story came out punctuated by sobs, and by the end of it even the nightjars had stopped singing.

The Countess had met her husband at a country ball while a guest at a shooting party. From the moment the officer offered his warm hand, led her to the dance floor, and looked into her eyes she was lost. Her parents, however, disapproved of her suitor, who was almost twenty years older. The couple conducted a secret courtship, leaving each other books on a bench in Hyde Park whenever he returned from battle, their love letters composed of words underlined in pencil. She barely spoke to any of the gentlemen her parents invited to the house in the hope of turning her head. Fearing she would never marry, they gave in, and the couple stood at the altar two days after her twentieth birthday. After they sealed their love on their wedding night, she lay in his arms with tears in her eye at the dreadful thought of their ever being parted. It turned out to be the cruellest of premonitions. Five years later she was sitting in the drawing room, embroidering the christening gown for the child she still hoped to have, when she received the news that her husband was missing in Sudan, presumed dead.

"I was a widow at twenty-five," she said, looking down at her hands.

She collapsed on hearing of her husband's death, and it was several months before the doctor allowed her out of the sickroom. The first thing she did was to go to the bookshelf and read all his love letters, and it was then that she vowed never to come out of mourning. As a result of her husband's distinguished military record, the Queen offered her a home at the palace. Without a body, it took another year for her to finally accept that her only love was never coming back, and from then on she took to surrounding herself with his memory. "I spent far, far too much on it all, of course. I was blind with grief," she said through her tears. For almost thirteen years she mourned him, ignoring all declarations from interested gentlemen, and turning her gaze away from perambulators, their tiny passengers too painful to bear.

About six months ago, the General, who had known her husband, approached her while walking in the Privy Garden, and suggested she sit down, as he had something important to tell her. She had no wish to stop, as it was a particularly cold day, but the man insisted. Clutching the neck of her black coat together, she sat on a bench in the piercing wind as he told her that her husband was very much alive and living with a woman and three children. He had seen him in a tobacconist while visiting relatives in the country, and was so surprised he followed him home. While it had been years since he had seen the man, he was in no doubt that it was him, adding that it was not uncommon for men to use the confusion of war to desert their wives.

"I didn't think a heart could break twice," the Countess said, staring ahead of her. She then bent her head and looked at her hands. "I turned grey almost overnight."

She told no one her secret. General Bagshot vowed he would keep it to himself, though she was never certain he would. "Sometimes I think I see my husband. I once went into some tearooms after him. But of course it's never him."

There was silence as they both looked at the silver moon. "Now you'll understand why it wasn't in the slightest bit difficult to swap apartments," the Countess added.

"You must feel very angry with him," suggested Mink.

The Countess turned to her. "Who? My husband? It was the General I was furious with. I wish he'd never told me. I'd finally found some contentment."

Suddenly the terrace door opened and a couple walked past hand in hand, laughing. Gripping her wet handkerchief, the Countess waited for them to be out of earshot before she continued.

"Of course my friends don't know and suggest that I come out of mourning and open my heart to a new romance. They mean well, but how can I marry again when I already have a husband? I am thirty-eight and will never know love again. And what is life without love?"

*

WHEN THEY EVENTUALLY RETURNED to the ballroom, Mink glanced around warily, hoping to avoid Dr. Henderson. But he was nowhere to be seen, having left immediately after his public disgrace.

"There goes the carrier pigeon and Charles I again," said the Countess, as the couple span past. "That man has hogged poor Lady Beatrice all night. Maybe I should ask Cromwell over there to intervene."

With a blatant disregard for tempo, and the correct placement of the feet, came the lobster and a gentleman dressed as Cupid in a gold tunic, a small bow slung across his back.

"I've never seen such appalling footwork," tutted the Countess, fanning herself. "They're almost as bad as Dr. Henderson."

The Princess stared. "They look as though they're trying to escape from quicksand." She then spotted Lady Montfort Bebb dancing with Sir Walter Raleigh, bunches of tobacco leaves hanging from his belt. "That looks like the Keeper of the Maze behind that fake beard," she said, peering at them. "I wonder what Lady Montfort Bebb would say if she knew she were dancing with a gardener."

The Countess leant towards Mink for a better view. "I'll make a point of telling her in detail tomorrow. Do let me know if you spot the dustman in disguise. I shall inform him Britannia is desperate for a dance."

Charles Twelvetrees strode past in his toga, looking for Silas Sparrowgrass again. He had just tracked him down to the refreshment room, where he had performed another magic trick. It wasn't until the homeopath had fled that the perplexed coroner realised that not only was he still missing his gold watch, but now also his best silk handkerchief.

The Princess and the Countess watched as Robinson Crusoe approached in a pair of knickerbockers, silk tights, and a monkey-fur coat tied with a belt from which hung a pair of pistols, a hatchet, and an umbrella. On one shoulder was slung a fowling piece, and on the other stood a stuffed parrot. Offering his hand to the Countess, Cornelius B. Pilgrim asked, "May I have this dance, Lady Bessington?"

Lightened by her revelation, and cheered by another glass of claret, she immediately accepted. As the pair made their way around the dance floor, the American propelled the aristocrat at a greater speed than was required to prevent her from swaying. Just as they passed the band, the Countess raised her head and looked at the one-eyed bird on his shoulder. Instantly she recognised the African grey parrot that she and Lady Beatrice had spent months training to call Mrs. Boots the most vulgar of insults. They had taken particular diligence in deciding the exact words. At first they swore at each other to see what they could come up with, but their language was too genteel, so they ransacked the dictionary. When that too failed to produce the filth they were after, they went to buy some pig's trotters from the drunk woman outside the King's Arms, and came away with a string of expletives that would make a cabman blush. When they repeated them to the bird, which had once belonged to a sailor, it raised its solitary eyebrow in shock.

Once it had recovered its composure, it set about learning the lewd insult, seduced by the lure of Brazil nuts. After months of coaching, the two women decided that the parrot was finally ready. They stood at Lady Beatrice's drawing room window overlooking Clock Court, eagerly waiting for their target. As soon as they spotted her scuttling across the courtyard with the gait of a startled pheasant, they moved the cage to the window and offered its inhabitant a nut. Recognising its cue, the parrot cocked its head to one side, opened its colossal beak, and squawked at the top of its tiny lungs the profanities that would be its last.

As the Countess gazed at the preserved bird, she suddenly remembered the look on Mrs. Boots's face, and let out an undignified snort. Next she tittered, then she sniggered, and the more she tried to forget the housekeeper's expression of horrified indignance, the more vivid it became, and she was no longer able to dance. She threw back her head, and Cornelius B. Pilgrim was obliged to hold her as she rocked with derision. Each time he asked her what she found so amusing, she was only able to squeak "the parrot" before she became convulsed again. Her laughter soon infected him, and he found his shoulders starting to shake. The bird began to dance, which only increased her hysteria. The howling pair soon created a logjam, resulting in a collision between the chaplain, dressed as Richard III, and the organist, who had come as one of the Princes in the Tower. The two gentlemen immediately blamed the other for the crash, and when no consensus could be reached they started to brawl. They were promptly ejected by the steward, who was forced to stand between them outside when an argument immediately ensued about whether Richard III really did kill the two little princes. Meanwhile, Mink accepted every dance she was offered in order to show her proficiency, lest someone thought her responsible for the calamitous Lancers. But eventually even she tired, and when four o'clock finally struck, the only thing left on the dance floor was a stewed gentleman's stocking.

CHAPTER XIV

A Surfeit of Anchovy Relish

SATURDAY, APRIL 16, 1898

INK woke suffering from the usual ruinous consequences of a ball. Not only did her feet ache, but so too did her head, as a result of all the champagne she had drunk to forget the humiliation of being the partner of the man whose antics were already known by the watchman when she returned to the palace. She forced herself to sit up when Pooki brought in her morning tea, and as she sipped it, she remembered Cornelius B. Pilgrim asking the Countess to dance. Wondering again about the mystery woman he was trying to impress, she threw back the covers, staggered over to the writing table, and picked up her pen.

She ate more than usual at breakfast, helping herself twice to the eggs, the smell of the kippers turning her stomach. Still thirsty, she rang the bell and asked Pooki for more tea. The next time she looked up from her newspaper the maid was standing next to her with a silver salver. On it was a glass filled with a swirling black liquid.

"What on earth is that?" the Princess asked, staring at it.

"It is soot and milk, ma'am. It is a cure for people who have drunk too much. The chimney sweep recommended it."

The Princess looked at her. "I'd rather have some more tea, if you don't mind."

The maid shook her head. "Dr. Henderson would not like it," she replied, leaving the glass on the table before Mink could protest. As the maid started for the door, she added, "That man should never have attempted the Lancers. No one knows how to dance it."

Mink span round. "How do you know about that?" she asked.

The maid stopped, frowning as she thought. "I think the first person who told me was the fishmonger."

"The fishmonger?" the Princess asked, eyes wide.

The servant raised a finger to her chin as she tried to remember. "Or maybe it was the sweep . . . No, I remember now, ma'am, it was the milkman. He said there were people who came off the first train from London this morning who were talking about it . . . And they were from Germany."

The Princess reached for more toast. "To make matters worse, he was dressed as Romeo," she snapped.

"That is what they were saying, ma'am. They found it very funny indeed, as you were dressed as Juliet. German people are known for their sausages, not for their sense of humour, so it must have been very amusing indeed."

"So it would seem," muttered Mink, buttering loudly.

The maid put a hand on her hip. "I would say it was even funnier than one of the Maharaja's comic songs, or that All Fools' Day when I hid behind the curtain all morning and you were looking for me, getting crosser and crosser. That gave me the worst case of hiccoughs that I have ever had," she continued.

The Princess put down her knife and looked up. "I'm sure the front steps need whitening."

"No, ma'am, they do not. I did them while you were recovering from your night of dancing," the maid said over her shoulder as she headed out. "When Dr. Henderson was not lost, that is."

*

MINK WAS JUST FINISHING HER toast when the front door-bell rang. Shortly afterwards Pooki entered the breakfast room, clutching the sides of her dress, and announced that Mrs. Boots was waiting for her in the drawing room.

"Why are you looking so nervous, Pooki?" the Princess asked. "Anyone would think it was that policeman."

But the servant didn't reply.

Mink found the housekeeper frowning back at the portraits of the ancestors. She turned and immediately got to the point. "The charge for the extra supply of water needs paying, Your Highness."

"It will be paid in due course," said Mink, raising her chin.

"Forgive my saying, but I've heard that one before."

"I've only been here four weeks!" the Princess protested.

The housekeeper crossed her arms underneath her enormous bosom, causing it to surge. "I like to have it upfront. Some grace-and-favour ladies disappear for months at a time, and I never see it until they're back."

"I'm sure they're not avoiding you, Mrs. Boots. They've probably gone to visit a relation."

Mrs. Boots raised an eyebrow. "They don't want to spend their money heating the place, that's their problem."

Suddenly she approached the Princess, lowered her voice, and asked out of the corner of her mouth whether she had ever seen a monkey sitting on top of the chimneypots.

The Princess blinked. "No, Mrs. Boots, I haven't."

"Do you drink much tea?" asked the housekeeper, taking a step closer.

The Princess looked at her, wondering whether the woman had been drinking something stronger. "We all drink a lot of tea. It's how the upper classes cope with the world, along with feeling superior to servants."

The housekeeper continued to press her. "Have you ever seen anything you shouldn't have?"

"I'm sure I've seen lots of things I shouldn't have."

Mrs. Boots smiled. "That does reassure me, ma'am. Pay me in a couple of weeks."

*

SHORTLY AFTER THE HOUSEKEEPER HAD been shown out, Mink heard the drawing room door open and hoped it was Cornelius B. Pilgrim. After thanking him for coming at such short notice, she spotted Pooki's look of confusion as she closed the door. The Princess immediately saw the reason. He had failed to bring in with him his hat and cane as English etiquette dictated on a brief visit to a mere acquaintance, having left them in the hall as if he were a friend about to stay for luncheon.

"Did you enjoy yourself last night, Mr. Pilgrim?" Mink enquired, offering him a seat. "I must say, I very much admired your Robinson Crusoe costume. You looked suitably deserted before asking Lady Bessington to dance."

The American smiled. "Oh, I had a wonderful time!" he enthused. "My only regret is that I sat out the Lancers. It looked so much more fun than the American version. That doctor sure can move. If you didn't know any better you'd think it ended in a bun fight. What a pity the band couldn't keep up."

Mink swiftly changed the subject. "I was wondering whether you'd made any progress in your investigation into the new ghost sightings, Mr. Pilgrim. In the event that I have to get a new maid, I may very well struggle to find one if they're still at large."

"I've been out every night since I arrived," he replied. "But it hasn't been easy having to keep it all secret. You wouldn't believe the number of people walking around the palace after dark. Some of them have spotted me with my equipment, and I've had to invent reasons why I was carrying it all."

"What sort of equipment does one use to catch ghosts?" Mink asked.

Cornelius B. Pilgrim sat back. He had several large nets in which to capture them, a ball of string to keep them in position, should he not be able to get close enough to cast them, and a pistol in the event that things got tricky. "And then there's the cheese."

The Princess raised her eyebrows. "The cheese, Mr. Pilgrim?"

"An eight-pound Cheddar. No one can resist a bit of Cheddar cheese, ma'am. Not even the dead."

"And have you made any progress with your cheese, Mr. Pilgrim?"

The American glanced at the floor. "So far I've only attracted Lady Bessington, and then there were the two footmen I caught in my net," he admitted. "But I haven't given up. I've just managed to get my hands on a phonograph, and hope to make my first recording tonight."

Pooki came in with some tea and the Princess walked to the window and looked at the view. Once the door was shut again, she asked how Mrs. Bagshot was.

"I sometimes hear her weeping in her bedroom at night," he said flatly. "She's finally started redecorating, which seems to be helping to take her mind off things a little. People react to grief in such different ways. Some cling onto every reminder, and others just want to clear everything out."

Slowly Mink turned round. "You do have my sympathies, Mr. Pilgrim. First you get caught up in the murder of a friend, and then you have to remain a houseguest of his widow. But now that I remember, you made Mrs. Bagshot's acquaintance first. She must have been a very fine-looking woman when she was younger."

"Oh, she was," came the immediate reply, followed by nervous laughter.

The Princess returned to her seat. "Was it love at first sight?" she asked.

Cornelius B. Pilgrim froze.

"I've been thinking about your kerasaurus, Mr. Pilgrim," she continued. "I couldn't understand why you donated it to a museum in England. The only reason I could come up with was that you wanted someone to see it. That person had to be someone you wanted to impress more than your rival palaeontologists in America. The answer could only be a woman."

There was no reply.

"And being as though this is your first trip to England, I presumed you must have made her acquaintance abroad, which brought Mrs. Bagshot to mind."

Still there was silence.

"Mr. Pilgrim, I fear for your trousers."

The American looked down, and, seeing the precarious angle of his cup and saucer, placed them on the table next to him. He took a moment, then hesitantly told his tale. He had met Mrs. Bagshot seventeen years ago, when he had just turned twenty-two and she was eighteen. She had accompanied her father on a business trip to America, and they were staying for a couple of nights as houseguests. At the time, her father was a senior figure in the company that made Patum Peperium, the English gentleman's relish, which had been exhibited at the Paris Food Shows in 1849 and 1855, and lauded with a *Citation Favorable*. Pilgrim Senior was the sole American importer, having seen a business opportunity in the spread that was the colour of a mudlark's legs. With boomtown Chicago trying to rival New York for European sophistication, there was no matching the man's ability to sell the virtues of the blended remains of a tiny fish with a blunt snout and sharp teeth. Such was his salesmanship, he was credited with starting the 1867 Great Chicago Anchovy Toast Craze, an achievement noted in his obituaries many years later.

At first Cornelius B. Pilgrim took no interest in the young Englishwoman, who barely spoke as they sat in the drawing room before dinner. What he didn't know was that her reticence was due to her dread of having to consume six courses laced with the ingredient that whiffed of a Swansea cockle-picker's socks, and which she couldn't abide. His eyes kept returning to the clock on the mantelpiece in the hope that the evening would soon be over. Much to his relief, once they had sat down to eat he was unable to see her due to the fashion for tall table decorations. It was only after the entrées were served that she finally spoke, such was her relief that her pheasant was untainted. There was no stopping her, and soon she had turned the conversation round to the world's first full-scale dinosaur models, displayed at the Crystal Palace in England, which she had recently visited. The sculptor Benjamin Waterhouse Hawkins had hosted a famous dinner inside the boat-like mould of his thirty-foot-long Iguanodon for more than twenty learned gentlemen, she added, with a peal of laughter. Captivated by her accent, Cornelius B. Pilgrim looked up and tried to see her through the foliage, but he caught only the glimmer of her diamonds. At the end of the meal, when she stood up and asked him whether he intended to spend his life in business with his father, he felt the full impact of her allure. Before he knew what he was saying, he announced that he was going to become a palaeontologist.

As soon as the ladies left the gentlemen to their cigars, Pilgrim Senior, already incensed that the pheasant had tasted of game, turned to his son, his palms outstretched, and demanded, "What about the anchovies?" Cornelius B. Pilgrim had now seen an escape route from a life devoted to a briny relish, and fought off his father's entreaties to stay with the firm. The port went round several times until it was clear that no capitulation would be brokered. When finally the embattled host suggested they join the ladies in the drawing room, his son immediately sat by the Englishwoman who had opened his eyes to a world of possibilities. They stopped talking only when each was given a candle to take upstairs to bed, silenced by the sudden realisation that they would be parted until morning.

Their conversation resumed at breakfast, when they both chose boiled eggs in the belief that they ran the least risk of contamination. They glanced at each other on discovering that the brackish taste had invaded the shell, and from then on all decorum was lost. While attempting to muffle her laughter, the Englishwoman snorted, which set off Cornelius B. Pilgrim. There was no stopping their uproar. Pilgrim Senior, already irascible from lack of sleep, immediately tried to put a stop to the racket. But his indignation only inflamed their mirth. The Englishman, affronted by his daughter's lack of manners, banished her from the table, and promptly ate five of the offending eggs in a bid to calm the turbulent waters. The visitors left that morning, a day earlier than expected, without a chance for the young couple to say goodbye. With a lump in his throat, Cornelius B. Pilgrim stood at the study window, watching the carriage leave. It was only when he shut himself in his bedroom to hide his unexpected tear that he discovered her note. On it was drawn a picture of Hawkins's Iguanodon at the Crystal Palace, and he smiled when he spotted the tiny anchovy caught in its prehistoric mouth.

It was he who sent the first letter. Unable to wait for a reply, he sent another, and then a third. When that too remained unanswered, he sent a fourth and then a fifth, until his father asked why he had permanently ink-stained fingers. He loitered about at home, waiting for the numerous appearances of the postman. But still nothing arrived for him bearing the mark of England. It was four months later that the reply finally came, written in the swirling script of the love-possessed. Her father had hidden his letters, she explained, and she had only just discovered them in his desk drawer. She begged him to continue writing, and, as she waited for his reply, she returned each day to re-read those he had already sent. But her father noticed the opened envelopes, their fingered edges worn out by desire, and burnt them. Each time he left the house, she hunted for more of the notes that made her tremble. But after months of finding nothing, she assumed the American's affection had died, and she accepted the first offer of marriage that came along, her heart forever torn.

Six years ago, when Pilgrim Senior heard of the death of his English supplier, he invited the couple to stay in memory of the man who had helped make his fortune. Cornelius B. Pilgrim, who had remained a bachelor during the eleven years that had passed since he had seen her, knew none of his love had faded the instant he saw her again. He chose the menu, replicating precisely the famous dinner Hawkins had held inside the mould of his Iguanodon. But despite the mock turtle soup, the *currie de lapereau au riz,* the woodcocks, and the Madeira jelly, Mrs. Bagshot made no mention of prehistory at the dining table, and left the conversation to her husband, who spoke only of himself. When, the following morning, Cornelius B. Pilgrim chose boiled eggs for breakfast, and muttered that they tasted of seamen's combinations, her eyes remained on her cutlets.

It wasn't until the visitors' luggage was being loaded that the pair finally found themselves alone in the library. Gazing out the window across the grounds, Mrs. Bagshot revealed that she had only just read his second batch of letters, having found them hidden in a cigar box on her father's death. She had taken them into the garden to read, where only the blackbirds heard the wretched sound of her sobbing. "I had assumed you'd stopped loving me when I never heard from you again." She then turned from the window and they looked at each other in silence, imagining the life they could have shared. When her eyes began to fill, she walked out to the carriage, and he stood alone, choked by the words that could never be spoken.

When he arrived in England to investigate the ghosts, and

found, much to his dismay, that she had already left for Egypt, he went on a pilgrimage to the Crystal Palace. He eventually found the Iguanodon, instantly recognisable from the tattered picture he carried in his pocket, except for the tiny anchovy in its mouth.

"And you never fell in love again?" Mink asked, after a pause.

"I couldn't," he replied, his head bowed.

"So your efforts to try and get to the bottom of the General's death were an attempt to help win her back?"

"Yes. But we've barely spoken since her return."

"Forgive me, Mr. Pilgrim, but if I were a police inspector I would come to the conclusion that his death rather clears the way for you."

He paused. "I suppose it does," he replied. Announcing he had to collect the phonograph, he stood up and left the room without waiting to be shown out.

*

AFTER HELPING HERSELF TO A cigarette from the tortoise-shell box on the mantelpiece, the Princess returned to her father's armchair. She sat back, staring at the floor as she smoked. She was still no nearer to knowing who had killed the General. Was it the Countess, who had only just got over her husband's death when he informed her that her love was alive and well and living with his new family? Did she fear that he would expose her humiliating secret, and that she would lose her home as a result of still being married? What about Lady Montfort Bebb, who resented his snipes about her piano playing, as it stirred her guilt at having survived the First Afghan War? Had he pushed her over the edge by sending all those tradespeople to her door for a joke? Or was it Lady Beatrice who blamed him for killing her doves, a wedding present from a man whose love she could never enjoy in public? Had General Bagshot discovered her marriage, and did she realise that he knew? Not only would she be ostracised by society if he exposed her, but she too would forfeit her apartments. But how could Mink suspect the three women whom she considered to be her friends?

Perhaps it was William Sheepshanks, who blamed the General for his mother's death? Or could it be the vine keeper, whose secret marriage the dead man may well have uncovered? Was Thomas Trout trying to protect the woman he loved from public exposure and losing the type of home he could never provide for her? Surely he would have some arsenic around the place to protect the vine against rats. Or had the American simply made up the story of their arguing to deflect attention away from himself, having killed the General in order to have Mrs. Bagshot for himself? And then there was Alice Cockle, who had lost her position as a parlour maid after he accused her of stealing.

Maybe it was someone else altogether. But who? She thought again of being parted from Pooki, the nearest thing she had had to a mother since losing her own. She should have hired a private investigator, she suddenly realised, and sold her grandmother's emerald earrings to pay for it. Why she hadn't thought of it before was beyond her. At that moment Pooki came in to change the flowers, but Mink kept her eyes on the floor, unable to look at her. The maid glanced uneasily at her mistress, silently picked up the vase, and shut the door behind her.

There was something that Cornelius B. Pilgrim had said that niggled Mink. Why, so soon after her husband's death, was Mrs. Bagshot redecorating her apartments, when she had never got round to it before, despite being a woman of such taste? Then it occurred to her. The Princess stubbed out the cigarette, fled from the house, and caught up with Cornelius B. Pilgrim outside the royal tennis court. "If Mrs. Bagshot is redecorating her husband's bedroom, would you mind terribly fetching me a tiny piece of the wallpaper?" she asked. "It's one of my favourite designs, and I'd like to find something that matches it. Wilderness House is in need of some cheer. I wouldn't want to bother Mrs. Bagshot over such a trivial matter."

"No problem," he replied, and they walked together to Fountain Court. Mink waited in the cloisters until he came back down, wondering whether she was right. "You're in luck," he said, handing her a blue-and-silver scrap he had found on the floor. "The decorators haven't swept up yet." Returning home, she lit one of the candles on the drawing room mantelpiece and held the paper into the flame. She blew it out, and there was no mistaking the smell of garlic. In that instant she knew.

She was out of the house within minutes, calling to Pooki to lock the front door behind her, and on no account to open it to anyone. She strode along Moat Lane, drawing the visitors' eyes away from their guidebooks. While she knew how the General had died, she now needed to find out why. Heaving open the door leading to Fish Court, she headed down the narrow redbrick passage to the Countess's apartments. Alice answered the door, tucking away a strand of hair that had worked its way loose from her bun.

"I wonder if I may have a word," said Mink.

"Her Ladyship is still in bed with a headache after last night's ball, Your Highness," she replied.

"It's you I wish to speak to, Alice. In private."

The maid's smile disappeared, and she pulled the door shut behind her. Glancing up at the windows of the other apartments, she led the way along the worn flagstones to the end of the courtyard, and went out onto Tennis Court Lane. Mink followed her through yet another door, and found herself in the abandoned Tudor kitchens, which had become a repository for bats.

"Not many people come in here," said the maid, wiping the top of an oak table with a rag and sitting on it. Suddenly she sneezed.

"This can't be the most hygienic place for you to be in, Alice, considering your condition," said the Princess.

The maid looked at her.

Mink raised her eyebrows. "I presume you are in the family way, Alice. It would explain why you happened to have a bottle of arsenic in your room."

A silent tear slipped down the girl's face.

Mink offered her a handkerchief and put her hand on her arm. "You're not the first domestic servant to have tried getting rid of an unwanted baby."

When her tears had receded enough for her to speak, the maid blew her nose and said she thought her world had ended when she learned of her condition. Following her father's death on the railway, she had given half her salary to her mother, who still had her three sisters and brother at home. Fearing she and her mother would end up in the workhouse if she lost her position, she had asked Dr. Henderson to help her get rid of the baby. But it turned out that the prescription he had given her was for dandelion tea. One morning, she was in Lady Beatrice's kitchen borrowing some arrowroot, when the cook went upstairs to answer the drawing room bell. She looked around for something to eat and spotted a bottle of arsenic, which she slipped into her pocket. "I never used it, ma'am," she said, shaking her head. "I would have rotted in hell."

Mink walked over to the neglected spit, almost white with dust, and looked at it. "It must have been quite a comedown for you to have gone from being a parlour maid to a maid-of-all-work," she said. "I expect you had your sights on becoming a lady's-maid."

The servant wiped her nose. "I would have made it too, if the General hadn't accused me of stealing and dismissed me. I was lucky the Countess took me on. She got me cheap, mind."

Mink looked at the teenager. "Were you still in their employ-ment when Mrs. Bagshot lost her baby?" she asked.

Alice immediately looked up. "Oh, ma'am. It was terrible."

From out of her mouth tumbled the story that she had kept to herself all this time. The day Mrs. Bagshot gave birth, the female upper servants gathered outside her bedroom in the hope of hearing a cry. When, finally, the baby wailed, it was their turn to weep, for none of Mrs. Bagshot's babies had ever survived. Rushing down to the kitchen, they told the others the wonderful news, and it was the only time the butler saw fit to take a bottle of his master's champagne to celebrate.

Several months later, Alice had just finished cleaning and trimming the lamps when she opened the drawing room door and saw Dr. Barnstable striding down the hall carrying the baby. With her mistress not at home, and the nurse on an errand, she wondered what he was doing. She stood at the window, watching him hurry down Fish Court, and heard Isabella whimper. She looked for General Bagshot and found him in the library, his head in his hands. Still clutching her cloths and scissors, she asked him why the doctor had taken the baby. He started, then told her that Isabella had suddenly taken ill. Dr. Barnstable had done his best, but he had been unable to save her. She told him that the baby must have come round with the fresh air, because she heard her cry as the general practitioner was leaving. But the General insisted that she was mistaken, as the man had just signed the death certificate. Standing up, he instructed her never to mention it again if she had any feelings for Mrs. Bagshot, as such nonsensical imaginings would make her fit for the asylum and she was fragile enough as it was.

The news quickly spread through the household that Isabella was dead, and when Mrs. Bagshot returned from her walk all eyes fell to the floor. The General immediately took her up to her bedroom, and even the cook heard the shriek from the kitchen. It was several months before she came down again, by which time the servants had been instructed never to mention Isabella's name again.

"I'd been dismissed by then," said Alice, clutching the Princess's wet handkerchief in her fist. "Shortly after the doctor had taken Isabella, the General accused me of stealing one of Mrs. Bagshot's brooches, a little frog with diamond eyes. Then he took me up to my room and found it underneath my pillow. Funny that."

"And you never told anyone that you heard Isabella cry?" Mink asked.

She began to doubt herself, the maid explained, and she didn't want Mrs. Bagshot ending up in the asylum over something she had imagined. "She was always good to me. Not like him. He caught me in Tennis Court Lane one night on his way back from his club. Pinned me up against the wall and lifted my skirts. Stank of booze, he did." When he had finished with her, he told her that if she ever told anyone he would inform her mistress that he'd spotted one of the soldiers going into her apartments while she was out.

"And now I'm carrying his baby, ma'am, and I'm going to lose my position all over again," she sobbed.

*

WHEN MINK RETURNED TO WILDERNESS HOUSE, she found the door open and Dr. Henderson standing in the hall, talking to Pooki.

"If you've come to apologise for your antics last night, doctor, forgive me, but I have absolutely no time to listen. And this door should be locked. I left strict instructions that it should not be opened to anyone," she said crossly.

But the general practitioner hadn't come about the ball at all. "The grocer's boy just told me that Inspector Guppy has arrived on the train from London and is about to arrest your maid," he said.

CHAPTER XV

Worse Than Harris in the Maze

INK strode through the cold cloisters of Fountain Court, wondering how she was going to confront her. She ignored the laughter of the excursionists buying cherries from the fruit seller and continued on, her heart tightening at the thought of what she was about to do. She turned up the steps, an empty basket hanging motionless in the stairwell. Standing for a moment outside the door to gather her thoughts, she rang the bell. Dora Cummings appeared wearing servant's mourning, and informed her that her mistress wasn't at home for visitors.

Mink insisted that she be seen. "It's a matter of urgency," she said.

The parlour maid hesitated, glanced at the caller's hat, then stepped back to let her in. As the Princess followed her across the hall, she noticed the intertwining initials on the marble floor. The servant showed her into the drawing room, perfumed by white lilies, then went in search of her mistress. Invaded by the scent of death, Mink stood at the window with its coveted view of the Thames. But all she could see was her task ahead of her. Sitting down on the sofa, she looked around at the modern Arts and

Crafts furniture, and then at the dated wallpaper, finally understanding why a woman lauded for her impeccable taste had failed
to change it.

"It's a pleasure to see you again," said Mrs. Bagshot from the
doorway, choked to the neck in widow's weeds. The Princess
watched as she came to sit opposite her, remembering the kindness she had shown her when she first arrived. For a moment the
Princess studied the crape on the woman's skirt, then raised her
eyes.

"Please accept my condolences, Mrs. Bagshot. Your husband
was good enough to give me a tour of the palace."

Mrs. Bagshot offered a thin smile. "He was very fond of the
place. Very few gentlemen are given a warrant. We were lucky in
that regard."

"I hope you don't think that my maid was somehow involved
in his death. Much was made at the inquest of the pies she made
for the residents' picnic."

"One hears all sorts of rumours, but I never believed that one
for a minute," said Mrs. Bagshot, shaking her head.

Mink sat back. "She was rather reluctant to come with me to
the palace. Domestic servants aren't terribly keen on the place."

"Finding a good maid is hard enough, let alone one who's
prepared to live here. I've been through umpteen, what with one
thing or another," said Mrs. Bagshot.

"Sometimes it's just little things that servants take, and you
never realise until months or even years later that they're missing," said Mink. "You look for a particular pair of earrings, and
when you can't find them, you wonder whether you've lost them or
someone has pinched them. And yet you can't believe any of your
servants are capable of it. I understand that you had a problem
with Alice Cockle."

There was a pause. "My husband found a little brooch of mine
under her pillow. I didn't for a minute think she had taken it.

I assumed it was one of the other maids who had put it there. You do hear about these petty jealousies amongst them. But I was unwell at the time, and didn't have the strength to get involved. I was very pleased to hear that Lady Bessington had offered her a position."

"I happened to be talking to Alice this morning," said Mink. "She says you treated her very well."

Mrs. Bagshot frowned and looked out the window. "I always felt guilty for not standing up for her, but I had other things on my mind at the time. I did like the girl very much."

"She remains very fond of you."

"She does?" asked the widow, turning back.

Mink nodded. "So much so that she never told you that she heard Isabella cry when Dr. Barnstable took her away."

The widow stared at her.

"Your husband convinced her that she was imagining it, and you would become mentally deranged if she ever told you," the Princess continued.

Mrs. Bagshot put her hand over her mouth.

"Did your husband lie to you about your daughter having died?" Mink asked.

There was no reply.

"Is that why you killed him?"

Still there was silence.

"Mrs. Bagshot, the police have come to arrest my maid, and she's entirely innocent. I'm aware that the wallpaper in your husband's bedroom contains arsenic."

The widow held her gaze, then gradually her eyes sank to her clutched hands. "God forgive me," she whispered.

Eventually she raised her head and looked out the window. She had no idea why she kept losing her babies, she said. Some died before she even realised she was in the family way. "But the pain of all those lost souls faded the moment Isabella was born.

She brought me a joy that I didn't know was possible. I even forgot the loneliness of my marriage."

It was she who suspected that the baby couldn't see. Isabella wasn't even three months old. She asked Dr. Barnstable to call, and he confirmed her terrible suspicion. When she wondered how it could be, he asked her about the failed pregnancies, as well as a number of intimate questions. "He said nothing for a moment, then turned to me and with the frankness of a butcher said that I probably had the loathsome disease. I asked him how it was possible, given that I had never been anything but loyal. In retrospect, it was such a silly question. I was in shock. To this day, I still don't know who my husband caught it from. It could have been anyone, a girl with a pretty bonnet he'd spotted in the West End, or one of the ladies who hang around Trophy Gate. I caught him with at least two parlour maids over the years. One would have hoped for a little more imagination from one's husband."

Once it had been confirmed that Isabella was blind, her husband wanted nothing more to do with the child. "I still thought she was perfect." Fearing his temper, she said nothing of the syphilis, and silently took the mercurial blue pills the doctor prescribed until the symptoms went away. Shortly after the baby's diagnosis, she returned home to find that none of the servants would look at her, and she knew at once that something was wrong. Her husband sat her down in her bedroom and told her that Isabella's heart had suddenly stopped, and that the doctor had just taken away her body so she wouldn't have to see it. "After that I went through what he always referred to as my 'hysterical phase.' I couldn't even attend the funeral. My friends went. They said it was extremely moving. Of course, my husband didn't want all that fuss made, but I insisted on it."

It was quite by accident, almost a year ago, that she discovered that Isabella might still be alive. She was rushing home through the rain when she noticed the soaked watercress seller still standing at the palace gates, his tray almost full. "He looked even thinner than usual, and I offered to buy the lot so he could go home." She suggested he accompany her home, as she couldn't carry it all, and, sheltering him with her umbrella, they started up the drive. The man finally stopped thanking her when they reached Fish Court, and he read the brass nameplate next to her bell.

He waited in the hall while she fetched some coins, and the footman relieved him of his cresses. But he didn't move after she told him to keep the change, and when, eventually, he got out his words, he told her he had something to tell her. "He looked in such a state I immediately showed him into the library." Clutching his sodden cap in front of him, he told her that when he had no means for a bed for the night he was in the habit of sleeping in an empty coffin at the undertaker's in East Molesey. One night, four years ago, he had just climbed in through the window when he heard a noise and hid behind a door. He watched through the crack as the undertaker's apprentice walked in carrying a sack, which he put inside a tiny white coffin, and screwed down the lid. Once the apprentice had left, he came out of his hiding place and looked at the nameplate. While he was not one for letters, he had never forgotten the name, and what he had witnessed had troubled him ever since. He had never told anyone, fearing the consequences of Mr. Blood knowing he had been sleeping in his premises. Nor did he want to meddle in other people's business, especially that of the rich. "I was just grateful that he told me and I asked him to keep it to himself. I bought from him regularly after that."

Mrs. Bagshot paused, her gaze drifting out the window. "Sometimes I wonder what the apprentice put in the coffin. Was it stones or a bag of flour, perhaps? Did he weigh it in his hands, wondering whether it matched the weight of a three-month-old baby? Did he pick up his own child to check? Did I, week after week, year after year, put flowers on the grave of a dead cat washed up in the Thames, weeping for its loss? And how much money was that man offered until he agreed to ruin my life?"

The two women sat in silence until Mrs. Bagshot continued.

She immediately went to find the apprentice, but Mr. Blood had fired him years ago and had no idea where he was. "So I went looking for him. I had to call on most of the undertakers in London, but eventually I found him in his lodging house. I told the housekeeper I was an aunt, and she let me go up to his room. He was in bed at the time. Of course he denied everything. So I got my husband's pistol out of my bag and pointed it at him, at which stage he lost control of his bladder and finally had the good grace to tell me the truth: Dr. Barnstable had paid him to fill the coffin with the weight of a small baby. He had no idea why, and just took the money, which a pickpocket stole from him anyway. I then cocked the gun and warned him that if he ever did anything like that ever again, I would find him and see to it that it was the last time."

She then went to see Dr. Barnstable, who denied it all. When she brought the matter up with her husband, he told her she was suffering from delusions that constituted the early signs of lunacy. "He said that if I persisted in wanting an exhumation he would have no alternative than to ask Dr. Barnstable to certify me. I then realised that he had been in on it all along. I expect you've heard what happened to Dr. Barnstable?"

Mink nodded. "He drowned in the Thames."

"Just before he died he brought me a letter, then disappeared. Mrs. Nettleship, his housekeeper, went round all the public houses looking for him. The boatman found his body the next day, his pockets full of stones. Having read the letter, I wasn't at all surprised that he had killed himself. His confession was very frank. My husband had paid him to take Isabella away to stop people realising there was pox in the family. He agreed to do it, not only because of his debts but because my husband threatened to report him for his drinking. But he said the guilt he felt over what he had done had only worsened his problem, and he found life intolerable. He gave me his profuse apologies, which is something, I suppose. Unfortunately, he didn't know where Isabella was. He had given her to a woman he'd never met before in the East End, whom he chose simply because she looked like his sister. He gave her some shillings, and told her to take her to a school for the blind.

"Anything could have happened to that baby. I had no idea whether the woman had simply pocketed the money and abandoned her. At first I just walked the East End looking for a blind girl, but it got me nowhere, apart from nearly being killed myself. My only hope was that the woman had a heart and did as Dr. Barnstable requested. So I visited all the homes and charities for the blind, first in London, and then further out. I kept going, hoping I would find her . . . Eventually I did.

"Of course her name had been changed, but I recognised her instantly. My husband was a very handsome man when he was younger. I'm pleased to say that she's only inherited his looks, and none of his temperament. She's four now, and seems to have a gift for the pianoforte. I became a patron of the school, and gave them as much of my husband's money that I could get my hands on."

She looked out the window, then turned back to the Princess, her face changed. Her symptoms returned about six months ago, she continued, looking down at her gloves. "He must have got himself reinfected. There's no stopping my husband when he wishes to enter my bedroom. I couldn't bear to lose another child . . ." she said, almost to herself.

Mrs. Bagshot stared at the rug for a moment, then turned her gaze back to Mink. "I didn't set out to kill my husband," she insisted. "The idea came to me one afternoon when I called on Lady Bessington while she was still living in these apartments. She was quite distressed, as she'd just lost a Killarney bristle fern. She'd only recently started collecting plants and said that they always died in one particular room overlooking the river. I thought it very odd, and asked her to show it to me. We went in, and she said that her cat used to sleep there, but it lost all its fur, so she put its bed in another room, after which it was fine. I looked at the wallpaper and guessed that it was arsenical. It was so old-fashioned it must have been put up decades ago.

"I'm sure you're too young to remember, but about twenty years ago the Queen reprimanded a gentleman for being late for his audience, and he said he had been ill during the night because of his green wallpaper. When it tested arsenical, she had every trace of wallpaper removed from Buckingham Palace. My mother did too in the house we were living in at the time. But of course it wasn't just green paper that had arsenical pigments. Doctors warned about all sorts of colours . . ."

Mrs. Bagshot fell silent, then continued her tale. "Lady Bessington was always complaining about the cost of heating her apartments, so I suggested that we swap, as ours was much smaller. Of course my husband agreed. Who wouldn't want such a view? Eventually the Lord Chamberlain gave in. He's a distant relative of mine, which helped. I had no problem persuading my husband to use the room as a bedroom, as it faced the river. We've had separate rooms for years because of his snoring. Lady Bessington didn't say anything about the room I slept in, but I didn't want to take any chances and had the walls varnished. It was a little tip I read in one of my medical books.

"I had no idea whether my plan would work. You read about these poor people who died from the lethal vapours of wallpaper, and it all seemed so random. But there was a chance, given his age and the poor state of his health. I heard him vomiting several times before I left for Egypt. It was a shock, nevertheless, when I received the telegram telling me he was dead. I thought I would be pleased. In fact, I collapsed."

There was silence.

"You didn't consider divorce?" the Princess asked.

"I couldn't bear the thought of all those women stuffed into the court's public gallery with their opera glasses and brandy flasks, feasting on the carcass of my marriage." She paused. "I must apologise for your maid having been dragged into this. Had she been charged, I would have immediately come forward. I couldn't have lived with that on my conscience too."

*

WHEN MINK RETURNED TO WILDERNESS HOUSE, she found the constable standing in the garden, smoking a cigarette. "The Inspector's inside," he said, with a jerk of his head. Searching through the rooms, she eventually found him in the attics, peering under a dustsheet. He turned on hearing her footsteps, and immediately demanded to know where her maid was.

"I've no idea, Inspector. But I do know how the General died," she replied, explaining he had been slowly poisoned by the arsenical wallpaper in his bedroom, which had been put up by a resident years ago. "I tested it by holding a scrap into a candle flame to see whether it smelt of garlic. It was one of those handy household tips I read in a magazine. Still, I'm sure you'll subject it to proper analysis. Perhaps if it had been green, someone might have suspected it earlier."

The Inspector continued to stare at her.

"I hope you weren't going to make an arrest on the assumption that no one would care about what happens to a poor Indian servant," she said. She looked at him in silence for a moment, then added, "I found my Sherlock Holmes book, by the way. I shall give it to you. You may find it useful. Now, in the absence of my maid, may I show you to the door?"

When the police eventually left, Mink sat down in the drawing room and stared ahead of her, unable to believe that it was finally over. She hadn't told the Inspector about the role Mrs. Bagshot had played in her husband's death. It would be impossible to prove, should she deny it. But what worried her more was whether a judge would take the General's behaviour into account. Feeling the urge for a brandy, she rang the bell and sat for a moment with her eyes shut. When there was no reply, she suddenly remembered that Pooki was still hiding, and she started hunting through the house. While opening her wardrobe, she heard the shouts of the excursionists, and, recognising a voice, looked out the window.

*

"I'VE GOT A RIGHT PAIR IN THERE," muttered William Sheep-shanks as the Princess paid him her penny entrance fee. "Been lost for ages. If you see a thin Indian woman with big feet and that doctor who messed up the Lancers, I'd be obliged if you'd escort them out. They've been causing mayhem, believe me. They're worse than Harris when he got lost in the maze in *Three Men in a Boat*. At one stage there were twenty-four people following them, assuming they knew the way out, including a Swiss Alpinist and a fellow from Stanfords, the mapmakers. I've been keeping a close eye on that doctor. He has the look of a tunneller about him."

*

IT TOOK A WHILE FOR POOKI to take in the fact that the police were no longer coming to arrest her. Sitting next to each other on the drawing room settee, Mink tried once more, repeating how the General had died and that she no longer had anything to fear. Finally the maid buried her face in her apron and sobbed so forcefully that she shook. She wept for the Maharaja, who had saved her life and taken her in all those years ago when no one else wanted her. She wept for her mother, whom she feared would die of shock if she were hanged. And she wept for the Princess, who loved her enough to save her.

"Most mistresses would have dismissed me, ma'am," she said,

drying her eyes. "Now I will live to see your wedding to that doctor, which makes me very happy." As she started to leave, she suddenly turned and planted a kiss on Mink's forehead. She then ran out, closing the door quickly behind her. The Princess remained where she was, head bent, letting a tear of relief tumble onto her dress.

CHAPTER XVI

The Princess's Dr. Watson

IVEN Dr. Henderson's spectacular disgrace on the dance floor, Mrs. Nettleship still hadn't dared broach the subject of his progress with the Countess. The humiliating incident had already been gleefully recounted in a report of the evening by the *Surrey Comet,* which endeavoured to solicit a comment from the perpetrator before going to press. But the housekeeper closed the door on the journalist, telling him that the general practitioner had more important things to do with his time than to defend himself against accusations of having two left feet.

As he sat down in the dining room for breakfast, she placed in front of him a pair of mismatching cutlets. No longer able to contain herself, she said, "You never used those hoily rags I left hout for you to stuff your codpiece with, Dr. 'enderson. I was wondering whether your 'eart his still beating."

The general practitioner picked up his cutlery. "I very much hope it is still beating, Mrs. Nettleship, otherwise I will be lying facedown in my cutlets any moment now. If indeed these are cutlets," he added doubtfully, peering at his plate.

"Beating faster than husual, his what I meant," she said.

He started to saw. "I am a little worked up that two of my

patients have just defected to the homeopath from East Molesey following the ball, if that's what you mean. I'm sure that man has my hat."

But the housekeeper persisted. "His there hanything you want to tell me habout matters relating to the 'eart, doctor?" she asked.

"I would advise plenty of fresh air, the avoidance of tea, and regular sea bathing," he replied.

The housekeeper clutched her hands together. "And what hof marriage, doctor?"

"I couldn't recommend it enough, Mrs. Nettleship," he said. "At the age of twenty-five, married women can expect to live another thirty-six years, which is six more than unmarried women. And mortality in unmarried men aged between thirty and forty-five stands at twenty-seven per cent, yet drops to around eighteen if they're married. I, for one, do not intend to put it off."

"Oh, doctor," she said, embracing him. "I can feel a proposal hon hits way!"

Gasping for air, Dr. Henderson struggled free. "Mrs. Nettleship!" he said, slamming down his knife and fork. "I fear your imagination has run away with itself. While I very much appreciate everything you do for me, my feelings towards you are those one would feel for an aunt. And not even a maiden one at that. I must inform you that I am not about to ask you to marry me."

The housekeeper recoiled. "I wasn't meaning me, Dr. 'enderson," she replied, a hand on chest. "I'd no more want your 'eart hif you hoffered hit. There was honly one love for me, and Mr. Nettleship his hon the bottom of the hocean with the mermaids. I was thinking hof Lady Bessington."

Dr. Henderson returned her stare. "Lady Bessington?" he repeated. "She's considerably older than me. Not only that, but she has an unnatural affection for ferns, and, I'm afraid to say, she still hasn't paid me for treating her corns."

The housekeeper frowned. "It's not 'er, then?"

"No!"

"Then oo his hit?" demanded the housekeeper, her hands on her hips.

"It's no concern of yours, Mrs. Nettleship."

She headed for the door. "Well, hit's a good job hit's not that princess oo went to the ball dressed as Juliet. Happarently she was standing hon the dance floor looking like 'er homnibus 'ad just left without 'er . . ."

*

DR. HENDERSON HAD JUST RETURNED from divine service when Mrs. Nettleship flung open the drawing room door.

"Doctor, come quick," she cried. "There's a maid come for you. She says Halice Cockle his 'aving a baby and Lady Bessington wants you there himmediately."

Grabbing his pocket case, as well as some linen thread for tying the cord, he reached for his hat and coat and rushed out. There was no doubt that the baby had come much sooner than he was expecting, he thought as he started to run, and he wondered whether she had done anything to precipitate it.

A huddle of servants stood in Fish Court whispering nervously, and he let himself into the Countess's apartments. As he tried to find the way to the attic, he heard a voice from one of the first-floor bedrooms.

"She's in here, Dr. Henderson," called the Countess. He walked in and found the maid in bed, her damp hair stuck to her white face, and her mistress sitting next to her, holding her hand. "I put her in my room," she continued. "I couldn't have her climbing all those stairs. I wish someone had told me she was in the family way. I just assumed she was getting stout."

The doctor asked the Countess to prepare a bath of hot water in front of the fire. Pulling off his coat, he rolled up his sleeves and washed his hands and arms in the bowl on the washstand. As he examined Alice, tears streamed down the sides of her face onto the pillow.

"You've got to save the baby, doctor. I didn't do anything to it, I swear," she said, looking up at him.

He asked the Countess to tie a towel to the bedpost so Alice would have something to hold on to, then told the teenager to turn onto her left side and draw up her knees. But still it wouldn't come.

"Alice, the baby isn't making the progress I would like it to; I'm going to have to use forceps," he said. But the girl became even more distressed. She was a Catholic, she wailed, and he would have to administer conditional baptism before going anywhere near the baby with such things.

"There isn't time, Alice," he urged.

"But it might be born dead!"

Announcing she would be back, the Countess left the room and returned with a cup of water. The doctor wet his fingers. "If thou canst be baptised, I baptise thee in the name of the Father," he said, feeling the baby's head. "And of the Son. And of the Holy Ghost."

He stood back, then turned to the Countess. "Pass me the forceps. Quickly."

With trembling fingers, she took the instrument out of the case and handed it to him. By now the maid's wails had developed into screams, and the Countess watched, both hands covering her mouth. Suddenly the baby appeared, and the doctor held the tiny girl to him, wiping her mouth and nose with a napkin. But there was no sound. He blew on her face, and patted her briskly. But it was no use.

"She's dead!" wailed Alice.

"Pass me that jug," he said to the Countess. She handed it to him, and he sprinkled some water on the baby's chest.

"She's still not making any noise," sobbed the maid.

The doctor tied and cut the umbilical cord, plunged the baby up to her neck in the bath by the fire, then sprinkled more cold water onto her chest. But there was no response.

"God have mercy," said the Countess, kneeling by the side of the bed and holding the hand of the maid, who had started to pray.

Laying the baby on the covers, Dr. Henderson pinched her nose, covered her lips with his, and gently blew until her chest inflated. He opened his fingers and watched as it fell again. He continued blowing and releasing until eventually there was a splutter followed by the indignant wail of a perfect newborn.

*

LATER THAT AFTERNOON, MINK FOUND the door to Chocolate Court near a former kitchen where Mr. Nice used to make hot chocolate for William III's breakfast. Her three friends were already sitting on the tiny patio, the tea paraphernalia on a nearby table covered with a white cloth.

"There you are, Princess," said Lady Montfort Bebb, her red setter lying at her feet. "I must say it's a little disappointing that no murder was committed after all. Things were just starting to liven up around here."

Lady Beatrice offered Mink a teacup. "I was rather looking forward to the trial. I haven't used my brandy flask in ages. What a pity it wasn't that American. Do you think there's any chance that he might kill someone before he leaves?"

The three women looked at her.

"How clever of you to have got to the bottom of it," said the Countess, turning to Mink.

"Quite so," said Lady Beatrice.

"We're extremely proud of you," said Lady Montfort Bebb. "At the very least it means we no longer have to endure Inspector Guppy and that unfortunate suit of his. Only the upper classes can afford to dress so badly."

The Countess lifted her cup. "Thank goodness I never used that room as a bedroom. It turns me quite queer just thinking about it. I understand that poor Mrs. Bagshot will be leaving us shortly to live near the school for the blind, where she's a patron. I shall miss her, of course, but I quite understand her not wanting to live here with all those ghastly memories." She leant forward and reached for a macaroon from the table. "Apparently several residents have already written to the Lord Chamberlain asking to swap apartments, and insisting that the palace covers the redecoration costs."

Lady Montfort Bebb turned to Lady Beatrice. "Perhaps you should put in a request. It would get you away from Jane Seymour, and give your nerves a rest."

She shook her head, stirring up the red feathers on her hat. "I wouldn't dream of it. It would confuse my doves. I still fail to understand how some of them went missing. I asked the butcher whether the General had sold him any birds, and he said it was a rumour started by the Keeper of the Maze."

Lady Montfort Bebb put down her cup and cleared her throat. "I think I can shed some light on what happened to them. I'm afraid to say that Wellington caught a number for his luncheon. I'd never seen such a guilty expression on a dog, and the game was up when I spotted some grey feathers around his mouth. I assure you I reprimanded him quite severely. I hope you will find a place in your heart to forgive us. Have you ever seen a more remorseful dog?"

Wellington wagged his tail.

Lady Beatrice fumbled with the clasp on her handbag and drew out a silk handkerchief. "Oh, I do," she muttered, dabbing an eye. "That is, if you'll forgive me."

"What on earth for?" asked Lady Montfort Bebb.

Lady Beatrice returned the handkerchief to her bag and closed it with a loud snap. "All those tradesmen and the milliner's assistant who came to your apartments. I'm afraid that was my doing."

"You?" demanded Lady Montfort Bebb, the skin under her chin wobbling.

"It was meant to be an All Fools' Day joke. I thought you might find it amusing. Things had been so quiet around here. Unfortunately I got my dates rather muddled," she added with a frown. "Perhaps Mr. Blood was a little too much. But you did say your psoriasis made you feel at death's door."

Lady Montfort Bebb looked at her for a moment in silence. "My dear, your heart is bigger than most, but unfortunately your brain is the size of a plover's egg," she said.

Lady Beatrice fussed with her false fringe, then turned to the Countess. "I expect you'll be looking for a new maid-of-all-work, what with that baby. I'm afraid to say you'll have a devil of a job finding one prepared to live here."

"Alice isn't going anywhere," she replied. "Her mother will look after the child, and she'll start work again as soon as she's recovered. I've even given her a little raise to cover the baby's keep. You've never seen such a pretty little thing."

Lady Beatrice and Lady Montfort Bebb looked at her in astonishment.

"At least you'll get a housekeeper if you marry Dr. Henderson, though I'd worry she'd frighten away all the callers," said Lady Beatrice.

"Marry Dr. Henderson?" asked the Countess, her mouth full. "Why on earth would I do that?"

"Didn't he propose to you at the ball while dressed as Romeo?"

The Countess straightened up. "Thankfully not. That man should never have attempted the Lancers. No one knows how to dance it. I quite upbraided him this morning for sending me roses. He looked quite taken aback. He said he knew nothing about them, and wondered whether his housekeeper was responsible. He apologised profusely and said he would have strong words with her. I assured him I would think nothing more of it if he waived his bill for my corns."

The door opened and the women turned to see Cornelius B. Pilgrim walk into the courtyard.

"Do have a seat, Mr. Pilgrim," said the Princess. "May I offer you some tea?"

The American declined and sat down next to a potted palm, smiling broadly.

"You look rather pleased with yourself," said Lady Beatrice. "I expect you're relieved that you weren't arrested on this occasion."

"Ladies," he said. "I have some exciting news. You're gonna love it."

Lady Montfort Bebb looked him up and down. "We'll be the judge of that, Mr. Pilgrim," she said.

He had spent the previous night hiding in a corner of Master Carpenter's Court, with all but his netting, string, revolver, phonograph, and eight-pound Cheddar cheese for company, he said. It had drizzled steadily, and he sat engulfed by the smell of wet cobbles, trying to avoid being spotted by the watchman on his rounds and the servants hiding in corners with their sweethearts. Eventually he drifted off, and when he woke he witnessed a terrifying vision: the Cheddar was gliding several inches off the ground towards Seymour Gate. Immediately his fingers reached for his gun, and when he finally gathered his courage, he set the phonograph, stood up, and began to follow it. He had almost reached the far end of the courtyard, and was just about to cast his net, when he realised that the cheese was not being carried away by a spirit with a penchant for Somerset curds, but by a pack of nefarious rats. He started chasing after it, and it was then that he heard a horrible noise behind him. Turning, he saw two small ghostly figures, one carrying a chain and the other a lantern. He stood transfixed, watching them as they murmured together in the swaying lamplight. Suddenly they let out a peal of hideous laughter that chilled him to the bone. Realising it was now or never, he took several steps towards them with his net, but the beings heard the sound of his boots and turned to look at him. For one ghastly moment they held each other's stare, and he advanced again. But the spectres took off, and by the time he reached them they had vanished. He sank to his knees in despair at another fruitless night of missed sleep and disappointment, the rain working its way down his collar. Deciding to return home, he was packing up his equipment when he wondered whether the phonograph had recorded anything. He wound it up and from out of its brass speaker came voices from the other side.

There was silence as the ladies stared at him. Taking her hand away from her mouth, the Countess asked, "What did they disclose? A cache of buried gold, perhaps? Or the existence of a will?"

"Was it a vile deed?" gasped Lady Beatrice, clutching the side of her seat.

Lady Montfort Bebb held up a hand. "Don't hold back, Mr. Pilgrim," she ordered. "We are braver than we look."

Cornelius B. Pilgrim paused. "It was Pike and Gibbs, the delivery boys, wearing old sheets and wondering who to haunt next."

The women looked at each other.

"I shall never tip that pair again," said Lady Montfort Bebb, gripping the top of her cane.

"And I shall never start to," said the Countess.

Mink leant forwards. "Congratulations, Mr. Pilgrim. We must inform the newspapers. It will do wonders for your career."

Lady Beatrice offered him the plate of macaroons. "How terribly clever of you, Mr. Pilgrim," she said. "I'm sure that will resolve my problem of finding a new parlour maid. And not before time, I can tell you. I found my cook asleep under the kitchen table this morning. Let me say how pleased we all were to hear that you weren't responsible for the General's death. We had complete faith in you. Have you met my daughter?"

The American smiled weakly, then glanced at the Countess from under his lashes.

"I expect you'll be leaving us shortly, Mr. Pilgrim," said Lady

Montfort Bebb, stroking Wellington's head. "You must come back soon and pay us all a visit. We English are nothing if not forgiving."

*

AS SHE RANG DR. HENDERSON's bell, Mink suddenly worried that she was overdressed. For some reason she failed to understand, it had taken her longer than usual to get ready, and she had tried on several hats before leaving the house, all just to thank him for hiding Pooki. How ridiculous she had been, she thought, as she waited several minutes for the door to open. Assuming no one was in, she was just about to turn away when Mrs. Nettleship appeared, her red hair dusted in flour. Looking the Princess up and down, she informed her that the doctor had been called to see a patient at the palace. "It's not hanother baby that needs being born, his hit?" she asked.

The Princess said it wasn't.

"That's a relief. They can't make up their minds whether they're coming or going 'alf the time. Some wants to stay where they are, while others wants to come out early, like that one Halice Cockle just delivered. Fit has a fiddle, despite what hit put the doctor through. A pretty little thing too, happarently, despite being so hearly. Usually they're has bald has Mr. Nettleship. Lady Bessington his much taken by hit, and even paid the bill. Poor Dr. 'enderson nearly 'ad a 'eart hattack."

Mrs. Nettleship then took a step towards her and lowered her voice. "I 'ope Dr. 'enderson hapologised for 'is hantics at the ball," she added. "I told 'im 'e should 'ave used my hoily rags to stuff 'is codpiece. But 'e took it hupon 'imself to use a stocking that 'ad shrunk when I boiled hit after 'e fell in the Thames. Happarently that was 'alf the problem. 'E was worried hit was going to drop hout, and 'e 'ad to keep moving. That and 'aving no knowledge hof the steps, hof course. E'll be most grateful that I hexplained hit to you. Shall I tell 'im you called?"

*

ARRIVING HOME, MINK FOUND ALBERT sitting on the front doorstep, dressed in his red velvet trousers. He stared back, blinked, and promptly dropped the penny bun he was eating. She immediately picked him up and, after she had finished stroking him, looked to see whether he was harmed. Anxious to get him inside, she rang the bell, but there was no reply, so she let herself in, wondering where her maid was. Slowly she headed down to the kitchen, the monkey still clutching onto her. She found Pooki walking towards Victoria with the concentrated look of a Bank of England counterman as she carried a saucer of milk laced with Madeira to keep out the damp. Still in the monkey's embrace, the Princess took a seat at the table and waited for an explanation. Eventually the tale emerged of how the servant had never surrendered the creature to the owner of the travelling zoo. "The Maharaja would not have approved of the state of that man's beard, ma'am." Instead she had hidden Albert amongst the luggage taken by the removal men, and made him a home in the attics. Unfortunately he escaped on several occasions when his curiosity got the better of him, as it had during his journey from India, when the captain offered him a mango and he fell into the ocean with excitement. He had taken a particular shine not only to the palace's chimney-pots but also to its housekeeper, for which she could offer no explanation.

The Princess sat for a moment in silence, watching the maid as she attempted to make fowl in aspic jelly. Suddenly she remembered where she had last seen those enormous feet.

"Were you the lobster at the ball?" she asked.

The maid looked up. "Ma'am. It was my dying wish to go to a ball. I had never been to one before."

Mink frowned. "I thought your dying wish was to go to the Royal Aquarium," she said.

"That too," Pooki replied, lining the copper mould with jelly.

"How on earth did you get a ticket?"

"One of Lady Montfort Bebb's servants pinched a batch and was selling them. Alice bought me one, as I had mentioned that it was my dying wish to go," said the maid, not looking up.

"And I suppose Cupid was the watercress seller?" she demanded.

"Alice bought a ticket for him too. I did not know he was going."

Mink let out a short, sharp sigh. "So," she said. "In a matter of weeks you've disobeyed my instruction to sell Albert, broken my long-standing rule about having followers in the house, made me take you to the Royal Aquarium, of all places, attended a society ball dressed as a lobster, and been a murder suspect."

The maid looked at the ceiling as she considered each offence. "Yes, ma'am," she replied, nodding. "I have done all of those things. But I did not kill the General."

"At least I would have got a new maid," muttered the Princess.

"Ma'am, you would not want another maid. She would not tell you the butterman's jokes," said Pooki, pointing at her with a spoonful of jelly. "Nor would she be able to save that very expensive sealskin jacket of yours from the jaws of moths."

*

MINK SAT READING THE NEWSPAPER in the drawing room, while Albert watched her from the mantelpiece, his late master's pipe in his mouth. After a while the door opened and Pooki came in with her sewing.

"Ma'am, I had a lot of time to think when I was in the maze," she said, sitting down on the sofa opposite her.

"That sounds ominous," said Mink, lowering her paper.

The maid threaded her needle. "I was thinking how impolite you have been to Dr. Henderson, which your father would not have approved of. But it made me very happy because it means that you are in love with him, even though he cannot dance and has no money, both of which are very bad things. But we have to overlook them. No man is perfect. It is a delusion ladies suffer while they are engaged, from which they recover immediately upon marriage. It is a trick nature plays to keep the species alive, because by the time their senses are restored they are in the family way."

The Princess raised her paper. "I'm not in the least in love with Dr. Henderson. I've never heard anything so ridiculous," she replied curtly. "By the way, I'm thinking of getting a bicycle."

"You are changing the subject, ma'am, which is what you always do when you know I am right. And anyway, you cannot afford one."

Mink raised her eyebrows. "They're not at all expensive. Everyone's got one."

"Even so, ma'am. The butcher has asked again for his bill to be settled, and another letter has arrived from Marshall & Snelgrove."

"I might be able to afford one shortly."

"I will have to seek another position if you take to wearing knickerbockers on a machine, ma'am," said the maid, picking up her needle. "I have my reputation to think of."

Mink leafed through the paper, searching for the advertisement she had placed in the hope of solving her financial troubles. "H.H. Princess Alexandrina, Private Detective. All enquiries to Hampton Court Palace," it read. She glanced at her Dr. Watson, a bay leaf sticking out of her boot to ward off lightning, and for a moment she doubted her resolve. Her eyes then fell to her silver cigarette case next to her, engraved with a woman hunting tigers on top of an elephant, and instantly she knew that anything was possible.

*

WEARING HER EMERALD EARRINGS, MINK headed out to enjoy the grounds that had been walked by countless monarchs. She soon found herself in the Privy Garden, and turned in to Queen Mary's bower, a low avenue of elms leading down to the Thames that had grown together to form a canopy. Lost in thought, she looked up to see Dr. Henderson coming towards her. He raised his hat, which bore the telltale bulge of a stethoscope.

"I wanted to thank you for hiding my maid," she said when they met. "Most people wouldn't have wanted anything to do with her, given the circumstances."

"I could tell you're very fond of her. We all have our soft spots."

The Princess lowered her eyes. "The problem with loving someone is that they always leave you, one way or another."

He paused. "If I were to win my love I would never let her go." Searching her face for a sign, he added, "Though I'm not certain she would ever find me suitable."

They both glanced away.

"I must apologise for my behaviour at the ball," he said with a cough. "You made such a charming Juliet. I rather ruined your evening. My instructor said it was almost impossible for a woman to forgive a man who had made her look ridiculous on the dance floor. I fear he was right."

The Princess looked at him, her chin raised. "To quote Capulet, doctor, I think you're past your dancing days."

"You're probably right," he said, his eyes tumbling to the ground. Stepping back, he wished her a pleasant afternoon, and continued towards the palace, his head bowed. As Mink watched him walk away, she suddenly realised he was carrying her heart.

"Dr. Henderson!" she cried, striding towards him.

He stopped and turned round.

"I was wondering whether you would be kind enough to give me some bicycling lessons," she called as she approached. "I'm hoping to buy a machine."

They stood, holding each other's gaze in silence, while so much tenderness was said.

Evening had fallen by the time they finished their walk. As Dr. Henderson escorted her back to Wilderness House, Mink heard a group of visitors leaving the King's Arms singing the "Shirt-sleeve Pudding Song," and she looked up at the cloud-draped stars and all she could see was diamonds.

Author's Note

*

The last and final warrants for apartments at Hampton Court Palace were granted in the 1980s. Two grace-and-favour residents still live there, as well as numerous palace staff, including the vine keeper, a woman.

Acknowledgements

*

There is nothing quite like writing a Victorian murder mystery to bring out the kindness of strangers. When I first had the idea for this novel, I was living in the Middle East and e-mailed several questions to John Sheaf, a local historian of Hampton. He very generously fired back replies, including one on Christmas Eve while preparing his turkey. I felt so indebted to that gentleman, I thought I'd better write the thing. Numerous other experts have also taken the time and trouble to answer my questions. I am particularly grateful to Professor James C. Whorton, Dr. Brian Parsons, Dr. Daniel Grey, and Professor Alastair Bruce, OBE. I am indebted to the late Ernest Law for his accounts of the palace, as well as to historian Sarah E. Parker, a specialist in the grace-and-favour period. I would like to thank the palace staff for their generosity when I stayed in Fish Court while carrying out research, and during numerous subsequent visits, especially Gillian Cox, Anthony Boulding, and most of all Ian Franklin, a marvel. Heartfelt thanks to all at Doubleday, particularly my editor, Alison Callahan, and, of course, Gráinne Fox, my super agent. And, finally, I would like to embrace the British Library and the Wellcome Library, not only for their collections but for their muffins.

THE TOWER, THE ZOO, AND THE TORTOISE

Set in the popular tourist attraction in present-day London, *The Tower, the Zoo, and the Tortoise* is an exquisite story of love, loss, and a one-hundred-eighty-one-year-old pet. Balthazar Jones has lived and worked in the Tower of London for the past eight years. Being a Beefeater is no easy job, and when Balthazar is tasked with setting up an elaborate menagerie of the many exotic animals gifted to the Queen, life at the Tower gets all the more interesting. Penguins escape, giraffes go missing, and the Komodo dragon sends innocent tourists running for their lives. Still, that chaos is nothing compared to what happens when his wife, Hebe, makes a surprise announcement. What's a Beefeater to do?

Fiction